Positively
Pippa

Books by Sarah Hegger

Positively Pippa

The Willow Park Series

Nobody's Angel

Nobody's Fool

Nobody's Princess

Positively
Pippa

SARAH HEGGER

ZEBRA BOOKS
KENSINGTON PUBLISHING CORP.
http://www.kensingtonbooks.com

ZEBRA BOOKS are published by

Kensington Publishing Corp.
119 West 40th Street
New York, NY 10018

All Kensington titles, imprints, and distributed lines are available at special quantity discounts for bulk purchases for sales promotion, premiums, fund-raising, educational, or institutional use.

Special book excerpts or customized printings can also be created to fit specific needs. For details, write or phone the office of the Kensington Sales Manager: Attn.: Sales Department. Kensington Publishing Corp., 119 West 40th Street, New York, NY 10018. Phone: 1-800-221-2647.

Zebra and the Z logo Reg. U.S. Pat. & TM Off.

First Printing: June 2017
ISBN-13: 978-1-4201-4243-3
ISBN-10: 1-4201-4243-7

eISBN-13: 978-1-4201-4244-0
eISBN-10: 1-4201-4244-5

10 9 8 7 6 5 4 3 2 1

Printed in the United States of America

To Kelly Le Clair,
because you always said I could do it

ACKNOWLEDGMENTS

A book is a journey, and it helps to have a great guide through the process. My heartfelt thanks to Esi Sogah for all she's done on previous books, and for her invaluable input on this one. I would be remiss in not acknowledging the other wonderful folk at Kensington and all they do to bring my book to life. This book also marks the beginning of a new journey with my agent, Nalini Akolekar. I am looking forward to where we go from here.

A huge thanks to Steven Mitchell and Xio Axelrod for being gentle, but firm, critique partners. Also to Terri Osburn, who made me the grateful recipient of her generosity.

And always to my family for all they put up with while I'm in the writing cave.

To the KickAss Chicks (www.kickasschicks.com), you ladies rock, and your love and support, and the laughs when I need them, make life so much richer.

Also to the members of Romance Writers Weekly, a group built on the notion that no writer walks this journey alone.

A big shout-out to Andrea Johnson both for coming up with Agrippina called Pippa, and for naming the book. Also to Crystal Delores Hernandez for giving me the name "Mugged" for the new coffee shop.

Finally, to you, the reader, I write the words and you read them, and together we make the story.

Chapter One

"Aren't you—?"

"No." Not anymore she wasn't. Pippa snatched her boarding pass from the check-in attendant and tugged her baseball cap lower over her eyes. Couldn't Kim Kardashian help a girl out and release another sex tape or something? Anything to get Pippa away from the social media lynch mob. She kept her head down until she found her gate, and chose the seat farthest away from the other passengers waiting to board the flight to Salt Lake City. Latest copy of *Vogue* blocking her face, she flipped through the glossy pages.

Peeping over the top of her magazine she slammed straight into the narrowed gaze of a woman three rows over. *Shit!* Pippa dropped the woman's gaze and went back to Vivienne Westwood bucking the trend.

Across the airport lounge the woman's glare beamed into the top of her head like those laser tracking things you saw in spy movies. Pippa buckled under the burn and slouched lower into her seat.

Look at that, Fendi was doing fabulous separates this season. And really, Ralph Lauren, that's your idea of a plus-size model? Stuff like this made her job so much harder.

Her former job.

Losing her show still clawed at her. Losing? Like she'd left the damn thing at Starbucks as she picked up her morning latte. More like her jackass ex with zero conscience had knocked it out of her hand. Framed, stitched up, wrongfully accused—judged, found guilty, and sentenced to a plethora of public loathing wiping out all the years spent building her career. Burning sense of injustice aside, she was stuck in this thing until it went away.

Angry Woman lurked in her peripheral vision. As sweat slid down her sides, Pippa tucked her elbows in tight and risked another glance.

Under an iron-gray row of rigidly permed bangs, the woman's mouth puckered up.

Back to *Vogue*. The knot in her stomach twisted tighter, and she checked her cap. What the hell? A baseball cap and shades always worked for other celebrities. Why not her?

Angry Woman squared her shoulders and huffed.

This could go one of two ways. Either Angry Woman would come over and give her a piece of her mind on behalf of women everywhere, or she'd confine her anger to vicious staring and muttering. Maybe some head shaking. *Please don't let her be a crusader for women. Please, please, please.* After two weeks of glares, stares and condemnation, Pippa had gotten the message:

Pippa St. Amor, the woman America loves to hate.

Right now, all she wanted was to sneak home and stay there until someone else topped her scandal. God, didn't *Vogue* have anything fresh? She'd make a list. Lists were good. Soothing. *Item one, run away from Angry Woman and hide in the bathroom. Item two, get your career back.* She moved *item two* up to first place, where it had been since she left home at eighteen, and gauged the distance between her and the bathroom door. She'd never make it.

Angry Woman lifted her phone and snapped a shot of Pippa.

Damn, she'd forgotten that option; this one by *far* the worst. God, she hated Twitter. And Facebook. And Instagram, and Snapchat, and whatever-the-hell new social torment site some asshat was thinking up right this minute. The ongoing public derision chipped off bits of her until she felt like an open nerve ending.

A friend huddled next to Angry Woman, long hair that was totally the wrong shade of brown and aged her by ten years at least. If Pippa had her on the show, Long Hair would be wearing a cute, hip cut, a fresh new makeup look, and mile-wide smile with her new sense of self.

The reveals never got old. There was something about a woman finally seeing her own beauty that made all the other crap that went with a television career worth it. Ray had ripped that away from her too.

Pippa was getting it with double barrels now. Lips tight, matching twin spots of outraged color staining their cheeks as they whispered over Angry Woman's phone. They both wore mom jeans. Up until two weeks ago it had been her mission to deliver moms everywhere from jeans like that. Along with those nasty, out of shape T-shirts they sold in three-packs of *meh* colors that had no business existing on the color spectrum. Angry and Long Hair were so her demographic. They'd probably seen the original episode live and watched it over and over again on demand or something. Maybe even watching it right this minute on YouTube.

YouTube! She hated YouTube, too.

Why didn't they call her flight already and get her the hell out of here?

You didn't sleep with the boss, and especially not in television. For four years. Ray had always been a bit sneaky, but to annihilate her career to boost his own? She hadn't seen it coming. But you couldn't rely on a man. How did she not get this by now?

Three minutes until boarding.

"Excuse me?"

Ah, shit, shit, shit, double damned shit in a bucket. So close, two minutes and fifty-five seconds. Smile and look friendly. "Yes."

Try not to look like you.

"You're that woman, aren't you?" Angry Woman narrowed her eyes, and Pippa leaned back in her chair, out of striking range.

"Hmm?"

"It is you." Long Hair planted her legs akimbo like a prizefighter. "I watched every single one of your shows. I can't believe you said those things, and I—"

Two minutes, thirty seconds.

"—should be ashamed of yourself. What you said is a crime against women everywhere. You made that poor woman cry."

Of course they cried. They were supposed to cry. The shows were edited to make them cry even more, but not the time to point it out.

"Shocking. And cruel. You're just a . . . a nasty bitch." Angry Woman got the last word in. She'd been called worse. Recently, too, and it still stung.

A man in the row opposite turned to watch the action. The three teens beside him openly stared and giggled.

I didn't say it, people. Okay, she'd said it, but not like that. *Editing, people.* Creative editing—the scourge and savior of television celebrities worldwide. She could shout it across LAX and it still wouldn't do any good. Until the next scandal broke and hers was forgotten.

"This is a boarding call . . ."

Thank you, Jesus!

"I'm sorry, that's my flight." Pippa creaked a smile and gathered her things. Handbag, phone, iPad, and coat. Her hands shook under the combined weight of several sets of eyes and she nearly dropped her phone.

No cabin baggage, not on this flight. Nope, this flight she'd packed just about everything she owned into the two heaviest suitcases on the planet. Paid extra weight without an argument. Anything to get the hell out of LA and home to Philomene.

Phi would know what to do.

Chapter Two

"Shit, Isaac. If the plumber needs quarter-inch pipe, get him quarter-inch pipe." Matt threw open the door to his truck as he half listened to another lame excuse. He could recite them by heart at this point anyway.

"No, I can't get the pipe. I'm at Phi's house now." He sighed as Isaac went with the predictable. "Yes, again, and I can't come now. You're going to have to fix this yourself."

He slammed his door and keyed off his phone. Smartphones! He missed the days of being able to slam a receiver down. Jabbing your finger at those little icons didn't have the same release.

When God handed out brains to the Evans clan, he must have realized he was running low for the family allotment and been stingier with the youngest members. Between Isaac and their sister, Jo, there could only be a couple of functioning neurons left. And their performance, like a faulty electrical circuit, flickered in and out.

He grabbed his toolbox from the back of the truck. This had to be the ugliest house in history, as if Hogwarts and the Addams family mansion had a midair collision and vomited up Philomene's Folly.

His chest swelled with pride as he stared at it. He'd built

every ugly, over-the-top, theatrical inch of this heap of stone. He'd bet he was the only man alive who could find real, honest to God, stone gargoyles for downspouts. Not the plaster molding kind. Not for Diva Philomene St. Amor. Nope, she wanted them carved out of stone and mounted across the eaves like the front row of a freak show.

"Hey, Matt," a kid called from the stables forming one side of the semicircular kitchen yard.

"Hey, yourself." He couldn't remember the name of Phi's latest rescue kid doing time in her kitchen yard. Kitchen yard! In this century. Diva Philomene wanted a kitchen yard, so a kitchen yard she got, along with her stables.

"I want a building to capture the nobility of their Arabian ancestors thundering across the desert." She'd got it. Heated floors, vaulted ceilings, and pure cedar stalls—now housing every ratty, mismatched, swaybacked nag the local humane society couldn't house and didn't want to waste a bullet on. A smile crept onto his face. You had to love the crazy old broad.

He skirted the circular herb garden eating up the center of the kitchen yard. A fountain in the shape of a stone horse trough trickled happily. He'd have to remind her to drain it and blow the pipes before winter. He didn't want to replace the piping again next spring.

The top half of the kitchen door stood open and he unlatched the bottom half before stepping into the kitchen. The AGA range gave off enough heat to have sweat sliding down its sides before he took two steps. He opened the baize door to the rest of the house and yelled, "Phi!"

He hadn't even known what a baize door was at nineteen, but the Diva had educated him because she wanted one and it became his headache to get her one.

"Mathieu!" The Frenchifying of his name was all the

warning he got before Philomene appeared at the top of her grand, curving walnut staircase. Thirty-two rises, each six feet wide and two feet deep leading from the marble entrance hall to the gallery above.

The soft pink of the sun bled through the stained-glass windows and bathed the old broad in magic. Her purple muumuu made a swishing noise as she descended, hands outstretched, rings glittering in the bejeweled light. "Darling."

She made his teeth ache. "Hold on to the railing, Phi, before you break your neck." It had taken a crew of eight men to put that railing in, and nearly killed the carpenter to carve a dragon into every inch of it.

She pressed a kiss on both his cheeks with a waft of the same heavy, musky perfume she'd always worn. She smelled like home. "You came."

"Of course, I came." He bent and returned her embrace. "That's how this works. You call, I drop everything and come."

A wicked light danced in her grass green eyes, still bright and brilliant beneath the layers and layers of purple goo and glitter. She'd been a knockout in her youth, still had some of that beautiful woman voodoo clinging to her. If you doubted that for an instant, there were eight portraits and four times that many photos in this house to set you right. Or you could just take a look at Pippa—if you could catch a quick glance as she flew through town. He made it his business to grab an eyeful when he could.

"I am overset, Mathieu, darling." She pressed her hand to her gem-encrusted bosom.

"Of course you are." The Diva never had a bad day or a problem. Nope, she was overset, dismayed, perturbed, discomposed and on the occasion her dishwasher broke down, discombobulated.

"It is that thing in the kitchen." She narrowly missed taking his eye out with her talons as she threw her hand at the baize door.

Her kitchen might look like a medieval reenactment, but it was loaded for bear with every toy and time-saving device money could buy—all top of the line. "What thing, Phi?"

"The water thingy."

"The faucet?"

She swept in front of him, leading the way into the kitchen like Caesar entering Rome in triumph. "See." He dodged her hand just in time. "It drips incessantly and disturbs my beauty rest."

He clenched his teeth together so hard his jaw ached. He ran a construction company big enough to put together four separate crews and she called him for a dripping faucet. "I could have sent one of my men around to fix that. A plumber."

"But I don't want one of your men, darling." She beamed her megawatt smile at him. "I want you."

There you had it. She wanted him and he came. Why? Because he owed this crazy, demanding, amazing woman everything, and the manipulative witch knew it. He shrugged out of his button-down shirt and pulled his undershirt out of his jeans. He was going to get wet and he'd be damned if he got faucet grunge all over his smart shirt.

Phi took the shirt from him and laid it tenderly over the back of one of her kitchen chairs. "This is a very beautiful shirt, Matt."

"I'm a busy and important man now, Phi. A man with lots of smart shirts."

She grinned at him, and stroked the shirt. "I am very proud of you, Matt."

Damn it all to hell, if that didn't make him want to stick

out his chest like the barnyard rooster strutting across Phi's kitchen yard. He turned the faucet on and then off again. No drip. "Phi?"

"It's underneath." She wiggled her fingers at the cabinet.

He got to his knees and opened the doors. Sure enough, a small puddle of water gathered on the stone flags beneath the down pipe. Good thing Phi had insisted on no bottoms to her kitchen cabinets. It had made it a bitch to get the doors to close without jamming on the stone floor, but right now it meant he wouldn't be replacing cabinets in his spare time.

"You should be out on a date," Phi said from behind him.

"If I was out on a date, Phi, I wouldn't be here fixing your sink."

"Yes, you would."

Yeah, he would. He turned off the water to the sink. "Have you got some towels or something?"

She bustled into the attached laundry and reappeared with an armload of fluffy pink towels.

Wheels crunched on the gravel outside the kitchen and Phi dropped the towels on the floor next to him. She tottered over to the window to stare. A huge smile lit her face and she gave off one of those ear-splitting trills that had made her the world's greatest dramatic soprano. Everyone, from the mailman to a visiting conductor, got the same happy reception.

He leaned closer to get a better look at the pipes beneath the sink. Were those scratch marks on the elbow joint? Neat furrows all lined up like someone had done that on purpose. He crawled into the cabinet and wriggled onto his back. They didn't make these spaces for men his size.

"Mathieu?" Phi craned down until her face entered his field of vision. Her painted-on eyebrows arched across her parchment-pale face. "I have a visitor."

"Is that so?" What the hell, he always played along.

"Indeed." Her grin was evil enough to have him stop his tinkering with the wrench in midair. "I thought you might like to know about this visitor."

The kitchen door opened. A pair of black heels tapped into view. The sort of shoes a man wanted to see wrapped around his head, and at the end of a set of legs he hadn't seen since her last trip to Ghost Falls—Christmas for a fly-by visit. His day bloomed into one of those eye-aching blue sky and bright sunlight trips into happy.

Welcome home, Pippa Turner.

Pippa wrapped her arms around her grandmother and held on for dear life. Thank you, God, she was home. She'd made it in one piece. Missing the bits taken off her by the women at the airport, the car rental lady, and a group glare from a bunch of tourists at the baggage carousel of Salt Lake City Airport.

Phi tightened her arms around Pippa, as if she knew. Of course she knew, Phi always knew. The ache inside her chest unraveled and unlocked the tears. Not once in this whole ghastly two weeks had Pippa cried. But the smell of patchouli oil wiggled underneath her defenses and opened the floodgates. Home. Safe.

"Ma petite." Phi stroked her back in long, soothing strokes. The jewels encrusting her bodice pressed into Pippa's chest, like they had all through her childhood. "My poor, sweet girl."

The tears came thicker and faster, gumming up her throat and blocking her nose until they roared out in great gasping sobs.

Phi absorbed it all, like Pippa knew she would. Quiet

murmurs and calming pats that eventually calmed the storm enough for her to speak.

"Now." Phi cupped Pippa's face between her pampered palms. "You will tell me all the dreadful things that man did to you."

The relief almost got her crying again, but Pippa dragged in a deep breath. She could tell Phi everything, about Ray, the vapid blond thing he was boning, her meltdown, the lies—all of it. She had a list of every last one. And Phi would believe her. Not like those sharks surrounding her in LA. "Did you see it?"

Phi's eyes clouded and her mouth dropped. "I did, my love, and it did not look good."

"I only watched it once, and I haven't had the guts to watch it since then." Pippa's stomach clenched up so tight she thought she might puke. She hadn't been able to bring herself to watch the footage a second time, and that one blurred nightmare viewing was enough to know it had to be bad. Plus, the angry women mobbing her everywhere she went pretty much gave the game away.

Phi's droopy mouth confirmed how bad.

"It was Ray." Her legs collapsed like overcooked green beans and she needed to sit. The heavy kitchen chair screeched across the stone floor as she pulled it out. "He wanted me gone and used the show to make sure it happened."

"But why?" Phi threw her shoulders back, looking ready to do battle for Odin. It was the same pose she'd been photographed in while singing Wagner in Milan.

For the first time since Christmas, a real smile curled around the corners of Pippa's mouth. Drama was hardwired into her grandmother. Her mother hated it, and her sister, Laura, did her best to flatten Phi's flare. Pippa loved it. It warmed her from the inside and gave her that bit of driftwood she desperately needed. When you were with Phi, you had to go with it.

"Ray wanted a younger piece of ass." Saying it out loud brought the slow simmer up to the boil again. She'd only turned thirty-two three months ago. How much younger ass did Ray want? The answer stuck like a phlegm ball in the back of her throat. Twentysomething and fresh out of journalism college. Probably Debbie Does Dallas U.

"Men." Phi snorted and thrust her chin out. The Aida angle, a touch of defiance and high enough to catch the glitter of the follow spot. The expression crumpled and Phi glanced down at the floor. "It's all about sex for them."

A grunt sounded from under the sink. Pippa's nape crawled as her brain sorted this new information. "Phi?" She was afraid to ask. "Is there someone here?"

Phi waved a hand toward the sink, looking way too arch to be innocent. "It is just Mathieu."

"Thanks, Phi." A deep, dark country-boy rumble from under the sink.

Just Mathieu! An hysterical scream of laughter gathered in Pippa's throat. Matt Evans wasn't *just* anything, and he was under Phi's sink listening to every word of this.

"Hey, Agrippina," said the voice from the floor.

Only one person, other than Phi, called her Agrippina and lived to tell the tale. Sonofabitch, and she'd thought her day was done messing with her. "Hey, Meat."

"Matt is fixing my sink," Phi said.

Useful information she might have appreciated . . . say . . . five minutes ago. She leaned back and peered around the side of the table. Sure enough, a set of jeaned legs stuck out from the cupboard. His white T-shirt rode up exposing a couple of inches of tanned, smooth stomach. Matt Evans still had a little something-something going on. A too good looking, seriously charming, hot as hell, cocksure son of a bitch. Seriously nice thighs under those jeans.

"Don't mind me," he said.

With Phi listening she might have launched into her men and sex theories.

"We need champagne." Phi leaped to her feet.

"Champagne?" Pippa dragged her eyes away from the sizeable bulge at the top of those thighs. Matt Evans was packing. "I don't think I'm in much mood for celebrating."

"Darling." Phi flung her hands out in front of her. "Never let them see you bleed. Tonight we drink to your homecoming, and poor, single Matt eventually getting a date. Tomorrow we plot our revenge."

In Phi's wake the baize door swung shut with a whisper across the stone floor. Tools clinked from under the sink.

"Are you going to come out from under there?" Pippa craned her neck and caught a glimpse of his firm chin, dotted with stubble.

"Is it safe?"

The edge of another weeping storm swept through her. "Probably not."

"Younger piece of ass, huh?" Matt chuckled softly. *Go ahead, rub it in, you smug shit.*

"Dateless, huh?" Hard to believe the man who girls had ripped one another's hair out for in high school was dateless.

Matt snorted a laugh. "Damn, it looks like someone cut this pipe."

Phi! Pippa dropped her head to the table with a thud that reverberated all the way to the back of her aching skull. The timing was too convenient to be believed. Not to mention the super-subtle way she'd worked into the conversation how unattached Matt Evans was.

"If you're done with the crying thing, could you hand me a wrench?"

Was she done with the crying thing? Tears stung her eyes and made her blink. Nope, she had a few tons of water left to shed.

"Wrench." A tanned hand emerged from the cupboard and curled his fingers in her direction. Oh no, he didn't. The last man to crook his fingers at her . . . had been Matt Evans. She hadn't responded that time, either.

She was done with taking crap. *Hello, Mr. Leg Man, here comes trouble, sashaying over the kitchen floor right at you.* Matt and his ogling were one of the best parts of coming home to Ghost Falls. Nothing like steady appreciation to lift a girl's spirits. Matt didn't do subtlety, either. Hot, naughty twinkle in his eye, small smile playing on his mouth, he'd hand out that sexy attitude in bucketloads. Her heels rang against the stone floor. She parked a four-inch heel right next to his hip, pressing her ankle in to get his attention. She lifted the other over and trapped him between her legs. Her pencil skirt pulled tight across her thighs.

The man between her thighs stilled. He loaded his voice with enough warning to tell her he was onto her. "Agrippina."

Through the opening where the sink trap had been she caught his eye, twinkle still there, daring her to do her worst. "Meat."

His eyes widened as he read her intention a split second before she opened the faucet to max. Water gushed out, straight down the downpipe. His body tensed.

Pippa leaped out of the way as he uncoiled from under the sink. Damn that felt good. Absolutely childish but so good. Turns out, Matt knew some very nasty words. She sprang back as he emerged, shaking his head like a big, wet dog.

"You think that's funny, do you?" She did. She totally did, and her grin said so. Strong hands fastened around her hips, whipped her right off her feet, and slammed her into a rock-hard, very wet chest. Her feet dangled a foot off the ground. Water spiked his eyelashes and dripped off the end of his nose. "That was not very nice."

Her blouse clung to her in a sodden mess as he held her in place. She wriggled to get free, mashing her breasts against him. The damp cloth between them vanished against the blaze of warmth coming off his chest. "You can put me down now." Damn, her voice got all breathy and girly.

He gave her an evil grin and lowered her to the ground, chest rubbing all the way. It felt so good, her little old toes curled in her kick-ass shoes. The smug shit knew it.

Matt stepped back and she got a good eyeful of him. Matt in his twenties had been hot, hot, hot. Today's Matt was a supercharged version with hard angles and sinewy muscle. He fisted the back of his T-shirt and dragged it over his head.

Holy shit! Hard ridges marched up his belly from his belt to expand into the hard slabs of his pecs. Those shoulders begged to have her sink her teeth into the muscle. Her mouth dried and her tongue stuck to the roof of her mouth.

He raised one dark eyebrow at her. "Well."

She folded her arms over her see-through blouse. "I see you've let yourself go."

"Liar. You were so checking me out." He laughed, a flash of white teeth that softened his harsh features.

The sound tugged at something buried deep inside her. It bubbled up under her chest and turned her mouth up at the corners.

The look in his topaz eyes warmed into hot, melty chocolate, and reminded her who was the girl here and who was the boy. God, it must be years since a man had looked at her like that. A look like that could make a girl's day a whole lot better.

Chapter Three

Matt gunned his truck down Headland Drive. Standing in the kitchen flirting with Pippa Turner had made him late. Correction, she called herself Pippa St. Amor now. Damn, the girl got more and more smoking with each year. She'd blown out of town two days after her eighteenth birthday and taken all that heat with her—about the same time he'd decided twenty-two wasn't too old to ask eighteen out on a date. Like he'd had time to date back then anyway.

Her tears had rocked him. The Pippa he remembered never cried. Not even when she was a freshman and that little prick Declan Sherman tripped her up in the hallway in front of the entire football team. Pippa had gotten up, picked up her books, and calmly kneed Declan in the balls. Declan minced around school for three days after that, and nobody ever messed with Pippa again.

Yet, today in Phi's kitchen, she'd gone to pieces.

He checked the clock on his console. Damn, late. Late didn't get the job done, and late meant people waiting for him. Not that Jo had ever managed to get anywhere on time, but that wasn't the point, as he often told her. He resisted the urge to call and check on Isaac. All his brother had to do was go and see Hank at Builder's Warehouse and pick up some quarter-inch piping. So why did his gut still burn?

Jo's teeth-ache orange VW Beetle was parked outside Bella's. Figured she'd be on time for this. Bella's was pretty much the only show in town for wedding and prom dresses. He'd come with his sister to choose a prom dress, too, and felt about as useful as he did right now. Bella senior had retired three months ago and left the shop to her grand-daughter. Conveniently also named Bella and a classmate of Nate's.

Maybe he should go and get the quarter-inch pipe and send Isaac dress shopping. He didn't quite get why Jo didn't bring Mom with her, but every time he asked, Jo chewed his ear off about how Mom always tried to take over. Always. Women used that word a lot, and he generally took it as a sign to stop listening.

Parked right in front of Bella's, Bets Schumaker climbed into her car. He waited for her to check her lipstick, finger-comb her hair, and adjust her blouse before she finally got her seatbelt over her and backed out. Slow enough for Matt to hear death breathing in his ear.

Bets smiled and waggled her fingers at him before burning rubber down the road, as if she'd seen the specter of death waiting to take Matt and wanted no part of that. He put five bucks on Bets calling his mom before the day was over.

God, this town! Not even charming enough to make a nostalgic Americana catalog. Of course, the only people who got nostalgic about small towns didn't spend their lives slowly rusting away in one.

Jo looked up from her phone as he opened the door. Chimes tinkled above his head as he stepped into Bella's. Just walking in made his balls shrivel. Bella Erikson had a thing for pink and she went wild with it all over her salon—

pink and those chandeliers with little dangly crystals on them.

Jo looked about as out of place as he felt, with her heavy biker boots and ragged tee.

Ah hell, she'd added to the tats running down her arms from shoulder to wrist. Not that he had anything against ink, but he would rather it didn't decorate his baby sister. He could hear Mom's meltdown already and she wasn't even here.

Bella bustled over to him with a big, candy-sweet grin on her face. "Matt."

A tiny blonde, Bella reminded him of a voluptuous Disney fairy with her big blue eyes and perky attitude. Bella always wore the same expression, like he'd handed her a winning lottery ticket just by being here. "So nice to see you again. How is your mother?"

"She's good."

He settled his weight on one leg and waded through her usual hi-how-are-ya ritual. Bella stuck to it with a sort of religious reverence. One by one she would go through each member of the family and ask. Wherever and whenever they met up. It was a little annoying, but kindly meant. It actually seemed as if she cared, because she certainly listened closely enough to the answer. Thank God, there weren't as many Evans kids as the Barrowses. Nine of them, at last count, and it looked like Mrs. Barrows had number ten beneath the hood.

"And Nate?" Bella went a little pinker around the cheeks at the mention of his middle brother. Nate had his pick of women, was knee-deep in them with his position as sheriff. It didn't hurt that he was the family pretty boy, either.

"Actually, he sends his regards." It was wrong on so many levels, but he could never resist. Nate would find himself facing one of Bella's pink casserole dishes before the end of the day. Honey sweet as she was, Bella needed to hang up her apron, for the safety of stomach linings everywhere.

"And Isaac?"

"He's good." Telling Bella that Isaac was still thick as pig shit wouldn't go down well. Actually, Isaac was far from dumb. Isaac was . . . apathetic. It was as close as he could get to his youngest brother's issue.

Bella's face creased in a concerned frown. "Have you heard from Eric?"

"Nope, not lately."

"I have." Jo unfolded from a pink, round couch thing. All legs and arms, tall for a girl and graceful. Not that you would notice with the whole gothic grunge thing she had going on.

"You've heard from Eric?" The world must be heading straight into the sun.

Jo shrugged. "He called me this morning. He's coming home for the wedding."

"Really?" Matt stared at Jo, waiting for her to tell him he was being punked. "We're talking about the same Eric here? Our brother, Eric. About my height, darker hair, a whole helluva lot uglier."

A smile lit Jo's face, and Bella giggled her twinkly, fairy laugh.

Damn, his sister was pretty when she smiled. She didn't do it enough. Not even when her dickwad fiancé was around. A girl ought to smile a lot around the guy she was about to marry. Okay, he wasn't a woman and most of the time barely understood what they were jawing about, but it seemed to him brides smiled a lot. They got this sort of glow thing. Jo didn't glow. She seemed . . . resigned. Grim, even. He'd tried talking to her, but she stonewalled him the entire way. He was her brother, for God's sake. How much help did she expect from her single brother who had barely enough sensitivity to walk into a dress shop without wanting to run for his life?

Maybe he should try and get Mom to see if she could figure out what was going on with Jo.

Phenomenally stupid idea. So stupid it made the skin of his nape crawl. His mother and Jo in the same room, unsupervised, and talking about feelings? Sweet Jesus!

"Okay." He smacked a grin onto his face. Jo was getting married. Happiest day of her life and all that. She deserved somebody here looking enthusiastic and he was all she had. Poor kid. "Let's get you a dress. How do we do this?"

Bella giggled and slapped him on the arm. "Jo has already picked out her favorites. All you have to do is sit over there and tell her what you think."

His gut went ice cold. Puke your lunch up cold. *Tell her what you think.* Oh God, no. He might be a caveman but even he knew better than that. "Great."

He let Bella shove him into a baby armchair with gold tassels all around the fringe. His knees ended up somewhere around his ears. If anyone asked him if their ass looked fat, he was out of here.

"You were late." Jo raised her eyebrow at him. Her piercing caught the light and winked. "So, I went ahead and made a selection."

"Yeah, sorry about that. I was fixing Phi's sink. And Pippa is home."

Jo and Bella swung to look at him, like he'd whipped his dick out or something.

"What?" they both yelled at once.

"Pippa. Her granddaughter. The one who does that TV show. She's home."

Bella sucked in a deep breath and her normally pink

cheeks went an even deeper shade. "I can't believe she would dare show her face here after what she did."

Okay, a picture was forming here. Pippa's tears, some of the things she'd said, and now this reaction from Bella. Bella saved butterflies and put bows on puppies. Bella did not look like she was inches away from grabbing up her tar and feathers and running a trollop out of town.

"Where else could she go?" Jo shrugged.

Bella bristled a bit more before settling down like a hen to roost. "Still, what she did was awful."

"What did she do?"

With twin looks of exasperation, they both swung his way again.

"You don't know?" Jo rolled her eyes. "Where do you live? Under a rock or something?"

"I've been working, Jo." The same thing he'd been doing every day of his life since he took over the business at nineteen.

"Here." Jo fiddled around with her phone and handed it to him. "It's had over two million views on YouTube. The thing went viral about five minutes after they yanked the TV show off the air."

Matt eyed the small screen in front of him. He wasn't so sure he wanted to see this.

"Oh, yes." Bella breathed out on an ecstatic little whisper and took the tasseled armchair next to him. "They stopped the show right in the middle and went to commercial break. And when they came back, all they showed was old reruns."

"What did she do?" Nothing could be worse than his imagination. Sick bastard that he was, he wouldn't be totally opposed to a Pippa strip show. Him and two million other horny bastards. The idea suddenly lost its appeal.

Bella leaned forward and put one slim hand on his knee. "She destroyed that woman."

"What woman?"

"He's never seen the show." Jo gave Bella a look that poured scorn on his unworthy head. "Well, you know it's like a makeover show."

"No." Sue him. He didn't watch television. He worked, he read, and he tried to get laid often enough not to get cobwebs between his dick and his balls.

"Okay, well, it's a makeover show. They find some woman—"

"Nominated by her family." Bella squeezed, her grip strong for such a tiny woman.

"Anyway," Jo said. "So, Pippa will feature this woman, take her shopping, get her hair and makeup done, and by the end of the show she's looking great."

"A bit like *Pimp My Ride*?"

Jo swelled indignantly before she caught on with a bark of laughter. "So, the last show, the one they yanked, Pippa had this woman called Annie on."

"Alice," Bella said.

"Right, Alice. But they called her Allie."

"That's right." Bella smacked her palms together in delight. "I remember because I was thinking that normally they call an Allison Allie, but in this case she was Alice and they called her Allie."

His ass might end up grafted to a pink velveteen chair at this rate. "So, Allie has her makeover?"

"Yes." Jo swung right back on track. "And it was going so well."

"I loved what they did to her hair." Bella leaned forward, her eyes sparkling. "She had all this gray—"

"And then what happened?" He only had one life to live

and he'd already tossed a fair amount of it away waiting for Bets to back out of her parking space.

Jo leaned toward him. "The woman—"

"Allie." Bella nodded.

"Allie is saying to Pippa how her life is such a mess, and how is a pair of shoes going to fix all that. And Pippa goes nuts."

Bella's eyes went wide enough for him to see into the back of her brain. "Completely lost her marbles."

"I mean, loses her shit." Jo made a bobblehead. "And starts telling Allie about how she needs to get her life in order, and how ugly she is—"

Bella snatched the phone out of his hand and pressed the Play icon on the video. "Here, watch it."

They must be having him on. Pippa did not lose her shit, not ever. Just ask Declan. He dropped his gaze to Jo's phone.

Pippa appeared onscreen looking that sort of effortless gorgeous that made him want to ruffle her up and get her hot and sweaty. All that red hair, so sleek and contained, begging his hands to grab fistfuls of it. Why the hell hadn't he watched this show? Pippa smoked from the screen, wearing some dress that wrapped under her breasts and around her waist. She had the sort of body that he would bet she tried to diet skinnier, but from his perspective her curves were perfect.

He tuned in to the words coming out of her full, red mouth. *"You're right, a pair of shoes can't change your life, or a pretty dress or even new makeup. Nothing you put on can really change you. You're fat, ugly, unwanted, and not worth loving, a dress is not going to make any difference. But for now, put the dress on, wear the pretty shoes and see if they help you find something you can love about yourself."*

Bella sucked in a harsh breath, as if she heard it for the first time.

Matt sat there. He hit the Replay button and watched again as her beautiful face with that bad girl mouth said those things. And he didn't believe it. Not for one second. "Pippa never said that."

Jo stared at him as if he'd lost his grip. "Hello, Matt. It's right there in front of you."

"I know." He handed her phone back to her. "I heard it, but I know Pippa. I've known her since Eric dated her sister and I would put my cock on a block she never said that."

Bella leaned forward and patted his thigh. "Perhaps because you like her so much, you find it difficult to believe. But she was always a bit stuck up."

He lifted Bella's hand and put it on the arm of her chair. "Sure, she was stuck up, full of attitude, and totally out of place in a town like this, but she was never mean."

"Fame changes people." Bella did a creepy big eyes thing.

Not Pippa. Not only did she have Phi to help her keep it real, Pippa had always been the same—a ball-busting, sexy-as-hell force of nature. Bella and Jo looked set to keep ripping into Pippa, and he needed to chew this one over. Alone.

"Let's see your dress," he said.

"But—" Bella creased her forehead into a frown and glanced at Jo.

He folded his arms over his chest and dropped his chin to his chest. Man signal for not-gonna-go-there.

Jo raised her eyebrows and breathed, "Oh-kay."

Four dresses and about eighty years later, he made his escape.

Three things bugged him as he drove away from Bella's. First, and God knows how he'd done it, but Isaac had managed to buy the wrong pipe and the plumber had left site,

with promises to return tomorrow. Which, Isaac the dumb
fuck, had believed. The plumber wouldn't have even tried
that shit had Matt been around. But Isaac, he liked to smile
at the world and was happy enough if it smiled back at him.
On Matt's dime.

Which brought him round to Jo and the dress he'd paid
for. What he knew about fashion you could write on the
head of a nail, but that dress was UGLY. He'd said the right
things, even managed to have Bella beaming at him in
approval. But that dress . . .

He stopped at the new traffic light on Eighth.

It had no shape. It hung straight down from her shoulders like a frilly feed sack. Not that he noticed, because he
was her brother and that was just wrong, but Jo had curves
in the right places.

And the glow thing, just not there. Jo had faced her reflection in the mirror with all the enthusiasm of a girl doing
the football team's laundry after a three-week road trip.

Thirdly, Pippa Turner bugged him, and he didn't give a
crap she called herself St. Amor now. To him, Pippa Turner
was Pippa Turner with the wild red hair and big green eyes.
She'd started off being a pain-in-the-ass kid at family get-
togethers, and ended up blossoming into a tall, cool drink
of water that made his blood thicken.

Now she was back in town, and the thought made him
tingle. Small towns didn't offer a lot in the way of romantic vistas, or even straight-up sex. He'd learned to take his
urges three hours away to a bigger town. Four Evans brothers,
all still single and hunting—Ghost Falls did not have the
range they needed. But Pippa Turner . . .

The thing with the TV show chafed like a badly fitting
boot. He made a hard left onto St. Amor Crescent, his tires
screeching their protest on the blacktop. If you had a question,
you asked. Straight up. No bullshit and this wondering and
picking at a thing in your mind—who the hell had time for

that? He pulled around the house into the kitchen yard, dodging the flock of chickens Phi kept because she liked the sound of them.

The top half of the door was open and he peered over into the kitchen.

Pippa was cooking something. At least, that's what he thought she was doing because she'd changed into a pair of jeans and her ass was in the general vicinity of the oven.

"Matt?" She turned and gave his happy eyeballs another feast. Her top draped over the generous curve of her breasts. "Did you come about the leak?"

"What leak?" He dragged his gaze up to her face. He liked it when she didn't wear a lot of makeup. Liked the starburst of freckles across her nose.

"My room." She motioned up the stairs, elegant, effortless. "It seems there's a bit of a leak."

"No." He certainly wasn't here about the leak. He'd told Phi to get the roof checked months ago. "I'll come round on the weekend and repair it."

"Okay then. So what are you doing here?" Direct and to the point, that was Pippa and she deserved a little of the same back.

"Jo showed me the thing."

"Your sister?" Her pale brow creased in a frown. Summer or winter, Pippa's skin stayed the same rich cream that didn't tan. It made him think how pale that skin he couldn't see would be. "What thing—oh."

She folded her arms over her breasts and dropped her head. Then, she turned back to her cooking.

"Did you say it?"

She shrugged and stirred the pot in front of her. "You saw the clip, so I must have."

Okay, he knew an evasive maneuver when he saw one, and he spent enough time with Mom and Jo to read a girl in flat-out defense. He unlatched the bottom half of the door and stepped into the kitchen. "Yeah, I saw it, but I know you and I don't think it's true."

"Really." At least he'd surprised a short laugh out of her. "And why's that?"

She took the pot off the burner and turned to look at him. Legs braced, arms crossed, and ready to fight. It was that red hair of hers, gave her a hair-trigger temper that taunted him to light the fuse. "It's not like you to be mean."

"I could have changed."

Now she was pissing him off. "So, you're telling me you said that shit?"

Her shoulders slumped and the fight bled out of her. "No, I just wondered why you cared."

Again, honesty was the only way he knew to break tough ground, and he had a feeling Pippa could be all kinds of rocky and unpredictable. "It didn't sound like something you'd say."

Her eyes widened, big, green, and beautiful. "And you know me so well?"

"Better than a load of people on the Internet."

"You're so full of yourself." Her top lip curled back from her teeth.

Some days, he'd give her that, but not now. "No, I'm not, I just don't do well with bullshit."

"Fair enough." She looked down at her feet and then up again. "I said it, but not the way it looked on the clip. They edited enough together to make it look pretty damning."

"Why didn't you tell people that?"

"I did. I released a press statement, but people believe what they want and the more noise I make, the longer this will go on."

That plain sucked, and he believed her. Fame might change some people, but those people maybe had a little asshole hiding inside them all along. Not Pippa, though, which meant she wasn't a total bitch. His dating calendar looked a little more cheerful. "Why did they do that? Whoever did the editing?"

She sighed and her face got that sad look. The same one Jo's wore in the dress shop. "That's a story for another time."

"Like on a date?"

Her head whipped back up and he got a small smile out of her. Made his chest glow like Iron Man.

"Are you asking?"

"Are you saying yes?"

She crinkled her nose up at him. "No. I'm not dating."

"Ever?" He moved to stand right in front of her, forcing her to look up if she wanted to maintain eye contact.

Her wide mouth almost smiled. "Not dating for now."

Matt could back off and let it go. Be a nice guy and let her deal with the shit on her plate. Except, he'd been backing off for so many years now, it was flat-out pathetic. She was single, he was single, and okay the timing could do with some tinkering, but YOLO. "What if one friend asked another out on an . . . excursion?"

She pressed her lips together but he caught the smile gaining ground in the twinkle in her eyes. Cocking her hip, she stuck her chin out at him, all smoking attitude and classy girl put-down. "You'll have to ask first."

And he grinned like a schoolkid. She had that effect on him. "Good to know."

Chapter Four

Pippa used the excuse of cleaning up the kitchen after dinner to get enough alone time to make her call.

Mundane things like dishes didn't even penetrate the orbit of Phi, so she toddled off with her wine, and a happy smile on her face.

The call went straight to Allie's voice mail, just like the other three Pippa had made, and she left another message. "Hi, Allie. It's Pippa. Look, I know this is probably really difficult for you right now, but could you please call me back? We need to talk."

Ray had stitched them both up good. Surely Allie had a little something-something inside her looking for some payback. God, Pippa hoped so.

Allie could set the record straight, without looking like a liar trying to save face. In the first shock of the episode hitting the air, Pippa had reacted. Sent out denials, issued statements, tried to hire a publicist—but in the end, it all got chewed up and spat out of the social media machine looking nothing like the way she had intended.

Pippa carried her wine to what Phi liked to call the salon. Until Allie called her back, her hands were tied. No point in wallowing in what-ifs like a teenager waiting to be asked to prom. Speaking of . . . Matt Evans had finally asked her out. All the times she'd come back to Ghost Falls and stayed with Phi, there had been Matt hovering in the background with his panty-melting smiles and hot eyes.

Of course, she'd say no when he asked, because she wasn't dating at the moment. Ray's betrayal still left a scorch mark right through the middle of her. The funny thing was, she'd started dating Ray because he felt safe. Not in the "to have and to hold" sense, but safe because falling in love with Ray had never been a consideration. Pippa didn't need a psychologist to show her the link between her carnival—now you see him, now you don't—dickwad father and her attitude to relationships. She got it, accepted it, and chose her career. Ray had been the perfect partner. They liked each other, got on well, and both understood the one rule: Career came first, relationships were a nice-to-have.

Boy, did he show her how that rule worked. The hurt surprised the hell out of her. Only a complete idiot dove back in the dating pool while their last burn still smarted. Only a sucker for punishment got back in the water—or someone who had Matt Evans asking them out. High school heartbreaker, football captain, president of debate, and all-round nice guy. Who hadn't totally crushed on him in this town? She'd certainly wondered over the years.

Timing had worked against them, and maybe that little voice deep inside warning Pippa not to go there. Still, she couldn't help thinking about it every time she went back to LA. What if, for once, she didn't have a boyfriend and Matt wasn't involved with someone else? The spark simmered low and constant between them. Probably because neither of them had ever done anything about it.

Nothing could come of her and Matt. Their lives couldn't be more different. He was all about home and hearth, and she was . . . she didn't know what, exactly, now that career was obliterated. If Allie called her back, at least she could do something about that part.

Maybe she and Matt could have coffee instead of a date-date. Or lunch. Middle of the day, she'd take her car and he could meet her there. No chance of candlelight, wine, or romance. No chance of action, either. *Shit, Pippa, get your head in the game here—life is falling apart all around you.* Lunch would be fine. Maybe have a glass of wine—although he probably drank beer. They could catch up about his family and her lack of a life and they'd be done.

Perfect. Except, according to Matt, he hadn't officially asked yet. She laughed out loud and Phi threw her a questioning stare. No way was she telling Phi about this afternoon's conversation. Phi already had her matchmaking tentacles unleashed. Her grandmother hadn't missed the byplay between her and Matt over the years. More like actively encouraged it.

Pippa put her glass and the bottle on the table in easy reach of Phi's chair. Swathed in a stiff organza cloud, Phi perched on her throne. No other word suited the huge, tall-backed, carved wooden monstrosity that sat central to a hearth large enough to take an entire tree. Every Christmas at Phi's they went large on the whole burning-the-Yule-log thing. Last Christmas she'd had the added bonus of Matt Evans shoveling the kitchen yard every morning.

"So tell me." Diamonds glittered from Phi's wrists. They always dressed for dinner at the Folly. "Let's start with that awful man and get it all off your chest."

Pippa toed off her heels and tucked her legs beneath her on the much more modest and comfortable rose-bedecked sofa. "Ray found a younger woman. She was ambitious, he wanted to get laid, and my show was the answer to both their needs."

Phi snorted into her wine goblet. "How boringly predictable. It lacks imagination."

Maybe, but it hadn't lacked punch. She took a sip of her wine. Phi may have appalling taste in evening gowns and furniture, but her cellar was excellent. She had her wine flown in by the crate from Bordeaux. "I don't really want to talk about it, Phi."

Those piercing green eyes snapped over to her and locked on target. With Phi, you never could tell whether she'd respect your wishes or plow right over them. "You're right, of course. Such a small man doesn't deserve any more of our time. How shall we spend the evening? We could drink our way steadily through several bottles of this excellent merlot."

"Or." And Pippa knew exactly how she wanted to spend the rest of the night. An old ritual, as dear to her as it was to Phi. A way to feel connected with home again. "We could look at the treasures."

"The treasures!" Phi's face lit up, and she bustled straight over to a huge, black oriental armoire. As a child, Pippa used to love looking at the lacquered images of dragons on the front and making up stories about the little etched figures fighting them.

Phi threw open the double doors with a sense of occasion. "Where shall we go today?"

"Russia." Pippa plunked her ass on a velvet cushion, eager for the journey to begin.

"Otlichno!" Philomene's "treasures" were all carefully housed on the rows of shelves. Each wrapped in a silk or velvet covering in a dazzling array of colors. It was like a peep into Ali Baba's cave of wonders. Phi stretched onto

her toes to reach the heavy silver tray and tea set on one of the top shelves.

Pippa got to her feet. "Let me do that for you."

"Pfft." Phi threw her a dagger look. "I am not that old, missy, stay where you are."

The silver rattled as she lowered it. Pippa sat poised to leap in with a save if needed.

Phi placed the tray on the ornate Louis XVI coffee table and took hold of the scarlet velvet draping. Pippa laughed and gave her a nod of encouragement. The game never got old, and right now it was the magic salve she needed on the place scraped raw inside her.

"*Doucement, ma petite.* Darling Nikita gave this to me mere days before Brezhnev made his move." Phi sighed and closed her heavily made-up eyes. Sapphire blue shadow glinted through her sooty false eyelashes. "Nikita loved the opera, such a fan. He gave me this set and assured me it had once graced the table of the last czar." The czar must have had some fairly hefty tables.

Phi whipped off the scarlet velvet cover and let loose a lusty, melodic trill. "Ah. How lovely it is."

They didn't make things like this anymore. The artistry in the bowl's shape and patterning reeked of lost skills and bygone eras. Pippa cradled the sugar bowl in her hand, carefully wiping it with the velvet before handing it to Phi.

Phi's gnarled fingers didn't have such a sure grip anymore. "See the work, *ma petite?*" Phi turned the bowl toward the light. "All the hours of engraving this must have taken."

Probably by some hapless Russian serf. Pippa nodded and smiled.

Phi dropped her head back and closed her eyes as she disappeared into her past. "I sang *Turandot* at the Bolshoi Theatre. A standing ovation. One of many that night."

Pippa smiled. She'd bet it had been. It took her back. Years of standing in her special spot in the wings of the great theaters of the world, listening to her grandmother's heavenly voice fill the space with its throbbing purity.

"Nikita had tears in his eyes." Phi's face softened into a smile. She handed the sugar bowl back.

Pippa reached for the milk jug, the next item in the ritual. "Phi, where's the milk jug? Did you take it for cleaning?"

Phi's eyes snapped open. "Of course not, I clean these myself. Not even June can be trusted with the treasures. Now hand me the milk jug."

Pippa moved the two large pots aside. One shorter and stouter for tea. A taller, more elegant version reserved for coffee or chocolate. The milk jug was missing. "It's not here."

"But it must be."

As far as Pippa knew, Phi was the only person allowed to open the "treasure trove." Pippa went back to the bureau and peered at the shelf where the tea set normally rested in state. Empty. An uneasy tendril snaked through her belly.

Phi's eyes grew larger. "Have I been robbed?"

"No." Pippa hurried back to her side. This was Ghost Falls, not exactly the crime capital of the world. What would anyone in this town do with a pre–Russian Revolution milk jug?

Phi's breathing grew shallow and rapid and her face reddened. "We must call the sheriff."

"Are you sure you didn't misplace it?" Pippa peered under the coverings of the other treasures.

Phi's bosom swelled. "Misplaced it? Me?"

No, it didn't seem likely. Phi guarded her treasures like the dragons on the cabinet. But still she was getting on in years, and . . .

Pippa didn't like the direction her thoughts were taking.

Phi's mind was as clear as a bell. "Has anybody been here lately?"

"Darling." Phi rose to her feet in a swirl of puce organza. "This house vibrates with people."

Maybe not vibrates, but Phi never lacked for visitors. "Anyone out of the ordinary?"

Phi tapped her fingernails against her chin. "Laura was here with the lovelies."

Pippa couldn't imagine her niece or nephew making off with Phi's treasures. Except, they were very young. "Could one of them have taken the jug by mistake? You know, kids are always fascinated by shiny things."

"Never." Phi's impressive pipes made the word boom around the salon. "I do not allow them to touch. When they are older, perhaps, but they do not share your fine appreciation for the treasures." Okay, totally childish, but still nice to know she was still Phi's "special girl."

Pippa had a vague idea of the monetary value of the treasures, but the stories Phi told suggested a lot. It didn't matter whether Khrushchev had given Phi the set, if it had belonged to the Russian royals, or some less well-known family. The set was old and solid silver and that alone made it valuable. "Any strangers?"

Phi gasped and clasped her hands to her bosom. "Last week, there were some men here."

"What men?"

"Matt sent over some roofers to check on my gutters. They said the gutters were fine but I will not be persuaded that the imp gargoyle is not spitting out more water than he used to."

"I'll call the sheriff." Pippa couldn't imagine Matt sending the wrong sort of man out to Phi's. "Or, maybe we should call Matt first?"

Phi's face grew redder. "I told him I do not like it when

he sends strangers here. But that dreadful woman needed him at her house."

It took her a moment to remember "that dreadful woman" was one and the same as Matt's mother. Nobody liked Cressy Evans, but "dreadful" might be a bit strong. "She's a bit overprotective."

Phi snorted. "The woman is like a carbuncle on her son's ass, slowly killing its host."

All right, then. Phi wasn't going to take a moderate approach. "So, should we speak to Matt first or call the sheriff?"

"Doesn't make any difference." Phi wilted into her throne. "Nate Evans is the new sheriff, and Matt will find out fast enough."

"Nate is sheriff? How the hell did that happen?"

"He's a changed man."

"He'd have to be." Nate Evans, of the permanent parking space on Lovers' Leap. Nate Evans who spent more time out of school than in. Nate Evans who was on the "do not date" of the mother of every daughter in Ghost Falls.

"Everyone deserves a second chance," said Phi, giving her a minatory look. Phi read her so well. "And he looks simply edible in that uniform."

Pippa let herself dwell on the mental image. All the Evans boys were hot, but Nate had something extra, in bucketloads. "Okay, so why don't I call the sheriff's office?"

"Do it in the morning." Phi fluttered her beringed hand over the tray. "Put it away. I cannot bear to see it so denuded."

Pippa wrestled the tray back into the bureau. "I think I should check and see if anything else is missing."

"I cannot." Phi's voice weakened—*La Traviata* style, weakened—but still, theatrics aside, this would be very upsetting for her.

"Okay, darling." Pippa pressed a kiss against her powdered cheek. Patchouli oil engulfed her. "I'll take care of it.

I'll make a list of what's missing and go around and see Nate in the morning."

Phi tottered out of the room, the wine bottle clutched in her hand. Pippa would go up and check on her later. After Phi had time to change into her sleeping attire. The changing of a diva was a lengthy process and she'd learned to honor it. Nobody busted in on the Diva before she was ready to be seen.

This thing with the missing milk jug worried her.

The feeling worsened as she checked the cabinet. One of the Queen Victoria napkin rings was not in the set of twelve, and two missing teaspoons—allegedly from the Vatican—had also gone AWOL.

Chapter Five

Pippa crawled out of her canopied yellow bed the next morning. Draped in yards and yards of buttercup and white organza with tiny little flowers and butterflies tacked onto the drapery, it was a bed for a princess. Phi surprised her with it when she was twelve. Unfortunately, Phi hadn't replaced the mattress since then either. Pippa recognized the lumps in this one from past visits. But it wasn't only the mattress keeping sleep at bay. Allie hadn't called back. She suspected Allie wasn't going to call either, and that meant another look at her action list.

The missing treasures bugged her too. It didn't make any sense. Sure, the stuff was valuable but it had limited marketability. It wasn't like taking an iPad and fencing it, or getting rid of a DVD player.

The treasures were unique, easily traceable, especially in this part of the world. Around two in the morning she'd come up with the theory that perhaps whoever took them didn't know that, and had no idea what they'd really taken. Which made her want to scream, because this person could be selling them for ten bucks in a back alley somewhere. Which then begged the question, why would anyone working for Matt risk their job for ten bucks?

The entire thing made no sense. In fresh, spring green, the happy bathroom mocked her mood as she stumbled into it. Ghost Falls was tiny, everybody knew everybody else, and Phi was like royalty here. Phi used the same cleaning lady she'd had for the last twenty years. Of course, she couldn't rule June out completely, but why now?

She snapped on the faucets to run water into the mammoth claw-foot tub. Phi didn't believe in showers, and there wasn't a single one in the house. God, what Pippa would give for a shower to wash away the fugue this morning.

It made sense to go and see Nate. He was sheriff here, he knew this town, and might have some ideas for her. Then again, he was the law around here, and she hesitated to escalate it to that level. Matt was the logical person to speak to. He knew Phi almost as well as she did. She wouldn't go in there all guns blazing, she'd take it easy, slow and careful, and see what happened.

The bath made her sleepier and she tripped over the curling edge of the delicate silk carpet as she tried to get dressed. Three times. You would think sooner or later her brain would register the fact that the end curled up. Jeans seemed too casual for her morning mission, so she opted for a summer dress, fitted on top and skimming an inch above her knee. She paired it with heels, because this was not a trip to the beach.

She checked her reflection before she left. Age appropriate, occasion appropriate, and looking cool and in control. So many women on her show got those things confused. Younger piece of ass was hosting *Your Look, Your Way* now, and God help the women on it, because the girl saw no reason not to dress everyone like a size two twenty-four-year-old. Pippa had to get her show back. It was everything she'd worked for, dreamed of.

She finished her hair and makeup. Battle armor in place, and ready to face central Ghost Falls. May God be with her.

Her phone buzzed and she glanced down. Allie's number. Her hands shook as she answered the call. "Hi, Allie."

"Um . . . no. It's not Allie, it's her husband. Todd."

Pippa sank onto the edge of her bed, knees shaky. "Hi."

"Look." Todd cleared his throat. "Allie asked me to call you."

Pippa got a sinking feeling in her gut.

"She got your messages, and stuff." Todd cleared his throat. His voice came back stronger, with an edge of determination. "You know what she's like. She's shy and all this stuff has been hell on her. People stop her on the street and ask about it. Everyone calling her all the time. It was hard enough to get her to do the show in the first place."

"I understand that, Todd." Pippa could hardly hear her own voice over her hammering heartbeat. Her entire life hinged on this call. "But she was there. She knows what really happened. Without her I'm—"

"She says she's sorry," Todd said. "She wanted to make sure I told you that, but she can't help you."

"But, Todd, she's the only—"

"She's sorry. We're both sorry, but this thing. It's gotta stop."

"I'm trying to make it stop," Pippa said—to the dead phone line.

Evans Construction's offices sat on a side street off Main. Pippa pulled her car into a marked parking spot and stared through her windshield. She may as well deal with this now, and give herself time to regroup from the Todd shutout.

The original office had grown to swallow up the two

buildings on either side of it. Matt ran all this and still fixed her grandmother's kitchen sink?

She pushed open a set of glass doors into a smart but modest lobby. Good, quality leather furniture, and a couple of discreet photographs of projects, but a lot like Matt himself—quiet, self-assured, and straight to the point.

A middle-aged woman sat behind a tall, wooden desk. "Can I help you?"

"Mrs. Cameron?" The school secretary seemed to have made a career move. The change hadn't extended to her tightly curled crop of aggressively chestnut hair.

Mrs. Cameron's purple mouth disappeared into a thin line. "Hello, Pippa."

Okay, then. Another ex-fan on the rampage, or was it Mrs. Cameron being the same Mrs. Cameron and taking no crap from anybody? It had to be tough taking the combined hormonal backlash of four hundred students between the ages of thirteen and eighteen. "You look well."

"Thank you." Frost coated the words.

"I wondered if Matt was in."

"Mr. Evans is a very busy man." Mrs. Cameron held up a finger and answered her ringing phone. "Evans Construction."

Well, she considered herself firmly put in her place. But Mrs. Cameron still had nothing on an LA casting agent. Pippa waited for her to finish her call. It was all in the delivery. Say it with enough conviction and the other person might come around to seeing things your way. "I realize he's busy, but he'll want to see me. Is he in?"

Mrs. Cameron's lips nearly disappeared, she pressed them together so tightly. "I'll check if he's in."

"I'll wait." Matt was here. Gorgons didn't guard an empty cave.

Mrs. Cameron picked up her phone and spoke to someone

on the other side, keeping her voice low enough that Pippa couldn't hear. She put the phone smartly back in its cradle, clearly not happy with the response. "Mr. Evans said he will see you now."

"Lovely." Pippa sailed past her with a smile.

"I saw your television program." Mrs. Cameron wasn't going to give up without a fight.

Pippa stopped and met her hostile stare. "Yes, I would imagine you did. There are a lot of people who saw the program, particularly the last one."

Mrs. Cameron sniffed and braced her shoulders, warming up for more.

"But unlike most of the people watching, you knew me before the show and have the advantage of being able to discern whether what you saw was the whole truth or not." She leaned forward and dropped her voice, forcing Mrs. Cameron to lean in to hear. "Not everything you see on TV is real. You told me that in high school."

"Agrippina." Matt's bass rumble skittered across her nerve endings. She really was going to have to cure him of that habit.

She jerked her chin at him. "Meat."

He got close and kept on coming, stopping right in her space and grabbing her hand. "This is a nice surprise."

Yeah, well, about that. She was going to send his day right into the toilet. "Is there somewhere we can talk?" She glanced at Mrs. Cameron, who wasn't missing a word of this. "In private."

"Sure." He kept hold of her hand and led her down a corridor deeper into the office. Warm and callused, his hand engulfed hers.

He'd been busy in the years since she'd left town. What used to be a dusty old building with a couple of offices had been transformed. At least a dozen people milled around in a large, bright central space. She nodded a greeting to a couple of familiar faces. Doors to glass-fronted offices led away from the central space, two glass-fronted conference rooms dominated the street side. "Did you do all this?"

He shrugged. "I had some help."

"I'm impressed." He'd built himself a small empire here. A long, long way from the lost nineteen-year-old forced to take over his father's business.

A woman passed her, sucked in a breath, and scurried away. *It only hurt if you allowed it to.*

Matt stopped and pulled her to a halt beside him. "Jill," he called the woman back. "You remember Pippa."

Jill . . . something, chemistry class, a year or two above her in school, and puckering up her face like she'd swallowed a lemon. "Yes."

"Hi, Jill." Because what else could she say, with Matt keeping her standing here like a turkey ready for its roasting.

Jill stuck her nose in the air and spun around.

Matt went rigid beside her. "Pippa's staying with her grandmother."

Pippa tugged her hand, she wanted out of here before this turned into a lynch mob. Another woman, vaguely familiar, peered around her computer monitor. It was easier to deal with the hate when strangers directed it at you.

Matt tightened his grip enough to keep her in place. "Pippa had a bad time in LA. She's come home to the people who know better than to believe the worst of her."

Matt the crusader. Always there for the underdog. God, she so didn't want to be his latest project. "Leave it."

"No." Matt glanced at her and away again. "Just for the record, ladies, she didn't say it the way it was aired."

Her crew! Of course! They would have the original footage, or at least know how to get their hands on it. Pippa wanted to smack herself in the head. She'd been banking on Allie coming through for her, but she should have looked to the people who had worked side by side with her for years. Surely they'd help her.

Jill frowned and a flicker of doubt crossed her face. The younger woman ducked back behind her monitor.

"But of course you guessed that, didn't you?" Matt smiled and walked away. Taking her with him, his strides so long she was forced to trot to keep up with him. He reached what she assumed was his office. It had better be, otherwise someone was going to be way pissed off to have their door slammed that hard. "How do you stand it?"

"I don't know." And she didn't, because most of the time it was more a case of grin and bear it. Never let them see you bleed or they'd attack. Which brought her back to Matt buckling into his armor on her behalf. "I ignore it, Matt, and I would prefer if you did the same."

"Why?" He loomed over her. Still topping her in her heels by a good four inches.

"Because the more fuel you give the fire, the brighter and longer it's going to burn."

He snorted and tugged her closer to him. "Bullshit. These people grew up with you, they know better."

"I'm not your pet project, Matt."

He raised his brows at her. "Maybe not, but you're in my office now, and I won't have people being rude to you."

Okay, that was kind of nice. When was the last time someone had stood up for her? A long, long time, for sure. Living in LA you got used to being a one-person army, and you counted your friends on one hand. Maybe the crew wasn't the best idea. Through the glass front of Matt's office Jill watched her, now standing next to the other woman, their heads close together. No prizes for guessing the topic of their conversation. Then again, her options were few.

"Look, you did a nice thing, standing up for me, but I . . ." She ran out of steam under the steady regard of his amber eyes. Not brown and not quite yellow, like the warm glow through a bottle of single malt. "Anyway, you might not be so keen about being in my corner once I tell you why I'm here."

"Oh?" Up went a brow and he released her hand to walk around his desk.

The warmth of his grasp still tingled along her skin. "It's about Phi, and those men you sent around last week."

"For her gargoyles?" He indicated for her to take a chair. The intercom on his desk lit up. He leaned forward and pressed the button. "I'm in a meeting, Mrs. Cameron."

The old dragon had a helluva lot of fight still left. "It's your brother. The sheriff."

"Thanks, Mrs. Cameron, I'm sure my brother, the sheriff, won't mind waiting a few minutes. And if not, I do know where he works." He looked up at Pippa. "Sorry, I had a lunch date with Nate, but he'll wait. Nate will do anything for a free meal."

Sometimes fate set stuff up for you. "Actually." She took a deep breath. "You might want to have him here."

"Why?" His eyes cooled and his face settled into harsh lines. "Did something happen at the Folly?"

She suppressed the desire to fidget like a schoolgirl under that look. Beneath the charm Matt was a tough customer, and a person did well to remember that. "I was going to talk to you first, but if Nate is here . . ." She finished with a shrug.

A sharp knock interrupted them and the door opened.

Holy shit! Nate Evans had grown up and done it good. Thank God, she was sitting down because Nate was a kick to the back of the knees. Darker than Matt, with the same chiseled features and lazy lion eyes. His body filled out his uniform like the thing was ironed onto every curve and ridge. Every hot inch of him yelled "real man." Quite a change from her years amongst pampered show cats. Dear Lord, the girls of Ghost Falls must be falling over themselves. Was that ink she saw peeping out of the rolled-up sleeves of his shirt?

Nate gave her his shy, little-bit-wicked smile. "Hey, Pippa. Heard you were back."

"Hey, Nate," she breathed. *Get ahold of yourself, Pippa, and stop simpering.*

Matt snorted and gave her a hard look over his desk. There went her breathing again, and a prickle of awareness arcing over the paper-strewn wood between them. The same sort of sensual nature's wake-up call she'd been avoiding by being with Ray for the last four years.

"Pippa was about to tell me something about Phi when you came in. She seemed to think it might interest you."

Back on track and about to get very uncomfortable in here. "Yes, it seems that Phi is missing some . . . things."

"Things?" Matt cocked his head. "As in some of her things have been taken?"

Ah, shit. Matt looked annoyed now, and why wouldn't he be? Asking a man if one of his employees was a thief was never going to be an easy conversation. "I'm not sure."

"Either they're there or they're not there, which is it?"

"Easy, Matt." Nate took the seat beside her. "What does this have to do with Matt?"

"I think this is where Pippa is about to ask if the two guys I sent over to check Phi's gutters made off with the family fortune."

Did he have to make it sound so dumb? "I wasn't suggesting anything of the sort."

"So, what are you suggesting? I took them?"

"Will you shut up?" Nate glared at his brother.

"No." Matt placed a firm fist on the edge of his desk. "This is my business and my reputation—"

"I'm not saying anyone stole anything." God, she had to get in here fast before this went even further south. "That's why I came to talk to you first. It doesn't make sense, any of it, and I wanted to ask your opinion."

Matt eased back in his chair.

"I bet you feel like a dick?" Nate threw him an evil grin.

"No, Matt's right. Anything that taints his reputation is bad for business," she said when Nate stared at her. "I'm not saying any of this right because I'm not sure what I'm saying."

Matt leaned forward in his chair and jabbed the button on his intercom. "Mrs. Cameron, could you bring in some coffee?" He sat back again and crossed his arms over his chest. "Why don't we start again?"

Nate waggled his fingers at the intercom. "And some cookies. I've been up since four and haven't had breakfast yet."

"Would you like me to get her to cook you breakfast?" Matt speared his brother with a glance.

Nate considered his suggestion. "You think she would?"

"Tell me about Phi?" Matt said.

So she told them, about the game, the missing treasures, and how she ended up here. Not blaming anyone, fact-finding.

Mrs. Cameron interrupted them with the coffee tray. She kept her gaze averted from Pippa, but gifted Nate with a beaming smile. "I sent out for some muffins, Sheriff. I know you don't get time to eat, and we need you to keep up your strength."

Nate Evans, Ghost Falls chick magnet and dragon tamer.

"What's she doing?" Matt peered over her shoulder.

Jill stood outside the glass wall, two blouses in her hand. Staring straight at Pippa, she put the blue one against her face and raised her eyebrows, took it away and replaced it with a yellow one.

God, not the yellow, it leached all the color out of her face. "She wants me to tell her which blouse," Pippa said.

"After the way she treated you earlier?" Matt half rose from his chair, ready to jump to her defense again.

"It's fine." Pippa waved him down again. "It happens . . . *used to* happen all the time."

"Really?" Matt glanced at Jill.

"I've had people stop me in the street, at restaurants. One woman even chased me into a fitting room." Pippa had never thought she'd miss that.

"So, there was nobody at the house between the roofers leaving and you arriving?" The caffeine seemed to kick-start Nate's sheriff brain.

"No." Pippa dragged her gaze off Jill, who was lifting and lowering blouses on repeat. "But I also have no idea when these things disappeared. It could have happened months ago." She turned back to Matt, who was focused on Jill through the glass wall. "That's why I came to you. I thought you might know more."

"Right." He dragged his attention back at her.

"You know there is another explanation." Nate blew on his coffee and took a careful sip. He added more sugar. "How old is your grandmother?"

"Seventy-eight."

Matt threw her a wry grin. "Don't you mean sixty-eight?"

It warmed her from the inside. Matt got Phi without judgment or condemnation. It was another of those things she liked about him. "It depends who's asking."

"Okay." Nate sipped and added more sugar. Pippa gaped as yet another spoonful of sugar went into his coffee. Damn men and their metabolisms. "There have been a couple of incidents around town—"

"Those were bullshit." Matt slapped his hand down on the desk. "The Diva's eccentric, always has been and you know how this town loves a bit a drama."

"What sort of incidents?" Pippa got a sick feeling in her stomach.

Nate settled down, happy with his cup, at last. "Times when she got a bit confused, misunderstandings. That sort of thing."

"Come on, Nate." Matt shook his head. "That was as much Bets's fault as Phi's."

She didn't give a crap whose fault it was, Pippa could do with knowing what these "misunderstandings" were. "What happened?"

"Phi left Bets's store without paying for something, a carton of milk and some eggs."

"Phi went grocery shopping?" Not the point, but still damn hard to picture.

"June was ill." Matt's tiny smile shared her amazement. You had to know Phi.

"Well, that explains it." Pippa really didn't like where this was going. It too nearly echoed the tiny concern nestling in the back of her brain. "Phi doesn't shop, never has. She probably didn't realize she had to pay."

Nate stopped with his cup halfway to his mouth and gaped at her.

"She always had minions when she was singing. They would take care of the payment, while Phi picked things out." It sounded stupid, but Phi's world was so different from everyone else's. "My mother or the housekeeper get her groceries. Her clothes are made for her and they have an arrangement. The thing with Bets proves nothing."

"It's not the only thing." Nate's gaze flitted from Matt to

her. "I've had to take her home once or twice. Found her on a walk, not sure where to go."

Phi had an excellent sense of direction, when she paid attention to where she was going. Which was not often. Pippa opened her mouth and shut it again. Trying to explain Phi was like trying to explain chaos theory. It didn't make any sense and further explanation only made you more confused. Jill shifted into her sight line with her alternating hangers. Blue shirt? Yellow shirt? Neither, the blue color was better than the yellow but they would both hit her in exactly the wrong place on her hips.

"Look, I have to get going." Nate stood, brushing muffin crumbs off his pants. "If you want to report a theft, I can do something, but until then . . ." He turned back to Matt. "I came to tell you I couldn't make lunch, and ask if you've heard about Eric."

Matt nodded. He kept his gaze on Jill's pantomime. "Yeah, Jo told me."

"I'll believe it when I see it." Nate snorted. Giving her a nod, he left, striding across the open-plan office and taking every female gaze with him.

Except Jill. The woman was relentless.

"Could you just . . . ?" Matt waved his hand at Jill.

Pippa turned to Jill. The woman got more enthusiastic as she noted Pippa's attention. "It won't take long." Pippa yanked open the door to Matt's office. "If you have to choose between those two, I'd go with blue. Yellow will clash with your skin tones."

Jill dropped her arms. "What do you mean, if I have to?"

"The shape." Pippa strode over and took the blue shirt from her. She held it against Jill's torso. "The bottom hits you right at your widest part. Go for something shorter."

"Really?" Jill held both shirts in front of her.

"Look." Gently Pippa turned Jill to face her reflection

in Matt's office wall. "We're all a bit broader across the hip. If you go below that area, your legs will look shorter and make you appear squat." She pressed the blue shirt against Jill's torso and lifted the hem slightly. "But if the shirt hits you higher and narrows under your bust . . ." Bunching up handfuls of fabric she made her point.

Jill's face lit up. "Oooh."

"And you look slim and put together."

There was the look, the one that made Pippa's job all worthwhile. She'd worked her butt off to get to the point she had been before Ray snatched it all away. Dammit, she wanted that back.

"You're right." Jill beamed and scuttled away with her shirts.

Matt loomed up behind Pippa. "You do that well, Agrippina."

The name-calling thing really should have stopped in junior high. "I didn't lose my job because I wasn't good at it . . . Meat."

He grinned. "I'm sure you were." He folded his hand around hers as he walked her out. "How long are you in town?"

"I'm really not sure." Behind Matt's shoulder, Jill waved.

Matt raised her hand to his mouth and pressed a kiss against her fingers. "Don't run out on me again."

Chapter Six

Pippa rode the thrill of Matt's parting all the way home—then she pulled into the kitchen yard and returned to earth with a thump. If not liking your sister made you a bad person, Pippa was in deep, deep shit. She'd tried, okay, maybe not that hard, but there didn't seem to be a middle ground between her and Laura. The sight of Priss Perfect Laura climbing out of her hybrid mom wagon made her bite back a groan.

Laura's beautifully cut linen shirt was neatly tucked into her sensible cargo pants. Functional for Mom-on-the-go, pretty enough to look attractive, age appropriate and cool. You'd think they could have bonded over a shared fashion sense.

Laura glanced up as Pippa drove into the kitchen yard, and then her torso disappeared back into the car again. Not even a fat ass to make Pippa feel nice and smug. Nope, Laura looked fantastic. Like she'd never even had kids.

Sam leaped out of the minivan. Eight years old and cute as a bug, his face split into a huge grin of greeting. "Hey, Pips."

"Hey, little man." Pippa grinned back. Maybe other people had nephews as cute as hers, but she doubted it. "Still up to your old tricks?"

"No." Sam shook his head slowly from side to side, his face serious. Then, he broke into another grin. "I got a whole new bunch now."

Daisy stepped up beside her brother, and Pippa got a bit woozy. It was like looking at herself at age twelve, standing there with her chin stuck out and her I'm-the-shit attitude blaring from top to toe. Seems she'd grown a mini-me while she was away.

"Hello, Pippa." Daisy gave her the teenage squint of death. Mini-me was mad as hell at her.

Pippa didn't give a crap. Daisy could be as mad as she liked. It was wonderful to see her niece again, and Pippa dragged her into a hug. Daisy's slim form stiffened but she leaned in a little to the hug. So, not a complete loss.

Sam threw his arms around her hips and buried his face in her tummy. "I missed you, Pips, where've you been?"

"Working hard." Pippa had missed their sweet faces too. She spent far too much time away from them.

"Or hardly working." Sam mumbled the words against her shirt.

"So." Laura loomed up behind her children. She and Laura shared Phi's red hair, but Laura kept hers smooth and neatly cut into a chin-length bob that looked the bomb on her. "You came home."

It stung that neither she nor Laura could get over themselves enough to do more than spit at each other like wet cats. No, you-look-great, so-do-you, I-missed-you, me-too—love, hugs, kisses. Not in this lifetime. "I came home."

"Staying long?"

The rest of her life if she didn't get this crap fixed. That would probably piss Priss Perfect off no end, the idea of Pippa under her feet for years to come. A familiar knot tightened in Pippa's belly. "I'm not sure."

"Have you called Mom yet?"

"I only got here yesterday, late." A little white lie. Why was she babbling out justifications?

"Mes enfants!" Phi flung open the kitchen door, blinding and bright in her hot pink lounge suit. "Did you see who's home?"

"Hi, Phi." Sam bounced right up to her and stopped. "I like your sparkles."

"Me too." Phi kissed him noisily on the top of his tousled head. "Life is simply not life without sparkles."

"Hello." Daisy approached more slowly, but the look on her face no less delighted.

"Daisy, darling." Phi dragged her great-granddaughter into a hug. "You get lovelier every time I see you. You're going to be a great beauty, just like your mother."

Laura huffed beside Pippa. "More importantly, Daisy, you're going to be clever and a woman who carves her own path in life. We do not define ourselves by our looks."

If Laura hadn't said it, Pippa would have agreed in a heartbeat. Or maybe if Laura had said it without that carrot-up-the-ass voice going on. As it was . . . What could she do? It was bigger than she was. "She'll never catch a rich husband like that," she said, low enough for only Laura to hear.

"Don't start." Laura threw her an icy glare and stalked after her children into the house.

Pippa followed, slowly. Her conversation with Matt and Nate needed some alone time to sort.

As she entered Laura placed her capacious purse on the kitchen table. That thing was half diaper bag, half Louis V, the real kind. They could have talked accessories. But no, they'd spent their teens trying to kill each other, and their twenties staying as far away from each other as they could. And their thirties, keeping it civil in front of the children.

She could do better than this. She loved Laura. They were sisters, even if they behaved like one of them was adopted.

"Nana, do you have everything you need?" Laura hauled an iPad mini from her tote. "I'll be going to Costco later and it's no trouble to pick something up for you."

Phi grabbed an oriental cookie jar off the counter. "I think I'm fine and Pippa can pick up anything I need."

"Right." Laura gave Phi a tight smile and shoved the iPad back into her mobile command center. "Pippa is here now." She made it sound like a bad thing. "I'll pick the children up at five thirty."

Not a minute before and not a minute after. Pippa approved of on time; it shouldn't bug her that her sister was the same. She was thirty-two. Time to stop the knee-jerk, tongue-pulling reflex action when Laura was around. "Unless you'd rather pick up Phi's things."

"No." Laura tossed her head. "I don't mind doing it, but I have enough on my plate." Laura put her bag on her shoulder. "Do you still have the toys I left here last time?"

Pippa gaped at her. Phi had a range of toys in the house. She could never pass an Internet site without ordering more.

Phi had seated Sam and Daisy at the kitchen table. She put three cookies in front of each of them. A chocolate, a peanut butter, and another one Pippa didn't recognize but it could have been raisin.

Laura struck. Snatching up the chocolate and peanut butter, she left the other one. "Nana." She took the jar from Phi and returned the fun cookies. "You know we only do approved snacks."

This liking-Laura thing would be a lot easier if her sister were only marginally less of a control freak.

Sam shoved his remaining cookie into his mouth.

Laura narrowed her eyes at her son's bulging cheeks. "You did make them to the recipe I gave you?"

Phi nodded. "Well, you know I don't bake anything, darling girl, but I gave the recipe to June."

"I'll fetch the toys." Laura slammed the cookie jar back down on the counter. "Daisy knows exactly how much time on each toy, and I wrote Sam's play instructions out for you last time. You do still have them?"

Phi nodded, obediently. Phi being all meek and mild should have had Laura on the alert. But then, you had to know Phi, and Laura had never bothered, because it never occurred to Priss Perfect that her instructions weren't obeyed to the letter.

Laura bustled out of the kitchen to find the approved toys. They sounded about as fun as a kick in the teeth.

"These are not the same cookies we get at home." Daisy popped the last bite into her mouth with a little smirk.

Phi puffed up her chest. "Aren't they? I'm sure June must have made them exactly to the recipe."

"Uh-uh." Daisy shook her head. She leaned toward Phi and whispered, "These have sugar in them."

"No." Phi leaned forward as well until their faces were inches apart. "I would never do that to your mother. June baked the cookies exactly as the recipe said."

Pippa bit back a giggle. June was no more in favor of Laura's mission to rid the world of the scourge of sugar than Phi. Pippa would lay her head on a block that there was even a little extra sugar in those cookies.

"Right." Laura charged back in and dropped a wooden crate on the table. Plastic was outlawed a couple of years back. "We're working on organizational skills and planning at the moment."

"Why?" The question got away from Pippa before she could stop it.

Laura's look of scorn could have seared steak. Only Pippa had been getting it for so long, she'd developed immunity. "These are necessary skills in successful home-work execution and laying the foundation for studying, later on."

"Ah." That's what you got when you were dumb enough to ask.

An alarm went off on Laura's phone. "I need to go." A gathering of gear and a few last-minute instructions and Laura was out the door. It bit her in the ass to do this, but Pippa followed her sister out to her car, the conversation with Matt and Nate still circling Pippa's thoughts.

Laura glanced at her in surprise. "Did I forget something?"

"No." It seemed disloyal to Phi to have this conversation, but if Phi was getting forgetful or maybe losing track of things, she was better off knowing. When she left here, *when*, not *if*, it wouldn't hurt to have some extra eyes on Phi. Even if they were the ever-scornful eyes of Laura. "Listen, have you noticed anything strange about Phi?"

Laura snorted and blipped her alarm.

"I mean more than usual." God, she could smack her sister sometimes. Phi was Phi, and it was a great thing to be.

"In what way?" Laura opened her car door and stood beside it with a let-me-get-out-of-here look on her face.

"I don't know." Careful does it with Laura. "Has she been more forgetful lately?"

Comprehension chased across Laura's face. "You're talking about the thing with Bets and the groceries?"

Okay, Laura knew, so it felt a bit less like talking behind Phi's back. "Yes."

Laura shrugged, climbed into her car, slammed the door, and opened the window a crack. "You know what she's like,

Pippa. God, you spent more time with her than you did with our mother. She's weird."

"Eccentric." The correction was automatic.

"Whatever." Laura pushed the starter button and her car purred to life. "Call Mom."

Laura's car wound down the long drive and disappeared through the tall stand of trees surrounding the gate.

Inside the kitchen, Phi was queen of misrule. Sitting at the kitchen table with Sam and Daisy unpacking the offerings in the crate. Looked like a total yawn to Pippa. Not a Barbie to dress up or a Ninja Turtle in the whole thing.

"You know what?" Phi sat back in her chair and tapped the edge of her chin. "I have an idea."

Sam's and Daisy's faces lit up. Phi's ideas were always the gateway to a whole load of fun. "We're working on organizational skills, and they're very important." She eyed Daisy and Sam in turn. "We should organize my costume wardrobe. The thing is an absolute mess."

Dress up! Pippa's favorite game with Phi, and by the way Sam hopped on his chair, his too. Daisy tried not to look excited, but failed as a huge grin split her face. Dress up with Phi—a wonderland of old operatic costumes, masks, props and makeup. Everything from feather boas to swords, and a huge, mirror-lined room to try them all out in.

Pippa's phone vibrated and she checked the caller ID. Her heart sank, as *Mom* popped up on her screen. Laura must have dialed from the car. "Hi, Mom."

"Pippa." Her mother could load that word with more reproach than Saint Peter. "You're home."

"Yes." Couldn't Laura have waited for her to call their mother first? Nope, that's not how Laura did things. "I arrived yesterday. I was on the verge of calling you."

Phi glanced at her inquiringly and Pippa waved them on. No dress up for ungrateful daughter Pippa.

"Yes," Mom said, and left the heavy silence hanging. "I imagine you're with my mother."

"Yes."

The only thing tenser than her relationship with her mother was the war raging between Phi and Emily. A pretty much one-sided war from where Pippa stood. Her mom kept a long, deep resentment going against Phi. Pippa understood, kind of. Phi was larger than life; growing up as her daughter couldn't have been easy. But then growing up as Emily's daughter hadn't been a cakewalk either. Emily had rules, and lots of them. Mainly to counterbalance her own chaotic childhood. Dragged across Europe during the summer while Phi was on tour and spending the school year in Ghost Falls with her father.

When she'd gotten old enough, Phi had taken her along. Pippa had loved those tours with Phi, thrived on them. Her mother still bore the grudge, after all this time.

"I saw your program."

And you failed. Her mother didn't even have to say the words to send them zinging down the phone lines. *I told you that you would fail and you did.*

"Yes, it's . . . complicated." How to explain that it all started with Pippa getting into a relationship with her boss? Emily would point out the flaws in that plan, calmly and efficiently. She would also point out how she'd never liked Ray and said so on many occasions. Pippa didn't need to hear what she was already living. "Things are not always put on air exactly like they happen."

"Are you saying it didn't happen?"

"No, it happened. Just not like you saw it happen."

Silence, punishing and heavy in the absence of any sort of reassurance. Just once, could her mother ask how she was, and resist the urge to tell her why her answer didn't cut it?

62   *Sarah Hegger*

"Are you coming to see me, or must I come there?" She made Phi's house sound like Sodom and Gomorrah. Which it must be for her mother. The plethora of vibrant color, the dramatic jumble of striking furniture. So at odds with the calm, tasteful tranquility of the home Emily had created around her girls.

"I'll come and see you."

"Fine." That word wielded so skillfully by women of all ages. "Please call first because I have a rather tight schedule and I'll have to fit you in."

Of course she did. Mondays at the retirement center, Tuesday bridge in the morning, followed by the week's baking in the afternoon. Wednesdays were spent at the local elementary school, doing what the teachers needed. And so the week went on. No point in asking if it had changed. Emily liked her routine and stuck to it. "I'll call the day before."

"Tomorrow's no good, I have a town council meeting."

"You're on the town council?"

"Yes, Pippa, I am a member of this community and have been for forty-odd years. I feel obligated to give back to it."

Unlike other people. People who left town and only visited sporadically. The sort of people who went to stay with their grandmother and not their mother. Those sorts of people did not know their duty and they sure as hell didn't do it. People like her . . . and the sperm donor she refused to call father. God. This is why she hated coming home, this right here with her mother, and earlier with Laura. For Phi, she'd be here all year round if she could. And Laura and her mother knew it. "I'll make sure I call first."

"Okay, good." Another awkward pause. "Are you all right?"

"Not really." *I'm shit, my career is in the toilet, my long-term boyfriend and his new piece of tail are the reason it's*

*in the crapper, and pretty much the entire nation thinks I'm
the worst kind of bitch.* "But I'll be fine."

"Call if you need anything." But not during any of
Emily's scheduled events.

Pippa hung up and stared at her phone. What a mess.
They went around in circles, the women in this family.
Emily was at war with Phi, she and her mother didn't get
on. You didn't need a degree in psychology to see the mud
bogging them all down. Was she as bad as her mother?
Holding on to past hurts and grudges, and building a bar-
rier between her mother and herself with them? Probably.
Her life. The giant cosmic joke of the day.

Was it any wonder she'd chosen to focus on her career?
Family, love, attachments—it all got ugly and messy, and
no matter how long you stayed away or how far you went,
those nasty claws reached out and dragged you back in.
Thumbing through her contacts, she found the one she
wanted and hit call.

"Pippa." The cigarette-stained vocals of the show's long-
time editor came down the line. "How are you, girl?"

"Not so good."

Jen sucked in a breath. "Listen, babe, what they did to
you was total shit. I didn't do the editing, I want you to know
that. Ray had someone else do it."

"Thanks for that." Outside the kitchen window a rescue
cat sunned itself beside the fountain. "Listen, can you get
your hands on the original footage?"

"Fuck! Just hang on." The phone clunked in Pippa's ear,
and then the sound of a door closing before Jen picked up
the phone again. "I love you, girl, you know that. Love you
like a sister, but what you're asking, it can't be done."

"Why?" Pippa's frustration bled into her voice.

"Ray, girlfriend. You know who his father is." Jen sounded
defensive now. "If I got that for you, my job would be over.

You know how this town works." The phone crackled as Jen sucked on a cigarette. "Girl, I shouldn't even be talking to you, but we go way back."

Not back far enough, apparently. Pippa hung up not long after. Jen couldn't, or wouldn't, help her. It didn't really matter which. Another door slammed in her face, and as angry as she was about it, Pippa understood. People had their own lives, and their jobs kept them fed.

Tears pricked the back of her eyes, and Pippa blinked them away. She couldn't give up, because right now that job of hers felt like all she had. All right, she had Phi, but the rest of the crapshoot of Ghost Falls—it couldn't be all there was.

Pippa glared out her bedroom window. Self-pity was for losers, and she was feeling sorry for herself. Ergo—great word and you didn't often get a chance to use it—she was a loser. And driving herself crazy.

Thick, laden clouds rumbled overhead and provided the perfect soundtrack to her mood. A mountain storm blew in late afternoon and gathered drama as the evening wore on. It really was quite breathtaking, the pewter clouds truncating the mountaintops to sit heavy and expectant. Lightning flickered through their center as the wind picked up speed and howled through the odd nooks and crannies of the Folly.

Phi's voice throbbed an aria, pure and deep from her room. A recording of *Turandot*. One of her finest roles. God, she'd been something in her time. Formidable. Her whimpering wuss of a granddaughter should try and be more like her.

Turandot stopped her lament and the house fell silent. Phi would be in her huge, pink bower of a bed, eye mask in place, hair tightly curled with bobby pins, about three inches of gunk on her face.

Pippa changed into her pajamas and climbed into her yellow butterfly bed. She'd been so excited the day Phi first showed it to her. The organza bed curtains swayed a little in the breeze, and butterflies danced and shimmered along its length. Wallowing was so not her thing. She needed an action plan, complete with options A, B, and C. It didn't matter if those options changed, as long as the plan was there and she could execute. She got out her iPad and opened Excel. Planning was her crack, her mac and cheese, her washed-out sweatpants.

Column one, goals—stop being a sucky baby, right at the top of the list.

Pippa planned until her eyes got gritty, and by the time she switched off her bedside light, the rock in her chest felt a whole lot lighter.

A gust of wind tossed a patter of raindrops against her window. She snuggled deeper into her bed. To borrow a line from another kickass chick, tomorrow was another day.

Chapter Seven

"Pippa." Matt cupped her cheeks and tugged her closer. He was going to kiss her. Her breasts tingled and her tummy tightened. The full sweep of his sensual bottom lip drew closer.

He focused on her mouth, eyes heavy with intent, and licked her forehead.

Wait. That couldn't be right. But he did it again. A wet, cold, slopping lick on the forehead. Except Matt wasn't here, because this was a damn dream and she was actually getting wet.

Pippa blinked open her eyes and got another drop on her cheek. The drops sped up, and she jackknifed into a sitting position. The bed on her left side was soaked. She scrambled out of bed and stood on the cold floor as more drops came down from the ceiling. Shit, the roof was leaking, right onto her bed. Goddamn it. Matt had mentioned something about the roof, and she'd let it slip her mind.

Waking Phi up was so not an option. The Diva did not rise until the Diva was good and ready. Well, the Diva wasn't getting a cold shower in bed. Pippa stomped out of her bedroom and into the hall. The place was darker than a sinner's soul with Phi's heavy drapes blocking out any light.

Pain lanced up her foot as she stubbed her toe on the claw foot of a large chair on her way to the stairs. "Shit."

No matter how much Phi didn't like to be woken, Pippa wasn't taking that staircase in the dark. She fumbled about, hit the wrong thing, which rocked against the wooden hall table, and found a lamp. Dim, amber light warmed the hall and gave her enough illumination to stagger down the stairs.

Phi had to have a bucket somewhere in this heap of stones. The kitchen was her best guess and she headed there.

She tried under the sink. Rags, detergents, rubber gloves, and enough dishwasher soap to wash years' worth of dishes, but no bucket. The stables would have a bucket. Pippa twitched back the kitchen curtain and peered outside. Rain bucketed down and dropped more water onto the sodden kitchen yard.

New plan, one involving boots and a raincoat. She went back into the hall. The damn hat stand stood skeletal beside the door, artfully draped in a couple of silk scarves and a tiara left over from dress up this afternoon. And beneath the scarves, an umbrella.

Thank you, Lord. Pippa snatched it up and went back into the kitchen. A glance at the kitchen clock told her what she already knew. It was I-should-be-sleeping o'clock. She loved Phi, really she did, but would it kill her grandmother to have something practical lying about, like a coat? Pippa cracked open the top half of the kitchen door. Wind whipped the door out of her hand and sent it thundering into the wall.

Three very wet hours—okay, maybe twenty seconds—later, Pippa wrestled the damn thing closed again. On to her third plan, which was nothing. She could sleep in the salon. On satin Louis XVI furniture.

The message light on the phone lit up the dark hallway outside the kitchen in eerie red blinks.

Instead of dreaming stupid hot, sweaty dreams about Matt, she should have gotten him to fix the roof. Matt, dry and at home, probably fast asleep. And that pissed her off so much, it made her head spin. She marched over to the phone and snatched it up. His number was right where she'd programmed it on speed dial. Phi wasn't the only diva in this house, not tonight.

He answered on the four hundredth—make that about seventh—ring. A sleepy, husky drawl that hit her straight in the girl parts. "Hello?"

"Hi, Meat, it's Pippa."

"Pippa?" Some of the sleepy drifted out of his voice and shuffling noises from the other side had her picturing him sitting up in bed. Was he alone? God, she hoped so.

"I'm wet."

Deep silence. "Pardon?"

The way he said it made her face heat. "I mean I'm getting wet because there is a hole in my bedroom ceiling."

He laughed. Deep-roasted and raspy and so damn gorgeous she clenched her thighs together. "I guess you called to tell me the roof is leaking."

"Yup."

"You know"—the phone crackled in her ear as he moved—"some people wait until morning to call the contractor."

"It is morning." A smile crept up her face. She'd dialed on impulse, never a great idea, but he was so good-natured about it. "And I was pissed off."

"Tell me about wet." Oh, he was bad and naughty. "Where is the roof leaking?"

"Um, it seems to be right above my bed."

"That's what I thought. I warned Phi about it the last time I was there." He yawned. "Want me to strap on a tool belt and rush right over?"

She closed down the Matt Pinterest board building in her head. "Nah, that's okay. I shouldn't have woken you up. I don't wake up cheerful at the best of times."

"Maybe that's because you don't go to sleep happy." He did great phone voice.

Her imagination took over the journey. Matt in a low-slung tool belt and not much more. Matt in a bath towel and not much more. Matt in bed, in absolutely nothing. *Stop already*. "Do you go to bed happy?"

"Sometimes." He chuckled, low-down and dirty. "Do you?"

"Not lately." As in years. As in the closest she could get to going to bed happy, was mildly contented. "Not in a long time."

"That's a pity. We should see what we can do about that?"

Her knees loosened and she leaned against the wall for support. The receiver slipped in her sweaty hand and she tucked it between her shoulder and her ear. "That sounds like you're offering."

"What if I was?"

Standing was overrated. She slid down the wall until her ass hit the cold floor. "I told you before. You have to ask first before I give you an answer."

"I'm asking now."

Did he just proposition her? And was she giving it way too much thought?

"Have dinner with me?" he said.

A tight curdle of disappointment gripped her gut. Dinner with Meat Evans was good, dinner would be . . . nice. "I'm not sure that's a good idea."

"I am."

"Do you always proposition women so fast?"

He laughed again. "Pippa, I've been trying to ask you out for years. You don't leave a guy a huge window of opportunity. And last time you were here, you disappeared to LA before I could get to you. So, in this case, I'm coming on strong."

"Oh." What had she been hoping for? "I'll think about it."

"What's to think about, it's only dinner."

It was only dinner, and she felt horribly let down. This warranted a stern talking-to. Pippa St. Amor didn't feel let down over men, because she didn't let them under her skin. And she had a crappy life to get back on track. She didn't have time and energy for relationships. Or dinner. "I should let you get back to sleep."

"Where will you sleep?"

"I'll grab a spare blanket and use one of the spare rooms. June doesn't make them up when there's nobody here, but it'll do for the few hours left." That should have been plan three. "I could have done that before and not called you in the middle of the night."

"I'm glad you called."

Her heart gave a leap. Keeping a cool head might be easier if he quit saying things like that. "I woke you up."

"It doesn't matter." More rustling from his side. "So have you had enough time to think yet?"

Crazy man. "No."

"Got an ETA on that?"

"Nope."

"Ah, I see, playing hard to get."

"Would you chase?" Something about Matt made this stuff come out of her mouth.

He chuckled. "I hadn't got that far in my thinking. We could always find out."

Pippa propped her bleary eyes open and winced at the

volume Phi put out. Another sleepy morning bath left her feeling half alive. She'd gotten dressed on autopilot, and made it into the kitchen about thirty seconds before Phi launched.

"We will shop." Phi had an armful of bangles on this morning that clashed through Pippa's head like the anvil chorus.

"Shop for what?"

Phi's eyes widened. She went green and sparkly this morning for eye makeup and it made the effect even more dramatic. "Your bedroom. Fate has interceded and encouraged us to redecorate that room."

A little extreme there. Some good sense was called for, if she could get her sluggish brain to come up with some. "Phi, all we need to do is dry out the mattress and wash the sheets. And it wasn't fate, it was a leaky roof."

Phi let forth with a trill to make the glasses vibrate in the cabinet. "Darling, you lack vision." Her bracelets crashed. "We will create a space in which you feel your heart can mend."

Seemed a lot to ask of some bed linen and a few pieces of furniture. And her heart wasn't really the problem. Ray had hurt her, for sure, but to break her heart, he'd have had to have held it in the first place. "Phi, I won't be here for long. Just until I can get this Ray crap sorted out."

Phi gave her a crafty smile.

"I know that look, Phi." Pippa wasn't as clueless as Laura. Her grandmother had something stewing in that fertile brain of hers.

"Ma petite!" Phi batted her sparkly green lashes. "You are too suspicious. It makes the skin wrinkle between your eyebrows and will give you horrid lines when you are my age."

"And besides." Pippa sucked back her coffee. "I am probably America's most hated television personality right now. Do you really think going out and about in public is the best idea?"

Phi smacked her hands down on the kitchen table. "It is the perfect idea. Never let them see you sweat, darling. Never. Now come along, grab one of those marvelous purses of yours, and let us away." With a flourish, Phi exited stage left, sweeping out the kitchen door and into the yard. She stood beside the car, tapping her foot.

Pippa downed her coffee dregs, snatched up her keys from the counter, and grabbed her purse. This was so not a good idea, but you could never tell Phi anything she didn't want to hear. It was going to be a damn bloodbath. The things she did for her grandmother.

Of course, Phi didn't want to shop in the meager offerings of Ghost Falls but insisted on driving an hour and a half farther to Salt Lake City. As they parked under a downtown mall, Pippa prayed her viewership in Utah was low.

Phi chattered the entire time. Sitting beside Pippa like a visiting princess. Wasn't the sky the most sublime shade of cerulean? What did that woman think she was wearing? Watch out, Salt Lake City. Pippa locked the car and followed in the wake of Hurricane Philomene.

They made it into Macy's on an empty elevator, Phi bobbing her head to the Muzak as they rode.

Pippa kept her head low as they wove through the women's section and into home goods. Thank God, it was quieter in here. Fewer people to turn and gawk. And gawk they did. Phi moved through a crowd like a radioactive ripple, leaving nobody undisturbed. People's gazes flitted right over her and locked onto Phi. If Pippa stayed in the slipstream, she might make it through this in one piece.

"Darling." Phi lighted on a display, arms pinwheeling. "Don't you just adore this?"

Pippa blinked to be sure she was seeing the right thing. "It's snot green."

"Snot green." Phi's voice reverberated off the ceiling. For the woman who could fill La Scala, Macy's on a Friday morning was a cinch. "It's olive."

No way in hell was she sleeping on that. "It went past olive several shades back."

"I can see you are going to be difficult to please," Phi said with a happy little titter, and charged on. "Stop."

Heads whipped around to stare.

Phi's hands went straight up in the air. "I have found it."

"Not if it's that horrible mustard thing you haven't." Pippa stayed well in the shadows as people's gazes tracked Phi around the store.

"Mustard." Phi snorted. "It is definitely old gold."

"It's mustard and those orange things all over it are even worse."

"Well, then." Phi jammed her fists on her hips and did a slow three sixty. "Miss Impeccable Taste, you pick something."

"Excuse me." A quiet voice came from behind Phi.

Phi whirled to reveal a slim twentysomething woman peering at Pippa. "You're her, aren't you?"

"I—"

"Of course she is, darling." Phi boomed across the store. "Are you a fan?"

"I am." The woman nodded, her mousy brown hair bobbing around her thin face. "I was wondering if you could . . . I mean if you're not too busy, and I'm not interrupting . . ."

"Speak up, dear." Phi increased her volume as if to make up for the other woman's quieter note.

The woman's cheeks went pink. "I was over there shopping for a dress and I . . ." She shook her head and went even pinker. "No, never mind, it's nothing."

"She has superb taste." Phi leaned forward and stage-whispered to the woman. "You would like to ask Pippa's opinion, wouldn't you?"

Was she not standing here? Had she disappeared into the comforters behind her? "I'm not sure—"

"Lead on, dear." Phi patted the woman's arm. "Let us choose for you the most exquisite of gowns. Something to highlight your exceptional good looks."

"Oh, well, I . . ."

Pippa had to give it to Phi. She had the magic. The woman seemed to shimmer, sparkle, and glow in front of them. Her rather plain features took on a light that had been missing before.

"Let's look at the dress," Pippa said before she changed her mind. "We were only arguing over sheets anyway."

The woman led them back into the women's section. "I'm Carly, by the way."

"Carly?" Phi pursed her lips. "Is that short for Carlotta, or Charlotte perhaps?"

"Umm . . . no." Carly's gaze flickered in Pippa's direction, a silent plea for help.

"Come on, Phi." Pippa tucked her arm through her grandmother's. "Nobody but you insists on naming people after operatic characters."

"Well, they should," said Phi, with a nod that indicated the matter was settled. She found an armchair in the fitting room and settled herself like a queen about to hold court.

"What's the occasion?" Pippa turned back to Carly.

The next hours reminded Pippa of why she loved this so much. When she'd started out, it had been all like this, that great moment when someone looked at herself and saw the potential come to life. Watching a woman find her mojo right in front of her. There was nothing like it. When she was working with a woman on her show, she had been able to forget the feral behavior that surrounded a career in television. The women on the show made everything worth it.

Carly ended up with a lovely, simple cocktail dress, a pair of jeans, two shirts, and a great little skirt that she could dress up or down.

The fitting room filled as they shopped and talked. More women poured in from the main floor, clutching all manner of items and standing patiently chatting with Phi while they waited for Pippa's attention. An attendant popped her head in for a while, and went away with a happy smile. She returned with a bottle of water for Pippa and a steaming latte for Phi.

Phi was in her element. Sitting in her chair, chatting to everyone around her.

"Not the black." Pippa replaced a top with another for a middle-aged woman.

Two young girls peered around the corner.

"What's going on?" The one behind craned her neck to get a good look.

"Looks like some sort of makeover thing," the one in front said.

Her friend looked at Pippa, and her eyes widened in recognition. Her mouth popped open and then she giggled. "Hey, it's that chick who spazzed out on YouTube."

Pop. The magic bubble imploded and reality whaled in like a prizefighter. Around her, women stopped, stared, whispered, as if they'd just received the same bitch slap. Like a smelly old dog, her reputation as America's most hated personality slunk back into the room.

"I think I'll take the black." The woman snatched back her top, and stepped away from Pippa as if she was contagious.

The eyes on her turned hostile, speculative, searching. For a time there, nobody had thought of her as the bitch who ripped into Allie. They'd been talking to the old Pippa. The real Pippa. God, this morning made her want that back even more.

Phi rose to her feet in a rustle of fabric. "Well, then, I think we will get to our own shopping."

Pippa followed Phi out of the fitting room like a criminal. It had been too easy to forget when she was doing what she loved best. Ray owed her big for this, and she was done taking it. Damn it, these women lapped up what she did. Lots of them needed it. Ray had no right to take that away.

"I think we should lunch in the village." Phi's name for Ghost Falls, and granted, the town was small, but not that small. Then again, it had been nothing more than a dusty outpost in the mountains when Phi grew up there.

"No." This crawling was old already. "We'll go to Lamb's, you love it there. But before then, we have some bed linen to buy. Only let's leave the butterflies on the bed curtains, I like those."

Pippa was done hiding.

Chapter Eight

"Woman spazzing out on YouTube." Who would have thought you could type that in and find anything. It might have been mildly amusing if that woman hadn't been her. Sweet Mother of God, how many hits had the damn thing received? Surely that comma in the views tally was in the wrong place.

After lunch with Phi, they'd picked out some bed linen without too much more fuss. A woman shopping for pillows had given her a glare, but that was about it. Pippa waited for Phi to go and have her afternoon nap before she braved YouTube. She'd stopped watching the clips and reading the articles after her abortive early attempts to set the record straight.

Pippa hit play. Five minutes later she was ready to puke. Seeing it again brought it all back. Shit, Ray had stitched her up good. He'd always been a skillful editor but this shit was masterful. No wonder women reacted like they did. She wanted to slap herself. Ray made her look hard, callous, and ruthless. She looked like she'd stripped Allie of her dignity and made her crawl. No great surprise that Allie didn't want anything more to do with her.

Pippa watched it again. And felt even sicker. She paused

the clip and studied her face. The camera caught her looking bitter and angry. Her eyes slitted and her mouth contorted viciously.

Someone had to have that original footage, and be prepared to give it to her. Flipping through her contacts, she weighed them up as she went. Maybe one of the cameramen? She tried texting this time.

"Hey." Matt stood in her bedroom doorway in jeans and a plain green tee. Her pulse did a weird flip thing as he smiled, soft and gentle and glad to see her. "What you doing?"

"Watching the woman who spazzed out on YouTube." She pushed her laptop across the bed toward him. "Have you seen it?"

"Yup." He stepped into the room, making it shrink around him. Pushing the computer closer to her, he perched on the end of the bed. They couldn't teach what he did to denim around the thighs. "You didn't say it, that's all I need to know."

Damn, if that didn't make her chest warm and tears prick the back of her lids.

His strange, lion eyes held her gaze. Honest, true, steady. Men like this were rare, nonexistent in her life of the last ten or so years. Her voice came out all gummed up and she cleared her throat. "Thank you."

He stroked her cheek with the back of his fingers. "It wasn't meant to make you sad."

"It was nice."

"Yeah." He shrugged and dropped his eyes. "So, I'm here to look at your ceiling."

"Oh." She stared up at the ceiling. A muddy stain oozed over the plasterwork. "It's not leaking now."

"Hmm." He tilted his head, the suntanned column of his

throat inviting a girl to bury her face there. "It's not raining, either. Do you think there could be a connection?"

"Smart-ass." She laughed, and it lifted some of the nasty fog in her head. Matt could always make her laugh. "I haven't watched it since the first time it aired."

"What made you watch it now?" He had this way of being, not judging or trying to fix things, that made him easy as hell to talk to.

Pippa spilled her day with Phi. "And I still have these tabloids calling me, all the time. They want to print my side of the story." As if! She made a rude noise. "And I finally made it onto *The Tonight Show*, as the opening joke."

He pulled the corners of his mouth down and shrugged. "You said it yourself, this shit will go on until they find something better to talk about."

"It can't come fast enough."

"You know." He got to his feet. "I think we're going to have to speed up the timeline on your whole hard-to-get thing." The subject change left her wrong-footed and struggling to make the mental leap.

"Normally, I would ask a couple more times. Maybe even do a bit of begging." He shrugged. "In a totally not desperate way, of course."

"Of course."

His eyes glittered, alive and alluring. "You would eventually be overcome by my manifest charms."

"Manifest charms? That's a lot of charms, Meat."

"Yeah, well." He grabbed her hand and hauled her off the bed. "You hang out with Phi long enough and shit rubs off."

"What are you doing?" She dug her heels in before he dragged her out of the room.

"We're doing the date thing, right now."

Pippa looked down at her baggy sweats. "I don't think so."

"You look fine for what I have in mind."

And what was that exactly? That wicked gleam was doing nice things to her libido. "I didn't say I would go on a date with you."

"True." He stepped right into her, heat coming off his big body in waves. "But we agreed that my charms would do the trick in the end and you would anyway."

Her body swayed toward him as if they were connected somehow. "I didn't agree to that."

"Sure you did." His eyes burned almost gold, liquid and hot. "Or you were about to, which is the same thing."

Going out with Matt or sitting on her bed feeling sorry for herself. No real contest. "Where are we going?"

"I'm working on it." He kept hold of her hand, a snug, right fit that radiated all the way up her arm.

"How about working on the leak?"

"Already taken care of." He led her into the hallway. "Phi," he yelled. "I'm taking Pippa out. Don't wait up."

"C'est merveilleux," Phi called back.

"Whatever that means." He frog-marched her down the stairs and into the kitchen. Snatching up a pair of runners, he handed them to her. "I insist on footwear."

"Okay." She slipped them on and trailed him to his truck. "How's the date plan coming?"

His grin started in his eyes and spread down to his full mouth like sunlight across the yard. "Do you still plan everything?"

"Doesn't everyone?"

He shook his head and smirked. "Don't worry about this plan, I think I've got it."

"As long as it involves alcohol."

"Figures." He snorted and opened the door for her. "Now I have to spring for a six-pack, and the gas."

"You sure know how to show a girl a good time."

"You bet ya." He slammed the door and jogged round to the driver's side. "We have to make a couple of stops and then it's off to Lovers' Leap for you."

"No." Pippa stared at him. Caught between a laugh and a sigh. Lovers' Leap, the high school make-out spot up above the Coleman farm.

"The view is spectacular." He failed the innocent look right out.

"Uh-huh." They drove out of the yard, through Phi's "verdant thicket" and onto the main road. "Just so you know, I've never been to Lovers' Leap."

He snapped his head round before turning his gaze back to the road. "You are kidding me, right? Every girl in town has been to Lovers' Leap. Some of them should be paying rent by now."

"Not every girl." She adjusted her sweats over her ankles. Some girls got the reputation for being stuck up. Even in a town where teenage boys vied for the attention of the small pool of girls at their disposal, some girls never got asked to go parking at Lovers' Leap. And why was this bugging her anyway? High school was years ago. Maybe because she'd been secretly hoping a boy would ask all through high school. Say, someone who was hot, popular, rumored to be in line for a college football scholarship, a senior not scared off by a fancy way of speaking, and a bit of a stick up the ass.

Well, he'd asked now. Or rather, dragged her into the car and was taking her there. God, her teenage heart would be swelling like one of those pink helium balloons they decorated the school gym with for the Valentine's stomp. At least the parts of that teenage heart that still clung to its romantic notions of love and forever. "They didn't ask because I intimidated them," she said.

A smile curled the corners of his mouth. "You mean because you were stuck up."

It didn't hurt when he said it with that smile. "That, too."

"And just so you know," he said. "My brother would have totally asked, but he was too chickenshit."

Deep inside, awkward teenage Pippa perked right up and tossed her ponytail.

"I know Nate wanted to." He frowned and gave it a bit of thought. "And Eric, for that matter, but he was a junior and scared you'd be freaked out."

"Eric?" The second Evans, good-looking like all of them, but super smooth and a little scary. "I wouldn't have gone with Eric. But Nate." She hummed as if giving it serious consideration. "With that whole bad-boy vibe he had going. Even though he was in my year, and maybe lacked the cool factor of Eric. I—"

"Should quit now." His jaw stuck out, not seriously pissed, but a little miffed for sure.

"I was going to say, I was holding out for the older Evans anyway."

"Me?" He stared at her, hard.

Her cheeks heated. "I had a bit of a crush on you."

He grinned and stared out the windshield. "I know."

"What?" Cocky son of a bitch.

His grin morphed into a laugh. Warm, deep with a little husk hanging on the end. "You used to go all cute and pink when I spoke to you."

"How would you know, you never spoke to me."

"Yes, I did."

"No, you didn't."

"Did too."

"Did not."

"Outside the science lab, you were practicing for some debate thing, and I was on my way to practice."

Pippa had to think hard. "You can't have that one. All you did was that chin thing."

"I'll have you know, a lot can be said with that chin thing." He did it right then.

"What was that saying?"

"That was 'hey.'"

"Then that's what you said."

"No." He shook his head. "I did this one." He did the identical chin lift thing again.

Pippa laughed. "It's the same."

"It's not. Watch." He did it again and she got nothing. They could be at this all night. Her earlier grump had disappeared like smoke. Being with Matt was an instant panacea to self-pity.

He pulled into the lot of Bets's Grocery. "I'll be right back."

"The truck's still running."

He stopped with one foot on the ground. "And?"

"The environment." Pippa rolled her eyes.

"I didn't want my date getting hot and grumpy." He gave her that killer smile. Okay, so no eco-warrior, but so sweet. "My date gets grumpy and I don't get lucky."

He jogged away before she could work up a snappy comeback. She nearly hung out the window and yelled that he wasn't getting lucky anyway. Two reasons why not: First, the parking lot was busy and the denizens of Ghost Falls would love that. And second, she hadn't decided if he was or was not yet. Which made it a damn good thing he hadn't asked her to go parking in high school or God alone knows where she might have ended up. Given the depth of her confused crush at the time, the back of his truck wasn't a far stretch.

Ten minutes ago, she'd been holed up in her room in Phi's house, wallowing in the sucking mud that was her life. She laid her head back on the rest. The hum of the engine lulled her, and the cool air felt great on her heated face.

Matt appeared at the grocery store door, his hands filled with bags. He nodded greetings across the parking lot as he strode toward the truck. Big, long-legged, loose-limbed, like he had his own soundtrack playing behind him. JT's "SexyBack" popped into her head. Yup, that was Matt. A rush of warm air came in through the door as he opened it. "Bets says to say hi."

Pippa nearly rolled her eyes. This town. She would lay money on Bets squatting behind her older-than-God cash register peering through the security monitors to get an eyeful of what happened next. "I feel like I should flash her or something."

Matt laughed and leaned over to put the bags on the backseat. "As much as I support that idea, it might kill her."

Pippa snorted. Bets and her three-pack-a-day habit would outlive them all. She could hear the old woman now. She slumped into a close approximation of Bets's posture. "Matt Evans was just in." *Cough, wheeze.* "Had that uppity Turner girl with him." *Cough.* "Turner is what they christened her and Turner is what I'll call her until some man changes her name."

Matt stared at her. "That is scary good, and totally not hot."

She grinned at him; her Bets was some of her best work. She peered around him at the bags. "So, what did you get?"

"The finest in romantic fare that Bets had to offer."

Romantic? She really liked the sound of that and she shouldn't. She didn't do romance. Romance led to love, and love led to people walking out without looking back. "A pack of Bud and a couple of Twinkies?"

"Something like that." He smiled and kept his eyes on the road.

They passed the town square, the lights to the sheriff's office still on. The Nate she remembered had been the town rebel. "Just how did Nate get to be sheriff anyhow?"

Matt glanced in the same direction. "He got into some trouble the year after he finished high school." His jaw tightened. "Bigger stuff, way bigger than I could deal with."

"And your mom?"

Matt shrugged. "She doesn't handle stuff like that well."

Nope, Cressy Evans didn't. She'd left the messy stuff to her oldest son. He must have been about twenty-three then. Already running his dad's business for four years.

"Nate was hit hard by Dad dying. He was always a bit wild, but that drove him over the edge. For a while there, I thought we might not get him back." Matt turned his attention back to the road.

Pippa heard the stuff he didn't say. He'd been worried about his brother, not able to handle the situation, and with nobody to turn to. "What happened?"

"Old Sheriff Wheeler got involved." Matt took the turn out of town onto Rural Sixty. "He gave Nate a choice, go to jail or go to the Academy." Matt shrugged. "Nate made the right choice. The smart choice. Did a few years in Salt Lake, then came home when Sheriff Wheeler got sick."

"Cancer, right?"

"Yeah." Matt shook his head. "Liver. Took him so fast. It was like he was fine one day and then, nine months later, we were burying him."

"But Nate's appointment is new. He wasn't sheriff when I was last here."

"Just this year." No mistaking the pride in Matt's voice. "We had another sheriff for a while, but he didn't take to Ghost Falls, and Ghost Falls wanted Sheriff Wheeler back. When the election came up, a whole bunch of people pushed Nate to run. He did and we now have one of the youngest sheriffs in the state."

"And Eric? What's he doing?"

Tension crept into Matt's posture. A subtle tightening around his shoulders. "Eric is in Denver, big property developer. We don't see a lot of him."

She gathered as much from the conversation she'd caught between him and Nate. "And Isaac works with you?"

"Yup." He said it quickly, slamming the door on that line of questioning.

It was better that way. Talking families and their issues smacked of involvement, and this was not that. The road wound through the mountains, breathtaking in their rocky rise against the darkening sky. "And you? Why aren't you married?"

He relaxed and flashed her a grin. "You asking because you're interested?"

"Interested in you answering the question, yes." It was hard to keep a stern face when he gave her that panty-melting grin.

"Didn't have much time for dating when I was learning the ropes of the business. I owe Phi everything for that." He slowed for the turn to the Coleman farm. "And you know about the woman shortage in this town." Shortage yes, but they'd have to be dead not to see the possibilities in Matt Evans. "All the women I liked were married by the time I got around to getting serious. Or moved away."

He slid a sly glance her way and she laughed. Smooth-talking son of a bitch. It got her every time. The truck jounced over the rutted road through the scrub oak. She clung to the dashboard, glad for the truck. "Was it always this bad?"

"Sure." Matt laughed. "I think it's Coleman's way of trying to keep the teenagers off his land. I'm convinced he comes out here and roughs it up every spring."

"People still park here?"

"I dunno." He eased around a bend. "It's been a while since I was up here."

He slowed for another hairpin and Pippa gasped. The view was unbelievable.

Matt stopped the truck and she stared. The road ended with the steep side of a canyon. Beyond it rose the wall of the Wasatch Mountains in every direction. Snow still clung to the higher reaches, laying a white carpet between the thin scattering of trees. "It's beautiful."

"And mostly wasted on a bunch of horny teenagers." Matt's face was still and carved as he stared at the view.

He turned to her, his eyes unreadable. Matt moved constantly, laughing, making her laugh, busy and always doing. The moment of stillness had a strange intimacy to it. It wrapped around her like an embrace, warming a place inside she'd almost forgotten about. A girl she didn't think she knew anymore. And Pippa panicked. No other word for the wash of soul-numbing fear that took her with it. She whirled around and grabbed for the bags. "What did you buy?"

"Provisions," he said.

In the crackle of plastic and opening of beer bottles, she got it under control. Tucked that part of her firmly where it belonged and accepted a sub, still warm in her fingers. "It seems Bets is branching out."

"There was a rumor earlier this year that another grocery store was coming into town. Bets upped her game."

Bread! Dear Heaven, carbohydrates. You had to love them. Pippa sank her teeth into the sub and chewed slowly.

Matt watched, a small smile playing around the corners of his mouth. "Good?"

"Great." She took a huge bite and he had to wait a bit for her reply. "This must be the first sandwich I've eaten in years."

He grunted. "That's too long."

"Tell me about it." And cheese, real cheese that melted on your tongue. "This is so good."

He gave a small huff of laughter. "Who'd have thought Pippa Turner was a cheap date."

She didn't care. The sandwich and the beer were enough to keep her happy for the rest of the night. She took a swig and savored the ice-cold bite of hops on her tongue. "Ray would disagree with you."

"Huh." He made short work of his sandwich and crumpled the wrapper in his huge fist.

"My ex, Ray." The sudden need to share didn't seem odd, sitting here with Matt, drinking beer, eating subs, and looking at the most incredible view she'd seen in years. Maybe ever. "He says I'm a tough date, always did. He used to like that about me."

"What changed?"

"I got older."

Matt swung in his seat to look at her. "Wanna say that again?"

"I got too told for Ray." Saying it aloud dragged the claws right through her gut. She was thirty-two, thirty-fuck-ing-two. "He wanted something younger, easier to control."

"Jerk."

It made no sense, but she was laughing. How did he make her laugh when baring her soul? "That about sums it up."

"And he deserves to lose you for it."

The intimacy crept back into the truck. A little tingle that started at the base of her spine and edged up to her nape. It sparked and jolted her nerve endings awake and made her brain stutter to a halt. Pippa breathed in, out, and went with it. "You think?"

"I think." He jammed his beer in the cup holder. "You're the real deal, Miss Pippa St. Amor. You're classy, clever, funny, and kind."

"I'm not kind." Is that the way he saw her? Thrilling, and a little intimidating. How did a girl live up to all that?

"Yeah, you are. The way you talked to the women in my office. The thing that bugs you the most about that YouTube thing? The other woman. Your dick of an ex laid you bare, stripped you down and shoved you in front of the nation to be hated. That gets to you, sure it does. You wouldn't be human if it didn't. But what gets you more is that the woman with you in that clip got hurt too." He turned sideways and laid his arm over the back of the seat. His fingertips brushed the ends of her hair. "And you take care of your grandmother."

"Not like you do. You're here all the time for her."

His finger curled around her nape, sensitizing the skin and sending tingles straight to her nipples. "I owe Phi, as well as the fact that there's nobody else on this planet like that old broad. But you, you just love her and you make sure she knows it in a hundred different ways."

"This is not me you're describing." He wouldn't be saying this if he spent a day with her in LA. It got hard to think with the stroke of those long, callused fingers on her neck.

"Sure it is. You call when you can. The little gifts you

send her all the time that tell her you're thinking about her. She shows them to me."

"You take care of your family." The waiting for him to move churned through her tight belly.

"We're not talking about me."

"What are we doing?"

His other hand took her beer and placed it in a cup holder. "Not sure about you, but I was getting ready to make my move."

"You're taking a long time."

"Just setting the scene, smoothing the way." A slight pressure on her nape brought their faces closer. His breath stroked warm and yeasty over her lips. "I forgot to add something to your list of finer qualities."

"What's that?" He had a beautiful mouth, the top lip fine and clearly etched, the bottom plumper and made for sinking your teeth into. "You're so hot, you make me ache."

Oh dear Lord, aching like she was? Not possible. His mouth brushed hers. Soft, seeking. Pippa increased the pressure, opening her mouth beneath his.

With a groan, he cupped the side of her jaw with his free hand and angled her head, taking the kiss deeper. His tongue brushed into her mouth, firm and demanding.

Heat shot straight between her legs at the silky glide of his tongue against hers. She tasted the slight tang of beer and male musk. Shit, she'd almost forgotten how great a man tasted. He exploded through her senses, nipples tight, moisture flooding her core. Raging, unsatisfied, and, yes, aching need. Her breasts swelled, between her legs a pulse pounded to get closer. She fisted her hands in his shirt and held on.

Her knee hit the gearshift but she kept on going. He had what she needed wrapped in denim and cotton and she was getting close to it. Her ankle banged against the driver's door, but she got it around him. Tucked her legs in between hard bits of plastic and metal and Matt. All of Matt, hot and hard beneath her thighs.

Her core grazed his erection. Her sweatpants thin enough to feel how hard he was beneath his jeans. Shit, she did this to him. And he made her so wet it was nearly embarrassing. If she could give a crap about anything else, but his mouth, his tongue, his hands fisted in her hair. The steering wheel pressed her tight to him, hard at her back. Matt even harder at her front.

His hands slid beneath her shirt, rough and warm on her back, his fingers digging into her skin and letting her know she did it for him, too.

The horn blared and Pippa leaped. Teeth scraped, and she nipped his lip, hard enough to bring the salty copper of blood to her tongue. "Shit." Her breath came out in pants that mingled with his in the tiny space between them. "Sorry."

"Totally worth it." His tongue darted out and licked away the tiny spot of blood. "Pippa Turner, you were well worth waiting for."

A warning bell tolled in her mind, but very softly. "Don't get all sappy on me, Meat."

"God forbid." He nipped her bottom lip. "You're too stuck up for that."

She laughed. "Yeah, but I'm not easy. Second base and no further."

He frowned and hummed as if in thought. "Okay. For the sake of clarity though, what exactly is second base?"

"Nothing under my clothes." Pippa needed to slow this down. Kissing Matt could get out of control too fast, and she liked this. She could handle this much.

He cupped her breasts and she gasped as the heat shot through her. "So this is okay?"

"Uh-huh." It came out as a breathy moan as he brushed her nipples with his thumbs.

"I can work with this." His mouth slanted over hers in another drugging kiss.

Chapter Nine

Pippa woke up feeling like one of those mattress commercials where the girl opens her eyes, sits up, and stretches with a great sappy smile on her face. That girl was her, and the sappy smile froze on her face. What the hell did she think she was doing?

She hadn't been thinking at all when she'd gone to sleep with the taste of Matt still on her lips. So horny her body had been alive in places she didn't know she had. They'd made out like crazy kids until her lips chapped and she ached from pressing into him. Then, Matt had helped her clamber back over the gearshift and brought her home. He'd walked her to the door and stayed for one more blistering kiss on the porch. She'd floated up the stairs like Cinderella.

But that was last night, and the good feeling was dissipating faster than the drops of condensation on her window. She couldn't get involved with Matt. Matt was Mister Small Town, Mister Family Guy—in as much as he took care of his mother and siblings. And she was out of here as soon as she could get her life back on track. Relationships weren't part of her future, and certainly not the sort of connection a guy like Matt would be looking for.

There was a damn good reason they'd danced around each other for all these years. There wasn't any future in it, and never could be. What if he developed feelings for her? That would make her the worst kind of bitch, to use him to get her mojo back and then blow him off. For the first time in twelve years, she didn't know exactly where she was going next. The future terrified her, looming like a black, amorphous blob of what-the-hell. Building a career took the kind of time and energy that didn't include a sexy man with a load of responsibilities. Rebuilding that career might take even more out of her. God, was it worth it? To start all over again?

Of course it was! Pippa St. Amor was making her comeback, and that meant flying solo. That's how she rolled. Ending up like her mother, bitter and angry at a man who'd walked out on her, wasn't in the plan. She liked Matt a whole hell of a lot too much to do that. She liked him a whole hell of a lot too much, period.

Her planner sat beside her bed and she grabbed it. This was her life. Time to get this train back on the tracks. She needed a refresher on her life goals or she could end up spending the rest of her life in Ghost Falls.

Twelve years in television had to count for something. She had pages and pages of contacts. People who owed her, people who said all she had to do was call. Time to find out who her real buddies were. She checked the time in LA. Shit, she'd slept late. LA was already bustling. She grabbed a quick bath and pulled on a pair of dress pants and a cashmere sweater. She took the time to do her makeup and her hair. This was Pippa St. Amor and she was back.

Downstairs, Phi bustled around the kitchen, doing something heinous to bread and eggs. Cooking was never Phi's thing, which made it damn lucky she had June to keep her fed and alive. It didn't stop Phi from experimenting, however, and trying to rewrite the laws of cuisine all on her own.

"What is that?" Pippa peered over Phi's shoulder at the smoldering lump of blackened bread.

"Italian toast." Phi prodded the mess with the edge of her spatula.

"Italian toast?"

"Yes, I used olive oil instead of butter and I mixed some pasta sauce in with the eggs. Like French toast, only Italian."

At least she'd gotten over her fetish with Thai fish oil. In theory, the Italian toast didn't sound so bad. "How much olive oil?"

"About a bottle. I thought I could use more, being as it's healthier for you."

And there you had it, the problem in a nutshell. "Why don't I make us some eggs?"

"Good idea." Phi grinned at her. She settled her banana yellow self at the table and folded her hands in front of her. "So, how was your date?"

"It was nice. I like him." Pippa whisked the remaining eggs and got the toast started.

"But?"

She moved the destroyed pan to the sink. June was an old hand at dealing with Phi on a culinary tear. "Phi, you know how I feel about getting involved."

"Because of your ridiculous father."

"Because my career is more important."

Phi blew a raspberry and cut the air with her hand. "Did Matt ask you to get involved with him?"

"No." He totally hadn't. Matt had been as into making out as her, but he'd never even said the obligatory "I'll call you" at the door.

"Maybe he only wants sex." Other people might think it

strange to have these sorts of conversations with their grandmother. They wouldn't if they had Phi for a grandmother.

"Matt is not that type."

Phi made another rude noise. "He is so that type. Do you think he's not married because the other women in this town are blind and stupid?"

No, and hadn't she had that exact thought? "Are you saying he's a player?"

"No." Phi pursed her vermillion, sparkly lips. Where the hell had she got that lip thing she was wearing? "Matt takes care of Matt, and he's no dummy about doing it."

Pippa turned back to her eggs. The dummy here was cooking eggs. She'd all but talked herself into a gentle scene where she let Matt go. At least her ego wasn't completely broken. "So you think I should carry on seeing him? In a casual sort of way."

"I think you should have a conversation with him. Underneath all that outrageous hotness is a brain and a man capable of using it."

"You make a good point."

"Of course I do." Phi tossed her head, nearly unseating her turban. "When you've had as many men as I have, you learn a thing or two."

"Don't want to hear it, Phi." Pippa kept her eyes on her eggs. Phi would tell her, as well. In great, gory, and skin-crawling detail.

"You're such a prude, but you make good eggs. Now where's my breakfast?"

June came in as they were finishing up. She looked at the pan in the sink and rolled her eyes. "You don't pay me enough for this shit."

"Of course I do, you silly old cow." Phi poured herself

more coffee and got settled in for her morning gossip with June.

Pippa took herself into the library. What would be called an office or study in anybody else's home was Phi's library. God, Matt must have sweated and sworn getting all those wooden bookcases in, and that silly little windy stair with all the curved bannisters. Just turned nineteen, his dad recently died and Matt had built this house for Phi. Phi could have chosen any contractor she wanted, even brought one in from a bigger city. Typical Phi, she'd chosen Matt, and tossed him the rope he so desperately needed. He said she loved her grandmother, and he was right. How could you not?

Damn, she needed to call her mother and make a time to go and see her.

Emily answered on the first ring. "Hello, Pippa."

"Hi, Mom. When can I come and see you?"

"I was expecting a call yesterday." Emily paused, left it hanging in the air for a moment. "I kept this afternoon free in case you did."

"So, this afternoon then?"

"Yes, I can make that work."

"Great, I'll see you then." Okay, hardest call of the day over. The rest, the favor-begging ones, would be a cinch.

Hours later, Pippa got ready to go and see her mom. She dressed carefully, feeling all the while like she was being called into the principal's office. To say Emily had rigid standards would be like saying Genghis Khan needed anger management. Even as she put on the right sort of blouse, Pippa wondered why the hell she bothered. It's not like she'd ever managed to gain her mother's approval. Something Laura seemed to get right without even trying.

The show debacle was bound to come up, and she still had no solution. She'd made over fifty phone calls. Got voice mail or an assistant every single time. It got more depressing the further she went down her list. Apparently, years in the business didn't count for much. She'd made the list with her most likely people to give her a hand at the top. One by one she'd gone through them. Of course, they might call back. Slim as it was, she clung to that hope. Twelve years had taught her this; they always took the calls they wanted to take.

Time to quit stalling and go and see Emily.

June was vacuuming when she got downstairs. "You going out?"

"Yes, I'm going to see my mother."

June pulled a face, never Emily's biggest fan. "Diva is upstairs, I'll let her know if she asks where you are."

June had one of those faces that had looked old at forty, and faded over the years since then. Not so much lined as careworn, the corners of her mouth turned down and etched into permanent lines of disappointment. June's brown eyes carried a world of secrets and life. She'd also been Phi's housekeeper since her early retirement almost twenty years ago.

"June, can I ask you something?"

"You can ask." June made a business of shutting down the machine and standing straight.

Not the touchy-feely type was their June, but you could always get the truth as she saw it out of her, whether you wanted it or not. "Have you noticed Phi getting forgetful?"

June snorted, and moved a chair out of her vacuuming path. "The Diva does things her way, wouldn't notice if she was. Why?"

"It was just something Nate said the other day."

"Our hot sheriff? What's his business with Phi? Has Bets been making trouble again?" June crossed her arms over her skinny chest and thrust her chin out. "I've a good mind to go over there and set her straight."

"It's just that some of Phi's things have disappeared."

June's eyes narrowed. "I've worked in this house for eighteen years, and I've never taken so much as a cup of coffee I didn't ask for."

Pippa stepped back from the vehemence on June's face. The fact that June routinely helped herself to the pantry and both she and Phi pretended it didn't happen was neither here nor there. Pippa hadn't meant to get her back up. "I wasn't suggesting you did." She gave June her most conciliatory smile. "I spoke to the sheriff about it and he said Phi sometimes wanders off."

"Is that all?" June got her vacuum hose in her hand again. "That old girl couldn't find her way out this house some days, but that ain't new. Every time I'm here she's lost something or can't find her way somewhere. It's Philomene." June tapped the vacuum into life with her foot. Clearly, they were done with the conversation.

"But anything out of the ordinary you've noticed?" Pippa had to yell over the roar of the vacuum.

"Seriously?" June bellowed back. "You want me to tell you if anything is different? In this house?" And she was off, pounding the vacuum against the baseboards. June cleaned well, if not gently.

Pippa groaned as she pulled her rental up beside Laura's minivan. She should have known her mother would invite Laura. Ever efficient, Emily never let an opportunity to kill two birds with one stone pass her by. The house looked great, like it always did. A neat two-story ranch house with green gutters marching in precision across its eaves. The yard could have been vacuumed by June on a rampage. Not a stick or leaf out of place, and all the flowers neatly contained to their beds. After the sperm donor's disappearing act, Emily had redecorated any sign of his existence out of the house.

Pippa walked up the central path to the porch. Pansies bordered the walk, one blue, one white, one blue one . . . what? Oops, was that a pink one? Nope, trick of the light, white and as it should be.

Two beautiful carved rockers flanked the porch on either side of the door. Throw on the left one, perfectly coordinated with the scatter pillows on the right, tonal but not matching, a tasteful sense of balance between them. Even if the placement would mean yelling the length of the porch to have a conversation with the person on the other side. Pippa had inherited her sense of style from her mother. She adored Phi, but restraint did not even enter the Diva's lexicon, not in any aspect of her life.

Pippa rapped the fox-head brass knocker, central and conveniently placed at eye level.

Her mother opened the door. "Pippa."

A lovely smile split Emily's face. A brief moment of being glad to see her that Pippa grabbed on to. Her mother drew her into a light floral-scented hug and kissed both her cheeks. She set Pippa away from her, green eyes cataloging every feature. "You look tired."

"It's been a difficult time."

Her mother loved her, Pippa knew that; it was sometimes hard to keep that in mind when Emily got judgmental or did the perfect thing.

Emily cupped her cheek. Silk and roses and Mom. "I'm sure it has. Come on in, tea is ready and I need to be at the Women's Auxiliary by five."

And that love often came sandwiched between Library Committee and Rotary Club.

"Hello, Pippa." Laura sat on a sand linen sofa, reigning

over a tea tray of fine china. Emily had been baking. Vanilla-scented air teased Pippa's taste buds.

"Hi, Laura. How are you?"

"Well, and you?"

"Fine, thank you. Sam and Daisy good? And Ian?"

"Everyone is fine, thank you. Do you still take your tea black?"

"Yes, no sugar."

"Isn't this nice." Emily took her seat on a coordinating floral armchair. Faded cabbage roses gave a pop of color against a background echoing the sand of the couch. "All of us together."

Pippa hunted for a topic not guaranteed to light the smoldering fuse. "Is the sofa new?"

"I told you she would notice." Emily accepted her cup from Laura and laid the linen napkin across her knees. "I had it reupholstered. I liked the old shape but the fabric was so dated."

"I suppose it's her job to notice things like that." Laura sipped her tea. "Or, at least, it was her job." First blood to Laura. A rapier thrust straight to the heart. "What is happening with your job?"

Emily dabbed carefully around her lips, not smudging her discreet lip color.

"I don't have it anymore." Pippa took a cookie and bit into it. Almond, vanilla, and sugar exploded across her tongue. "These are wonderful."

"Yes." Emily sipped and dabbed. "But wickedly fattening. I tend to stay away from them."

"Well, it's not like I have to worry about the camera adding pounds for the moment." Pippa got it in before Laura could take another cut at her.

"I have been thinking about that." Emily laid her cup on

the table and waved Laura and the teapot off. "Perhaps if you wrote a letter to the media and explained what happened?"

Wouldn't it be great if it were that simple? "They're not interested in the truth, Mom. It's all about selling papers."

"I'm sure they would print it if it came from you. I drafted something for you to look at." Emily folded her napkin and laid it beside her teacup at a right angle. "I e-mailed it to you yesterday."

"I haven't checked my e-mail." The cookie got lodged in her throat and Pippa took a swig of tea to wash it down. "Since the episode aired, I've been inundated with request for interviews and comments from angry fans."

"What made you say it?" Laura curled her lip up in disdain.

Pippa sucked in breath and prayed for patience. "I didn't say it, Laura. At least not the way it was aired."

"Are you saying they misrepresented you?" Emily almost frowned but kept it clear of an actual skin crease.

"They edited out the parts that explained the bits that you heard."

Laura made a scoffing noise. Sisterly love. It warmed a girl from within.

"You should sue." Her mother gaped at her in amazement. Well, almost gaped, because Emily never did anything quite so gauche.

"If I sue, it will only get worse." As satisfying as it would be to get her own back. "And the best thing I can do is lie low until this all goes away."

Laura poured more tea into her cup. "If it goes away."

Enough already. Laura of the perfect life, great kids, and wonderful, supportive husband. "What is your problem?"

Laura smirked and sipped her tea. Happy to have gotten the reaction she was playing for.

"Now, girls." Emily made a vague hand motion between

them. "Let's all have a lovely cup of tea together. There is no need to fight."

Actually, there wasn't. Pippa looked at Laura and smiled. "Sorry, I'm just tense."

Laura nearly swallowed her teacup whole. But, she was quick to bounce back. "No, it's my fault, I'm so angry for you and it comes out wrong."

"There now." Emily sat back and folded her hands on her lap. "It makes me so happy to see you girls getting along so well."

Pippa snuck a look at the clock on the mantel. Forty-five minutes to play along before she broke for freedom. Without smacking her sister in the smug jaw. "Where are the kids this afternoon?"

"My children." Laura labored the word a bit. She disapproved of the term *kids*. "Are spending some time with Philomene. Although frankly I'm not sure for how much longer she can be trusted with them."

Pippa stared. What the hell was going on in Laura's head now?

Her mother turned back to her. "Laura tells me you have some concerns for my mother's grasp on reality?"

Chapter Ten

Matt missed the days of punching the hell out of his brothers for their stupidity.

Isaac lounged in the chair on the far side of his desk, bottom lip stuck out like a four-year old. "He didn't have the pipe. I thought it would be better to have him off-site. I made a judgment call."

You made the wrong one. Matt swallowed the bellow. "Ordinarily, I would agree with you. But that plumber has too many jobs lined up right now and he'll take any gap we give him. Did you get a date when he'll be back on-site?"

Isaac shifted in his seat and stared out the window at the near-empty parking lot. "He said he'd be back."

"But when, Isaac? We built this business by meeting our deadlines. I'm not going to let that slip now."

"*You* built this business," Isaac said, almost too soft to catch.

How many times were they going to go through this? "Isaac, if you want out, nobody is keeping you here."

"And do what?" Isaac's gaze swung back to him. Anger simmered in his eyes. "We both know I didn't make two years in college."

Somehow this was Matt's fault too. Along with the fact

that Isaac hated this job. He couldn't figure Isaac out, didn't know how to give him what he needed. Bone-tired snuck up on Matt and lodged behind his eyes. "I can't talk about this now. I'm due at Mrs. St. Amor's place."

"Surprise, surprise." Isaac glared at him across the desk. "You're like that crazy old broad's lap dog. Or maybe there's another reason you're in such a hurry to get over there?"

The Ghost Falls jungle drums had been doing their thing. Pulling up to Bets's shop with Pippa in the car was the equivalent to taking out an ad on the front page of the *Falls Crier*. He'd also made no secret of his long-standing crush on Pippa. "You got something to say?"

"Nope." Isaac folded his arms over his chest. "I said all I wanted."

Matt studied his brother's set, bitter face and the yell of frustration clogged up like a bad steak in his throat. When had they gotten to this, him and Isaac? When had Isaac stopped looking up to his big brother, and put the blame for all the shit in their lives at Matt's feet instead?

Matt was so sick of it. Their father died, tough break, but they'd all lost a dad, not just Isaac. There'd been no time for Matt to grieve. He'd been nineteen and responsible for his four younger siblings. Yeah, he'd screwed up a thing or two. Okay, he'd screwed up a lot, but kids didn't come with a step-by-step guide, and he'd tossed his energy behind putting food on their table. Turned down his scholarship to Utah State, because that's how their dad raised them. Man up, do what you have to do. No excuses, no whining.

The irony of his internal whining didn't escape him. Isaac had gotten less of their dad's attention than any of them. Even though Jo was the youngest, she was Daddy's girl. While Isaac was growing up, Dad had been too busy keeping his struggling construction company afloat. The others were still clueless as to how close they'd come to losing everything. Eric may have suspected, because he was a sharp son of a bitch, but the others didn't know and Matt aimed to keep it that way.

Isaac wasn't wrong about the something else luring him to Phi's. He had to get to Phi's because she hated men on-site without him. But the idea of Pippa being there put a little more fire in his belly. Before Pippa left town this time, Matt had plans for her and her smokin' body. Even the thought got him a bit hot. Isaac's sulky face worked better than a cold shower.

"You know how much I owe that crazy old broad." He gentled his tone. He didn't want to get into it with Isaac. "If this doesn't work for you and you want to do something else, we can talk about it later."

"Jesus, Matt." Isaac lurched out of his chair, his body tight with anger. "You sound like a guidance counselor. Just give it a fucking rest."

"Well, this is like a time warp." A voice they both knew well came from the door.

Matt spun around.

Eric stood in the doorway, dressed in the fanciest suit Matt had ever seen. He didn't know much about suits, but he'd bet the farm this one had a price tag on it that would make his eyes water.

Pippa would know who made that suit.

Shit, he'd missed his pain-in-the-ass brother. Matt stepped toward him, Eric met him halfway, and they did that awkward half-hug, slap-on-the-back thing. Women had it so much easier. They just hugged and kissed and got it done.

"You look good." Matt stepped back and eyed Eric. And he did. Eric had been working out. That pound on the shoulders nearly knocked the air right out of him.

"So do you." Eric turned to do the same man-I'm-really-glad-to-see-you pounding thing with Isaac.

"Well, look at you." Isaac whistled through his teeth. "All dressed up and pretty."

"Shut up." Eric grinned. "I see you two assholes are still fighting."

"Can't let my older brothers walk all over me." Isaac shot a loaded look in Matt's direction. What was up with that anyway?

They chatted a bit. Ragged on Eric some more for his fancy duds, and then Isaac excused himself with another death glare at Matt.

Eric twitched the seam of his fancy suit pants and took the seat Isaac had shot out of earlier. He raised his brow at Matt. "So, Isaac?"

"He'll get over himself." Maybe, but talking this shit over wasn't going to make it go away. "I couldn't believe it when Jo told me you were coming home for her wedding."

"Seriously, Matt?" Eric's gaze, eyes a darker brown than his, met his over the desk. "She's my sister, too. Where the hell else would I be when she got married?"

When he put it like that, Eric had a point.

"Anyway, what the hell is up with Jo getting married? That asshole?" Classic Eric, straight to the point.

A little something unraveled in Matt's chest. He could talk to Eric. They butted heads a lot, but Eric understood responsibility. "She says she loves him."

Eric shook his head. "Can he even support her?"

The muscles in his neck tightened at Eric's question. "Who the hell knows, but Jo doesn't care. She'll work beside him and they'll be partners."

"Fuck." Eric breathed long and slow. "Should I kidnap her and drag her back to Denver with me?"

Yes, yelled the primal big brother inside him. He laughed and shook his head. "You know Jo."

"Yeah."

Mrs. Cameron bustled through the door, breaking the

awkward silence. "Eric Evans." She put the tray on Matt's desk and turned to stare at Eric. "Well, look at you."

Eric stood when she entered. He grinned at the older woman. "Hey, Mrs. Cameron."

Matt flat-out stared as Mrs. Cameron went all pink and giggled. How the hell did Eric do that? Nate was the looker, Isaac the joker, and him? He didn't really know. Mr. Responsible, maybe? But Eric had the magic. Could weave a spell around any woman within fifty feet. He could turn it on like a faucet, and you could hear the knees weakening.

"Are you staying long?" Matt could have kissed Mrs. Cameron for asking what he'd like to know.

"I have some time." Eric gave her the player smile again. "I'm here for Jo's wedding and to have a chat with my big brother."

"Hmph!" Mrs. Cameron could pretend all she liked, but she was melting like she always did. "See if you can talk him into not working quite so hard."

Say what? Matt stared at her rigid back as she clumped out of his office.

"Mrs. Cameron is working for you?" Eric raised a dark brow. "Does she make you write lines if you piss her off?"

"I try not to piss her off."

They shared a look. One of those snatches into boyhood that he didn't get a lot of. It felt good. "She got laid off a couple of years ago with the school board cutting costs. She supports her mother and that waste of space son of hers. I offered and she took it."

Eric cocked his head and studied him like he was a bug on Eric's windshield. "You're a good guy, Matt."

Mr. Responsible? The good guy? These are not things that got a man laid. He shrugged off the compliment. "You wanted to talk to me about something?"

Eric glanced behind him at the busy office. "You up for this now?"

"Sure." Matt got that tight feeling in his gut. Eric had something big on his mind. "I have to go and see Phi in a bit, but I have five minutes."

Eric's face split into a genuine smile. "How the hell is the Diva?"

"The same." Phi was reliable as clockwork in her eccentricity. "Still a pain in my ass, demanding I go over there every time she needs a lightbulb changed."

Eric chuckled. He got it. He didn't ask why Matt still went. He understood obligation and honoring a debt.

"What's on your mind?" Matt liked to get straight to the point. They were the same in this, too.

"You." Eric sipped his coffee. "I want you to partner with me on something."

Matt sat back in his chair. Not sure he'd heard right. Along with the lady-killer smile, Eric had the family money gene. He worked hard, sure, but lots of people worked hard. Eric had this way of seeing a deal coming five miles off. And maybe he'd lost his mind a little as well.

"In Denver?"

"Doesn't have to be Denver." Eric shrugged. "But it would help if you could be closer to my office."

Definitely lost the plot. How could Matt leave Ghost Falls? Shit, his family got into enough crap when he was around. God only knew what they could manage if he was in Denver. "Eric." He stared his brother down. "I can't leave Ghost Falls. You know that."

"No." Eric eased back in his chair. "I know you think you can't leave Ghost Falls. It's not the same thing."

Wouldn't that be great if he believed it? He shook his head and laughed, not that he found it funny, but the conversation was making his gut clench. "Who would look after the family if I left? You?"

Eric's eyes flashed at the subtle taunt. Surprisingly, he kept his cool. "Maybe they don't need anyone to take care of them anymore. Isaac is grown, Jo's getting married. Shit, even Nate has got his crap sorted now."

"And Mom?" His words hung in the air between them.

Eric shifted in his seat. "Look, hear me out before you shoot me down."

"Okay." Matt sat back in his chair. Whether he agreed or not, Eric would have his say.

Eric leaned forward, resting his elbows on his knees. "This area is about to hit a boom." The old razzle-dazzle tone crept into Eric's voice. It was impressive, and even Matt wasn't totally immune. "The view, the whole quality-of-life thing. You have Denver and Salt Lake City within a couple of hours from you. There's money to be made here and I want in before other people start paying attention."

"You planning on developing Ghost Falls? McMansions and strip malls?" That stuck in Matt's craw. The place might be small and kind of lost, but they liked it that way. For the most part.

Eric read him like a book. "Don't get that face, Matt. I was raised here, and I'm not going to blast in like some big property developer and turn it into a crappy suburb of Salt Lake City. I want to do this right, do it well, and in a way that benefits me and the town. And I want you to do it with me."

A tingle teased along Matt's spine. Now his brother had him even considering the idea. Sure, he did well enough. Business was steady, but Eric was talking major growth, for the town and everyone in it. "If what you say is true, then I would benefit from being just about the only contractor in town."

Eric reached inside his coat and pulled a thumb drive from the inside pocket. "You've done great with this business, Matt, don't get me wrong. But you can field, what, five crews?"

"Four full. Six if I subcontract."

"I'm talking hundreds of homes here. And businesses and services around them." Eric slapped the drive on his desk. "Just take a look at that. Before you turn me down. Look at that, and think about it. I can run this without you, but I'd rather do it with you. You're here, you know the town even better than I do and I trust you."

The tingle morphed into a slither of excitement. Matt liked what he did, but the feeling of being trapped was still there. Eric scratched it all up again and made him twitchy. "I can't leave Ghost Falls."

"Matt." Eric sat back again, his face deadly serious. "You turned down a football scholarship for the family. Don't be a stupid dick and turn this down too."

Anger, hot and sharp, surged to the surface. Eric with his expensive duds and big-city attitude coming in here and passing judgment. Man, that bit.

"I don't want to fight." Eric held his hands in front of him.

Matt still wanted to take his head off, but they were in their thirties now. Generally, you needed to think before you threw a punch. "I did what I had to do."

"I know that." Eric stood and pushed the thumb drive closer. "And nobody knows better than me what that cost you. This." He tapped the drive. "This is for you. This is your second chance and don't piss it away because you want to take a swing at me."

Of course, Eric would know that look on his face. It actually made him laugh. They were only a year apart; they read each other easily. And before he could think it through anymore, he nodded. "I'll take a look."

"And we can talk further?"

"I'll take a look." Eric was a pushy bastard. If you gave him an inch, he'd take the whole damn mile. Still, the drive lay small and innocuous against the burgundy leather of his desk blotter. A chance for him. A chance for something more than Ghost Falls and Mr. Responsible. His finger closed around the drive. "You know it's pointless."

"I know you think so." Annoying son of a bitch. Eric grinned at him. "Now, why don't you take me on a ride along. Time to get reacquainted with the Diva."

Eric used to chip in with the construction crew in the summer before he started college. He was a great favorite with Phi.

Matt shoved the drive in his pocket and got a cocky grin from Eric. "Just looking."

"Look carefully."

Pippa's belly did an honest to God flutter as Matt's truck pulled into the kitchen yard. He climbed out, tall and broad, and stopped a moment to chat with the kid Phi had walking her rescue horses around the yard. The sorry-looking nag, fur moth-eaten, dragged its feet like it was off to meet its Maker. Still, Phi gave her horses the same sort of love she would a thoroughbred. Made their last years on earth happy ones.

"Is that Mathieu?" Phi trotted into the kitchen.

As if she hadn't been calling the guy all morning. "Yes."

"Who's that with him?"

Funny thing, Pippa hadn't noticed anyone with Matt. And more the fool her, because that someone was dressed in Hugo Boss—if she guessed right and she nearly always did—and smoked across the yard like a *GQ* center spread.

"Eric?" Phi squealed and nipped out the door as if she were half her age. She had her arms open wide as she approached the eleven. The eleven notched up to twelve with a smile that made Pippa's knees buckle.

"There's my diva." He enfolded her grandmother in a

hug. Phi was a tall woman but Eric Evans made her look like a young girl. Phi was giggling like one too.

"You're such a flirt." Phi slapped him on the arm. "Don't ever stop. At my age, a girl needs something to look forward to."

"Hey." Matt's whisky baritone dragged her eyes away from the window.

A giggle built in Pippa as color rushed to her face. He leaned against the doorframe, wearing a sexy, naughty grin that catapulted her straight back to last night and made her want to rub up against him like a cat. "Hey, yourself."

"I brought Eric." He jerked his head to where Phi was still firing questions at Eric.

"I see that."

"He came in this morning. Surprised Isaac and me."

"Pippa Turner." Eric shouldered his way past Matt and entered the kitchen in a swath of cashmere and charm. "Or should I say Pippa St. Amor?"

That smile should be condemned as deadly. "You can say whatever the hell you like as long as it's followed by how good it is to see me."

Eric flashed perfect teeth in his tanned, carved face. Yup, definitely a threat to women everywhere. "It's always a pleasure to see those legs, Pippa. And the rest of you." He swept her into a citrus man-scented hug. "How the hell have you been?"

"She's been great," Matt said. "And you can put her down now."

"Oh, Mathieu." Phi bustled into the kitchen. "Stop peeing on Pippa's leg and let's have a drink."

"It's ten in the morning." Pippa disentangled herself from Eric. Matt stood beside Phi and glared at the back of his brother's head.

"And?" Phi hauled glasses out of the cupboard. "Where

does it say we cannot drink to celebrate the return of the prodigal?"

"How am I the prodigal?" Eric's dark eyes were still doing a thorough inventory of Pippa. Normally, she'd have given any ogling jerk-off a good reason to keep his eyes to himself, but Eric had a way of doing it that was totally non-creepy and made a girl want to prance like a show pony. Except, her attention was more on Matt, and the thunderous look on his face.

If Matt had been giving her the same ogle Eric was, she'd be shoving him up against the wall and demanding he deliver on the silent promise. And she was supposed to be keeping her distance.

Pippa went to fetch the champagne. Fortunately, Phi was not much of a drinker. Despite her big talk.

Eric shrugged out of his beautifully cut coat and laid it over the back of a chair.

Phi squealed and grabbed his arm. "Eric, is that a tattoo? Show me."

God, her grandmother was irrepressible. Pippa threw Eric an apologetic look. "You don't have to."

"Yes, he does," said Phi.

Eric chuckled and rolled back his sleeve with sharp, decisive wrist turns. "I had it done a while back."

Tanned, muscular forearm appeared under the crisp, white shirt. The kind of arms a girl would like to gnaw on. Pippa stepped closer to get a better look. At the tattoo.

"I have more ink." Eric grinned at her. "Wanna see?"

The Evans flirt for sure and up to his old tricks. It made her laugh.

"I'll leave you to catch up with Eric." Matt shoved his hands in his pockets. "I'm going to check out how my guys are doing."

"Oh." Phi swung back toward him. "They did a wonderful job. Such nice boys. You can send those ones around anytime. The dark one." Phi shivered and went pink. "I do like a man built like he could toss you around the bedroom."

"Right." Pippa cut this short, before Phi elaborated. "So, Eric, tell us what you've been doing."

Matt stopped with the baize door half held open. "I'm afraid you're going to have to wait to hear what Eric's been doing. I need you to show me the problem."

She swung around and stared at him. Matt knew exactly what the problem was. He'd seen it last night.

"You'd best go." Eric gave her a prod in the back. "My brother's getting territorial."

Was he? Matt's jaw could break rock it was so tight. His eyes bored into her, daring her to refuse. It shouldn't be at all thrilling, but it kind of was, and very flattering. She followed his fine ass out the kitchen and up the stairs. Heat burned below her skin. She hadn't taken full advantage of her chance to get her hands on that ass last night. Next time—

Wasn't she the one explaining to Phi an hour ago how she needed to nip this thing in the bud? Now she was building scenarios in which she could get both tight butt cheeks in her hands.

Matt strode into her bedroom and went right to the leak.

His men had plastered it over, and Pippa could only barely discern the sheen of new paint. She joined him, letting her eyes stray along the strong column of his neck. It tasted as good as it looked. Pippa cleared her thick throat. "They did a good job."

"Yup." Matt grabbed a small set of steps propped against the wall and one-handed them over to the spot. He stretched up and lightly touched the repair. Where to look first? The inch of ripped stomach exposed by his tee riding up, or the convenient eyeful of package right in front of her. She had that pressed against her last night too. Damn it!

She was never a crotch watcher. What the hell was she doing? "Um, Matt?"

"Yup." He ran his fore- and middle fingers over the plaster-work. Magic fingers. "Matt, can we talk?"

He looked down at her. Topaz eyes, guarded and watchful as they studied her. "Okay."

"About last night."

"Ah." He dropped his hand and descended the steps. He put them neatly against the wall beside a closed paint can and a tool-strewn tarp. "I'll take those away with me when I go." He folded his arms over his chest and lowered his chin, almost to his chest. The age-old man pose for getting ready for a verbal takedown.

"Last night was . . . great."

His stare didn't waver. "And?"

"Why do you think there's an and?" She played for time.

He shrugged one shoulder. "Because with a girl like you, Pippa, there's always an and."

"I'm a woman not a girl."

"Duly noted."

And he was back to staring at her. "I don't think . . . I mean, I'm sure that we shouldn't . . ." If he'd help her out here, this would be so much easier. "I'm not looking for anything right now."

He dipped his head to stare at the ground and raised it. "By 'anything' you mean what? A relationship? Sex? More crazy hot making out?"

"A relationship?" Pippa pounced on the word with a long exhale.

"But making out some more is good?" He shoved his hands into his pockets.

"What? . . . Um . . ."

"How about sex?"

"Yes. No. You're messing with me." She caught the telltale gleam in those wicked, gold eyes.

"Yeah, Pippa, I'm messing with you." He strode toward her, gripped her arms, and tugged her closer. "I didn't like you flirting with my brother."

"Everyone flirts with Eric."

"True." His grip on her arms was nice, secure and firm. The whiff of laundry detergent and musky male went straight to her knees. She put her hands against the hard ridge of his pecs. Seriously nice. She allowed her fingers to drift a bit.

"Last night was hot." He crowded closer. "I had wood for hours." Her sex clenched in response. "I've wanted to make out with you for years, and it was everything I imagined and more. But"—he dipped his head and pressed his forehead against hers—"I know you have a life and career, and you'll be getting back to it. My life is here in Ghost Falls." He slid his nose along her cheek until his breath huffed hot and ragged in her ear. "But if you want to mess around until you go, or maybe more, maybe less. I'm good with that." He sucked the lobe of her ear into his mouth. Hot and wet. "I'm so down with that."

Her body was so down with that too. She leaned into him. Her breasts swelled against the hard line of his chest. And she got her hands on that tight, gorgeous ass. "Okay."

"Okay what?" He bit her ear, hard enough to get her attention.

"We can mess around. Maybe more."

"Maybe a lot more." He pushed the hard ridge of his cock against her belly.

Man, that was not fighting fair. She hadn't had sex in so long, and he was hard and beautiful and big. She rubbed against his erection. No choice, had to be done. "Okay. But nothing serious, because I don't do serious."

He groaned and stepped back. "Nothing serious, but not with your grandmother and my brother downstairs at the time." He palmed his erection and adjusted himself with a slight wince. Ah, hell, she wanted to do that. "Pippa, babe." His voice husky and horny. "You gotta get that look off your face."

"Right." She shook her head to clear it. "You're right."

"Tell me about your plan to take your career back."

"Hm?"

"Your plan." A grin split his face. "Your plan to get back in the game."

"How do you know I have a plan?"

"Pippa." He shook his head slowly from side to side. "You always have a plan."

Except now, with him. No plan. Clueless.

Chapter Eleven

Pippa checked her messages before she went downstairs to make dinner. One of her calls had been returned. She dialed voice mail, her finger difficult to control as it shook over the little buttons.

"Ms. St. Amor." A young, female voice, chirped into her ear. *"This is Brittany at Mr. Carlson's office. I'm afraid Mr. Carlson is out of town for the rest of the month. On vacation. And he's out of cell reach. He won't be able to get back to you until he returns."*

Pippa jabbed the Off icon. "Bullshit."

Bryan Carlson never took a crap without his cell phone. Miserable bastard. She'd helped him get his first AD job on her show, thrown her weight around for him. She tossed her phone onto her bed. Too restless to settle, she paced the room.

"I didn't say it," she said to the room. "God, you so busy condemning me for something I didn't do."

Doors, all of them, slammed in her face and locked tight. Not one call back. Not a damn one. Allie hiding out, her editor scared for her job, and the cameramen pretending like her text never even existed. When they turned their backs on you, they went deaf and blind as well. And why was she surprised exactly? It's how it worked. She knew that. When you're out, you're out. Twelve years of her life gone, just like that. She almost wished she had said those things. Had done what Ray had rigged.

No, she didn't, because Allie had been sweet and lost and looked to her to help her find her inner Cleopatra. Allie knew what happened, she'd been there and heard the exact words Pippa said. Maybe she could insist Allie speak out.

No, she couldn't do that. Allie flinched at her own shadow. She had no place in a shitstorm like this one.

Social media. God, it made her life so much harder. All that instant access to millions of unsolicited opinions. All those millions of voices commenting on something she was innocent of. God, her head was going to explode with this crap.

She tapped the Twitter app. So many damn notifications. Some self-flagellation demon had her tapping the top one open.

Elena@elenigirl22—@pippastamor boy did you have us fooled! #numberonebitch #shameonyouPSA

"You know what?" she said to the phone. "If you want to talk about something, why don't you talk about the truth? Wouldn't that make a nice change?"

Pippa@pippastamor—@elenigirl22 I never said it! #getyourfactsstraight #askpippawhatshesaid #justiceforpippa

"Shit!" Pippa stared at her phone. That had been incredibly stupid, but the desire to—just this once—yell back had her finger hitting tweet before her brain could haul it back.

Ah, well! It was done now. The only good thing about social media is it moved so fast, her tweet would probably get lost in the shitstorm within seconds.

Pippa checked her e-mails. She tried to squash the little surge of hope when she saw she had messages. *National Enquirer* was not giving up. Too bad she wasn't going to play. She hit delete and tossed her phone back on the bed.

Where was Matt to take her mind off this shit when she needed him? Working and getting on with his life, and best she do the same. He hadn't called in two days either, because they were keeping it—whatever it was—strictly easy.

Bing went her phone. Okay then, maybe not so lost. But did she really want to read the response?

Rachel@rachelmews—@pippastamor we love you Pippa #askpippawhatshesaid #justiceforpippa

penny@pennyknowsbest—@pippastamor we know you didn't say it. We miss you #askpippawhatshesaid #justiceforpippa

See, that was nice. Maybe everybody didn't hate her after all.

Pippa@pippastamor—@pennyknowsbest @rachelmews thank you ladies, I appreciate the support #askpippawhatshesaid #justiceforpippa

That last hashtag had a nice militant ring to it. She'd spent all this time trying to find help behind the scenes, when it was the fans who really counted. The fans who would see you through.

"Pippa." June's voice, strident and demanding. "You better get your ass down here."

Would it kill June to say please? She stomped over to

her door, then stomped back and snatched up her phone. Following the sound of voices, she entered the salon.

June's craggy face was creased into a frown.

Phi sat on the floor in front of the treasure armoire, and rocked. Back and forth, back and forth, her shoulders heaving as she sobbed.

"What the hell happened?" Pippa threw June a glance as she ran to Phi.

Her grandmother was tiny, sunken in her arms. Phi was so much larger than life it was difficult to think of her as vulnerable.

"I dunno." June twisted her fingers together. "I came in here to clean and found her like that."

Pippa tightened her arms around Phi's shoulders. "What is it, Phi?"

"It's gone." Her face a mess of smeared makeup and tears, Phi held a velvet box in her clenched fingers. "They took my fob watch."

Pippa pried Phi's fingers open and took the box from her. It was empty. The circular indentation in the velvet stared up at her accusingly. The fob watch, another favorite treasure, given to her by Prince Rainier of Monaco with the royal coat of arms etched beside the message on the back. Gone.

A surge of lava-hot rage roared through Pippa. How dare they touch Phi's treasures? Take them from her as if they didn't mean a lifetime of achievement and accolades. A life spent bringing the gift of her voice to people all over the world.

"I didn't touch it." June stuck her chin out.

Pippa didn't give a shit about placating June. Someone had put their hands on Phi's stuff and it ended. Now. Today.

"She had it the other day." June took a cautious step closer. "I picked it up in her room and put it back."

"Is that true?" Pippa gentled her tone with Phi.

Her grandmother sobbed in earnest. Her false eyelashes drooped over her eyes, mascara gummed in the skin folds. "I don't know."

"I saw it." June's voice grew more confident. "Right beside her bed. I put it away. Straight away."

"Why?" Phi's shoulders shook so hard, it was difficult to contain it.

"I don't know, darling." Pippa stroked the knots of her spine. "But I'm going to find it, Phi, I promise you that."

It took hours to settle Phi into bed with her restorative scotch. She kept looking at Pippa with big, green eyes and asking "why?" Pippa would give her right arm to have an answer for her. It didn't make any sense and it was so wrong it made her teeth ache.

Phi was loud, flamboyant, and a real handful, but she was also one of the kindest people on the planet. She rescued horses, dogs, chickens, and people. All gathered under her protective wing and treated to her special brand of wonderful. When Pippa last checked, the Diva had her feathered purple eye mask on and snored softly. Phi would sleep till morning. The restorative scotch was a generous triple.

Another trip to Nate was in the cards. This had to stop. But before then, she wanted to make sure of a few things.

It felt disloyal to make the call.

"Agrippina." Matt's voice hummed down the line, and shivered across her nerve endings.

"I need to ask you something."

Matt's voice changed timbre as he sensed her mood. "What is it?"

"It's Phi." Dammit, she was going to cry. It made her so angry to see her grandmother hurt like this. "More of her treasures have disappeared."

"My guys?" Matt was alert and tense.

"Can you vouch for them?" Pippa got it in quickly before he went down the wrong track.

He growled down the line. "Pippa, I wouldn't send anyone over there who I didn't trust. I'll check with the guys anyway, but as far as I know, they only went into your room." He sighed. "What the hell is going on in that house?"

"Someone is taking her stuff. Matt?" This was so wrong. Phi was as sharp as a tack, but she had to ask. "Do you think she could have misplaced them?"

"Phi." He paused. "Maybe."

"I'm worried, Matt." The idea of losing Phi to senility throbbed raw and painful in her chest. "I need to search this house, top to bottom. Just to make sure she hasn't misplaced them. You know—"

"I'll be right over."

The phone went dead in her ear. Pippa changed her shirt to a nicer one, drew the line at changing into a sexier pair of jeans, but lost the battle not to freshen her makeup. Or put perfume on. Matt liked to bury his face in her neck and draw in deep breaths. Shit, she was twisted. Her grandmother was in crisis and she was thinking sex.

It didn't take him long. He rapped gently on the kitchen door.

"She's sleeping." Pippa let him into the house. He stayed on her heels, big and radiating warmth and comfort. "I don't want her to know I'm doing this."

Matt stopped her and stroked his finger down her cheek.

"I know. We'll do it quietly, and go and see Nate in the morning if we find nothing."

"We?"

"We." He gave a firm nod. "But, I don't think we're going to find anything here."

"Really?" Pippa didn't want to face the possibility of Phi getting forgetful, or losing her incredible mind. "Because she's seventy-eight and—"

"Sixty-eight." He smiled down at her. "The age on her bio and I'm sticking with it."

He was such a good man. The sort of guy a girl could lean on. Her heart gave a little thump of "if only." Enough of that! Pippa didn't lean, and especially not on a man. "Where should we look first?"

They started with the kitchen. June kept things neat and orderly, and it didn't take too long. They moved into the salon. Pippa checked the treasure trove one more time. Opening each of the treasures, just to be sure they weren't put away in the wrong place.

Matt worked alongside her. He'd built the house and knew all sorts of strange little hidey-holes Pippa didn't even know existed. Phi had built her drama into every inch of the Folly.

By the time they reached the third-floor attic, Pippa was grubby and exhausted. They couldn't do Phi's room with her in the house. She would have to find another time to get it searched.

"You could ask June to distract her," Matt whispered as they tiptoed past Phi's room. They needn't have bothered. An act of God couldn't wake the Diva. But they did it anyway.

"I don't think I can. June has been with her for years, but someone is taking things from this house and I don't know who it is." Pippa couldn't believe it could be June. Pleasant, the woman wasn't, or even amicable, but she'd been with Phi for so long it made it almost unthinkable. Yet, stuff was disappearing and with no obvious suspects, she had to consider everyone.

He nodded. "I'll start in the attic." Blowing out a harsh breath, he opened the door to the attic stairs. "Why don't you get us something to drink? It's going to take some time."

Pippa got them both a bottle of water and rejoined Matt in the attic.

Matt had called this one right. Phi threw nothing away. It all ended up in the attic, waiting for some needy soul. Phi had enough stuff up here to furnish a small house. Everything from furniture to pots and pans, stacked in pile after pile and covered with sailcloth. The dust clogged up her nose as they moved things around, and she sneezed.

"Bless you." Matt looked up from going through the drawers of an old chest. Dust and sweat streaked his face. Damn, he totally rocked the workingman look. Pippa grinned at her own thoughts.

"What?"

"You're a nice guy, Matt Evans."

He pulled a face. "Two words a guy never wants to hear applied to him. Nice. Guy. You might as well go ahead and friend-zone me."

"I wouldn't go that far." Looking at Matt, Pippa took a sip of water, her mouth dry from dust.

He quirked a brow at her. "Oh, really?"

What a terrible flirt! And thinking of flirts . . . "Tell me about Eric."

"What do you want to know?" Matt lost some of his perk.

"Why doesn't he come home more often?"

"My mother." Matt bent to search beneath an old swan-shaped child's bed. It had been hers back in the day. "At least, that's my best guess."

"Your mother?" Cressy Evans had followed her sons around like a shadow. Always there, always standing guard. More than one teenage girlfriend had run the gauntlet of Cressy and come out bloodied at the other end.

Matt shrugged. "She's needy."

Cressy was cling wrap. Pippa kept that to herself. Men and their mothers, a place you did not go.

"She used to drive Eric crazy. He took the first road out of here after college and built a life for himself in Denver. He does very well." Matt pulled a face. "He does extremely well. When he first started, he lived in a house with five other guys, so he could afford to send money home to get Isaac and Jo through college."

"Isaac went to college?" Forget good guy. Matt Evans needed canonizing. He'd raised his siblings after his dad's death. Cressy went to pieces and Matt stepped in. And apparently, Eric, too.

"For all the good it did." Matt gave a vicious twist to a cover and sent a cloud of dust into the air. Pippa hid her nose in her arm.

"Sorry, Isaac gets to me." Matt's hair was dull beneath a thin layer of dust. "He's the smartest of all of us and yet he can't seem to get it together enough to make something of his life. I haven't a goddamn clue what to do with him."

"And you have to do something?" Pippa gauged his reaction carefully. So far, Matt had been pretty open, but she was about to step right into his space. The sort of place only a real girlfriend went. She did it with her women on the show, but they had to take it—more or less.

Matt narrowed his eyes at her, his broad shoulders tight with tension. "Of course I do."

"Isaac is a year or so younger than me, right?" A terse nod from Matt. "So, maybe it's up to him to find that thing and do it."

He stilled, and Pippa tensed, waiting for him to tell her to butt the hell out.

"You sound like Eric." He huffed out a laugh. "Except Eric keeps telling me I have to get out of here and let them all sink or swim."

Eric might be on to something. "Why don't you?"

"Jesus." He shook his head. "Try and picture that. My mother didn't get out of bed for three weeks after my dad died. Didn't even make the funeral. It took me another six months to get her out of the house."

Leaving her son to organize a funeral and take care of the other children. At least Emily hadn't done that after the sperm donor disappeared. Nope, Emily had launched into a frenetic "new beginning." Pippa was starting to get why Phi had such a resentment for Cressy.

"Isaac." He smacked his palms on his jeans, leaving dusty sprints behind. "Well, Isaac is stuck. And Jo." He frowned and ran a hand through his hair. Dust motes hit the air behind him. He looked sad, and confused.

"She's getting married, isn't she?"

"Yup."

"You don't like him."

He barked out a dry laugh. "He's a musician." Matt twisted his mouth around the word. "Who doesn't play an instrument, have a band, or even write songs. Now he's in Montreal, at the Jazz Festival to network and further his career."

"Okay." Pippa was getting a not-so-good picture here.

"And Jo paid his way there." And there it was. "Fuck." The word exploded on a soft breath. "I hate talking about this shit." He strode to the small dormer window and stared into the night. "I could even accept the guy was a total loser if Jo was happy."

Pippa closed the distance between them. She wanted to

wrap her arms around those big, strong shoulders and ease some of the burden. He'd carried it a long, long time. It wasn't her thing though. They weren't a couple, or even a hookup. "How do you know she's not happy?"

"Hey!" He spun to look at her. "You could help me out with something."

"Okay." Not if it involved Cressy she couldn't. Cressy never missed a chance to give her the death stare.

"I went wedding dress shopping with Jo the other day, and she chose this dress . . . the ugliest dress I've ever seen. Couldn't you like . . ."—he made a vague waving motion with his hand—"do your thing and get her a nice dress? One that makes her look as beautiful as she is."

It didn't sound like a dress was going to do for Jo what she needed, but this was in Pippa's wheelhouse. "I could do that."

A beautiful smile lit his face. "I know it's only a dress, but maybe if she felt beautiful . . ." He shrugged. "I mean, it's her wedding day. A girl should feel like a princess, right?"

"Right." Such a good guy, with such a great, big heart in that gorgeous body. Men like Matt could almost make her believe in the happily-ever-after thing. She took his face between her hands and forced him to bend his neck a bit. "You are the nicest guy, Matt Evans."

He curled up his lip in disgust.

Pippa laughed and pressed her mouth against his. "And you're dead sexy, too."

His arms came around her and tugged her closer. He hummed his appreciation against her mouth and sucked her bottom lip between his.

"And you kiss like a bad boy."

"This is getting better and better." He pressed his hips

against her. His cock hardened against her belly as she pushed closer. He so had her number with this stuff.

"But you talk too much."

That seemed all the invitation Matt needed to take over the kiss. His tongue plunged into her mouth, firm and demanding. And wonderful.

Pippa mated her tongue with his, savoring the taste and feel of him. She wanted him. Lust, pure and unadulterated, curled up from her belly and spread to her breasts and between her thighs. His hardness against her was a visceral reminder of their sexes, and Pippa relished every delicious difference. The way her breasts flattened against his chest. The cradle between her thighs where he fit so perfectly. His big hands almost spanning the width of her back.

He groaned and shifted his weight. His hand trailed beneath her shirt and found the skin of her back. Firm, slightly rough from working with them, his hands created thrilling abrasions over her skin. He slid his hand up to rest on the side of her breast.

Pippa twisted in silent demand. Heat shot through her as he cupped her breast. She filled his hand, pressing into it.

His touch sure and steady through the fabric of her bra. He brushed her nipple with his thumb.

God, it felt so good. Her knees buckled and she grabbed his shoulders for support. Her breast swelled as he played, eager for his touch, so sensitive she wanted to throw back her head and moan.

He pulled her bra cups down and bare palm touched naked breast. Hot and firm. His other hand slid into the back of her jeans to cup her ass. "I love you city girls with your tiny panties."

Her tiny panties were drenched, and Pippa rubbed against his erection. Shit, he was even harder than before.

They had to break the kiss to come up for air. Harsh pants filled the tiny space between their mouths.

"We can't do this here." The words came out with claws on them when every firing neuron she possessed was all for pushing him to the ground and riding him until the ache between her thighs went away.

"You're right." He took her mouth in another blistering kiss, plumping and squeezing her breast. "But you feel so fucking good." His fingers slid into the crack of her ass. He dipped his knees to get the leverage needed to slide them into her heat. "Shit, you're so wet."

He tugged his hand free, and Pippa whimpered her objection.

Then his mouth was on her breast, sucking her nipple deep into his mouth, and his hands were on her jeans. The buttons popped and he slid his hand over her mound. His fingers dived under the tiny scrap of fabric and found her again.

She was just about there, when he slid between her wet folds, pushing a finger deep inside her, his mouth working her nipples.

"Oh God." It ripped from her in a whimper as he played her clitoris, working another finger deeper inside her.

"Let me make you come."

"Yes." She gripped his hair as his fingers moved over her. Sliding through her wet heat easily, pushing her closer to the edge. Her knees gave as she came and he caught her against him.

Holy hell. Pippa melted against him in a happy heap as her legs had checked out. Best orgasm ever, and she still had all her clothes on.

Gently, he covered her nipples with her bra and lowered her shirt. He eased his hand away from her slowly.

Pippa cupped his cock through his jeans. He pulsed hard and thick in her hand.

Matt placed her hand over his, pressing her to him before taking it away.

She didn't know if she could do the same for him, but she was damn sure going to give it a try. "But—"

"We can't do this here," he said. "But soon, baby, soon we're going to do this and do it right."

And it would be so good. Her sated body hummed low-level at the idea of their bodies moving together. "Soon."

Chapter Twelve

Pippa checked in with Twitter while she waited for Matt.

The outpouring of love and support brought tears to her eyes. Tweet after tweet from people telling her how much they missed her, how they'd never believed what they had seen. It provided the salve she needed for the raw place left after all the scorn and hatred.

Matt didn't waste any time collecting on his promise about his sister's wedding dress. He called her first thing the next morning and arranged to pick her up in an hour. Nothing from any of her contacts. Who needed them anyway? She would make her comeback through her fans. Three hundred and twenty-eight people loved her, stood behind her.

Matt's truck swung into the kitchen yard, right on time. He hopped out and strode toward her. She could stand here all day and watch that man move. The smile he gave her made her girl parts tingle. "You ready?"

"Yup."

"I really appreciate you doing this. Jo almost lost her mind when I told her."

Pippa stopped. "In a good or bad way."

"A good way." He leaned in and kissed her cheek. So sweet and familiar, like they'd been doing this for years.

They had, sort of. "Okay."

He opened the door for her.

Pippa stared up at the cab. Her skirt wasn't designed for the graceful hopping in and out of pickups. It was much more of a being-handed-out-of-a-limo affair, hugging her curves to the knee.

Matt eyed the skirt, then the running board, and grinned. "Would it be totally screwed up if I told you how much I want to watch you wiggle and struggle to get in there?"

Dork! And how could you get mad at this man and stay that way? "You're a pig, now give me a hand."

He went for her ass. Of course he did. Why mess with eating the salad when the steak was on the table? "I don't think so." She gripped his hand in hers. "We'll do this the civilized way."

He helped her into the truck, grumbling all the way. "Great skirt." He shut the door and trotted around to the driver's side. "I've always had a thing for your legs."

As if that was news. Pippa laughed because he always checked out her legs.

"So, Jo's on board with this?" Her gaze strayed to the pull of denim across his thighs. Who knew a girl could get a bit silly about thighs? And forearms. A girl could lose herself in the play of sinew and muscle between his elbow and his wrist. Not to mention the thick ridges of vein curving beneath his tanned skin.

"Totally." He turned out of Phi's drive and onto the highway. Only three cars passed them on their way into town. Matt did the finger-lift hello each time. So different from her LA life where it was wall-to-wall, I-want-to-kill-you traffic all the way. Where, most of the time, nobody really cared if you lived or died. "I owe you for this."

"What did you have in mind?" *Ask me, ask me!* Her libido yelled its head off.

"Dinner?" He turned to her with an eyebrow lift. "Like a proper date? Tomorrow night?"

As opposed to a hectic make-out session in his truck or the dusty attic. "Somewhere nice?"

"You got it." He smiled at her and turned back to the road.

"A place I can wear heels and not feel overdressed."

His smiled broadened. "Wouldn't miss it for the world."

A date. She was in the mood to celebrate. A chance to get all her war paint on, wear something pretty. What girl didn't love that idea? Not this one, for sure.

"For the record, I like you fine in jeans." His long fingers tapped the steering wheel. "But seeing you all dressed up, that's good, too."

Oh, he was going to get it, no holds barred, all out tomorrow night. Everything from her underwear to her jewelry.

His phone rang, and he gave her an apologetic grimace as he answered. "Hey, Mom. What's up?"

Did the woman have psychic powers or something?

"Isaac?" A frown creased Matt's face. Pippa didn't want to think it, but he looked hot when he was pissed.

The frown deepened and radiated down to a clenched jaw. Make that very pissed. "What do you mean he didn't go into work?" He listened for a while, his body still and tense. "No, I can't come now."

Cressy's voice came as a tinny mumble over the phone, but the pitch was an unmistakable whine.

"I'm busy," Matt said. "Going to meet Jo. At Bella's."

The way he parceled out information intrigued her. Matt

was keeping secrets from his mother. Then again, if Cressy were her mother, Pippa would have left town and not come back. Not too far from what she had done, actually.

"I don't know why she didn't ask you." Matt switched his phone to the other ear and turned into Main Street. "You'll have to ask Jo that."

More whiny tone from the other end of the phone line set Pippa's teeth on edge.

"Because I'm not going alone," Matt said. This should be good. Pippa stared out the window, but kept her ears perked.

"Pippa," he said. "Yes, Turner, but she calls herself St. Amor."

Cressy squawked on for a bit before Matt cut her off. "Because it's her stage name. I don't really care why. If she wants to be called that, we call her that."

Pippa laughed, on the inside. Deep, deep down on the inside. Good luck to Matt's future wife, whoever the poor woman might be. She remembered Cressy from the LDS socials held at the big community center attached to the church. Cressy used to have this way of sidling into the social and staring down any girl who dared dance with one of her sons. Strangely, Jo had been pretty much left to run wild.

"Gotta go, Mom." Matt hung up on Cressy mid-whine. "My mother."

"I got that. And she's not happy."

Matt shrugged and pulled his face into an easy smile, which didn't quite reach his tawny eyes. "She's not happy about a lot of things. Isaac is at home, and not going to work."

"Do you need to go?"

"No." His body language said the exact opposite. "I needed him on-site this morning. We have a job that might go late if we don't get our thumbs out our ass. But I promised Jo."

How many pieces of this man were there? Certainly not

enough to go around. "Why don't you leave me with Jo?" she said. "It will probably be better if you're not there."

He shook his head as he turned into Eighth. "Jo needs me." And Cressy needed him, and it sounded like Isaac needed him too.

"I got this, Matt." She touched the warm skin of his arm. "This is what I do and I'm good at it. You come in, get Jo and me reacquainted, and then go deal with your brother and the site."

"Really?" A flicker of hope played around his eyes.

"Really." Pippa squeezed his arm to reassure him, and also because it was a seriously hot arm and why let an opportunity go to waste?

"Thanks." He whipped into a parking spot three doors down from Bella's. "This is what Eric doesn't get. He thinks I can leave here, but it's never going to work."

He could leave here. She opened her mouth to agree with Eric, and snapped it shut. Whatever this thing between them was, it wasn't about sharing burdens and life stuff.

Matt walked around the truck to open her door. He'd given up seventeen years of his life to take care of his family, a football scholarship, and God knows how many other small parts of what he wanted. It wasn't right.

And it so wasn't any of her business. She took his hand to slide off the seat.

Bella bustled over as they opened the door. She saw Pippa and stopped. "Pippa."

"Hello, Bella." All the women in the family were named some version of Bella. This one, had been Rosabella in high school. Her mother, Arabella, and her grandmother Clarabella. Now she was Bella, like her shop.

"Hey, Bella." Matt eased in behind her. "You remember Pippa?"

"Um . . . sure." Bella put her hand out. "We were in school together."

"Pippa is going to help Jo with her dress," Matt said.

Bella dragged her eyes away from Pippa and blinked at him. "But Jo already chose a dress."

This could get ugly, especially if the dress was paid for. Bella had every right to insist they stick with the dress Jo chose. So, why the hell had Matt brought her here today if the thing was done? He needn't think he was getting out of dinner, either.

"I tell you, Bella." Matt dropped his head, and gave it a slow shake. "I've been thinking about that dress nonstop."

Bella frowned at him and threw Pippa a fleeting glance.

News to her, too. Pippa shrugged.

"It's the one she wanted," Bella said.

"Yeah, I know." Matt gave a rueful grimace and rubbed the back of his neck. He could add an "aw shucks" to that performance and get away with it. "I just think she could do better. You know what I mean?"

Bella folded like a cheap deck chair. "Sh . . . sure."

"She's such a pretty girl, and I want a dress for her that makes her look like a princess."

The cocky bastard used the same line on her. Pippa empathized with Bella as the other woman melted into a warm puddle of goo. "Of course you do."

"I don't know much about this stuff." Matt went right on spreading it with a paddle. "Pippa agreed to rescue me."

Only so she could drown him later. Pippa tossed him a glittering smile.

He winked at her. Matt Evans was such a smug, cocksure, too-charming-for-his-own-good son of a bitch. Someone should take him down a notch or two. She hid her grin, because she was the right girl for the job.

Bella was no help. Fluttering her lashes, and squirming like a Labrador puppy as she asked after his family. Bella went through each member, one by one. Taking a little extra time on their smoking hot sheriff. What woman wouldn't?

"You leave it with us." Bella patted his arm. Clearly, the arms fetish was another thing they had in common. "Pippa and I will get Jo into a dress that makes her shine like the diamond she is."

Matt's topaz eyes gleamed liquid gold as he gazed at Bella. "Of course, I'm happy to pay for any inconvenience this causes. I mean if you've ordered the other—"

"Pffft." Bella batted her hand at him. "We can talk about that later. The important thing is to get Jo into the right dress."

"Is Jo late?" Matt glanced around the shop.

Bella shrugged. "She'll be here."

"It's just that I promised to introduce Pippa and Jo and—"

"I'll do it." Bella beamed at him.

Matt turned his jelly-knees smile on her. "Only if that's okay with Pippa."

"It's fine. You go on now." Pippa shook her head. When it came down to it, she was as bad as Bella.

"Thanks, Bella, you're a sweetheart." Matt leaned down and kissed her on the cheek. "You girls play nice, now." With a quick hug for Pippa, he disappeared out the door and into his truck.

"You should so charge for the first dress," Pippa said.

"Yeah, I know." Bella sighed. "But he's just so, so . . ."

Pippa sighed. "Yeah, I know."

"I thought I was going to marry an Evans brother when we were in high school." Bella gazed out the window as Matt got his sexy ass into his truck.

Not Pippa. In high school, all Pippa wanted to do was get the hell out of Ghost Falls. Maybe if the sperm donor hadn't left her freshman year she might have felt differently about it. Probably not.

Bella shook her head and turned back to her. "So." Her pretty face tightened. "How've you been?"

The thing is, Pippa could slap on her TV smile and give Bella all the brittle layers of glamour she had in her. Except, Bella was one of those truly nice people. Sweet ran right through the core of her, and Pippa didn't want to do it. "I suspect we both know how I've been."

Bella's manic smile flipped upside down and she winced. "I saw."

"Everyone saw." The idea of sweet, nice Bella looking at that clip and making the inevitable conclusions made her want to crawl away and hide.

Bella leaned forward on a waft of fresh, sweet perfume. "Matt doesn't think you said it."

Good to know. "I explained it to him."

"No, before then." Bella waved her hand over her shoulder. "When we were in the shop with Jo before. We showed him the clip and he said straight away that you didn't say it."

Huh! That needed some more thought. It made her feel good, though, that Matt had taken her side before she'd explained. "Well, I didn't say it." Bella deserved an explanation. "I said it, but I didn't say it."

"What did you say then?" Bella cocked her head.

"I can't even remember the exact words anymore, but Allie asked me how a pair of shoes could make her life different. And I said something like, 'You're right, a pair of shoes can't change your life. Neither can a pretty dress or even new makeup. Nothing you put on can really change you. The answer is inside you. If you believe you're fat, ugly, unwanted, or not worth loving, a dress is not going to make any difference. The only thing that can change that is you. But for now, put the dress on, wear the pretty shoes, and see if they help you find something you can love about yourself.'"

"But on the clip, you said—"

"They edited out enough of it to make it sound really, really bad."

Bella's big blues were even wider. "That's dreadful! You have to say something. Don't let them get away with that." She clenched her fists, a militant light in her eyes. Who knew sweet Bella had teeth?

"I tried that." And she had, there were rules about doing what Ray did. "But the ratings on the show were off the charts, and a scandal is always more interesting than the truth. Ray has some powerful friends." Pippa didn't want to bore Bella with all the other details that played almost constantly through her mind. How Jen was scared for her job, or her conversation with Allie's husband. "It seemed better to leave LA and live to fight another day."

"Of course it did." Bella bubbled back into sugar right before Pippa's eyes. "You did the right thing."

Had she? There were girls who would have stayed and fought, manned up and gone toe to toe with Ray and let the mud stick where it fell, but she wasn't one of them. Being back in Ghost Falls made her feel like taking a swing back. Here she reconnected with that feisty eighteen-year-old who had streaked out of town like a meteor on a straight trajectory to stardom. LA Pippa would never have sent that tweet, and never have discovered how much support she had in the real world.

"Would you like to look around?" Bella flushed. "I made some changes since I took over."

Pippa really looked at the shop for the first time. It had changed since the days of Bella II, aka this Bella's mother. The racks of twin sets were banished to a small corner near the back of the store. Her eagle eye homed in on a line of clothes on the front rack. "Bella." Nothing thrilled Pippa like beautiful styling. Fabric and cut, the two absolute must-haves. "You have some great stuff in here."

"Really?" Bella's eyes shone. "You're not just saying that?"

Pippa strode over to her find and flipped through the hangers. "I am definitely not just saying that, Bella. This is gorgeous." She tugged a silk sheath out and held it up. "Do you have this in my size?"

Bella did a little happy tap dance on the spot. "Do I ever."

Chapter Thirteen

Pippa kept her distance as Jo blew into Bella's bristling with antagonism.

Bella took it all in her stride. Sweet, lovely, and an instant panacea to whatever bug Jo had up her ass. Probably a bug that strongly resembled Matt Evans. The damn man had that way with him. A little charm, a little good ol' boy, a smidgen of helpless and they were all putty in his hands.

"Hi, Jo." Time to get the meet and greet over with. If Jo didn't want to do this, coffee was always an option. Coffee and cake. Lots and lots of cake, with calories oozing off the plate and into her mouth. Ray said she was packing on the pounds anyway.

Jo had changed in the years since Pippa had seen her. Gone was the pretty princess in her frilly pink dresses. Jo sported a biker grunge look, complete with a beautiful scrolling of ink up her arm. The eyebrow piercing—not so much.

"You're back." Jo packed a whole lot of attitude into two and a half words.

"Matt said you weren't happy with your dress." Bella charged straight in there, candy-coated balls to the wall.

"Which means Matt isn't happy with my dress." Jo stuck her lip out.

Her second year on the show, Pippa had dealt with a woman named Carly. Carly didn't think she needed a makeover, and resented the fact that her mother did. It took Pippa three long weeks to come to the inevitable conclusion, you could lead a horse to water . . . "Okay." She shrugged and smiled. "If you're happy with your dress, that's all that counts. It's your day, after all."

Jo blinked at her. "Yeah."

"Do you have this in red?" She turned back to Bella.

Bella's gaze flitted between her and Jo. "No. Red is not a big seller around here."

"I don't know why he wasted everyone's time." Jo clumped her big-ass boots farther into the shop. "Why didn't he say he hated it when he was here?"

"You know men." Bella fluttered her hand and turned back to Pippa. "I do have it in the most awesome midnight blue. It would go great with your complexion."

"Do you hate the dress?" Jo fiddled with the edge of her eyebrow piercing.

Bella gave her a gentle smile. "I think you could wear a garbage bag and look beautiful, Jo. But, it really doesn't matter what I think, or even Pippa. It only matters what you think."

Damn, Pippa had underestimated Bella all these years. It was too easy to look at Bella and see pretty and harmless. If she was staying in Ghost Falls, getting to know Bella better would be top of her list. Friends, at least good ones, had been thin on the ground in LA. "She's right." Pippa kept her shrug light. "Midnight blue?"

"It's not one of the most requested colors, but I think it really brings the fabric to life." Bella flipped through the hangers with a practiced flick of her wrists.

"I hate blue," Jo said.

"Really?" Pippa stole a smile from Bella's arsenal. "Because you could probably wear most shades of it, with your skin tones."

Jo shifted her weight onto one hip. "I like black, it goes with everything."

"It sure does." Bella produced the shirt. "Here we go."

Pippa examined it. Bella was right on the money. The deep, almost purple hue gave the fabric a rich, luxurious quality. "I am so trying this on as well."

"And I have a great pencil skirt that would look fabulous with that." Bella bustled over to another rack.

Jo edged closer. She really was a beautiful girl with her mother's delicate bone structure and porcelain skin. You didn't have to like Cressy to acknowledge she was a very lovely woman.

"What's so special about it?" Jo pointed at the shirt.

"The cut." Pippa laid the shirt on top of a row of hangers. "You see these darts here. They taper the shirt in underneath the bust. It gives you a narrow waist and draws the eyes away from the widest part of me. In my case, my hips."

Jo glanced down at Pippa's hips. "They don't look wide to me."

"Then I've got the right outfit on." Talking clothes was her crack and Pippa smiled. "Also, years of television will keep you on a diet."

Jo had a killer body to go with that face. All long legs and sleek lines. God, she'd love to get the girl into a long tube of ivory satin. Nothing elaborate, nothing too over-wrought. A perfect simple foil for Jo's looks. "You don't have my problem," she said. "You have near perfect proportions."

Jo blushed. "I have a fat ass."

"You most certainly do not." Bella appeared with a gor-geous gray pencil skirt in her hand.

Pippa itched to get her hands on it.

Bella turned and stuck her booty out. "I have a curvy ass because I'm an hourglass." She swiveled back with a grin. "But I've got a rack to balance it."

"Gimme." Pippa nearly snatched the hanger from Bella.

"Maybe, I could . . . like, try the dress on for you." Jo shrugged and tugged at her eyebrow ring.

"If you like," Pippa tossed over her shoulder as she headed for the fitting room.

Bella followed her halfway and stopped beside Jo. "I have your dress in the back. I haven't made the alterations yet, so I could pin it for you."

"Okay." Jo stomped into the fitting room beside Pippa and yanked the curtains across.

Bella danced over and gave Pippa a quick high-five. How had she missed out on Bella all these years?

Pippa did love the skirt and she hurried into her fitting room to try it on. It fit like a glove. Bella had guessed her size perfectly. The woman had mad skills. In her previous life, she would have found a way to steal those kinds of skills for her show.

Curtain rings clattered as Bella entered the fitting room next door. Fabric rustled as she pinned Jo into the dress.

Pippa pulled her clothes back on, kept the skirt firmly by her side, and went to sit on one of the pink velveteen divans.

With Bella's impeccable taste in clothing, it seemed odd the decor had survived. It still looked like an eighties music video in here. Then again, Bella senior was stuck like glue in her ways.

Bella opened the curtains and Jo stepped out.

Dear God in Heaven.

Pippa schooled her features into neutral lines. It had to be the ugliest dress in creation. Ice white, so bright it hurt the eyes to look at the thing. It exploded around Jo in a myriad of ruffles and bows and goofy things that Pippa didn't even have a name for. A great wad of fabric obscured the line of her waist completely. Huge capped sleeves ballooned out from her shoulders to her wrists and ended in more of those marshmallow puffs.

"What do you think?" Jo stuck her hands on her hips. Her biker boots poked out from the bottom of the dress.

Pippa thought the designer should be shot. She made a business of studying Jo. "Are you happy with your dress?"

"It's a dress." Jo shrugged.

Warning tingles shot up Pippa's spine. A wedding dress should never be just a dress. Even the most low-key bride wanted to look good on her wedding day. Damn, Matt owed her lobster and Moët & Chandon for this. She raised her eyebrows in question. "You want my honest opinion?"

Jo hesitated, and nodded.

"I think you could do better."

"Why?" Jo's face clouded over with a brewing storm.

Make that lobster and Moët for the rest of her natural life. "That's a lot of dress." More dress than mortal man could stand. "And you're getting lost in it."

What had Bella been thinking, ordering that thing? Pippa threw her a quick glance.

Bella shrugged apologetically. "Jo picked it out of a magazine and we ordered it for her."

"You hate it, don't you?" Jo crossed her arms over her chest, obscuring her face with the sleeves.

There wasn't a nice way to say this. "Yes."

"And you?" Jo whirled on Bella.

"I think it's the ugliest dress I've ever seen," Bella said. "On the most beautiful girl in Ghost Falls, and that makes me mad as hell."

"Well, damn." Jo glowered down at her boots. "You could have said something before."

Bella stared at her and Jo had the grace to blush. "Okay, maybe not." Her head whipped around to Pippa again. "But I bought it, so now what do I do?"

The magic question, and it brought joy to Pippa's day. "You let me give you a couple of dresses to try on."

"I have the perfect dress." Bella flat-out ran across the store to the formal dresses. Pippa would bet her head Bella did.

Three dresses later, Pippa's warning tingle had grown into a yell.

Jo didn't like the satin on one dress, lace was "old lady" on another. Jo glared at her reflection in dress three, working hard to find something she didn't like. Good luck to her, because she looked incredible. Long and elegant, the dress molded Jo's curves in rich, ivory silk. The designer would have wept for joy to see Jo wearing his dress. It was a perfect synergy of girl and gown. Nothing elaborate, no distraction from the lovely girl wearing it. Pippa had even gotten a bit teary-eyed when Jo first emerged in it.

She and Bella exchanged a glance, having their very own *Say Yes to the Dress* moment. Jo—not so much.

Matt, the arch manipulator, knew all along the problem had nothing to do with the dress. Son of a bitch was going to hear from her, in minute detail, what she thought of his clever little ploys. "Jo?" She moved to stand behind Jo in the mirror. "You look amazing."

Jo pulled a face at herself.

"And I think you know you do."

Jo's hazel eyes met hers in the mirror. She glanced away again and back.

Tell me. Pippa clamped her teeth down on the shout.

"The dress is okay."

"The dress is beautiful." Bella eased over on silent feet. "And you look beautiful in it."

Jo studied the toe of the neutral-color pump Bella had put on her feet.

Bella clapped her hands together and Jo jumped.

"I tell you what," Bella said. "I think we need coffee and we need cheesecake with it. I'm going over to Mugged to get both. Why don't you get out of that dress, and I'll be back."

Jo met both their gazes in the mirror. Indecision teetered precariously on her face, and then she nodded.

Pippa let out the breath she'd been holding. Now they were getting somewhere. While Jo changed back into her normal clothes, Pippa texted Matt. *You owe me big.* Let him chew on that for the rest of the day.

Her Twitter app showed fifty-six notifications.

Jo reappeared and clumped over to the divan to tie her boots.

Pippa backed off and waited. She got the feeling you couldn't rush Jo.

Bella got back with the girl talk supplies. She arranged them on the table in front of the divan before popping over to the door and flipping the sign to CLOSED.

Jo sipped her coffee and ate half her cheesecake before she was ready to spill her guts. "I don't feel like a bride."

"How does a bride feel?" Pippa sipped her latte. Rachel and her café, Mugged, were new in town. Another great discovery that bore further investigation.

Jo shrugged. "Giddy. Excited. Happy." Holy crap. Alarming, but not entirely a surprise. "The thing is"—Jo sat back in her chair as she grabbed a deep breath—"I'm not sure I want to get married."

"Is it nerves?" Pippa had seen her share of brides, done

a few shows on them too. Not her first rodeo, so there was more to this than wedding jitters.

Jo shook her head. Long hair fell over her cheek and obscured her face. "I don't love him."

It wasn't the first time Pippa had heard that, either.

Bella's eyes were huge in her face. She made an oh-shit face at Pippa.

"Then you shouldn't marry him," Pippa said.

Bella sucked in her breath and hid behind her large, cream topped coffee.

Jo turned to glare at her. "Just like that."

"We're talking about the rest of your life here. So, if you don't love someone, it seems a long time to commit."

"I could get a divorce if it didn't work out." Jo gave her coffee a belligerent slurp.

Pippa let Jo's own words sink into her brain. Sometimes you had to know when to keep your mouth shut.

Jo leaped out of her chair on a strangled noise. "You're right. I know you're right. But I said I would and he's all excited about the wedding." She stopped and pulled a face. "That's a lie. He couldn't give a fuck about the wedding. He hasn't asked me one thing about the plans. It's just that . . ." Jo struggled in silence for a while, and paced. "Matt didn't want me to marry him, but I fought him until he gave in. And my mother." Jo let out another of her wounded animal noises. "I'll never hear the end of it from her."

Pippa would bet money on it. "Those are going to be difficult things to handle," she said. "But not good enough reasons to get married."

Jo threw herself back in the divan. She turned her head and gave Bella a small smile. "Why didn't I talk to you before?"

Bella shrugged. "I was here."

"And you?" Jo turned to Pippa. "How could you have said those things to that woman and be so nice to me?"

Pippa had to laugh. "Jo, people are never what they seem. I'm learning that more and more every day."

Matt gave the bolt a vicious twist and tried not to picture Isaac's neck as he did it. Day three and the plumber was still not back on-site. The owners were starting to give him are-you-going-to-be-done-in-time faces. At least the wife was; the husband did everything except roll his eyes and mutter "contractors."

He really hated the assumptions that came with his job. The contractor tells you this date, add three weeks or a month. The contractor gives you a price, tack on another thirty percent for unwanted surprises.

This business that he'd clawed out of the gutter had been built on meeting his price and hitting his target dates. You might not get the cheapest price from Evans Construction, but you got one you could take to the bank and you moved into your house when they said you would.

And Isaac was missing. He'd packed his car late yesterday and not been seen since. The brief text early this morning to say he was fine had sent Mom into a fucking frenzy.

Matt had to leave the office and go around and calm her down. Of course, yesterday with Jo and Pippa and the dress had come up five minutes after he walked in the door. He loved his mom, he really did, but the best thing he did was move out of that house as soon as he could.

He'd tried to call Isaac eight times and the call always went to voice mail. So, he concentrated on what he could fix: the lack of a foreman at the Barrowitz house. A call into the plumber got that asshole moving at least, but he would need to find someone to oversee this job until Isaac got back from his little walkabout. Isaac hadn't even called him to say he would be missing. Mind you, if Isaac had called, Matt would have taken a chunk out of his ass and told him to get the rest of it on-site.

Footsteps crunched over the sand and Eric popped his head around the doorframe. "Hey."

"Hey, yourself." Matt got back to his plumbing. He needed to get these pipes in the wall so the drywallers could get started.

Eric crouched down beside him and watched him work for a while. "Got a spare wrench?"

Matt sat back on his haunches.

Eric traced the line of pipes with the tops of his fingers. "Why don't I get started on this section while you work over there?"

"You still remember how?" Matt eyed the fancy shirt and designer jeans his brother sported.

Eric threw him a grin. "I still remember how."

"Toolbox is over there." Matt jerked his head to the center of what would one day be a kitchen. "Need to get these in so they can drywall. Cabinets are expected in a couple of days."

Eric strolled over to the toolbox and bent to select a few tools. He stuffed a couple in the back of his jeans. The right ones, too. Matt didn't mean to check on him, but Eric didn't look like he knew an elbow from a coupling.

Eric glanced up and caught him staring. He shook his head and chuckled. "I still keep my hand in."

"Oh, yeah?" Matt got back to his section of pipe, check-ing the angle of drainage before fitting another coupling.

Eric kneeled, not looking fussed about getting dirt on his fancy jeans. "Did I tell you about my house?"

"Nope."

Eric lifted a section of pipe into place and clamped it. "I found this piece of land outside Denver. Beautiful place, right on the edge of a cliff." He sat back and got a faraway look on his face. "When you stand there, it feels like you could see forever. No neighbor in sight."

Matt could picture the spot, the kind of place he'd like to have. Maybe with a water cannon mounted on a deck that could shoot down any stray family member heading his way with a mind to complicate his life.

"Designed my own house." Eric grunted as he gave the wrench a twist.

Matt sat back in surprise. Eric used to doodle as a kid, everything from Transformers to fruit in a bowl. "You designed your house?"

"Yup." Eric stood and went over to fetch another section of hot water pipe. "Figured I'd built enough houses to know exactly what works and what I want."

It made sense. Matt would like that, to sit down and design something from scratch. He'd have a big kitchen, big enough for a family. Except he was missing the wife part in this scenario. Like he had time for a wife. "Have you started construction?"

"Yup." Eric crouched nearer to him. He really was quicker on the plumbing than Matt. The old competitive edge stirred and he got down to it. "But I'm doing it myself."

"What?" Matt nearly pinched his finger in the joint.

"Myself." Eric glanced at him quickly and back to his work. His face got a bit red. "I mean, everything I can do. I want to put myself in my house. Know what I mean?"

Matt did know what he meant. He just never thought Eric would have the same dream.

They worked in silence for a while. Eric manned the blowtorch, which pretty much meant the end of conversation. Eric flipped off the torch and pushed his goggles back on his head. "What's next?"

"Bathroom." Matt grabbed the toolbox and headed up the stairs.

Eric fell into step behind him.

"I'd like to see your house," he said.

"Yeah?" Eric actually sounded surprised and Matt turned to stare at him.

"Yeah."

"Cool." Eric shrugged but a dumb little smile turned the corners of his mouth up. "Bring your tools."

"I'd like that."

"Me too."

They were not much into big displays, he and Eric. This was nice, though. It felt right.

They got to the first bathroom and he showed Eric the blueprints. Eric nodded and got straight to work. It used to be like this in the days before their dad died. He and Eric trailing their dad onto site and chipping in. Shit, he'd been driving Bobcats before he had his license.

"You heard from Isaac?" Eric broke the silence.

"Nope. You?" Matt looked up from his drain to where Eric was putting in the ball joint for the shower.

"Nope." Eric's fancy pants were streaked with grit now. "But I never hear from Isaac anyway. No reason he would call me now."

"Mom's having a meltdown."

Eric snorted and glanced his way. "Mom's always having a meltdown."

Something about Eric's tone made Matt want to defend his mother. Never mind that he'd been thinking the same thing moments before his brother arrived. "She's alone, Eric. She has a lot on her plate."

"No, she's not." Eric tossed a wrench into the toolbox with a clatter. "She has you. She's always had you to pick up where Dad left off."

That sounded so wrong, and combined with the throwing of tools pissed him off enough to get him to his feet. "What the fuck does that mean?"

"Come on, Matt." Eric put his hands out in front of him. The same placating gesture he'd used the other day in Matt's office. "All I'm saying is she leans on you. All the time. For everything."

"She doesn't have anyone else."

"She's a grown woman. You were a kid and that didn't stop her from making you her little replacement husband."

Eric should shut his fucking mouth now before Matt put his fist in it. His mother did not treat him like a surrogate husband; she needed him and she didn't have anyone else. Who the hell else was going to step in and help her out? Not Eric, he'd been eighteen and heading for college. Nate was too busy tearing a strip through town and Isaac and Jo were too young. So, she'd turned to her oldest son. Her nineteen-year-old son.

Damn! He'd been a kid himself. Why exactly was he ready to smack Eric for something he'd thought a million times himself? He turned away and grabbed a trap to install for the bathtub. "She needed me."

"And you were there for her." Eric's voice came from right behind him. A firm hand landed on his shoulder. "I've thought about this a lot, Matt. I'm not giving you shit about it. You did what you had to do, what Dad had raised you to do. But it's seventeen years later and she's still leaning on you."

"Yeah." What else could he say? It was the goddamned truth and there were days when the weight of his mother's expectations hung around his neck like an anchor. An anchor keeping him here, stuck. The thought rattled his cage bad enough for him to shrug Eric off and stalk over to the window. The rough ground in front of the house needed leveling and landscaping before the owner moved in. Another job to add to the growing list. "Isaac should have called."

"Yeah, he should have." Eric got back to work, the soft clang of metal on metal sounding from behind Matt. "But I get why he didn't."

Jesus, what was Eric? Some kind of fucking Buddha or something? "Why?"

Eric laid down the showerhead and stood. "You're gonna want to deck me for this as well. So, before I say anything, consider yourself warned."

Matt braced for impact and jerked his chin for Eric to continue.

"It's you, Matt. You're so perfect all the time. It's like you don't have the normal shit the rest of us struggle through."

"What?" Matt couldn't believe he was hearing this crap. He had enough shit on his plate, only his eyeballs were still clear of it and they were clogging up fast.

"Something needs to be done and St. Mathew steps up. A problem comes up and St. Mathew whips on his white horse and fixes it."

Damn, that stung enough to smack the breath from his lungs. "What the fuck are you talking about?"

"Nothing ever gets to you, Matt." Eric jammed his hands in his pockets. "Like now. You should be screaming a blue streak about the shit Isaac pulled. But no, you're here, keeping the project on track, soothing Mom, being perfect."

"I'm not perfect." He would get mad, but this shit was too far out of left field to make any impact. "And what else can I do? The job has to get delivered. Mom is Mom."

"You can do something for yourself." Eric's voice went low and intense. "You can call Isaac and tell him either he get his ass back here, or he's fired. You can tell Mom to call one of that pack she hangs out with and cry on their shoulder. And you can tell me to fuck off."

It surprised a laugh out of him. "Get the fuck out of here."

"Too late." Eric flashed a quick grin. "I know what you gave up for us. I was there and I know you better than anyone. I saw you after you made the call to turn down your scholarship."

The one and only time he'd gone out and gotten deliberately, messily, puke-his-guts-out drunk. He had a vague memory of Eric handing him a glass of water as he finished tossing his cookies.

"But this martyr shit is getting old now, and so are you."

"I'm thirty-six." Hardly out to pasture yet.

Eric took a wary step closer. "And if you don't do something, next time we have this conversation you'll be forty-six. Fuck, Matt, when was the last time you had a woman in your life who wasn't your mother?"

"I have plenty of women in my life."

"Real ones." Eric pinned him with a hard look. "Women you give a shit about and not ones you bone and move on."

Eric had a way with words. Matt shook his head to clear them out of his brain. Pippa's laughing green eyes popped into his head. He was all big talk in front of her, but there was a woman a man could lose himself in. Except she had another life waiting for her that didn't include him, so he was safe.

Safe? The word clattered around his brain. Why the hell did he need to be safe?

Eric's eyes burned holes right through to the back of his brain, and left a smoking trail of nasty truth behind them. "You just want me to go into business with you."

It was lame and half-assed and Eric snorted and pulled a face. He deserved the derision. "That's bullshit," Eric said. "And we both know it. I can get any contractor to work with me on this. I want you, because you're my brother and I trust you. Most of all, Matt, I need to give you something back. You have no idea what it does to a man to know your entire life is built on someone else's life-changing sacrifice."

That sent him reeling. Matt had to grab hold of the wood framing to support his weight. "Everything you've built up, you did that, Eric."

"Yeah." Eric nodded. "Because you gave up your dreams, everything you ever wanted, to see the rest of us through."

"I was glad to do it." Did Eric not get how proud of him he was?

Eric looked at him, his eyes a little damp. "Always glad?"

Maybe not. Matt shrugged, his throat too thick for words. He didn't do this feelings shit. It wasn't him. Life got tough, he cracked a joke, threw down a little charm— and a beer—and eased on out of it.

Eric bent to pick up his wrench. "Let's get this done."

Chapter Fourteen

Twitter was up to over two hundred notifications now. Pippa had glanced at them earlier.

@Abby454 tweeted: Nice to have you back @pippastamor #sayitlikeitis #askpippawhatshesaid #justiceforpippa

She should check the others but Pippa had hit a snag in her preparations for her date with Matt. The dresses lay on her bed waiting for her to decide. You couldn't go wrong with your basic little black number, short and clingy and oozing classy sex appeal. The thinking man's sex bomb, and Matt kept a keen brain behind his Bob the Builder exterior. Then again, he wasn't one for subtleties and nothing said "take me" like the red one. Also short, because he was clearly a leg man, with a hint of cleavage and a rebel yell packed into each stitch. Or blue. Not the obvious choice, but then again, neither was Matt her obvious choice of a date. This was your shimmer and sparkle dress, the subtle come-on showing enough skin to tip opinion in favor of "Yes, she really does want me."

She'd never taken this long to get dressed before. There was a perfect dress for every occasion and she owned every one. A lot of them gifted to her by grateful stores and designers during her show.

The deathly silence from her contact list screamed there would be no help there for Pippa St. Amor. Well, she'd done it without them before, and she'd do it again. The idea of Ray getting away with what he'd done to her and Allie was getting tougher to swallow with each passing day. She was glad she'd tweeted that message. It had given her an idea; a sneaky, Ray-worthy idea. Ray had opened Allie and her up to public ridicule. Maybe it was time to use that little tactic against him.

Back to tonight. Red. She was not in the mood for subtle or sophisticated, and after that stunt he'd pulled with Jo, Matt deserved a full helping of sit up and beg. She slipped into a white lace push-up bra and matching thong. Never match your underwear to your dress, total overkill. The combination of virgin white underneath the devil red dress was perfect. Now you see the bad girl, now you don't.

The doorbell gonged through the house in the imitation of Big Ben's chimes. Right on time.

"I'll get it," Phi sang out. Of course she would because Phi was even more excited about tonight than Pippa. Her grandmother took personal responsibility for having set the entire thing up. This date was years in the making for Phi. Pippa wasn't sure whether it would disappoint or delight Phi that this was only a hookup between old sort-of flames.

Pippa wriggled into the red dress and adjusted the cup of her breasts. Five-inch nude sandals added the final touch.

The murmur of Matt's baritone drifted up the stairs as he spoke to Phi.

Pippa took her time coming down the stairs.

Her leg man did not disappoint. His gaze ate her up from top to toe and lingered in between, not missing an inch of skin as she descended toward him. "Holy shit."

"Succinct, and lacking finesse, but I'm certain Pippa understood." Phi patted him on the cheek.

Pippa did some staring of her own, much more subtle, but he was hard to miss all dressed up in a black jacket and pants with a deep blue dress shirt. He leaned in to kiss her cheek and she sucked in a breath of Calvin Klein's Eternity as his cheek pressed hers. "You ready?" he murmured against her ear.

Uh-huh, Pippa was ready and she nodded.

Phi clapped her hands to her bosom. "I won't wait up."

Matt led her out to a sleek, black Jaguar parked on the circular drive outside Phi's house. He'd even used the main entrance for the occasion.

"This is yours?" She eyed the car with appreciation.

He gave her his country boy grin. "I don't always rattle around in a truck. Tonight I'm taking my lady out, and she's a classy sort of girl."

Pippa laughed as he helped her into the low-slung seat. The inside of the car was pristine and filled with the smell of leather and Matt. He folded into the driver's seat, big and hot, and looking like he belonged there.

"Where are we going?" Pippa clicked her seatbelt in.

"We have a bit of a drive." Gravel crunched beneath the tires as they glided away from the house. "The best Ghost Falls has to offer is The Crank, and while they do make the best burger around, I thought I could do a bit better." Wincing, he glanced over at her. "After leaving you with Jo yesterday."

"Yeah." Pippa turned to glare at him. "About that?"

"I tell you what." He took her hand in a warm, strong clasp. "You can bitch at me all you like, and I deserve it. But let's make tonight about you and me. Not Phi, my mother, my sister, or even my dipshit brother. Just you and me."

"Okay." She didn't get all dressed up in a killer red dress

and heels to spend the night talking about a man's family. They'd certainly taken their time getting around to this date and tomorrow could bring a whole raft of nasty surprises. Maybe they only had tonight. This beautiful man was hers for one night, to do with what she liked. The hot look in his eyes told her he liked a lot. "I can do that."

"Good." He watched the road with her hand tucked in his, resting atop his hard thigh as he drove.

The silence in the car was easy but expectant as he headed out of Ghost Falls and over South Mountain. The view of the valley to their left made her catch her breath. A hundred lights twinkled like Christmas beneath them, and disappeared into the low black night all around them.

"Did I tell you how incredible you look?" He gave her hand a small squeeze.

"No."

His teeth flashed white as he laughed. "You look . . . perfect."

"You don't look so bad yourself."

"Eric got hold of me," he said. "He didn't think my T-shirt, jeans combo would cut it."

"Really?" She played along with a look of amazement.

Matt shook his head slowly. "And they were my best jeans, too. No paint stains on them or anything."

They headed into the ski hills around Ghost Falls. It made sense the fancier restaurants would be up here. They catered to the out-of-towners, only in for the skiing and snowboarding and with enough money to meet their prices.

Matt drove for about forty minutes before pulling up in front of a low glass-and-wood structure, perched on the edge of a cliff that offered a panoramic view of the mountains all around them. Even at this time of year, the parking lot was full. People came up here to hike in summer, or just enjoy the endless blue skies and clear days.

A valet took the keys as Matt opened the door for her. Matt's hand pressed warm and intimate in the hollow of her back as he led her into the restaurant.

Pippa looked about her with interest. "This place must be new."

"Only a year old." Matt gave his name to the sleek, twentysomething blonde manning the reception. "It's part of why Eric wants to develop this area. It's becoming more and more popular as people move farther out. We even get people making the trip from Denver and Las Vegas."

Her old hometown looked to be heading for the development loop. "It would be a shame to ruin it with hotels and resorts."

"Eric doesn't want that to happen. It's part of his plan." An edge of tension crept into Matt's voice. Not anger, but something else.

His face gave nothing away. Pippa followed the hostess through the busy restaurant.

About two-thirds through the dining room, it happened. A woman glanced up from her dinner companions, her eyes widened, and she sucked in a breath. Leaning forward, the woman whispered to her friend across the table. From there, it seemed as if a wave swept the diners. One head after another swung in their direction. Some not sure why, but sensing interest from their fellow diners and wanting to know.

Not tonight. Pippa raised her chin and straightened her shoulders. This was her night, hers and Matt. The first, honest-to-God, get-dressed-up-and-all-excited date she'd had in years. And with a man she'd been circling for long enough to be embarrassing. She'd be damned if she let Ray and his bullshit ruin this for her too.

Matt held out the chair for her, and took the seat opposite.

He'd given her the best seat, the one with the view outside and the dining room behind her.

Hundreds of eyeballs burned into her back and Pippa shivered.

"Are you cold?" A brief frown chased across Matt's handsome face. He stilled and glanced around them. His jaw tensed as he came to the right conclusion. "Damn, I didn't think of this."

"Ignore them." Pippa waved her hand in front of his eyes. "It happens all the time. I'm used to it by now."

He eyed her skeptically, not at all convinced by her glib explanation. That made two of them. She fidgeted in her chair as he ordered their cocktails. She forced her voice to sound chipper. "So, Eric has plans for the area?"

"Yeah." Matt dragged his gaze back to her. "He has this plan and he wants me to be a part of it."

Pippa caught the flicker of excitement deep in his eyes. "That's great."

He damped it in a blink. "Not gonna happen, though. I have too many responsibilities here to follow Eric to Denver."

"You would be based in Denver?"

"For a while." His eyes shifted back to the restaurant. "We haven't really hammered out the details."

As if the heat on her back wasn't enough, she could see by Matt's expression the scrutiny hadn't lessened one bit. Her lovely evening was heading south faster than she could stop it. Pippa ducked behind her menu. This would go away, eventually, and she would become old news. Not tonight, apparently. "I'm starving."

Across the table, Matt tensed and his eyes narrowed to a point behind her shoulder.

"You're Pippa St. Amor, aren't you?" Pippa swung round to catch a middle-aged brunette beside her. The woman's mouth screwed up into a tight ball of dislike.

Pippa's heart hit her sexy shoes and stayed there. "Yes, I am."

"I can't believe you would—"

"Lady." Matt's deep rumble cut her off. "Do you know either of us?"

"I know she's Pippa St. Amor." The woman paled as her gaze flickered to Matt.

He radiated pissed off from every stiff line of him. "But that's her name and that's all you know."

Pippa tried to motion Matt to stop. It never did any good anyway.

He shook his head at her. "You saw something on TV or the Internet and now you're over here to share your opinion."

"She had no right—"

"And you know for a fact that everything you ever see on TV or online is the God's honest truth."

"No, but—"

"Exactly." Matt leaned forward, his gold eyes smoking holes in the woman. "You go back and look at that clip again. And while you're getting your panties in a wad about it, ask yourself if you've ever seen Pippa do anything like that before. When you come up with the answer that you haven't, then ask yourself if you're so sure what you're seeing is the truth."

The woman shifted and frowned. "She said awful things to that poor woman."

"I've seen it," Matt said. "And I'll give you this, it's bad and it makes Pippa look like the worst kind of bitch. But I know Pippa, so maybe I have the advantage over you, and I know she would never, ever say that to another woman."

"But I . . ." The woman opened her mouth and shut it again.

"You still here?" Matt's voice was quiet but lethal.

The woman backed away from the table and returned to her companions.

Back at her table, the woman dug out her smartphone. Likely doing exactly what Matt had told her to do.

"Right." Matt's jaw was set so tight it was a wonder it didn't crack. "What will you have?"

His defense of her had come straight from the heart. However pointless against the flood of condemnation, he'd still done it. Pippa went all warm and gooey inside. "Matt Evans, you really are the best kind of man."

Matt blushed, and it was kind of adorable. The lack of a snappy comeback indicated more than anything how much the incident had gotten to him. Pippa motioned the waiter over. "We'll have the crab cakes and the bruschetta to start. Followed by your filet mignon." She glanced up at Matt. "And make it to go."

"Pippa?" His brows lowered over his eyes. "Don't let this crap disturb our evening."

"I have no intention of letting it." She got to her feet. "I hope you have wine at home."

A big smile spread across his face. "I have wine. Bets's finest."

"Then we're good."

The waiter's eyes jumped about like a panic-stricken squirrel. "Madam, we don't—"

Matt tucked a folded bill in his hand. "I'm sure you do."

The waiter glanced down and his head snapped up again. "You're quite correct, sir. We do, indeed."

They waited for their food in the restaurant bar. Glances still slid her way, but Pippa washed them down with an excellent dirty martini.

It took a little longer to get to Matt's home. A modest ranch style a few blocks away from his mother's house. Still too close in Pippa's opinion.

A delicious tension had filled the car from the restaurant, and mingled with the mouth-watering aromas coming from the bag the restaurant put together.

"I have a confession." Matt opened her car door and helped her out.

Pippa braced for impact.

"It's not my car." He pressed the fob to activate the alarm. The Jag gave a subtle wink and a blip to let them know it was locked.

Beautiful as it was, the Jag was not Matt. "Eric?"

"Got it in one." He took her hand in one of his, the other carrying the takeout bag, and led her onto a lit porch.

Her belly fluttered as he put the key in the lock. How long had it been since she'd been on a proper date? Gotten naked for anyone but Ray? Gotten naked for Ray, for that matter. Maybe the white underwear didn't send the right message. Exactly what was the right message?

She followed him into a central hallway and through the right-hand door into a sitting room. You didn't need to be an interior designer to recognize bachelor minimalist. A large leather sofa, big-ass TV, and an ugly-as-sin tree branch coffee table. The carpet sank beneath her heels in an indiscriminate blur of beige. No-nonsense blinds closed off the windows from the street.

Matt shrugged out of his jacket. "Fire?"

"Lovely." It came out of her mouth on an enthusiastic burst of noise. Damn, she was skittish. So much for her woman-of-the-world exterior when inside she was quaking like a sixteen-year-old virgin.

Matt raised a brow at her.

Pippa's face heated. He had so busted her.

He tugged his shirt out of his pants and knelt to light a fire. His dress pants tightened over the bulge of his thighs. "Why don't you make yourself comfortable?"

Pippa perched on the edge of the couch. Then scooted her butt back to look more relaxed. A match caught and she jumped a bit. All this big talk and underwear planning and she was getting ready to hoof it.

"Pippa." He leaned his elbows on his knees and stared at her. "I'm not going to jump you."

A stupid titter got away from her and she jabbed her nails in her palms.

"I'll get some wine and plates. Why don't you open the bag?" He stood and walked to the shadowed end of the room. A light snapped on in an open-plan kitchen. Again, very basic from what she could see from here. Plain, serviceable appliances, standard countertops—neat, but a little dated. The entire place gave off a temporary vibe, like a long-term rental.

"Have you lived here long?" Her fingers fumbled with the tie on the bag. Dammit, why did they have to tie it so tight?

"About ten years." He opened and shut cupboard doors. "My mom wasn't keen on me moving out, so I stood it for as long as I could."

He'd done well to last that long. Pippa took containers out of the bag and arranged them on the coffee table. Flames flickered and caught in the fireplace.

Matt prowled closer, plates and glasses in his hands, a bottle tucked under his arm. He placed it all on the coffee table and straightened. His warm lion eyes searched hers for a moment and he cocked his head. "You're nervous."

"No. Yes. I—" Pippa forced breath into her lungs. "Scared shitless."

He took hold of her hands and tugged her up. "Nothing is going to happen here that you don't want. You know that, right?"

The nice-guy thing got her every time. He slipped his arms around her waist and pulled her into a hot, Matt-scented hug.

"I know that." Her words were muffled by his shirt.

"This doesn't have to be a big deal, Pippa. You, me, whatever happens or doesn't happen, I'm okay with it," he said.

"I haven't done this in a while."

"Dated?"

She nodded.

"Messed around?"

"That, too."

"More?"

"Definitely a little short on practice with the more."

His laugh rumbled through his chest against her ear. "They say you never forget. Just like—"

"Don't say riding a bike."

"Pippa." He brushed her neck with his nose. "I've had a thing for you since you left town at eighteen. For damn sure, I'm gonna make a move on you."

"And this is supposed to relax me?"

"More like fair warning. A kind of statement of intent. And when I make that move, then you get to make a choice." He put her at arm's length. "But for now, I'm hungry, so can we eat?"

"We can eat." The knot in her gut unraveled and she returned his smile. "Any ETA on that move you plan on making?"

"Nah." He shrugged. "I'm a go-with-the-moment kind of guy." He let her go and dropped onto the carpet between the table and the fire.

No way that was happening in this dress. "You got something comfortable I could borrow?"

"Sure." He moved to get up.

Pippa waved him down again. "Laundry this way?" She pointed at the kitchen. "My best bet at something clean, right?"

"Damn, you're smart."

Pippa held her arms out to her sides and did a slow turn. "Get a good look. See Pippa all dressed up." She strolled over to the kitchen, feeling relaxed enough to put a little extra swing in her step. "Now she's gone."

"I have the picture burned in the back of my brain," he called.

The laundry was off the kitchen, as per her guess. A neat pile of folded clothes sat on top of the dryer. She grabbed a tee and a pair of sweats from the pile. Getting out of the dress went much faster than wriggling in. Her toes gave a grateful throb as she eased her heels off and slipped on a pair of sports socks. His clothes drowned her, and her ex-producers would have a shit fit if they caught sight of her outfit. Shapeless chic. She rolled up the waistband to clear her feet and grabbed her dress and shoes.

Matt was pouring the wine when she padded back into the sitting room. This felt more like her and Matt, relaxed and easy with no expectations and no tension.

She sat cross-legged beside him and took her glass. The fire laid a warm glow across her as Matt handed her a plate. Loaded. Good thing she had eating pants on, because it looked incredible. She paused in the middle of the first bite to let the light lemon aftertaste of the crab cake linger. "You've been here ten years?"

"Yup." He went straight for the meat. "I don't spend a lot of time here."

"It shows."

His bark of laughter didn't even have a tinge of resentment. "My mother is always after me to let her decorate. Even Jo tried to get in here."

The long fingers of Cressy. She gave him kudos for resisting.

"This is just a place to keep my stuff, eat, sleep." He

shrugged. "One of these days I'm gonna do what Eric's doing and build my own place. Up from the ground and do everything myself."

"Is that what Eric's doing?" She tried to picture Eric in a tool belt and failed.

Matt nodded and put his plate aside. He'd already eaten everything on it. God, he must have been hungry because she was still working away at hers. "Here." She handed him half her filet. "I'll never eat all that."

"Are you sure?" He frowned down at his plate. "Because we didn't order dessert or anything."

"I'm not a dessert girl," she said.

He gaped at her.

"Seriously." Pippa laughed. "But I'll swap you for your crab cake." She nabbed the last one before he could say anything. "Tell me about this thing with Eric."

He stopped, fork midway to his mouth, as if considering her request.

Pippa finished her dinner while he spoke. The note of excitement was back in his voice. He kept it locked down tight, but it came through every now and again. He'd studied Eric's plans in detail. A lot of detail for a man who claimed he wasn't going to do anything about the offer. "Anyway." He put his plate on the table and grabbed her hand. "It doesn't matter."

Ah, but clearly it did. Pippa kept her eyes on his fingers laced through hers. The Matt she remembered from school had been driven, focused, intent on getting out of Ghost Falls and leaving a trail of dust behind him. When Eric dated Laura, she'd gotten to know Matt a bit better, but four years in your teens was a big gap to bridge. Still, his scholarship had been everything to him. He'd worked so hard to make it happen, on and off the football field.

His calm acceptance of the rest of his life bothered her.

Sure, part of her got that people could be happy doing exactly what they were doing, but there was that buzz to Matt when he spoke of Eric's offer. It jibed with what came out of his mouth.

"Hey." He pressed her hand. "You still with me?"

"I'm still with you." She nodded and let him tuck her into his side.

He leaned back against the table and lifted her knees to drape her legs over his thighs. Pippa stared into the mesmerizing dance of the flames. Matt gave off a lot of body heat. His thighs beneath her were rock-hard. "This is nice."

"Yeah." He tightened his arm around her shoulders.

The niggle about Eric wouldn't go away. "Matt—"

"Nope." He dipped his head into the crook of her neck. "No interrupting. I'm getting ready to make my move."

Her brain emptied as if someone had pulled the plug. Sharp tingles of heat prickled beneath her skin.

He brushed the sensitive skin of her neck with his firm, warm mouth.

Heat radiated from that point, making her boneless, her skin awake to his touch.

He hummed against her neck, making the prickling thing go a bit crazy. "You always smell so good."

"It's Dior."

"No, it's Pippa." He stroked up her spine to cup the back of her neck.

His mouth was doing incredible things to her and she tilted her head to give him better access. Her nipples pushed rigid points against the soft cotton of his tee. A pulse beat between her thighs. All he had to do was this and she was ready to get some skin-on-skin action.

He brought her head around, so Pippa had to turn toward him.

Their lips stopped, almost touching but not quite. "How's my move going?"

"Really well." Pippa couldn't wait any longer and dipped in for the kiss.

His grip tightened in her hair. His kiss rocked through Pippa, and took any lingering doubts with it. His mouth was firm and demanding on hers, and lit her from the inside out. He took and she gave in a tangle of teeth and tongues.

He gripped her hips and pulled her to straddle him. He was hot and hard through the fabric of his sweats. The heat in her cranked up another notch and she sank her hands into the silkiness of his hair.

She felt powerful, sexy, desired. Sinking against his erection, his groan rippling through her, letting her know he wanted her as badly as she wanted him. This beautiful man wanted her, and knowing that made her wet and achy at her core.

He slid his hand beneath her sweats and cupped her bare ass cheek. "Pippa." He tore his mouth from hers. His breath came fast through parted lips, his eyes bored into her. "Baby, I gotta see what you've got on under these. It's been driving me crazy the whole night."

"All night?" Man, it was crazy hot to tease him like this.

"All night." He gripped her ass and dragged her onto his erection. "You in that dress, me getting horny thinking about how little it hid."

Pippa sat back on his thighs.

His hungry gaze swept down to track the motion of her hands as she tangled them in the hem of her tee. She inched the fabric up. Cooler air hit her belly, her ribs and finally her breasts as she hauled it over her head.

Matt sucked in a breath, his eyes riveted by the swell of flesh over the cups of her bra. Big, hot hands covered her breasts, dark against the pale ivory of her skin.

Her breasts swelled at the touch, desperate for more, and Pippa arched into the caress.

His hands firmed, plumping her, sliding his fingers under the lace to tease her nipples.

"Your turn." Her voice came out in a breathy rasp. She worked the buttons free on his shirt as he touched her. Pushing the fabric off his shoulders she opened her treat. God, he was beautiful. Sculpted, hard, and made for her to touch. She spread her hands over the swell of his pecs, giving her fingers a happy walk down the corrugated ladder of his abs to his waistband.

Matt shrugged his shirt off.

Pippa needed his hands on her naked flesh and she reached behind her to unclasp her bra.

The cups sagged forward and he brushed the bra away. He jackknifed up, taking her back and down to the floor. Resting his weight on his elbow he watched his hand as it moved over her breasts, taking a little time to pluck her nipple to aching hardness before sliding down her belly. Lower, until his fingers rested just inside the rolled-up waistband of her sweats.

Not close enough. Pippa bucked her hips to move his hand farther.

"Damn, Pippa." He slid her pants down her legs, coming up on his haunches to yank them off her feet and send them sailing across the room. He crouched there, his eyes so hot on her they almost burned. He dipped his fingers under the edge of her thong.

Pippa held her breath, need pounding between her thighs. She arched into the first dip of his fingers between her soaking wet folds. He slid easily into her, his thumb playing with her clitoris.

She almost went off under his hand.

"I need to see you." Impatiently he tugged her thong off.

Pippa yanked at his pants. "And these."

Matt shucked them, and his underwear. Firelight bronzed

his skin. The beauty of him made her suck in a breath—a man in his prime, hard muscle, taut skin, and big all over. He crouched beside her, spreading his big hands over her belly and down into her heat. It was so hot, watching him as he watched his fingers drive her crazy. His cock stood thick and hard from the apex of his thighs.

Pippa wrapped her fist around it, and he hissed. Dropping his head forward to watch her stroke him, still touching her, still driving her fucking crazy. Bringing her close and backing off again.

"Now." She squeezed his girth. "Inside me now."

Matt moved over her, pushing her legs wide to rest between them and forcing her to relinquish her grip on him. He snatched up his pants and took out a condom. Fisting the base of his cock, he stroked the condom down his length.

Pippa writhed as she watched. She'd no idea seeing a man touch himself would drive her out of her tiny mind.

He opened her wider, spread her legs, and watched as he slid inside her.

Pippa stretched to accommodate him. It had been so long, and he filled her so deliciously.

His gaze flicked up to her as he flexed, driving himself to the hilt.

"More." Pippa half raised herself, desperate for him.

His jaw clenched, tendons strained in his neck as he withdrew and plunged again.

Pippa sank her nails into his forearms. "I want it all." She didn't want slow and careful, she wanted him to take her hard and fast. She was so ready for him, she didn't know how long she could last.

The control stripped off Matt's face and he let go. The carpet scratched her hips as he pounded into her, filling her completely. Her orgasm built deep inside her, she clenched around him to keep the tight connection.

Matt brought his thumb to her clitoris. Two, three strokes against the distended bud and she was there, shattering around him, her back arching to take him deeper.

He tensed and came on a guttural shout that she felt all the way through her.

"Jesus." He let his weight rest on her, his breath rasped in her ear. "That was too fast."

Pippa shook her head. "That was perfect."

Chapter Fifteen

Matt waited until Pippa shut the door behind her before he put the car in gear and drove away. He hadn't wanted to let her go home. The idea of keeping her wormed into his brain and got stuck. And then freaked him the hell out.

Not ten minutes after he'd made love to Pippa, he wanted to start all over again. The itch inside him to get deeper under her skin, to unravel the mystery of her kept growing.

Instead, he did the cuddling thing, and that ramped the twitch into a burn. Pippa had felt right in his arms. Tucked up to his side, her head in the crook of his neck, it felt peaceful, and like she belonged there.

This was not how he rolled. He liked a woman, and he pursued her. If she was on board with the idea, they hooked up—once, twice, however many times it took to work her through his system. The nagging pinch in his gut tightened. How many times would it take to get Pippa out of his system? Pippa had always been different. She had this siren's call for him, drawing him closer every time she drifted into his life again.

He pulled up to the front of his house and climbed out of the car. Eric might have called it right at the site. Keeping

things light with Pippa wasn't going to work out for him
at all. Maybe some part of him had always known that.

The debris from their carpet picnic still spread across his
lounge. He grabbed up plates and glasses and carried them
through to the kitchen. Pippa had left his sweats and T-shirt
neatly folded over the back of the couch. The subtle fragrance of her still clung to the fabric and he pressed the
shirt against his nose. The woman smelled like sin and
heaven all in one massive wallop.

Pippa shut the door and blinked in the harsh light of the
hallway chandelier. It looked like Phi had every light in
the house turned on. "Phi?"

A crash pulled her to the salon at a run.

"Phi." Her grandmother stood in the center of the room
in an emerald velvet housecoat. Not a hint of makeup on
her face, bird's nest hair squatting on her head. "What
happened?"

"I threw it." Phi's voice shook, and not vibrato. Whatever
was going on here was beyond theatrics.

Pippa followed her pointing finger to the smashed re-
mains of a Wedgwood shepherdess. "Why?"

"I want my stuff back." Tears seeped out of Phi's hot,
angry eyes. "You didn't tell me about all the things they've
taken."

No, she hadn't. Pippa had kept that her little secret and
it seemed Phi had found out. "I didn't want to upset you."

"You treated me like a child." Phi swiped at her tears.
"Like a doddering old woman not worthy of your respect."

"No, Phi, I tried to protect you."

Phi vibrated like a tuning fork. "Protect me? Me?" She
ended on a shriek. Phi protected her vocal chords like a
broody Rottweiler. Shrieking meant she was way past

upset. "I have faced down a packed opera house hissing at my performance of Carmen. I have made conductors weep the world over. Hardened stagehands get the hell out of my way. Whom do you think you're protecting? Some limp-minded old woman?"

"I . . ." She'd treated Phi like she couldn't handle the truth. "You're right. I should have told you. I kept thinking I might find them somewhere here, or they might reappear and then this would all go away."

"Did you take it upon yourself to decide I had imagined the entire thing?"

"Yes."

"That at my advanced age, I had misplaced them?"

It sounded a lot better in her head than it did coming out of Phi's mouth. Yes to all that and Pippa nodded.

"Let me tell you something." Phi jammed her hands on her hips. "I remember the words and the music to every opera I have ever sung. I can still name the cast members of every performance I gave, and some of the crew. And yet my granddaughter, my precious flesh and blood, took it upon herself to cosset me like an aged dog."

The Diva poked through Phi's tirade and Pippa breathed a sigh of relief.

"I am a mere sixty-eight years old, need I remind you. And a robust sixty-eight at that."

"Phi, you're seventy-eight and we both know it."

Phi fluttered both hands at her. "Age is merely a number, it's how I feel that counts."

"I'm sorry, Phi." Pippa took a step closer. "I should have told you, and I should never have thought you might be losing your marbles."

Phi's shoulders inched away from her earlobes. "I am wroth with you, Agrippina, but I shall forgive you."

Pippa stepped into Phi's open arms. "I really am sorry."

"What we have is special, Pippa," Phi whispered against her hair. "I have always been honest with you, and I demand the same from you."

It was true. Phi told the unpretty truth whenever it needed telling.

"My daughter does not understand me," Phi said. "She blames me for so many things. Some of them justified, and some of them merely her own unhappiness. But you?" Phi held her at arm's length for a second. "You and I were soul mates from the moment you came into the world. Do not fuck with that, Agrippina."

"I won't." Phi's love was her anchor, always had been. The unconditional acceptance of who and what she was, from a woman who spent her life flipping the bird at others' opinion of her. There weren't many people who had it this good. Pippa tightened her hold.

"Now." Phi disentangled herself from Pippa's embrace. "Was Mathieu a multiplatinum artist or a one-hit wonder?"

Chapter Sixteen

Pippa stood beside Phi as Nate got to work. It was a beautiful thing to behold. His broad shoulders flexed and released beneath the official mud color of his sheriff's uniform shirt. What the man did for a pair of chinos ought to be illegal.

Phi leaned toward her. "If it doesn't work out with Matt, you could always tap that."

"They're brothers." Pippa choked back a snort of laughter.

"I had a set of brothers once." Phi got a dreamy smile on her face. "Spaniards. Three of them. Hung like—"

"You're sure there's nothing missing from the rest of the house?" Nate turned around, his cheeks red.

"I'm sure." Phi nodded. "I checked all my jewelry again this morning, but if you would care to come up to my boudoir and verify, I could be persuaded to let you."

The tips of Nate's ears went red as he cleared his throat.

"Ignore her." Pippa took pity on the poor guy. As sheriff, he must get hit on fifty times a day. If she wasn't so hot for his brother, she might be buying a cat and tossing it up a tree on a regular basis.

Nate let loose with a panty-dropping smile in Phi's direction. "I'm not man enough for the Diva."

"Nobody is, darling." Phi let go a window-rattling trill. "But I keep trying until I find one."

Nate's blush spread to his cheeks. "Can you give me a description of the missing items?"

"Sure." Pippa motioned him over to the sofa. "Why don't I get us some coffee and Phi can tell you what they look like."

Phi chuckled like a gutter whore. Panic flashed across Nate's face. "I'll get the coffee." She pushed Pippa toward the sofa. "You stay and make eyes at the sheriff. I see he brought his handcuffs."

"She doesn't mean it," Pippa said as Phi floated out of the room. "She does it to get a reaction."

Nate breathed out low. "And she gets it. Every time."

Pippa got down to describing the missing pieces.

Nate wrote it all down, his hand crabbed awkwardly around the pencil as it crept across the page. She slowed down so he could stay with her.

"Sorry." He glanced up at her. "I suck at writing."

"I could . . ."

A hard glance shut her up again. Nate didn't want help. Matt must have had his hands full managing all that testosterone when they were both teens.

Matt hadn't called or texted, and she was getting a needy-girl feeling. Even worse than Matt not calling was her obsessing about it. They were taking things easy. No promises, no commitment, just scratching an old itch. Checking her phone like a crushing tween was so not part of the plan. It sat like a cold lump in her gut.

She'd already checked her phone about sixteen times. Only one call, and it was from a number she didn't recognize. Notifications from Twitter were growing like weeds. The support warmed the cold place Ray had left inside her. Phi came back in, and brought the rich aroma of freshly brewed coffee with her. Tucked beside the coffee was a plate with June's latest batch of cookies. Looked like every woman in this town fed the sheriff. Not that it showed. Pippa would lay money on a set of washboard abs under that shirt. They must run in the family, because she knew from personal experience, his older brother had a killer set.

Nate left after painstakingly writing down every missing item. He gulped down his coffee and ate most of the plate of cookies on his way out.

Phi excused herself to go and manage June—more like pester June into bickering with her.

Pippa checked the unknown number again. They'd left a message. It was probably another of the sleazy tabloids trying to find a way to reach her. Then again, maybe one of her contacts had grown a pair. A lot of them had unlisted numbers.

Pippa retrieved the message.

"Hi, Pippa. This is Chris Germaine. My people showed me the YouTube clip, and now the disastrous Twitter thing . . ." The message broke into Chris Germaine's signature chuckle. Holy shit, it really was Chris Germaine. *"I know you are probably hiding from the media, but please give me a call. I have something interesting I want to chat to you about. It will be worth your while."*

Pippa dropped onto the sofa as the voice on the message recited a number and repeated it. Mohamed, that thing in front of you is the mountain and it's coming your way. Holy, holy, holy shit. She checked the time. New York was two hours ahead, but it was still the middle of the afternoon there.

Pippa had to key in the number three times as her fingers fumbled. Even then, she hit one wrong number and got Salvatore's Pizzeria instead. Finally, the call clicked through.

"Hi, if you have this number, you know who this is. Leave me a message."

The beep caught her wrong-footed. "Um, hi, Chris. Germaine. Ms. Germaine." *You're such a dork. Get it together.* "This is Pippa Turner." Damn, shit, fuck. "I mean, you know me as Pippa St. Amor, because that's my stage name. Actually, it's my grandmother's stage name. She's really—" Get. A. Grip. "I'll shut up now. I'm . . . uh . . . returning your call."

Sweat trickled down her sides as she ended the call. "Well, you just made a dick of yourself," she said to the empty room. Hopefully, Chris Germaine was used to that sort of thing. You didn't get to be such a huge household name without dealing with ridiculous fangirling.

She picked up her phone to call Matt and tell him. First, the amazing news about who had called her, and second to make him laugh at her phone message. Her finger hovered over his contact. Did taking it light mean she could call him for a chat, to share her news? Screw it. She wanted to talk to him. They were friends . . . with benefits . . . maybe. She hit his contact.

Voice mail again. "Hi, it's Pippa. You'll never believe what I just did. Call me when you get a chance. Or not. Whatever. Okay. Bye." It must be her day for lame voice messages.

What Twitter thing? Pippa replayed Chris Germaine's message. Disastrous? God, she'd have enough "disastrous" to last a lifetime. Her Twitter notifications had invited all their friends and family and were multiplying faster than bacteria. Seven hundred and twelve! No, make that one thousand and three.

Big Ben chimed from the front door.

"Good morning, Pippa." Her mother smiled from beside

Laura. "Sorry to drop in unannounced, but we thought we might have a chat."

Alarm bells clanged in Pippa's brain. *I thought we might have a chat about your behavior today. I thought we might have a chat about that boy I saw you with. I thought we might have a chat about your clothing.*

Laura's smug expression sealed the deal on doom. Pippa led them into the salon. "I'll go and get Phi."

She glanced at her phone. No way. That couldn't be right. Twitter must be broken or something because the notification number in the little red circle next to the app kept climbing.

"Actually." Emily perched on the edge of an armchair, back clear of the rest, legs neatly folded to one side. "We thought we might speak with you alone for a minute."

Laura sat exactly the same way as their mother. It was like one of those age progression photo series.

Emily drew a plastic folder from her Kate Spade. "Laura and I have been speaking about what you told her."

Pippa tried to remember the last conversation she'd had with her sister that went past a few snide remarks and the banal.

"About Philomene." Laura managed to inject a vocal eye roll in there.

"What about Phi?" She itched to open Twitter, but an air of complicity hung about her mother and sister, and if this had to do with Phi, she needed to pay attention.

Emily opened her folder and pulled out a bunch of glossy brochures. "If my mother is no longer able to care for herself, I think we should be looking at alternatives." She tapped one French manicured finger against a brochure. "I think this one looks best, it has a music program and they arrange for trips to the theater twice a year."

Pippa tilted her head for a better look. "The Meadows."

Scrolled out in fancy script across the top, *"offering assisted living for your loved ones in their twilight years."*

"You're kidding, right?" Pippa glanced from her mother to Laura and back again. They had to be yanking her chain. The two of them had cooked up some scheme to put Phi in an old age home. Part of her wanted to laugh, but the other part was too pissed off to even force a polite smile.

"She's getting old." Laura shrugged as if they were talking about a family dog, and one they didn't even like very much. "This house is an upkeep nightmare."

"She has June for that." Pippa stared at her sister. How they shared blood was a mystery.

"Perhaps not right away." Her mother slid into the heated silence. "But spots in these facilities don't come up all that often, and we should get her name down."

"Mes filles." Phi arrived in the doorway, resplendent in a buttercup yellow dress with huge red poppies crawling all over it. She must have changed from the lounge suit she was wearing for Nate. "What a lovely surprise. We should have a little cocktail to celebrate."

"No, thank you, Mother." Emily's spine jerked even straighter. "It's barely past lunchtime and I don't want a drink."

"Oh." Phi's happy smile dimmed a bit. "Laura?"

"I don't drink in the afternoon."

"I'll join you," Pippa said. "What will you have?"

Phi's smile widened. "There's my girl."

Battle lines drawn. Laura and Emily on one side, Pippa and Phi on the other. Four grown women who couldn't be in a room together for two minutes without the universe getting out its magic pen and drawing playbook scrawls all over them.

"I shall mix us up some Manhattans." Phi strolled over

to her large globe bar and flipped open the top. "Are you sure you won't join Pippa and me?"

"I'm sure." Emily's lips disappeared into a tight pucker of disapproval. "Mother, Pippa remarked the other day about some of your bits and pieces going missing."

Phi measured rye into her cocktail shaker. "Indeed. My treasures seem to be disappearing at an alarming rate." She replaced the top with a clank, and sailed to the door on a cloud of patchouli. "I shall fetch some ice."

"They were stolen. You just missed Nate, he was here taking her statement," Pippa said.

"You called the sheriff?" Laura's spine snapped straight. "Because our weird grandmother lost some ugly antique crap?"

Pippa saw red for a minute. She glanced down the passage to the kitchen to ensure the baize door was shut. "Phi is as sharp as ever and her treasures are worth a lot of money."

"You can't be sure of that." Emily rearranged the brochures on the table. "She's eighty."

"Seventy-eight," Laura said.

"Sixty-eight." Pippa glared back at her sister.

Laura snorted. "Please, not even her press agent believes that."

"If Phi wants to be sixty-eight, then she can be sixty-eight. A woman who dragged herself out of Ghost Falls to become the most renowned diva in the world gets to decide whatever age she wants. As for these"—Pippa snatched up the brochures—"put them away before you upset her."

"Pippa." Her mother took the brochures from her. "You aren't being rational. Your defense of your grandmother is laudable, but not based in reality."

"Pippa always defends her." Laura crossed her ankles.

"You're talking about putting her in a home." Pippa

lowered her voice before Phi heard. "You can't expect me to sit here and let you do that."

"That is not your decision, Pippa." Her mother raised her chin. "She is my mother, whatever you may believe, and I am her primary caregiver."

"You never see her."

"And you live in Los Angeles."

Her mother had her there. "I still spend a lot of time with her and if anyone should know if she needed a care facility, it would be me."

"You don't see her for what she is." Laura sniffed and got to her feet. "You're so caught up in the diva bullshit it blinds you."

"It's not bullshit." Pippa stood, damned if she'd sit while her sister loomed over her. "She may be a bit over the top, but she *is* a diva."

"Was." Her mother's quiet voice carried a knife-edge. "Now she is an aging woman living in a monstrosity of a house. Even if she didn't misplace these items, it still supports my case. Someone is taking advantage of her and she can't see it."

"You're not putting Phi in a home."

"With all due respect, Pippa"—Laura went to stand beside Emily—"you're not the one making that decision."

"No." Phi's voice came from the door. Her hands were full of a tray of cocktail glasses and the shaker. She strolled forward and placed the tray on the coffee table. Silence dragged the air out of the room. "I believe the decision maker here is me." Phi's face was devoid of emotion. She picked up the shaker and poured two Manhattans. "Emily, dear. I am neither a doddering old fool nor a senile old bat. I appreciate your concern, but I don't require any help."

"Mother." Emily's face paled. "I am not suggesting that. I merely think it's time you considered your future."

"How kind." Phi passed Pippa her glass.

Pippa nearly chugged the entire thing.

"Pippa, dear." Phi raised her eyebrow. "I thought we had the discussion about me needing your protection."

Damn, she'd done it again. Pippa tipped her glass back and took the dregs in one sip. Her eyes teared up on contact. Phi made these things strong enough to drop an elephant.

"You can't stay in this house on your own forever." Laura crossed her arms over her chest.

Phi sipped her Manhattan, paused, and gave a happy nod. "Dear, I am rarely alone. I have many friends who come to see me all the time. June takes care of the house, and you bring the lovelies around a few times a week."

"You know what I mean." Laura stuck to her course. She was determined, Pippa had to concede that. It also took balls the size of boulders to face down a sweetly smiling Phi. Opera casts and crews the world over had learned a sweet Phi was deadlier than a vitriolic one.

"Yes, I do," Phi said. "I have become an embarrassment to you and you would like to tidy me away."

Emily paled and tucked her skirt under her thighs.

"Oh, for God's sake." Laura threw her hands up. "Do you always have to be so damn dramatic? You're not embarrassing anyone. We're worried about you."

"Like hell you are." Pippa helped herself to another blast of courage from the cocktail shaker. "You don't give a crap about Phi. You only come here when you need free babysitting."

Laura hit her with an eye-searing blast. "And you would know this because you saw it in your crystal ball all the way from LA."

"My job is in LA."

"Was, Pippa." Laura's mouth turned up in a smug smile. "Your job was in LA before you screwed that up."

"Girls." Emily pressed her fingertips to her forehead. "None of this is helping."

"On the contrary, Emily dear." Phi lowered herself onto her throne. "I think a touch of honesty around here is very refreshing."

"You would." Emily came as close to shouting as she ever did. "You thrive on the drama."

"Indeed I do." Phi sipped her drink and leaned her head back. "It beats the tight-lipped, tight-legged approach."

"Must you always be so vulgar?" Emily rose to her feet. Her hands clenched and unclenched by her sides. "I despise your vulgarity."

"As did your father," Phi said.

Laura and Pippa sucked in a breath together as Phi jack-booted straight over sacred ground.

Emily trembled with emotion. Eyes fever bright, her mouth worked before she managed to get any words out. "Don't you dare speak about my father?"

"He was my husband, dear. I believe that entitles me to talk about him."

"He was your convenience, until you left him to pursue your career."

Phi made a small moue with her mouth. "Perhaps, but it still does not make it my fault your husband left *you*."

Pippa choked on her Manhattan. Phi had done it now.

"Leave him out of this." Emily's hands clenched into fists. If her mother took a swing at Phi, she was going to have to step in.

"Gladly, Emily dear," said Phi. "When you can do the same."

"Mark left because he couldn't stand you!" It burst out

of her mother on a jet stream of narrow-eyed fury. "All your drama and performing, all the time."

"Darling girl." Phi paled, and put her glass down on the table. "I know you believe that, but maybe he left because being part of a family did not suit him."

"Wow," Laura drawled. "Like father, like daughter."

"Seriously?" Pippa turned to stare at her sister. "You're going to take this and have a shot at me?"

"If the shoe fits?" Laura shrugged.

"How are the two in any way comparable?" Pippa really wanted to hear how this had gotten twisted in her sister's mind.

"You left Ghost Falls so fast, we didn't even spot your dust." Laura grabbed the shaker and poured herself a glass. "You wanted to be in television, and you couldn't wait to leave here." Laura downing Manhattans left Pippa momentarily speechless. "You never stopped to ask if I needed you or Mom needed you." Laura slammed her glass back down on the tray. "You were out of here too fast to know."

"You and Mom have never needed me." Shit, they had each other on their bitch bicycle made for two. "You were the perfect pair. Mom and her mini-me. There was no room for anyone else in your little club of perfect."

Emily turned to stare at her. "Pippa, I—"

"Of course Mom needed you. You're her daughter." Laura's cheeks were bright red. "She needed every one of those Mother's Day cards you sent to Philomene. Every call you didn't make to her, and made to Philomene. And when your life turns to crap, do you ask your mother for comfort? No. You come here. The only person who ever mattered to you was Philomene."

Emily made a weird whimpering noise and slumped back on the sofa.

Pippa stared, struck too dumb to think. Her mother had

Laura. Since they were kids, Laura and her mother. "She had you."

"And she wanted her other daughter, too." Laura grabbed for the shaker again. Ice rattled against the stainless steel as she shook the last drop into her glass.

"All those times it was *'never mind, Laura can do it,'* or *'Laura will come with me,'*" Pippa said. Not once had it been Pippa. Pippa didn't fit the plan.

"Oh, please, you've never had time for Mom or me. We were always too boring for Pippa. All you ever wanted was her." She jerked her head at Phi. "You didn't come back here for one of my children's births. Not one."

"I sent gifts." She hadn't come because she thought Laura would rather eat her own young than have her by her side.

"Great." Laura threw her a withering glance. She turned to Emily. "I think you should drive. I've had enough of this shit."

Emily trailed Laura to the door. She stopped in the doorway and glanced behind her as if she wanted to say something. Strain pinched the corners of her mouth. Then, Emily turned and followed her daughter to the car.

"Wow." Pippa turned to look at Phi.

Phi looked devastated. Pale face, eyes haunted, and her shoulders slumped to protect her heart.

Pippa's chest constricted on a tight squeeze. "Ah, no, Phi, please don't cry." Tears stung the back of her eyes. "Because if you do, I will."

And she burst into tears.

Chapter Seventeen

Pippa stretched next to Phi on the Diva's huge bed. *Toiles* cherubs cavorted on the canopy above their heads.

"I didn't know she cared." Pippa slurred the words a little. She and Phi had limped upstairs with another pitcher of Manhattans.

Phi heaved a big sigh. "Of course she cared, darling. It can't be easy living under the shadow of your younger sister."

"Say what?" Pippa turned her head to stare at Phi. "I think you've got that the wrong way round. I was always in Laura's shadow."

"Really." Phi raised her eyebrow. Except the makeup had smudged the eyebrow pencil and it went a bit demented on the end. They'd shaved Phi's eyebrows off when she was younger and her brows had never grown back again. "Laura was such a quiet, contained child and then you came along."

Quiet, contained, and perfect. Their mother's little darling. Oh God, she was pathetic. Still resenting her sister for being her mother's favorite at thirty-two. Maybe she needed a good round of therapy to get the hell over herself.

"You were a firecracker from the moment you opened your eyes." Phi gave her deep, throaty chuckle. "All wild red hair and big sparkly eyes. You walked before your first birthday and spoke before any of us were ready for it. Laura was a quiet child, unassuming. She got lost in the background."

Pippa shook her head. That couldn't be right. Years of teachers asking her if she was Laura's little sister, expecting her to be the same and then bemoaning the fact that she wasn't.

"No, Phi. Laura was the star. Who was homecoming queen? Laura." She took a sip of her Manhattan. "Who was captain of the cheerleaders? Laura. Most popular? Laura. Spring Carnival princess two years in a row? Laura."

And who made Mom quietly glow with pride. Laura.

Phi snorted. "Who created an uproar that went all the way to the county education department when she wrote an article on teen pregnancy in the *Falls Crier*?"

"Okay, that was me but—"

"Normally they give the front page to the prom queen, but that year they didn't." Phi took a sip of her Manhattan. "The prom queen was relegated to a tiny picture in the corner, while her younger sister took lead article."

She'd forgotten about that. It had been a great article though. "Okay, that one time."

"Who was voted most likely to succeed?"

"Laura—"

"Was voted most likely to marry and stay in Ghost Falls." Phi finished her sentence for her. "You don't see it, darling girl, because you are always surging forward with your eyes on the next mountain. I was the same, so don't even think of arguing with me." Phi grabbed Pippa's hand and folded it in hers on her chest. "We have a light inside us, Pippa. We were born reaching for the stars and we spend our lives trying."

"My star fell." Pippa finished her third Manhattan, or maybe her fourth.

"And mine burned out." Phi's chest heaved up and down on a sigh. "But we still had it, that one glittering, beautiful moment when the world lay at our feet. Laura has never had that."

"She never wanted it."

Phi huffed a soft laugh. "Maybe not, but it still doesn't stop her from envying it."

Pippa felt a twinge of sympathy for her sister. When she looked at Laura, all she saw was a mother in command of two great children, with a wonderful dentist husband who kept them all more than comfortable. She tilted her head to the side. What if she looked at it from a different angle? Maybe Laura was not so content with her perfect life. From this angle, the *toile* cherubs looked like they were peeping up the lady's skirt. They were peeping up her skirt.

"I need you to listen to me, Agrippina."

"I'm right here."

Phi pinched Pippa's fingers between her own. "Really listen, you hardheaded minx."

"Okay." Phi's voice had grown very serious. There weren't many times when Phi dropped all the drama, and when they happened, it was worth listening.

"I had a wonderful career," Phi said. "I lived a life so full, I have more stories than I have time to tell them."

Pippa turned her head to Phi. A soft smile played across her grandmother's face. "It was glorious. The fame, the money, the men." She gave Pippa a nudge and a wink. "But I fucked up."

"Phi, it creeps me out when you swear."

"Get over it." Phi's grip tightened on her fingers. "I was

so wrapped up and warm in my glowing light, I left my little girl out in the cold." A tear snaked down Phi's weathered cheek. "She needed her mother and I was off being fabulous for the rest of the world."

"You said Mom didn't want to come with you."

"I convinced myself of that." Another tear traced through Phi's heavy foundation. "Because it put a hitch in my gallop to have a young child trailing behind me. I told myself that she was better off with her father, he could take better care of her. It was only later. Much later. When Laura came along, I saw what I'd done."

"Phi, you've never told me any of this."

"I don't like to think about this." Phi sniffed and smeared makeup over her cheek as she wiped. "I moved back here to try to make a connection, but it was too late then. Emily was all grown up and she had Laura. Then, you were born." Phi smiled. "And I saw a chance to do it all again. Do better this time. Be the mother I could have been to Emily." The smile faded off her face. "But that was even more of a snarl, because Emily feels as if I have taken you away from her. After Mark left"—Phi shrugged—"we all became even more entrenched in our roles."

"He left because he was weak and pathetic. And Mom and I never got on, not like you and I do." Pippa pictured her mother's face. Laura's angry accusations rattled around in the back of her mind. There was enough truth in them to make her fidget.

"Now I see you making the same mistakes, my sweet protégée. You have your eyes on your star and it has given you tunnel vision. Look around you, Pippa. You have been given this chance to reevaluate and take stock. Before you charge blindly after your light for a second time, take a breath, have a good look around, and see if you can do anything different."

Pippa sucked in a breath and let Phi's words join the

swelling chorus in her head. A soft snore from Phi provided a welcome distraction. She eased the empty glass from Phi's hand and put it on the tray. She didn't feel tipsy anymore, just sad.

Pippa covered Phi in her cerise satin throw and took the tray back down to the kitchen. Maybe one of those times when she'd asked Phi to come to a school event, she might have asked her mother instead. For sure, she could have sent her mother a Mother's Day card. Except Emily had never seemed that interested. Emily always looked so contained without her, as if her younger daughter was a foreign and frightening land. What if it was more a case of her younger daughter had opened an old wound and made it bleed?

Sure, she could blame Emily and say she was the mother, and she should have known better. Except Emily had been young when she had her children. Pippa was ten when her mother was thirty-two. Did she have the maturity at thirty-two she expected her mother to display?

This family shit was messing with her head.

She needed a distraction.

A couple of Manhattans over the limit, Pippa caught a ride with the kid who worked in the stable. She forgot his first name almost immediately, but got that he was a member of the Barrows brood. He was sweet, though, and knew the way to Matt's house. Good thing, too, because she hadn't paid of lot of attention to where Matt went the other night.

Matt sat on a bench on the porch with his feet propped on the railing. As she stepped out of the car, he lowered his beer and gave her his big, Matt smile.

Right there was exactly what she needed. Pippa jogged up the garden path and took the porch stairs at a leap. Until she asked the Barrows kid to bring her here, she hadn't even known this was what she needed. Pippa walked straight up to Matt and straddled his lap.

He tensed, and then his arms came around her back.

Pippa tucked her head into the crook of his neck and took a deep breath of Matt.

"And hello to you, too." His deep voice rumbled through her ear.

"Hi." He was big and warm and Pippa relaxed against him.

He stroked her back. "Bad day?"

"Uh-huh." She nodded and pressed her nose into his neck. "You smell . . . perfect." Earthy and warm with a trace of something woodsy. It beat the hell out of all the expensive aftershaves and colognes that surrounded her in LA. He smelled real.

"Your nose must be blocked, because I was working on-site all day." Matt took a pull on his beer and offered her the bottle.

Pippa shook her head. "I'm already a few Manhattans down."

"Hence Wheeler Barrows driving you over here."

"Wheeler?" Pippa popped her head up to look at him. "They named that kid Wheeler Barrows?"

The corners of his eyes crinkled as he grinned at her. "All the other Barrows kids have a name that starts with *B*. I guess they got creative with him."

That was Ghost Falls for you. Pippa tucked her head back in its happy spot.

"Are you gonna tell me what's wrong?" His hands cupped her butt.

Rehashing her day was about as appealing as getting off his lap. As in, not at all what she had in mind.

His thighs were hard beneath hers and heat came off his

broad chest and soaked through the fabric of her shirt. "Tell me about your day instead."

"Okay." Her head rose and fell as he took a breath. Pippa snuggled closer and wedged her arms into the small gap left between his lower spine and the back of the seat. "Isaac is still MIA. Eric had a text from him to say he was alive, but my mother is freaking out." *Figures*. "Not so much about Isaac going missing, as the fact that he texted Eric and not her. I managed to get the plumber back on-site today, and the slippery bastard is trying to tell me he's not going to finish on time."

"What did you say?" This felt nice. A sort of how-was-your-day-dear type of nice. She could have this, for this short moment.

"I told him he would finish on time if he ever wanted to work one of my jobs again."

She'd have guessed something along those lines. Behind Matt's easygoing exterior lay forged steel. It made her feel safe when she was with him.

He took another pull on his beer.

She caught the subtle waft of hops as he blew out a breath. "I also spoke to Jo today. She's not sure she wants to get married."

"Yeah, I picked that up from her." This was Jo's show; Pippa wasn't going to out the girl until Jo was ready to do it herself.

"At least that butt-ugly dress is gone," Matt said.

Pippa caught a stirring against her spread thighs. "Matt?"

"Yes."

"Are you getting wood?"

"Yup." He tightened his hands on her ass. "It happens when you straddle my lap."

A delicious shiver snaked right through the core of her.

Her nipples tingled with a new set of possibilities. Pippa tilted her hips forward and brushed his erection.

Matt hissed in a breath. "That's not helping."

"Are you getting harder?"

"Yup."

"Then it's doing exactly what I want it to do." Pippa flicked her tongue over the skin of his neck. He tasted salty and hot to the touch.

He slid his hands under her skirt to grab her butt cheeks, bare on either side of her thong.

Heat built beneath her skin. She needed this, and her clamoring libido yelled at her to get on with it. Pippa looked up at him. "Wanna mess around?"

"And more." He slid a finger under the string of her thong. His eyes glowed darker and hotter.

His erection prodded her thigh. Damn, she could do him right here on this porch.

He pressed her forward to rock her against him. "Mrs. Parsons is peering around her lounge curtains. Why don't we take this inside?"

"Yes, please."

Matt's beer bottle clattered to the porch as he stood with her still in his arms.

Pippa wrapped her legs around his waist and held on. "I like this whole alpha man thing you have going on here."

Matt kicked the door shut behind him. "Then you're really gonna like what I do to you next."

"Yeah?"

"Oh, yeah."

Their mouths were close enough for his breath to wash hot over her lips. The tiny space between them tingled with possibilities that made Pippa tense in his arms. She wanted to kiss him, but the suspense was making her so hot, a pulse throbbed between her legs.

His face was tight with lust, his eyes burning holes into her.

He'd barely touched her and she was so wet and horny she didn't know if they were going to make it up those stairs.

"I liked what you did the other night just fine."

Muscle bunched between her thighs and under her hands as he climbed the stairs. "I left a few things out."

"You did?" His breath came faster now. Pippa's pulse pounded in response. "What things?"

"I need to know how you taste." His fingers brushed under her thong, slipping easily through her wet heat. Her core throbbed in response to his words. "You'd like that, wouldn't you?"

Shit, this man was going to talk her into an orgasm.

"Yes."

He dropped her on the bed and Pippa fell with her skirt up and legs splayed.

Matt's scorching gaze cataloged every inch of her. He caught the edge of her panties and tugged them down her legs. "Let me see you."

Pippa dropped her thighs open on a soft moan. She'd never done this for another man, but the look in Matt's eyes was hotter than hell. It made her feel like she was his next breath.

Matt stroked the rigid line of his cock through his jeans. "Wider."

Pippa parted her legs until she was fully on display for him.

Matt sucked in a breath and dropped to his knees beside

the bed. Big, rough hands gripped her hips and dragged her onto the wet, seeking suck of his mouth.

"Oh God." Pippa arched into the first swipe of his tongue over her folds. Her clitoris ached and swelled for his touch.

He hummed against her and it nearly pushed her over the edge. Long fingers parted her as he laved her. He took his time, driving her nuts with his tongue and teeth until she was a writhing, panting mess. Her hands grabbed hanks of his hair as her hips jerked against the rhythm of his mouth.

"I want you to come." He swirled his tongue around her clit and then sucked.

Pippa went screaming over the edge, her back arching and her fingers digging into his scalp. She stopped breathing as her orgasm rocked through her entire body.

"Damn." It was the first word she was able to speak. She lay spread over his bed like a rag doll wrung limp by what he'd done to her.

Matt stood and stripped off his shirt.

Pippa propped herself on her elbows to get a better look at the beautiful ridges and lines of his body. He shucked his jeans and underpants and knelt on the bed between her legs. His hard cock almost touched his belly button as he smoothed a condom over his length.

Shit, if she'd known what Matt was capable of she might have delayed leaving Ghost Falls. Or at least made more of an effort to get him into bed sooner.

Pippa needed full body contact with all that naked flesh. With a quick tug, her shirt came off followed by her bra. Matt helped her wriggle out of her skirt.

He fisted his erection and leaned down, one hand beside her head. Slowly, he guided his cock inside her.

Pippa stretched around him, his slow pace nearly driving her nuts as he worked himself in.

He dropped his gaze to watch her take him. His jaw

clenched so tight, the muscles along his shoulders and biceps flexed.

Too slow. Pippa wrapped her thighs around his hips and tilted her hips.

With a soft hiss, he slid all the way home. "Jesus, Pippa. Don't move."

To hell with that. Pippa wanted to move, wanted to drive him crazy.

He withdrew and angled his hips and Pippa jerked in response. Heat coiled in her belly as he drove into her, stroking her where she needed him. She'd never come from penetration alone, but she could feel it building with each thrust.

He held his body rigid, the fight for control all over his tight features.

It made her crazy to know she did this to him. Matt was straining to hold himself back until he made her come again. He increased his speed, his breath coming in soft grunts above her.

Her orgasm built slower than the last one, spreading from where his cock touched and up through her belly. Her nipples jutted hard as her breasts bobbed with each thrust. The need to come swept through her, tightening her walls around him.

"That's it, baby." He worked his cock deep into her.

Pippa exploded around him, her body arching off the bed.

He let go, pounding into her until he came with a shout.

Slick with sweat, his forehead pressed against her. Their panting breath mingled as he gently brought her down, fucking her slowly until the last aftershocks receded.

Matt rolled onto his back and took her with him. He slipped out of her as she nestled in the crook of his shoulder.

She felt every inch of his slick skin against hers, registered the slowing pulse of his heart right through to her spine. The connection was otherworldly, intense and a little bit scary.

He rolled, taking her over onto her back, and lay beside her. His big hands stroked the damp hair off her face. Something flickered through his eyes as he stared into hers. Something she sensed neither of them wanted to acknowledge. "I'll be right back."

She watched his tight ass as he walked into the bathroom to get rid of the condom.

Pippa stared at the ceiling. That had been incredible, mind-blowing, and more than sex. Matt Evans had rocked her world, again. Except there wasn't any room in her life for world-rocking right now. She needed to get her shit sorted and claw back the ground Ray had cost her.

Matt slid back into bed, tucking them both beneath the covers. He turned her on her side and tugged her into the crook of his big body.

She should say something, crack a joke, lighten the mood, but she had nothing.

His arm curled around her, keeping her close to him. "Stay," he whispered against her ear.

"Is that part of keeping things light?"

"Sure." His hand spanned the small of her back. "Everybody has to sleep sometime."

Part of her brain mumbled about what a bad, bad idea this was. The rest of her didn't care. "Okay."

Matt's breath deepened, and his muscles relaxed into sleep.

Pippa stared at the play of evening light through his bedroom blinds.

Shit. She was in so much trouble.

Chapter Eighteen

Matt woke to a bed full of Pippa, and his phone buzzing from the nightstand. Spitting out a mouthful of red hair, he grabbed his phone.

The phone stopped. He had a missed call from Jo.

Actually, he didn't get a lot of sleep. Three rounds of mind-blowing sex followed by Pippa the bed hog meant very little sleep. She tossed, turned, and nearly kneed him in the balls a couple of times before he got the message and retreated to a safe distance. When you had Pippa in your bed, you needed a king-size mattress to contain all that redhead. How long had it been since he'd woken up with a woman? Taking his urges outside of Ghost Falls came with a built-in excuse to get up and leave.

His phone started up again.

Pippa muttered, flung out an arm, and caught him on the bicep.

"Hey, Jo, what's up." He kept his voice down as he got his legs over the edge of the bed and sat up.

"Matt?" Jo ended his name on a massive sniff.

Not even eight in the morning and Jo was crying. He took the phone outside his bedroom. "Hey, Jo-Jo, you okay?"

"It's her." Jo's voice rose to a wail.

She meant their mother, and his gut tightened in response. Jo and their mother together always spelled drama in great big letters across the sky. They must have been at it since dawn, or maybe since the night before. "What happened?"

"We got into a fight," Jo said. "And then I told her I wasn't even sure I wanted to get married. I told her I'd been talking to Pippa about it. She lost it, Matt."

Matt thunked his head against the passage wall. This wasn't good. He got it. Cressy felt insecure and alone and needed her family around her. But, for God's sake, her kids were all grown up now and she needed to let go.

"Where is she now?" As if he really needed to be told. He felt tired right down to his bones and not from his active night.

"Locked in her bedroom."

Ah, the well-known tyranny of the locked door, attention withdrawal, hunger strike, massive sulk. Matt hit his head against the wall a second time. Cressy had them all by the balls. "I'll be right over."

Jo gave a big sniff. "Thanks, Matt. You're the only one she'll talk to."

"Put some coffee on, and leave her alone." He hung up and gave the wall another smack with the back of his head. It was like his mother had ESP or some shit like that. She sensed something happening in his life and pulled her crap.

Pippa's eyes were open when he went back into his room. This might be his favorite Pippa look, sleepy, tousled, and in his bed after a great night together.

"What is it?" She pushed her wild red hair out of her face.

He thought about lying, but this was Ghost Falls and Cressy's tantrums weren't quiet. "My mom's having a meltdown. All over Jo."

"Ah." She nodded as if she got it.

It didn't surprise him. His mother didn't see the point in keeping her crap inside the family. He didn't blame Eric for getting the hell away from this shit. Even Nate only went home when he couldn't get out of it. "She found out Jo asked you for advice about getting married."

Pippa chewed on her bottom lip, as if weighing something up. "And?"

"And she lost it."

"Because Jo made a decision without her, or because I was involved."

"A little bit of both. They got into a fight."

Pippa nodded, slowly, as if her mind was still working. "Do you need to go?"

Of course he needed to go. Who else was going to get his mother out of the bedroom and talking to Jo again? In one piece. He bit his tongue to stop the hot words from escaping. Shit, that wasn't fair. Pippa didn't bring any of this on. He'd asked her to help Jo. "Yup. She's locked herself in her bedroom and won't come out."

He grabbed his jeans from the floor and tugged them on. He'd have a shower at his mom's house, after he talked her down from the ceiling. "I'm sorry about this. It's not the way I wanted to wake up with you."

"Then don't go." Pippa shrugged.

Matt wasn't sure he'd heard her right. He had to go, he didn't have any choice. It pissed him off that she didn't see that. Pippa grew up in this town. She was here when his dad died. She knew how this went. But she didn't know how far his mom would and did take this shit. Only he knew that, and maybe he should tell her. But he didn't have time. "Look, help yourself to whatever you need and . . ." Fuck, she didn't have a car. He snatched up her cell phone and keyed in his brother's number. "What the hell is up with your phone?" Who had that many Twitter notifications?

Pippa could handle it. "Call Eric and see if he can give you a ride home."

He leaned in and gave her a quick kiss on his way out the door.

"Wow, that pretty much sucked," Pippa said to Matt's empty bedroom. Empty because Matt was long gone. His boots had clumped on the floor and the front door had slammed behind him. His truck had started up with a diesel roar and he was gone. At least he hadn't tossed some money on the dresser as the door had smacked his retreating ass.

Pippa ripped the covers aside and climbed out of bed. Even Ray, the betraying dickhead, had better morning-after patter than Matt Evans.

Cressy had called and Matt had jumped. How old was he exactly?

"Thirty-six," she told her reflection in the bathroom mirror. "A little old to be tied to Mommy's apron strings."

Her hair stood all around her head and makeup smudged beneath her eyes. Enough to send any man running home to Mama. No way was she calling Eric to give her a ride home.

She stomped over to the shower and snapped it on. The hot water worked some magic on her, and by the time she was toweling herself off, she'd come down from boiling hot to low simmer. Still, total dick move on Matt's part.

Maybe she could have been a bit more sanguine about it if last night hadn't been so spectacular. More than sex spectacular. There had been a connection between them, some deep, inherent sense of right about her and Matt. This feeling right here was why she avoided those sorts of connections.

Pippa grabbed up her clothes and got dressed. She dragged

Matt's comb through her hair and dug a hair tie out of her purse to pull it back into a ponytail. More than that would have to wait until she got home.

The doorbell went as she was coming down the stairs. She opened the door to find Eric standing on the doorstep.

He didn't look like he'd just rolled out of bed . . . at all. Hair still damp from the shower, but immaculate in a button-down and jeans. She could see the thread count on that shirt from three feet away. Eric Evans was one class act, and a smokin' one at that.

"Hey." He jerked his chin at her. "Got a message from Matt that you needed a ride."

Damn, her face got so hot she must be radiating. "I could have walked."

"Not even Matt is that dumb." Eric held the door open for her and motioned her forward. His low, sleek Jag sat in front of the house like a pedigreed cat.

"He went to see your mother." It sounded a bit like she was making excuses for him.

Eric must have thought so too because he snorted as he held the door open for her. "Did you even get a cup of coffee?"

"No."

"Let me buy you one." His carved face split in a charming grin that was so Matt, it hit her straight in the knees. "I'll even toss in a pastry of some kind."

"I don't like pastries." Eric could talk a rat out of the cheese board.

"Then why don't I buy you Craig's famous breakfast feed trough and we can bitch about my brother."

How was a girl to turn down an offer like that? Craig made breakfast for truckers and hungry mountain men. The other part of the offer didn't sound too bad either.

Eric started the Jag and it growled into life. The car fit the man perfectly. Maybe she was messing around with the wrong brother. Except, as gorgeous as Eric was—and there was no denying that—he didn't do it for her. Not the way Matt did. Her eyes teared up and she blinked the wet away. No crying. This thing with her and Matt was just fooling around. No sense getting all emotional about it. It clearly didn't mean the same thing to Matt. There went her eyes again. Damn it. She *liked* it this way—easy, no attachment, temporary. She stared out the window to keep her face hidden from Eric.

"What was it this time?" Eric turned on the radio.

Classical music whispered through the interior. Music to soothe the savage beast.

"Something to do with Jo and her wedding."

Eric grunted and kept driving.

Craig's Truck Stop made the best breakfast in town, which was a good thing because the diner shut after lunch every day. The banquettes and tables lining the walls were older than evolution. The few tables in the center looked only slightly better. Rumor had it Craig had bought the furniture when the old Roadhouse closed down forty years ago. The place was nearly full, and Eric found them a table near the back.

The cracked leather of the banquette snagged the back of her thighs as she shifted under Eric's steady gaze. "My brother is a pushover," he said.

That pretty much summed up what she was thinking and Pippa nodded.

The only investment Craig had made over the years to his diner was a fancy coffee machine, and whoever manned it had a way with a latte that soothed some of her shitty morning.

"But you have to understand my mother." Eric sipped his

coffee—straight up, black and strong. "She's got him by the throat."

Pippa knew all this. It didn't ease the burn, however. "And he never says no?"

"Not that I've seen." Eric stretched his arms over the back of the banquette. He hid some impressive muscle beneath that shirt, and the tat, which she still hadn't seen. "Look, you're mad and you have a right to be, but my mom . . ." He shrugged. "She knows exactly which buttons to push with all of us. Mostly with Matt because he's the oldest. He took the most fallout, took it for all of us."

"Okay." Either the coffee or Eric's calm presence worked, because she felt better.

The waitress arrived at their table and slid two platters at them. Food definitely made the world look better, and after her active night, she was hungry. Matt was a several-times-a-night kind of guy, and she hadn't gotten much sleep.

Eric salted his eggs. "She's got Matt in a corner. Every time he tries to make a break, she pulls the I-don't-know-what-I'd-do-without-you thing. Matt's a good guy, he doesn't want to hurt her."

Pippa took a bite of eggs. Just the way she liked them. "I get that, Eric, but sooner or later you have to cut ties. Know what I mean?"

He nodded and got down to breakfast. Eric ate with a sort of neat precision that made the food disappear. "I know exactly what you mean, and so does Matt. It may not look like it to you right now, but he does know it. He just doesn't know what to do about it."

"He could have tried not going over there this morning. Or at least waiting until I was out of his bed." She couldn't help the blush.

"You know." Eric put his knife and fork together on his

empty plate. "Not many people know this, and we certainly don't spread it around, but she made several attempts on her life after my dad died."

Pippa snapped her mouth shut. He was right. Nobody knew that.

Eric shrugged. "I don't think any of them were serious attempts, more like a bid for attention. Matt didn't want any of us kids to know. He still doesn't know that I know."

Shit.

"So, when she locks herself in her room . . ." Eric pushed his plate away and leaned forward on his elbows. "I'm not trying to make excuses for him. Matt does need to deal with this before it takes over the rest of his life. I just thought you should know."

Which led to her next question. "Why?"

"He likes you. He's always had a bit of a thing for you. It would be a shame if you kicked him to the curb without giving him a chance to make it up to you."

Pippa hadn't gotten that far in her thinking yet. "You're a good brother."

Eric's handsome face went still and serious. "I owe my brother everything, Pippa. Everything. He's going to make some woman very lucky to have him one of these days. I don't want to see him blow a good thing before it's even had a chance to grow."

Heat burned up from her neck and over her cheeks. "I'm not that woman. This thing between Matt and me, it isn't serious."

A smile flitted across Eric's face. "If you say so."

Chapter Nineteen

Matt sat in his truck and stared at the house he'd grown up in. He'd left his bed, and the woman in it, to get over here and sort this out. So, he really should get his ass out of the truck.

Jo peered out the kitchen window and raised her hand in greeting.

"Damn." Part of him wanted to turn his truck around and get out of here. Seventeen years he'd been sorting crap out in this house. He had some vague memory of a time when stepping into the house didn't fasten claws around his neck. He sighed and climbed out of his truck.

Jo opened the kitchen door, and stood there with her arms crossed and her shoulders hunched.

"Hey." He raised his chin at her.

Jo unclenched her arms and came in for the hug. He loved his sister, really he did, but shouldn't her fiancé be here and doing this stuff for her? Which raised a good point. "What's this about you not getting married?"

She sniffed and pulled away from him, scrubbing her hands over her eyes like a four-year-old. With her head bowed and her slumped shoulders, she didn't look a lot older than that. His baby sister. He pulled her back for another hug.

"I was talking to Pippa at Bella's." The words got a bit muffled by his shirt. "She's really easy to talk to."

Yes, she was. And really easy on the eye and really, really nice to wake up with. "What did she say?"

Jo shrugged. "She didn't say much. I was trying on the dresses and I didn't feel like a bride, and then I got to thinking that was because maybe I didn't want to be a bride."

He thanked God for that, and took a deep breath. "And why's that?"

"I'm not sure I love Lance."

That made it time to say good-bye to Lance the Loser. "And now?"

"I dunno." Jo wiped her cheeks with the back of her hand. "I mean, I must have wanted to marry him, otherwise I wouldn't have said yes."

"It sounds like you should talk to Lance." If he pushed, Jo would shove back. Still, even making the suggestion made him want to spit it out of his mouth. "Is he coming back soon?"

"He didn't say."

Matt did a slow ten count in his head. "But, he'll be back before the wedding."

"If there is a wedding."

"Jo." He gripped her upper arms to get her to look at him. "You gotta level with me. Either you want to get married or you don't, and if you're this unsure, then maybe that's your answer right there."

She peeped through her lashes at him. "You won't be mad?"

Where the hell had that come from? "Why would I be mad?"

Jo shrugged and dropped her gaze to her feet.

"Jo-Jo? Talk to me." This used to be so much easier when

she was little. He bent his knees to see her face. "Do we need to go to the treehouse?"

Jo gave him a wet chuckle. "It's still there."

"Come on." He tugged on her hand. "It'll be easier to talk up there anyway."

"She's still in her room." Jo jerked her head toward the house.

The grip around his throat tightened. "I'll see her before I leave."

Getting his six-four frame into the treehouse took some doing, but Matt managed it. Jo scampered in behind him. The old treehouse creaked and groaned under their weight, but he and Eric had built this thing strong.

"So?" He waited for Jo to get settled. "Why would I be angry with you?"

Jo picked at a splinter of wood, her face difficult to read from this angle. "Not so much angry as disappointed."

Something Eric had said to him piped up in his head. "Why?"

"Because you always seem so sure of things." Jo sighed. "You make decisions, never look back, and I know you worry about us all the time. I mean, with Mom the way she is and all."

He did worry about them. It was his job. Or was it?

"Dad died," Jo said. "And you stepped up, and it's been that way ever since. Just once, I wanted to do something that wouldn't need you to rescue me."

She knocked the wind out of him. "You do lots of stuff that doesn't need a rescue."

"Oh, yeah." Jo raised her eyebrow. "Name one."

"You graduated with a four point oh GPA."

"You sat with me and did my homework, nearly every night."

Night after night, so tired from working all day it had

been hard to keep his eyes open sometimes. "You got your job at the bar on your own."

Jo pulled a face. "We both know I should have gone to college instead."

He'd even tried to fill out the applications for her, but Jo didn't want that. "You could still go to college."

"You're doing it again." Jo glared at him. "Stepping in and being my fixer."

He shut his mouth.

"Don't you ever feel like you don't know the answers?" Jo cocked her head as she looked at him.

Christ, most of the last seventeen years had been like he was caught in a pinball machine. "All the time, Jo."

"Really?" She frowned and went back to working at her splinter. "Because you never seem that way."

Jo had always been his baby sister. He got that she was growing up, but he didn't really understand what that meant. Jo was a woman now, with her own strengths and weaknesses and she didn't need her big brother to fix things for her anymore. "Jo." This honesty thing was a fucker. The desire to make her world happy and keep her feeling safe was set deep inside him. "I was nineteen when Dad died, and so scared and shocked, I didn't know what I was doing."

"You never looked it," Jo said.

"Yeah, well, I felt it." It was weird admitting these things. He'd always protected Jo, from everything, including himself. "Dad's business was in the toilet, Mom was . . ." He shrugged. "Mom wasn't coping and you guys were so young. Jeez, Jo-Jo, you had your eleventh birthday three days before Dad had his heart attack. Somebody had to step up or we were all screwed."

"You turned down that scholarship to do it."

God, why wouldn't she look at him? He needed to see her face, gauge how this was all going down. "Yup."

"Do you regret it?"

Every day of his life until that dream drifted out of age range. "Sometimes. I loved football, I wanted to go to college."

"But you still did it." Jo looked at him. "You're like a saint, Matt, and that makes the rest of us look like screwups."

Matt tried to take that in. It was the second time someone had called him a saint in the last three days. Eric accused him of being stuck, and keeping the rest of them stuck with him. How had they all gotten this screwed up? It had broken him to make the call that would end his scholarship chances. He had driven out to Lovers' Leap after the call and sat in his truck and cried like a baby. Cried for his chance gone by, cried for the loss of his dad, cried because he was so fucking scared of the load that had landed on his shoulders. Part of him was pissed with Jo for saying that, but the bigger part was shocked. Reeling.

"I'm not a saint, Jo-Jo." He managed to find some words to express the crap tangled in his head. "I was mad as hell about the way things turned out. It still gets to me. I'm thirty-six, running my dad's old construction company and living in the same town I grew up in. I want out too sometimes. I want my life to be the way I dreamed it would be when I was a kid." He shook his head. "I'm not a saint."

"I love you, Matt," she said. Her words made his throat dry up. "And I feel like I owe it to you not to get into any more shit."

"You don't owe me anything." His throat was so tight it was hard to work the words out. "I did what I had to do."

"Nope." Jo's dark hair swished around as she shook her head. "You did more than that. Plenty of people wouldn't have done the same as you. They would have left it to Mom to cope." Her face lost its soft look. "She should never have let you do it."

"She was a mess." Hadn't he said the same thing to himself? So why the need to defend his mother?

"She was the mother," Jo said.

Matt didn't see it as quite as cut and dried. Maybe because he was older and had noticed more of how things worked with their parents. Dad had been the tower on which their mother leaned. When he was taken away, and so suddenly, their mother collapsed. Matt had known what his dad would have wanted him to do and done it.

"Enough about me." This conversation made his skin feel too tight over his bones. "Now that we've gotten it clear that you shouldn't get married because you don't want to disappoint me, what are you going to do?"

"Call off the wedding?" She said it like she was asking his permission.

It was all great and good to tell him all this crap about not wanting to be a burden, but that went two ways. If Jo wanted to stand on her own two feet, she needed to get up off her ass. "Don't ask me, Jo. This is all on you."

She frowned as if that hadn't occurred to her. "I want to call off the wedding."

"Okay, then."

"And pay you back for all the money you've spent on it so far."

Wow, she really did have it in her head to go all out. "That's not necessary."

"Yes, it is." Jo set her jaw in a stubborn line. All the Evans kids had that way of sticking their jaw out, like they were bracing for the punch.

"Dad would not have made you pay it back," he said.

"You're not Dad." There was no arguing with that. If she

needed to do this, then so be it. "I can pick up extra shifts at the bar until I pay you back."

"Okay." The idea of taking her money didn't sit right, but their conversation had gotten him thinking. It rang too close to what Eric had said. Maybe it was time to step back a bit and give everybody some room to breathe. Isaac had taken that room for himself, and maybe Matt needed to let him do it.

"I enrolled in an online college." Jo dropped her head again, hiding her face.

He stamped hard on the urge to go paternal and congratulate her. "Studying what?"

"I'm not sure yet, but something in the sciences." Jo shrugged. "I don't know yet, but I figured it was time to get back on the horse and see where that led me."

Jo had more brains than all her brothers put together. She wasn't so hot on the street smarts, though. She did have a way of getting herself into trouble. Maybe it was time to give her the space to get herself out of that trouble. "Let me know if there is anything I can do."

She rolled her eyes at him.

"What?" He shrugged. He couldn't change seventeen years of habit in one small conversation.

"Are you going to take Eric's offer?" Jo asked.

"I don't know." This conversation was certainly giving him a new perspective. "I need to think about it."

"You should take it," Jo said. "I think you need something like this to get on with your life."

She smirked at him and shuffled out of the treehouse through the hatch and down the ladder.

He went much slower, his big feet scrabbling for traction.

Jo dropped to the bottom and stared at the house. "Are you going in to see her?"

"Yup."

He strode toward the house. He couldn't put this off much longer. His mother already knew he was here. She would have heard his truck and would be waiting for him.

"Matt?" Jo stood where he'd left her, arms crossed. "What if you didn't go?"

"Where?"

"Into the kitchen."

He glanced back at the house. A curtain twitched at the upstairs window to his mother's room. "I don't know."

And that's why he went, because it scared the crap out of him what might happen if he didn't.

As afternoon gave way to evening Matt let himself into his house. Tired didn't begin to cover it. Sitting in his mother's kitchen, trying to keep track of business and keep his mother stable had eaten up his entire afternoon.

He'd been a dick to Pippa this morning. Eric had called him, special-like, to let him know. He really needed to talk to her, but first he needed to grab a bite to eat and a shower. His mother's desperation clung to his skin.

Condom wrappers littered the floor next to the bed and he bent and snagged them. His mother had a way of barging into his house and cleaning. Pissed him the fuck off, but sometimes you had to pick your battles, and he got a clean house out of this one. Pippa's perfume clung to the sheets in a subtle reminder of their night. And just like that, he didn't feel so tired anymore.

Chapter Twenty

Once she started reading, Pippa couldn't stop.

#getyourfactsstraight #askpippawhatshesaid #justice-forpippa were trending all right. God, how could she have been this stupid? All the positive tweets had been lost amongst the deluge of scorn and outright derision.

@bigboy wanted to know, "How did the Kool-Aid taste as you rammed it down your throat?"

@jenniferkearns went with a simple but effective, "fuck you, Pippa bitch"

@christyroth suggested she go into politics if she wanted people to believe her bullshit

@graeme_parker thought #justiceforpippa meant being stripped naked and paraded through LA.

From one tweet to the next she went, the nausea growing with each one, as if the venom seeped out of her Twitter feed and sank into her bones. Her chest tightened, and she went into the yard. Breathing deep, she dragged much-needed air into her lungs.

Her wobbly legs dropped her ass onto the side of the water trough fountain. Damp seeped through her jeans, but she didn't care. This was so much worse than before. She should never have believed she'd hit rock bottom because where she was three days ago was a long way up from here.

Like the instrument of her deliverance, Matt's truck cleared Phi's "verdant thicket" and entered the yard. Until he drove up, Pippa hadn't known how desperately she wanted to see him.

Strong and sure, he came toward her.

She walked straight into his arms. The world stopped spinning as his steady heartbeat drummed against her ear.

"Are you okay?" His voice came from above her head.

Pippa shook her head. She was far from okay. Suddenly she was all of thirteen again, watching her dad load his packed bags into the family station wagon. Lost. Alone. Terrified.

Matt tightened his arms about her. "Man, I needed this," he said.

So did she, and the idea terrified her enough to get Pippa out of his embrace. "Bad day?"

"I'll show you mine, if you show me yours." A ghost of Matt's cocky smile flitted across his mouth.

Pippa crossed her arms over her chest, as if she could contain the screaming pit inside her. "I pretty much killed my already dying career on Twitter. Now your turn."

Matt frowned and stepped closer. "What?"

Not really wanting to say the words out loud, Pippa handed him the phone.

"Fuck." Matt's thumb scrolled from one screen to another. "How did this start?"

"Someone tweeted me." Her stupidity crawled like a poisonous spider all over Pippa. "I responded. I was desperate." Matt kept scrolling. "I wanted people to know my side of the story. Everywhere else I went was a dead end. I thought . . ." She shrugged, because she pretty much hadn't been thinking, otherwise they wouldn't be having this conversation.

"But you told me to leave it alone. That the less you said, the sooner it would die," Matt said.

"I know that." It sounded too much like a criticism and she didn't need it right now. Everything she'd worked for, ever wanted was even deader than before and it had been barely twitching before this.

"Look." Matt pushed his hand through his hair. "This looks bad. I don't know much about this stuff, but this isn't pretty." He cupped her shoulders and pulled her closer. "But I know you, Pippa. You're tough. A fighter. You can recover from this."

"How?" Pippa blinked at him, staggered by his naïveté.

"I don't know." He dropped his hands. "What I'm trying to say is it isn't the end of the world."

"It's the end of my world." Pippa's voice rang across the stable yard.

"No, babe, it's not." He tried to take her hands but Pippa evaded him. "Look." He frowned. "I seem to be saying all the wrong things today. Why don't we have a beer, and talk about how to fix this."

"This can't be fixed." Pippa crossed her arms over her chest. Part of her knew she was being unreasonable. Matt didn't come from her world. He had no idea what the reper- cussions of this would be, but she was so fucking scared. "And you're not the person who could fix it anyway."

"Okay." Matt's eyes went hard and cold. "That certainly put me in my place."

Damn. She hadn't meant to sound that harsh. Pippa opened her mouth to correct it.

Matt slashed his hand through the air, silencing her. "No, it's fine," he said, but it clearly wasn't. She'd hurt him, and guilt mixed uncomfortably with all the other rioting emotions inside her. "It seems to be everyone's day for telling me to butt the hell out of their lives. I've got the message."

He turned and stalked over to his truck.

Pippa stood and watched him back out of the yard. Part of her wanted to stop him, and another part knew this was how it always was. This was what she knew. Pippa standing alone against the world.

Her phone rang as she walked back into the kitchen. Chris Germaine's number flashed up on her screen. She let it ring, and then changed her mind. Might as well see what else her day had in store for her. Her finger shook as she accepted the call.

"Hi, Pippa." Chris Germaine's robust, husky voice vibrated down the line. "You're a difficult lady to get hold of."

Not hard enough, apparently. "I'm hiding."

"Yes." Chris lingered over the *s* in that one word. "You've had a rough time."

That was one way of putting it. Pippa shut the kitchen door. "Some days are better than others. Today is probably the worst."

"Uh-huh." Chris spoke to someone on the other end of the line, her words garbled. "So, let's put our cards on the table." Her voice came back, stronger and with less background noise. "It seems your producer has been a very naughty boy."

Pippa stopped dead. As far as she knew that little secret was still inside the show's bubble. "You know about Ray?"

"We know all about Mr. Ray Brightly."

Pippa needed to sit down before she fell down. "Oh?"

"There were some members of your crew who were not at all happy about what went down," Chris said. "They have been very active on your behalf."

"Really?" This was news to her.

"That's when they came to me," Chris said. "Allie wasn't too happy about what aired either and she's also stepped forward."

"Allie?" The same Allie who wouldn't take her call?

"Actually, Allie is royally pissed off," Chris said. "It seems she's considering a lawsuit against the show."

Pippa tried to picture that, meek and sweet Allie getting mad about anything was far enough of a stretch. Thank God she'd sat down already, because her knees had melted.

Phi slapped open the baize door and paused in the doorway. She caught sight of Pippa and dropped the pose. Her stage whisper was loud enough for the back row of any amphitheater to hear. "What is it?"

Pippa waved her to silence, trying to concentrate on what Chris Germaine was saying.

Chris kept talking public apologies and shows being taken off the air. Past tense. As if they'd already happened.

"Are you still with me?" Chris sharpened her tone.

"No." Pippa shook her head to clear it.

Phi was making faces at her, trying to find out what was going on.

Pippa dropped her eyes to the kitchen table and drew in a deep breath. Then another, and her mind slowed down enough to process. "I didn't hear anything after you told me Allie was considering a lawsuit," she said. "This is rather a lot to take in."

Chris chuckled. "Right. Pull up your big girl panties and listen. I am going to say it all again."

"Okay." Mental check on the big girl panties.

"With Allie threatening the lawsuit, and your cameraman still holding the original footage, the show agreed to a public apology. Ray is not producing anymore, and that woman they hired to replace you has gone back to serving cocktails."

"Uh-huh." She nodded at the table.

Phi banged her knuckles on the table, her eyes bugging out of her head.

Pippa caught her hand and held it, twisting her fingers with Phi's for support.

"The public apology aired last night," Chris said. "Along with the real footage of what happened. Given a few editing bits and pieces for dramatic effect."

"Right." Because if the public really saw the hours of boring that happened to get the forty-five minutes that hit the air, they'd be asleep already.

"Now." Chris cleared her throat. "You and I both know that even with all that, this is going to take some time to die down. There will still be some people who insist on believing the worst."

It was the God's honest truth. It came with the job description and Pippa made a noise of agreement.

"But something you said on that last show got me thinking. Just a second." Chris spoke to an unseen body on her end. "I'm back. I have a million things going on. Where was I?"

"Something I said on the last show intrigued you."

"Right. You were talking about how it takes more than a pair of shoes to turn a life around. I agree with you. It's part of why I find these makeover shows so facile. No, I can't come now. They are just going to have to do it without me."

Pippa figured that last part was not aimed at her. "I believe that," she said.

"And you're right. It takes a total transformation to make any real change in a life," Chris said. "Which is why I've been stalking you. I have a show in mind, with you as the host. We take a woman for a year. Give her the tools to make real changes in her life, part of them cosmetic but the bigger part internal."

Pippa opened her mouth and a strange squeaking noise came out. It was like Chris Germaine had reached inside her head and plucked out a dormant idea that had been lurking there for the last few years.

It must have been the right sort of noise because Chris kept on talking. She went on about financial backing, selection processes. A lot of it washed right over Pippa.

She met Phi's intense green gaze. Her eyesight wobbled as a wash of tears filled her eyes. This couldn't be happening. Dreams did not, as a rule, come true. You made them happen. You hustled, you fought, and you hung tough and made them happen. You didn't get phone calls out of the blue that handed them to you.

"Damn it." Chris's sharp bark dragged her back to the present. "I have this all written down in a proposal for you to look at. Let me courier it to you and you can have a few days to look it over before we speak again. Yes, I'm coming now." Chris near bellowed that last part. "I have to go, but I want to know that you're interested. Before I go any further, let me hear you say yes or no."

"Yes." It came out whisper soft and silly.

"Great." It sounded good enough for the formidable Ms. Germaine. "I have to go, before they lose it over here. We'll speak in a couple of days. And Pippa—I said I was coming now—stay off Twitter." Chris hung up.

Pippa had the phone pressed to her ear for a while as she listened to silence.

"Merciful God our Father." Phi exploded from her seat. "Tell me what the hell is happening before I have a shit fit."

Pippa shook her head, trying to make the words come out. "That was Chris Germaine."

Phi's eyes widened. She didn't need to be told who Chris Germaine was. The most powerful woman in television needed no introductions. Starting as a talk show host, Chris has grown her brand on the principles of inner growth and authentic living, leveraging that into a massive industry. "And?"

"I need a drink."

"Darling." Phi spread her fingers over her bosom. "You've come to the right place then."

"Make that a few drinks," Pippa said.

"This calls for whisky." Phi got to her feet and did a quick double take out the window. "And look, here is dear Matt." She raised a brow at Pippa. "Again."

Pippa swung round to see Matt getting out of his truck. His face looked drawn and tired as he let himself in the kitchen door.

"Hey." He jerked his chin at her, and stuck his hands in his jeans pockets.

As pissed as she was, he was still the person she wanted to share her news with. And he shouldn't be. "Hey, yourself."

Phi's head swung between them like she was watching a tennis match. "I sense a little malcontent," she sang out.

"Can you give us a minute, Phi?" Matt managed a smile for her grandmother.

"Indeed." Phi patted his cheek. "A man should always know how to grovel. And once you are done, Pippa has received some stupendous news."

She bustled out the door in a cloud of patchouli.

Matt jammed his hands in the back pockets of his jeans. "Stupendous, huh?"

"You here for anything particular?" Pippa wiped her damp hands on her jeans. Still sweaty from how tight she had been holding the phone. The fluttering in her belly was all Matt, though.

Matt tilted his head. "Yeah, I'm here to grovel. Dick move on my part storming off like that."

"Gee, Meat." She played it cool on the outside. Inside, total mess. "That's big of you to admit."

"Yeah, you're right." His shoulders dropped a bit. "It's been a helluva day."

"What happened?"

He shook his head, as if clearing his head. "Tell me your stupendous news instead."

Pippa tucked away the part of her that wanted to pry and gave him her news. Telling Matt brought the excitement bubbling to the surface again.

"That's great, babe." The big grin he gave her filled her cup to the brim. He waved his fingers at her phone. "Will it fix the other thing?"

"Not right away." Pippa took another mood swing to the dark side. "But it does mean my career isn't dead."

"Then, you're golden. Back on track."

That was exactly what it meant. Back on an even better track than before. So, why wasn't she doing a victory lap of the kitchen. "Yeah."

"So, when do you leave?" He bunched his shoulders around his ears and dropped them on an exhale.

"Leave?" Pippa sunk into a chair. Of course she would leave. Chris Germaine's offer meant she was out of Ghost Falls again.

"Sure." Matt came closer. "Your future is out there. This town has always been too small for you."

"I don't know," she said. "We didn't talk about the details."

"I'm very happy for you, Pippa." Matt crouched at her

feet. Grabbing her hands, he raised first one and then the other for a kiss. "You've worked hard for this. You deserve it."

Beautiful topaz eyes stared at her, his sincerity clear for her to read. But lurking at the back, something she was afraid to acknowledge, a sort of resignation.

"I was never coming back for good," she said.

"I know." He squeezed her hands. "You never made any secret of that. I guess, I let that detail slip my mind."

The elephant charged into the room and squatted between them. "But I'm not gone yet." Pippa tried for perky. "We still have a bit of time."

"Babe." The regret in Matt's gaze took the air out of her. "I'm happy for you, really I am, but I need to get real with you here. Earlier, the reason I stormed off was because I'd had a shitty day, and all I wanted to do was be with you. And you . . . you have your own stuff, and I'm not part of it."

"My career is everything to me." His life was Ghost Falls, hers was LA, and they were further apart than the miles that separated the two places. Stuck here, hiding from her world, Pippa had allowed herself to be pulled into a bubble of her and Matt. Their fairy tale had come to an end.

"We both knew what we were getting into. Nobody made any promises," Matt said. "But I gotta level with you. I never expected to feel the stuff for you that I do. I think we need to call this one before either of us . . ." He grimaced. "Before I get in too deep."

But what if both were already in too deep?

"Neither of us is naïve enough to believe we have a future. It wasn't what we signed on for." He shrugged. "I don't want to ruin your big news, babe, because I really am happy for you. But the selfish part of me, the bit that needs to protect me, thinks it's best for both of us to get out before we start wanting things we can't have. The things we want, Pippa, they don't mesh. Both our lives are too complicated."

"You're right." Pippa managed to find her voice. It tore a strip off her to admit it, but he was right. She was leaving. He was staying where he'd always been. "We're keeping this light, remember."

His eyes called the lie for what it was, but he still managed a smile. "Sure. Keeping it light."

"And you're not the only one in danger of . . . feeling more." Her voice wobbled and she cleared her throat. "It's stupid to carry on and risk . . . more."

"Yeah." He rose and moved away from her, staring out the window through the heavy silence. "For what it's worth, I wouldn't change a thing. Getting to know you, Pippa, making love with you, one of the best things I've ever done."

Tears gathered beneath her lids and she blinked them away. "Me too."

It wasn't supposed to be this hard to walk away from Matt. When she'd gone into this thing, she'd thought she could handle it. A quick, hot-as-hell affair with Matt Evans and then back to life as normal. Except, she had the sneaking suspicion that normal was never going to feel the same again.

"Whisky!" Phi swept through the door. She stopped with the bottle raised. Her gaze skittered to Pippa and Matt and back again. "Too soon?"

"No." Pippa dredged up her voice. "But I really don't feel like a drink anymore. I think I might be coming down with something." Like a massive dose of heart-sore. "I think Matt has to get home anyway."

Matt stared at her, silently asking all sorts of questions, and Pippa nodded. This was the only way it could be. They'd had their time. Short and sweet as it had been, it was over. She'd make a list, pros and cons, possible scenarios and solutions. Lists always helped her sort through the confusion.

"Mathieu?" Phi took a step toward him. "Have you done something you shouldn't have?"

Matt met her stare, his eyes dark and unreadable but his face set in grim lines. "I'm more of a beer guy."

Pippa got to her feet, her limbs clumsy and not working right. She was relieved she made it through the door without banging into anything. "I'll see you around, Meat."

"Take care, Agrippina."

Chapter Twenty-One

Pippa woke from the two hours of sleep she'd managed to get the night before. Yesterday had started as a disaster, gotten worse, and then that call from Chris Germaine. Her dream had been handed to her on a platter. If anything, she should have been up last night, her mind cycling with ideas for the new show.

She spent most of the night obsessing over Matt, which was so dumb it made her teeth ache. Not even after his betrayal had she spent this much time thinking about Ray. Matt had called it right; they were drifting into dangerous territory. Far better, and less messy, to make a clean break now while they both still could. Except, it didn't feel clean to her. It hurt, dammit.

She was so pathetic it made her want to puke. Pippa stomped into the bathroom and snapped on the bath faucets.

The pipes clattered and groaned and . . . nothing.

"Really?" Pippa glared at the dry faucet. A small trickle of water tinkled out and stopped. Damn this ridiculous house. It was as temperamental as its owner.

Pippa tried again, just in case. The pipes groaned like a lactose intolerant after a cheese binge. Pippa stomped over to the bathroom door and yanked it open. "Phi!"

Sarah Hegger

Phi was not the only one in this house with an impressive set of pipes on her.

"Mon ange." Phi's voice floated up the stairs from the kitchen. Sweet enough to bring Pippa's hackles up. Phi was up to something.

"There's no water."

"Of course there is," Phi said.

Pippa opened her mouth to yell her complaint down the stairs and snapped it shut again. Phi could hold a bellowed conversation all day if she had to. Pippa tramped down the stairs and shoved open the baize door.

"Angel." Phi beamed at her. "You're not dressed."

Pippa glared at her grandmother. "Really? How am I supposed to get dressed if I can't have a bath? And can we please put in a shower?"

"Showers are vulgar." Phi pursed her lips and tapped her forefinger against her chin. "I see the problem. I know!" She snapped her bedazzled fingers. "Coffee. We will start with coffee and then apply our minds to the solution. See, we have a visitor."

Pippa stared blearily at Jo, sitting at the kitchen table with a smirk on her face. "Hi. Nice pj's," she said.

"Thanks." At least they matched and didn't have anything embarrassing on them. Pippa threw herself into a chair at the kitchen table.

Phi put a mug in front of her. "There we are, darling. You're always so much more charming when you have some caffeine."

True that. Pippa took a careful sip of her coffee. Thank God, June must be here somewhere because the brew didn't strip her throat on the way down. "The water isn't working in my bathroom."

"Really?" Phi did that chin tapping thing again.

Pippa smelled a Phi-shaped rat. She may be one of the

greatest voices in the world, but Phi was a truly horrible actress.

"My water was fine," Phi said. "Josephine, would you see if we have water here in the kitchen?"

Jo opened her mouth to protest her new name. Pippa shook her head at her. It wouldn't do any good. Phi had decided Jo was a Josephine, and not even the arrival of a valid birth certificate would change that.

Jo stood up and turned the faucet on. Water gushed out. It reminded Pippa of the time when she doused Matt as he—

"I'll use your bathroom," she said to Phi. She was worse than pathetic. Next thing she'd start doodling his name all over her notebook and decorating it with hearts. What she needed was a list. A list of all the reasons why taking the Chris Germaine job was the best thing for her. For good measure, she'd follow that up with a list of all the reasons why her future was not in Ghost Falls. Then she could combine the two and prove to herself that Matt calling this thing quits was the best decision for both of them.

"June is cleaning in there." Phi pulled a regretful face, so false it made Pippa want to laugh. The old bag was up to something.

"Then I'll wait."

"Or," said Jo, coming in right on cue. "We could call Matt and ask him to get over here. Urgently."

Pippa glared at her, then turned the glare on the real culprit, disemboweling fruit at the counter.

"What?" Phi opened her eyes wide.

"Is that why you're here?" Pippa turned back to Jo. "Because Phi dragged you into one of her schemes?"

"What scheme?" Jo had good game face, but Pippa was an old hand at Phi and her antics. She kept her level stare going and Jo blushed and dropped her eyes. "Only partly."

Jo rallied but her blush stayed. "I wanted to tell you that I broke off my engagement this morning."

"Really?" Pippa studied her face for signs of heartbreak.

Jo looked composed, relaxed even and missing that tiny storm cloud over her head.

"Are you okay?"

"Yup." Jo smiled. A little wobbly around the edges but still there. "I think he was relieved, to be honest."

"Stupid ass." Phi hacked a strawberry in half, and threw the good bit into the trash. "He has no idea the treasure he has tossed away."

Pippa got to her feet and took the knife away from Phi. She'd never get any fruit for breakfast at this rate.

"Men," Phi declared as she took her seat at the head of the table, "often need to be reminded of what they really want."

Ah, here it came. Pippa kept slicing the tops off the strawberries. Phi had a built-in radar for what she called "troubles of the heart."

"Yes," said Jo. "They're very stubborn about what they think they want."

Pippa dropped her strawberries into the colander and moved on to the pineapple. Jo had potential, she'd give her that. Delivery needed a bit of work, but she was quick to take her cue.

"You're so right, Josephine." Phi raised her voice until the horses must be able to hear her. "They tend to act impulsively, and often require a push in the right direction. Do you know any men such as this, Josephine?"

"Er, yes." Jo jumped on her line with gusto. "In fact, I do. You know the other day I was saying to my brother, Eric, that our brother Matt—"

"Seriously?" Pippa turned to stare at them.

Big eyes from Phi, but Jo had the grace to drop her gaze to the table.

"I appreciate the effort." Even though it felt like dragging fishing hooks under her nails. "But Matt and I are fine." She turned back to her pineapple. Almost did a Phi on it, her hands were shaking so badly.

"What does fine mean?" Jo asked.

Good question, and Pippa shrugged. "We were a fling, a for-now thing. There's no big relationship or anything. I'm leaving, he's staying, end of story."

"Then why is Matt in such a bad mood?"

He was? Pippa put the knife down before she took a finger off.

"Do you hear that, Agrippina?" Phi was not going to give this up without a fight. "Mathieu is aggrieved. Why do you think that is?"

"Probably has to do with his mother." Damn! Stupid thing to say with Jo sitting at the table. Pippa spun around to apologize. "Jo, I'm sorry. I meant—"

"Oh, please." Jo waved her off. "You don't need to pretend with me. I'm an old hand at the Cressy guts-in-a-vice style of parenting. She's launched a hunger strike over my broken engagement."

Phi gave a sigh that shook the rafters. "That woman needs to find something else to fill her mind."

"Couldn't agree more." Jo toasted Phi with her coffee mug. "Right now she is demanding Eric and Matt dance around her. I left before she could start on me."

"Did she like your fiancé?" Pippa wasn't sure why she asked, but she needed to know more.

Jo made a rude noise. "She can't stand him. She wouldn't even have him in the house."

"Then why?" Pippa turned back to her fruit and washed it

all under the working faucet. Cressy had always been difficult to figure out.

"Power," said Phi. "Information is power and she loses it when she is not the first to know."

"You could be right." Jo got up and refreshed her mug. She brought the pot over to Pippa and topped her up as well. "The guys get the worst of it. Eric laughs her off, but Matt . . ." She ended on a shrug. "He's so used to taking care of her, he's buckling into his armor before he even thinks about it."

"Very noble," Phi murmured.

Jo snorted. "Actually, I think it's a bit pathetic. Matt is nearly forty."

Thirty-six was not nearly forty, but not the point.

"It's time he broke the chokehold she's got on him," Pippa said. She didn't want to leave here and think of Matt stuck in his mother's boa constrictor grip.

Phi heaved another window-rattling sigh. "This, I cannot disagree with. It is the curse of the nice guy." She perked up straight in her chair. "Did I ever tell you about that Italian lover I had?"

"Which one?" Pippa sipped her coffee and brought the fruit to the table.

"Massimo." Phi stared off into the distance with a tiny smile. "Wonderful lover, so creative and caring, really inventive with his—"

"Anyway." Pippa got in quick because Jo looked a little green.

"Yes, indeed." Phi gave a bordello chuckle. "Anyway, he had a mother such as yours." Phi tapped the table in front of Jo. "She did not want him consorting with a performer, such as me."

"What happened?" Jo plucked a hunk of pineapple out of the bowl.

"He moved to Milan," Phi said.

"Because of his mother?" Jo chewed the pineapple and snagged another piece.

"Oh, no." Phi flapped her hands in the air. "He had a house there, and he was engaged to a young girl who lived two streets over from his house."

Jo blinked at Phi and then Pippa.

"And your point is?" Laughter built inside Pippa. Jo had no idea of the mental gymnastics of Phi.

"That nice men are often taken advantage of by grasping women." Phi finished with a hand flourish. She wrinkled her nose at the fruit. "Are we not having eggs?"

Pippa rose and grabbed a pan from the cupboard. The caffeine had soothed the rough edges off. "Are you staying for breakfast?"

"Of course she is," Phi answered for Jo. She leaned in to the other woman and winked. "Pippa is a marvel with the egg."

Pippa bit back her snort as she grabbed the eggs from the fridge, adding a few more for June, who was likely to appear at around the time they were ready.

"Call your brother about the pipes," Phi said from behind her.

"Phi." Pippa turned to glare at her grandmother. Her heart sank as she caught the fanatical gleam in Phi's green eyes. Phi might break the entire house to get her own way. She sighed and went back to her eggs. "At least give me a chance to get dressed first."

"Like I said, nice pj's." Jo laughed.

"Yes." Phi hummed and tapped the table. "But a dash of makeup and a little spritz of perfume would not go awry. Men are visual creatures, not subtle."

Pippa could feel their eyes on her back.

"You're right," Jo said. "I'll call in a little bit."

"But do not leave it too late," Phi said. "Because the lovelies are due here this morning and a man cannot woo with children underfoot."

"There will be no wooing here today." Pippa really had to draw the line somewhere.

Jo smirked at her.

Phi pressed her hand to her bosom. "Of course there will, darling."

Why did she bother? Pippa gave her eggs a vicious jab.

Matt sipped his coffee and wished he could mainline it.

"Sweet Jesus." Eric dragged out a kitchen chair and straddled it. "She's gotten worse."

"Yup."

Their mother was in full meltdown mode this morning. She'd barely given him a chance to get the coffee on before she started.

"How do you stand it?" Eric's hands tightened around his mug.

Matt shrugged, because right now he wasn't. The desire to yell at his mother rode him hard.

"Hey." Nate appeared in the kitchen door. "What's going on?"

"She called you, too?" Eric swung his gaze to their younger brother.

"Yup." Nate looked from him to Matt and back again. He growled and moved to the cupboard and snatched out a mug. "I'm too fucking busy for this shit."

Weren't they all? Coffee burned Matt's mouth as he took a huge slug.

"Wanna give me the Cliffs Notes?" Nate added cream to his coffee and three heaped spoons of sugar. Shit, his brother must work out like a demon to keep that sugar off. At least

Matt hoped so, because otherwise he was going to get seriously pissed. More pissed. Four times he'd pulled out his phone to call Pippa. He ached to hear her voice, watch the way her sparkling green eyes took the situation in, assessed and cut straight to the heart of the matter. But he'd done the mature thing with Pippa, the right thing. The only thing he could do really. He didn't want to hold her here. He knew too much about how that felt.

"Mom's having a shit fit because Jo broke off her engagement," Eric said.

Nate gaped at him. "What the fuck?"

"Exactly." Eric shook his head.

"She hated the idea of Jo getting married." Nate stared at Eric and then Matt. "Didn't we have one of these about six months ago when Jo first told her she was getting married?"

"Yup." For the first time probably since his dad had died, his mother's issues were not the most pressing thing on his mind.

His phone rang. Jo. He almost didn't hit accept, thinking for a minute their mother had decided to gather the clan. In the end habit kicked in and he answered the call.

He was heading for the door before Jo finished speaking.

"Where the hell are you going?" Nate called after him.

"Phi's," he yelled back. And Pippa. That got him moving faster.

A chair scraped behind him. "You'll need my help," said Eric.

Chapter Twenty-Two

Matt let himself into the kitchen. Pippa wasn't there, but the fresh floral scent of her lingered and her fancy purse sat on the kitchen table. He shouldn't be this anxious to see her. Her new job meant she was going away and soon. It didn't bode well that after only a night spent without her, he was as excited as a puppy with a tennis ball, but she sat like an effervescent bubble under his rib cage and he scanned the kitchen for any further sign of her.

"Mathieu, darling." Phi flung herself into the kitchen. She batted her lashes at Eric. "And your delicious brother."

"Phi, you're such a flirt." Eric kissed Phi on both cheeks. "We both know I'm not man enough for you."

"Sad, but true." Phi twinkled up at him.

Eric never struggled to find something to say. He opened his mouth and some player-smooth comment drifted out. Damn, what Matt wouldn't give for that gift. "Jo said you had no water?"

"Such a lovely girl, your sister." Phi beamed at him. "She popped around this morning for a visit. It has simply been ages since I have seen her. And now I have two of her brothers in my kitchen."

"The water, Phi?" Phi was as demanding as his mother,

tying him up in the same sort of knots. But with Phi, it felt different. Across the kitchen she was giving him a coy look out the corner of her heavily made-up eyes, and he grinned. Sly, conniving, and kind enough to give you her last dime. How she made him smile all the time beat him. Pippa had that gift too. She could walk into a room, any room, and light it right up. Which was why she needed to get the hell out of Ghost Falls and stay out. This town was too small, too cramped for the arc light that was Pippa.

"Don't you growl at me, Mathieu." Phi batted her lashes. "I am tempted to pout at you."

Matt's belly gave an uneasy clench. Phi had been talking to Pippa. He so didn't want to get into this with Eric watching like his favorite team was in the Super Bowl. "Phi, I—"

"I do not like it when my plans are overset," Phi said to Eric. "All the careful planning and plotting required."

Eric grinned. "What did he do?"

"I don't think this is a big share session." Matt tried to cut the whole thing off at the pass.

"He and Pippa have been wrenched apart." Phi gave it some hand action to illustrate.

"Wrenched?" Eric raised an eyebrow over at him.

You couldn't wrench apart what didn't exist, but the explanation would be lost on Phi. He kept it cool on the outside, but inside he was a squirming mess. "Let me look at that water."

"In Pippa's bathroom." Phi waved her hand in that general direction.

Matt knew he'd been had. He should be mad as hell at her. Firstly, though, he could never get mad at Phi and stay mad. Secondly, his brain locked onto Pippa and he took the stairs two at a time. He bypassed the bathroom and hung around the door to Pippa's room.

She lay stretched out on the bed, tapping away at her iPad.

Matt drank her in. The way the sun hit her hair and turned it to copper flame. The long, lush lines of her body that no man with a pulse could resist. He kept it quiet so as not to startle her. "Hey."

She jolted a little anyway and turned her head to him. "Oh, hey." She tucked a strand of hair behind her ear. "Are you here to fix the bathroom?"

"Yeah."

"Okay." She swung her legs over the side of the bed and sat up. "Jo must have called you."

"She did."

Damn, but he was like a dumbstruck teen with a huge crush.

"The bathroom's through there." She fiddled with the edge of her iPad, not quite meeting his gaze.

"I know." He should go and fix whatever Phi had done to that pipe. Fortunately, the Diva didn't know enough about plumbing to cause any major hassles.

Eric's full-throated laugh drifted up from the kitchen.

"How are you?" he said. Jesus, his super-sharp repartee was getting marginally better.

"Fine. You?" She put her tablet down on the bed next to her and stood.

Her shorts left most of her glorious legs for him to drool over. *Wrong thought, buddy.* His body didn't get the memo because even now he could feel the slide of her satin skin under his palm.

"Matt?" Pippa cocked her hip and stared at him.

"You're beautiful." The words jet-propelled out of his mouth before he knew he was even thinking them.

She blinked and raised her chin. "What the hell, Matt?"

"Yeah, I know. I shouldn't have said that." Damn, this was awkward. There was so much to say that needed to be said, but it jammed in his brain. He scrubbed his fingers over his scalp. "But for what it's worth, it's true. You are beautiful. Any man thinks that when they look at you." And now he was babbling. "I still think that. Maybe always will."

"Don't do this." Pippa took a shaky breath. "What you said before, about not getting in too deep, you were right. It's better this way."

"I know." Then why didn't it feel better? He took a couple of steps into the room. Honest to God, his feet moved without him directing them. This woman drew him, like she had a super power. "But I wish things were different."

Pippa took a few steps and met him halfway. Her green eyes soft and reflecting back at him all the confusion he had going on inside. The need to hold her was like a physical ache.

She blew out a long breath. "So much for keeping it light."

"Yeah." He needed to get it together here. "I'll go and see what Phi did to the plumbing."

"She's on a mission." Pippa half followed him, and stopped in the doorway.

"I got that. She's pouting." Matt forced an easy smile on his face. It felt a bit fake from his end, but Pippa responded with a small smile of her own.

Pippa made a jerky motion toward the stairs. "I'll be downstairs if you . . . need anything."

You, naked, sweaty, and panting under me. So not the right answer to the question. He shook his head and backed into the bathroom.

Pippa crossed her arms over the hollow ache in her chest. She'd expected to see Matt after the scene with Jo and Phi, been braced for it. Then, he appeared in her bedroom doorway and she couldn't breathe anymore. Couldn't think straight.

He wasn't making it easy, either.

She knew that look in his eyes. It had been beamed at her pretty constantly since she came home. Matt was still hot for her, and keen to scratch that itch. If she was really having this lighthearted, friends-with-benefits thing with him—no problem, right? They hook up, have a great time, and end of story. Not quite the way it was working out.

Friends with benefits didn't cuddle and talk about their lives. Spend time with each other because it felt good, comfortable, safe. Those things got messy, fast. The sex was great, off the charts, but the connection . . . the connection was the biggest problem of all. He got her. A deep-down understanding of her that didn't need words or gestures. And she got him.

Pippa took the stairs at a near run. If she gave herself half a chance, she'd be back up there with Matt.

Phi and Eric were making goo-goo eyes at each other over the kitchen table.

Eric was far more her type. Groomed, urbane, sophisticated, yet with that aura of I'm-so-much-trouble on the end of him. Why couldn't she be attracted to Eric? She threw herself down on the bench beside him. Who knows? Maybe some of that hotness would trigger a response.

He smelled great. A touch of sandalwood overlying warm male. Pippa took an appreciative sniff.

Eric turned to grin down at her. "Are you sniffing me?"

"Yup." She bumped his shoulder. "You smell great."

"Smell." Phi threw her head back and growled. "Such a raw, sexual response to a man."

"I'm not having sex with Eric," Pippa said. If Phi saw her plan with Matt heading south, she was very likely to switch targets. And that's all they needed right now, Phi on a mission to fix her up with Eric.

Eric huffed a soft laugh. "Are you sure?"

"Quite."

"Well, damn," Eric murmured. His naughty eye twinkle must drive the girls nuts. "There go my plans for later."

Wheels crunched over gravel outside and Phi raised her head. A smile bloomed over her face and she got to her feet and scurried for the door. "The lovelies."

Seventy-eight and she still moved like a teenager. Pippa must have lost her mind to think Phi was losing her memory. As for Laura and Mom, they so needed to get over themselves. She needed to concentrate on her own mess right now. Work. She'd throw all this energy into the new project with Chris. Later.

"Darlings!" Phi sang out.

Pippa answered Eric's questioning look. "Laura and her kids."

"Laura?" Eric shifted on the seat and his gaze darted to the door and back to her.

Had his voice gone a little higher? Pippa studied his face. "That's right, you and Laura were engaged."

"Not officially," he said, his eyes fixed on the door. "She broke it off."

Seeing someone else squirm for a while eased her snarled insides. "And why was that? Laura never said."

Eric raised his brow. His smooth, unreadable mask firmly back in place. "Then she must not want you to know."

"Ass," Pippa said.

"Maybe."

Sam clattered into the kitchen, his hair windblown and his cheeks blooming. "Pippa," he yelled. "Phi said you were still here. Mom said you would be gone, but I didn't believe it. Daisy agreed with Mom, but she always does."

He skidded to a stop right next to her chair and stood there, rocking from his heels to his toes.

"Hey, Sam." Pippa cupped his chin. Her nephew was a great kid. Full of life and energy. His mouth firing off faster than a machine gun. She really should spend more time with them. "What have you been up to?"

Sam's eyes went big, his mouth opened on a delighted inhale. "I have a new fort."

"Really?"

"Yes." He nodded and wriggled closer to her. His little body gave off a surprising amount of heat as he pressed against her leg and went into a description of the fort. It seems Blake had come up with the idea, and Aaron's dad had built it. Something about Liam that she didn't catch and Liam's sister. Somewhere in the names flying at her, Pippa got lost.

"I'll be back to fetch them in a couple of hours." Laura hit the kitchen spewing instructions. "Make sure they eat a healthy snack. I'm not sure those cookies you had last time—" She stopped just inside the door and stared over Pippa's head.

"Hello, Laura." Eric stood. "Nice to see you again."

"Eric." His name came out in a garbled squeak. "H . . . hi."

"Is this your son?" Eric motioned to Sam, who was staring at him and catching flies.

Laura nodded.

"Hey, Sam." Eric held out his hand. "I'm Eric."

Sam's shoulders went back and he shoved his small hand into Eric's large, tanned one. "I'm Sam."

Laura dragged in a deep breath and dropped her head. When she raised it again, all the messy bits had been tucked away again. "And this is my daughter, Daisy."

"Hi, Daisy." Eric gave the girl a sexy-as-hell chin lift.

Daisy's mouth dropped open and her eyes widened. Poor

kid. Eric was a whole lot of man candy for a tween to take in. "Hi," Daisy breathed.

"You look well, Eric." Laura snapped her sunglasses shut and slipped them into a case.

A smile played around the corners of Eric's mouth. "You look better than good."

Laura went red. "Yes, well, thank you. I have a wonderful life."

"I can see that."

Eric was so playing with her sister. Pippa felt a small twinge of guilt, like maybe she should rescue Laura or something. This was way too much fun, though. It had been so long since she'd seen her sister anything less than poised and in command.

"I'll go and fetch the toy box." Laura jerked her head at the baize door.

Phi watched her with a smirk. "You do that, dear."

"Right." Laura squared her shoulders. "I'll go and get it."

"Need a hand?" drawled Eric.

"Not from you." Laura went bright red. "I mean, no, thank you."

The baize door swung shut on her twitching ass.

"Do you know my mom?" Daisy ventured closer to Eric. She flushed, as if she couldn't believe her own daring.

Eric smiled at her. "I used to know her very well. I grew up here, I'm Matt's brother."

"Is Matt here?" Sam bounced on his toes.

"He's upstairs in my bathroom," Pippa said.

God, Sam must leave her sister wrung out by the end of the day. The kid gave off more energy than nuclear fusion.

"Cool." Sam ran through the door and his feet clattered up the stairs. "Maaatt!"

Matt's deep rumble sounded in response.

"It's me, it's Sam Johnson and I'm coming to help you." Sam's excited chatter drifted down the stairs.

Daisy rolled her eyes and slouched into the chair opposite. "My brother is so lame. He couldn't help Matt if he tried."

"We men like to pretend we know everything." Eric winked at her. "I'm going to see if my brother needs a hand."

Daisy kept her stare on him as he strolled out of the kitchen. "Did my mom, like, date him or something?"

"Your mom was engaged to him, or something," Phi said.

"Nooo." Daisy glanced at Pippa for corroboration. "What happened?"

"She liked your dad better," Pippa said. Laura hadn't met Daisy's dad until a few years later, but a little lie sometimes didn't hurt. And Laura had liked Patrick better; she'd married him and dumped Eric's fine ass.

"Hmph." Daisy shrugged, but a happy light danced in her eyes. "He's pretty hot, for an old guy."

"He most certainly is." Phi clapped and smiled at Daisy. "What would you like to do today?"

"It's Earth Day." Daisy screwed up her nose. "Mom wants us to do an activity to show our appreciation for the earth."

"What a lovely idea." Phi rocked on her toes. "We would pick some fresh herbs from the knot garden, and dry them. They would look enchanting hanging from the rafters of the kitchen." Phi's eyes glazed over, lost in the beauty of her new plan. "We could pick them, dry them, and tie them with beautifully colored ribbons. Then we could get Matt to suspend them from the rafters."

That would be quite some feat in a couple of hours. Pippa hid her grin.

Daisy leaped to her feet, another captive to the magic

of Phi. "That would look so cool, like an old-fashioned kitchen."

"Where is my gardening bonnet?" Phi glanced around the kitchen.

Daisy danced over to the row of pegs inside the laundry. "Here it is, Phi. Do I have to wear mine?" She reappeared with the object in hand. It had been a few years since Pippa had the misfortune of seeing the gardening bonnet. Carmen Miranda would have blushed at that one. A huge floppy-brimmed hat, festooned with ribbons and drooping under the weight of plastic fruit and silk flowers. There was even a honeybee on a stalk sticking out like an antenna on one side.

Phi placed it tenderly on her head and tied the wide yellow ribbon beneath her chin. "But, of course you must wear yours," she said to Daisy. "I know we have Botox now to keep the march of years at bay, but a good complexion will keep you smooth and fresh for longer."

"Mom says Botox is poison." Daisy produced a pretty straw hat and dragged it over her hair.

"Poison for wrinkles." Phi checked her reflection in the mirror beside the door and grabbed a wicker basket from the floor. "Now, let us gather roses while we may."

"Herbs, Phi." Daisy's voice drifted back into the kitchen. "I thought we were picking herbs."

The baize door opened and Laura edged back into the kitchen with her box of toys. She narrowed her eyes at Pippa as if Pippa had killed the lot of them and buried their bodies in the garden. "Where is everyone?"

"Sam went to find Matt. Phi and Daisy are picking herbs, and Eric went to see if Matt needed help." Pippa kept the prickle out of her voice. Why did Laura always have to look at her like she was in trouble?

"What is Eric doing here?" Laura lowered her voice to a hiss.

"He's home for Jo's wedding." Pippa leaned back in her chair, out of the arc of wrath beaming from her sister's eyes. "Matt came to fix the pipes today and Eric came with him."

"Did you invite him here?" Laura's mouth puckered up.

Pippa stared at her. Laura was seriously losing it. Over Eric Evans. "Of course not. And even if I did, what's the big deal?"

Laura reeled back and gathered up her purse. "You have no idea, Pippa. No idea what that man . . ." She twitched her dress straight and patted her hair into place.

"No, I don't," Pippa said. "Because you never told me why you broke off your engagement."

Laura sniffed and grabbed the case with her sunglasses from her purse. She opened it and snapped the sunglass arms out. "I don't want to talk about it."

There you had it. The same response Laura had given her all those years ago. "Shouldn't you be over it by now?"

"What?" Laura's eyes bulged. "Of course, I'm over it. I'm a happily married woman with two wonderful children. Why would I give Eric Evans a second thought?"

"Why indeed?" Pippa let a smug smile creep over her face. It wasn't often, if ever, she caught Laura on the wrong foot. No, it wasn't nice, or even very grown-up. But damn, it felt good.

Laura nearly took an eye out getting her sunglasses on her face. "I don't want to see him here again." With that, she sailed out of the kitchen, leaving a trail of pissed-off behind her.

Interesting.

Pippa got up to see Laura stop and say good-bye to Daisy before getting into her car and spraying gravel as she left.

"Laura gone?" Eric's voice came from right beside her, and Pippa jumped.

"Just what did you do to my sister?"

"Me?" He pressed a hand to his broad chest. "I'm the injured party. She dumped me."

Pippa tried to see past the naughty glitter in his eyes. "Maybe," she said. "But sometimes a man makes it impossible to stay with him."

"You'll have to ask Laura." Eric folded his arms over his chest.

Damn. There went her chance of finding out anything. Laura would be ten feet buried before she gave Pippa any details.

"Okay, well that's fixed." Matt pushed open the baize door. He stood in the doorway, one hand still on the door, his other full of his toolbox. His gaze flickered from her to Eric and back again. "Everything okay?"

"Yup." Pippa wanted to check if there was a smudge on her face.

Matt did not look happy about her and Eric chatting. "I guess I'll see you around."

"Okay." Laura and Eric had been a welcome distraction, but the ache was back in full force.

Eric's dark eyes gleamed as he looked from her to Matt. "What's going on?"

"Nothing." She and Matt spoke at once.

Eric raised his eyebrows. "There's a whole lot of nothing in this room."

Chapter Twenty-Three

Matt's phone rang as he turned out of Phi's driveway, on his way to the work site. Goddamn plumber had miraculously found time in his schedule, after a few not-at-all-veiled threats. He hit the answer to his Bluetooth without checking caller ID.

Eric glanced across at him and shook his head.

"Mathew?" His mother's quivering voice explained the headshake.

"Hey, Mom, what's up?" He pulled a face at Eric. The guy could have tried harder than a headshake, for his brother.

His mother took a damp breath. "Darling, I know you're really busy, but if you could find some time to come around, I would be very grateful."

Claws tightened around his throat. "I need to get to site, Mom. I've got the plumber there and he—"

"I understand." She gave a watery titter. "Your business is important and you've worked so hard."

Eric rolled his eyes and shifted in his seat.

"I'll come round after I've made sure the plumber is working," Matt said. He pulled a come-on face at Eric.

Eric groaned.

"That would be lovely. Shall I cook dinner?"

Eric shook his head, so hard his hair fell in his eyes.

"Um . . . no." Matt glared at him. What the hell? Dinner was dinner.

"Oh." His mother laughed, not convincingly. "I'm sure you have plans. Can't expect to keep my handsome boy all to myself."

His morning coffee seared the back of his throat. "I'm having dinner with Eric."

Eric widened his eyes in a say-what.

"He's buying." Matt gave his brother an evil grin. "Up at one of those new restaurants on the mountain."

"How lovely," his mother breathed. "I would love to go and have dinner there. It's been so long since I had the chance to get all dressed up."

Don't you fucking dare, Eric beamed at him from the passenger seat.

No worries, there. Matt grinned at him anyway. Let the bastard squirm. "It's a business dinner, Mom."

"What business do you have with Eric?" Her tone sharpened, and he could picture the way her brown eyes would narrow. "Eric's business is all in Denver."

Eric made a "duh" face.

Shit, backpedal fast. He couldn't deal with his mother if he told her about Eric's offer. "Mom, you should know by now, that's guy talk for a boy's night out."

Eric winced and looked like he might lose his breakfast.

Sue him, he was working off the hoof here.

"You're late getting into work today," his mother said. "Is everything all right? Can I do anything for you?"

"No, Mom." He smirked at Eric. His brother was going to spring for great wine as well. And they were taking that kick-ass car of his, too. "I had to pop into Philomene's first."

Eric threw up his hands.

"Oh?" said his mother.

Snap went the trap, and Matt pounded his palm against the steering wheel. Goddamn it, she'd laid down the wires and he went tripping right through them.

"You went there before work?" The way she tightened her mouth came down the phone line. "Interesting when you need to be on-site so urgently."

Matt pulled off the road; his tires kicked up dust and small stones as he jerked the truck to a stop. He balled his hand into a fist. How much damage would it do if he pounded the console? Not worth the effort to get it fixed and he breathed out a big sigh.

"She didn't have any water, Mom." Shit, he sounded like he was pleading with her now. Thirty-six years old and still scared to piss his mommy off. There had to be a word stronger than *pathetic*. *Fucked*. That just about covered it.

"I might not have water," said Cressy.

Matt rolled his head to ease the tension creeping up his neck. He didn't have time to go around there this morning. He had to get to site. "Do you have water?"

"Yes," she whispered. "That's not what I mean."

"Mom, I'll be there after my site visit."

"Fine," she said. "I understand."

Eric hit the End button on the console. "Five, four, three—"

"Fuck it!" Matt jammed the truck in gear and did a one-eighty back onto the road.

"Less than three seconds," Eric said. "That's impressive."

"Shut the fuck up." Eric was right, they both knew it, which was why he wanted to smack his brother in the smug mouth right now.

"We were just there this morning," Eric said. "How bad could it be?"

Matt didn't know. His brain said even Cressy would struggle to find that much drama in the two hours he'd spent at Phi's. His guilt said different. Maybe if he'd gotten there fifteen minutes earlier that first time, right after Dad died, he'd have been able to stop her before she got to the bottom of the Ambien bottle. "You don't know what the hell you're talking about," he said.

"Yeah, I do." Eric shrugged. "She took that overdose seventeen years ago and she never lets you forget it."

Matt veered out of his lane and yanked the truck back on the road. Eric knew about that? He took another quick look at his brother.

Eric raised one dark eyebrow.

"I know, Matt." Eric stared out the windscreen. "She made sure I did."

"Fuck." Cressy had told Eric about that? After he'd gotten her to agree that the other kids shouldn't know because their world was fragile enough. It shouldn't mean that much, no big deal. They were talking ancient history here. But it lit a slow burn in Matt.

The calls to him, all the time, were a pain in the ass. No two ways about that. Every time her number popped up on his caller ID, he got that tight feeling in his gut, but as long as she called him and not the others, it made it bearable.

Sure, she got Nate worked up every now and again, jerked Jo's chain every chance she could, but Cressy saved the worst for him. He didn't like it—hated it, in fact—but if it meant the others got a free pass, he could deal.

"She told you." He had to say the words out loud, to be sure he really understood the first time.

Eric glanced back at him. "You didn't know?"

"No." His hands tightened around the steering wheel, ready to snap it in two. "She told you!"

Matt pulled into his mother's drive so fast Eric grabbed for the dash. "Jesus, Matt. Wanna tell me what this is all about?"

"She told you." How many times had he said that now?

"So she told me." Eric shrugged and smoothed down his three-hundred-dollar haircut. "I don't get why this is a big deal."

Eric wouldn't, but he didn't expect him to. He flung open his door and strode over to the house.

As he yanked open the kitchen door, Cressy spun to greet him with a smile. "Darling!"

His mother was still beautiful. They got their dark hair from her. Jo had inherited that effortless grace that inhabited every movement. Right now, he had to get it together before he lost it. She was still his mother, and his dad had entrusted her into his care when he died.

"You told Eric." He was halfway across the kitchen before he realized it.

Eric stepped into his path before he got to his mother.

Her eyes went huge behind Eric's shoulder. "What did I tell Eric?"

"About the overdose."

Eric held his hands out. "You need to calm the hell down. This is not that big of a deal."

"I never told Eric." Cressy's gaze darted to the side, and she took a step back.

"Yeah, you did, Mom." Eric spoke over his shoulder, keeping his big body between Matt and their mother.

Cressy paled. Her hands fluttered up in a helpless gesture and her big brown eyes swam with tears. "I couldn't help it, Matt. I was so upset one day and Eric was leaving."

"Step back." Eric put his hand in the middle of Matt's chest and exerted pressure.

Matt eased back. As much as he would like to swing at Eric, he wasn't mad at his brother and Eric was right. Scaring a woman was a dick move. He knew better and this was his mother. He took three steps back and put the table between him and Cressy. "Mom." He dragged in a deep breath. He needed to calm down and have this conversation. "We agreed that you wouldn't tell the others."

"Eric was leaving," Cressy sobbed. "He didn't understand how much I needed him. He still doesn't understand."

Matt grabbed the chair back and held on tight. The wooden edge dug into his palms. "You didn't need Eric, you had me."

"Matt, darling, there is no need to be jealous." Her eyes lit up like a birthday candle.

The chair screeched across the floor as his grip tightened. "I'm not jealous."

"Matt?" Eric stepped closer to him. His body tight and controlled, but ready to step in if he had to. Eric was getting ready to tackle him down if he needed to. Fuck! He wasn't this man. He didn't lose his shit and lash out. He was not the sort of guy who needed his brother to maul him to the floor before he got his crap together.

He nodded at Eric. "I'm okay."

Eric's shoulders eased down an inch. He was still wary, but standing down.

"I'm not jealous, Mom. I'm mad as fucking hell."

Cressy's eyes widened.

Yeah, he'd shocked her. Shocked himself a bit while he was at it. "You had no right to tell Eric about the overdose because he had enough to deal with as it was."

Eric had felt guilty as hell, going off to college while Matt stayed at home and held down the fort. He'd nearly pushed Eric out the door to get him to go. Eric had been all for staying with him and helping out. Why hadn't he let him?

Matt looked at his brother. They could have been mistaken for twins. Same height, same build, same hair. Of course, Eric was a smooth son of a bitch and a snappy dresser, he also had a prettier face, but they were cast from the same mold. And it didn't end with the physical similarity. Only a year separated them, not even. Eleven months between the two of them. Yes, Matt had shrugged on the mantle of big brother and forced them all to get on with their lives.

He'd done the right thing. It wasn't that itching at him. If he had to do it again, he would still have insisted Eric go to college, and Nate go into the police academy. Still made Isaac and Jo get good grades and stick with their sports.

Eric and Cressy watched him as he teased the thought out from hiding.

Their dad had died and Matt picked up the entire burden. All seven thousand tons of it. The failing company, the staggering mortgage, the kids, and their mother. Could he have done it differently? Maybe let Eric take up some of the strain and pull in harness with him? Eric had tried. They'd gotten into more than one fight about it. Matt had turned him down every time. Patted himself on the back for being such a good guy as he did it. In the process, he'd cut his brother out, and set himself up as the martyr.

"I'm sorry," he said to Eric.

Eric jerked his head back. His eyes widened as he took on what Matt really meant. "Damn, Matt there is no need for you to apologize to anyone. You did it all, bro. You did it all."

"Maybe I didn't have to."

Eric shrugged, and a small smile tilted his mouth up. "No, you didn't have to, but you did and it is what it is. I'm more interested in what happens now."

"I don't know." His legs went iffy under him and Matt dragged out the chair and flung himself into it. He couldn't be his mother's pillar anymore. When Pippa left she would take the best part of his day with her. Seventeen years he'd spent living a sort of half-life, and he didn't want it anymore. He'd picked a hell of a time for an epiphany. "For the first time in seventeen years, I haven't got a fucking clue."

"Don't swear, Matt." His mother edged closer to him. Her gaze flickered between him and Eric as she tried to get a handle on what was going down.

"They say that's the beginning of wisdom." Eric gave him a smart-ass grin.

Dick! Matt threw his head back and laughed.

"I don't understand the joke." Their mother folded her arms over her chest. Surer of her ground now, she made one of those rapid-fire transitions of mood and persona.

"I'm tired," Matt said to Eric. "I want something else."

Eric snorted. "I'll bet."

"I want . . ." He picked his words carefully, aware of Cressy picking this all up. "My life, whatever that turns out to be. I want something different. More."

Eric nodded and grabbed the chair across from him. "It isn't about this specific offer." He tapped his long fingers on the table. "If you don't want to do it, don't do it." Eric shrugged. "I don't care about that. It's about you doing something you want to do."

"What offer?" Their mother's tone grew shrill as she stepped up to the table.

"I want you to think about what you want," Eric said.

A lump stuck in his throat, and his eyes stung. If Eric didn't stop this shit, he was going to cry. Eric had been there all along, standing on the field and waiting for Matt to shoot him the pass, wide receiver to his quarterback.

"I'll think about it." He grinned as Eric raised his eyebrow. "Properly this time."

Chapter Twenty-Four

Pippa needed a frontal lobotomy. Or a kick in the pants, whatever came first. Here she was, looking at the best career opportunity of her life, everything she'd ever wanted and more, and she was second-guessing herself. She didn't like Ghost Falls, dammit! You couldn't even call the place quaint. It was a tired, dusty collection of lost America in the middle of the mountains. The views were spectacular, but once you'd seen the mountains four thousand times, they lost their appeal.

She couldn't get out of here fast enough once she'd graduated high school. Why the hell was she even thinking about staying? Phi was part of it. Although Phi would kick her ass for even thinking this way. And Laura and her mom. Laura's anger the other day had found a mark. She hadn't been a good sister, or aunt, or even daughter. She'd stayed away, assuaging the guilt with the idea they didn't want to see her anyway. Except, behind Laura's titanium bitch barrier, lurked hurt. There were all hurt, flotsam in the sperm donor's wake. With her mother and Laura, a tight two-man unit, of course she turned to Phi for comfort. Phi had always been her safe place, somewhere she fit and didn't feel like an appendage.

The chat with Phi squatted in her brain and refused to let her go. Sure, Laura had been prom queen and sat on the Founders Day float for three years running, but Pippa had garnered her fair share of attention and wafted out of town on the fumes. This introspection thing sucked. It was easier when you got to tell other people what was wrong with their lives.

And Matt Evans. He was the kicker. He made her want things she'd never even considered before. This thing between her and Matt scared her. It came with a blaring Klaxon warning her back from danger. Somehow, Matt had snuck past light and easy and charged straight for serious.

Commitment. A serious commitment to one man. Something she'd never considered before.

The proposal for the show with Chris glared up at her from the bed. Pages and pages of wonderful ideas and thoughts. Pippa tidied them into a neat bundle, lined up the page numbers, and settled herself to read.

Downstairs the horses' hooves churned up gravel as they were taken out to the large pasture behind the house. Framed by the expanse of the French doors off her bedroom, the horses danced into view, Wheeler Barrows opened the gate, and his charges shot through. Throwing off far more energy than their age would suggest. The ugliest collection of horseflesh in one place, but here and living out their final years under the sunshine of Phi's huge heart.

Wheeler stopped and pressed his face against a scraggly gray mare's. Nice kid. Rumor had it, his mother was pregnant with her tenth. Would making babies be all that bad? Depending on the man making them with you.

Right back to Matt.

She snapped the pages in front of her and locked her gaze on the first line.

Chris Germaine's vision. Pippa forced herself to read the

first line. The woman wrote as beautifully as she spoke.
Her sage brand of clear-thinking wisdom leaked off the
page. The series would pick three women and follow them
over the course of the year. Look at their life challenges,
their current situations, and their dreams. Help each participant find their truth and put them on the path toward living it.
A life changer for whoever took part.

How would Mrs. Barrows feel about something like
this? Did any woman really want all those children?

Pippa read on.

Chris made more and more sense. The series wasn't
aimed at making life changes for the sake of making them,
but helping women find what made them happy and do
that. Even if, like Mrs. Barrows, kicking out one child after
another was what she aspired to. To help her be happy with
her choices.

So, how happy was Pippa with her choices? Or lack of
choices because she was pissing herself off with her dicking
around.

"Pippa?"

What the hell? June's voice sounded wrong, high and
strained.

Pippa shot to her feet and into the hall. "June?"

"Pippa, you better come!" June's voice came from Phi's
bedroom.

Gooseflesh crawled over Pippa's skin as she ran across
the hall. June was talking to Phi, begging her to wake up.
Pippa froze as her head caught up with her. And then she
sprinted into Phi's room.

June leaned over the bed. "Wake up, Philomene, can you
hear me?"

Pippa shouldered June out of the way.

Phi lay on her bed, crumpled onto her side like a tired
child. "What's wrong with her?"

June grabbed up the phone. "I'm calling nine-one-one."

"Phi, it's Pippa." Phi's skin was warm to the touch. Her chest rose and fell as she breathed. But she was pale, horribly pale and waxy. Pippa touched her face, patting her cheek lightly. "Wake up, Phi."

June made the call behind Pippa. What she said barely registering.

"She was looking at her jewelry." June appeared at her elbow. "You know, the special stuff she keeps in there." June pointed to the box tipped on its side, strewing its glittering, gaudy contents all over the riot of roses across Phi's carpet. "The tiara is missing."

"The tiara?" Pippa shook her grandmother by the shoulders. The bones were thin and frail beneath the gold silk Phi wore today. "What tiara?"

"The one she wore to her audience with the queen." June's hands fluttered toward Phi and then she snatched them back again. "Her favorite one."

Why wouldn't Phi wake up?

Pippa shook her harder.

Phi's body shuddered under her hands.

"Don't hurt her," June wailed.

Pippa's vision went black and she dragged in her breath. Hurt her grandmother? Hurt Phi? She turned on June, ready to rip her apart for even suggesting something that stupid.

Tears tracked down June's weathered cheeks. The older woman didn't mean anything by it. She loved Phi.

Dear God, let Phi be all right.

A siren wailed in the distance, and Pippa's heart leaped. They were coming. Help was on the way.

She plucked a quilt off the edge of the bed and laid it over Phi. She didn't know what else to do. What were you supposed to do? Her middle school emergency response lessons flashed through her mind. Check for a pulse? Check nothing obstructed her airway.

Pippa bent down to press her ear to Phi's nose and mouth.

Breathing crackled softly. Her pulse beat beneath the skin of her throat.

Phi had to be all right. She had to be.

The siren wailed closer, splitting the still afternoon with its raucous shout.

Pippa crawled onto the bed beside Phi. Body warmth. Would that help? She didn't know, all she knew is she needed to be close to Phi. Press her life force against her grandmother and hope to reach inside that silent shell.

Phi was fragile in her arms. Old. Aged. Weak.

"Please, Phi." Pippa pressed her lips to Phi's ear. "Please, darling, be okay. I need you. You know how much I need you."

Car brakes screeched and gravel clattered. June's voice rose from downstairs.

She didn't know when June had left the room.

Heavy steps on the stairs and then a hand, strong and big on her shoulder, covering her entire joint.

"Pippa." The hand burned hot against her. "It's Nate. You need to let me see her."

Nate? Phi would have loved to know Nate Evans was in her bedroom. It would have made her year. "I don't know why she won't wake up." Pippa's voice broke on the last. Wet, sticky tears tickled her cheeks and over her jawbone.

"I know, sweetheart." Nate pressed her to the side and away from Phi.

Pippa nearly darted right back.

His grip firmed and he ducked into her eyeline. "I'm gonna see what I can do, Pippa."

His eyes, not quite Matt's eyes, warm and reassuring. Pippa scrambled off the bed.

Nate bent over Phi, hiding her grandmother with his broad back.

Pippa edged to the side, keeping Phi in sight, as if that would keep Phi with her.

"The ambulance is on the way," Nate said. "But she's breathing and her pulse is steady. How long has she been this way?"

She didn't know. Why didn't she know? Pippa's mind scrambled, she had to know, had to tell them all—

"I found her." June stepped up beside her. "It can't have been more than five minutes. I was in her bathroom. She made this strange groan and I heard her jewelry box fall. I came to check on her."

"That's good, right?" Pippa asked Nate. Her hand crept around June's dry, thin fingers.

June squeezed, not hard enough to hurt, but firm and telling Pippa she was not alone.

Her mother and Laura! She needed to call them.

"The tiara is gone," June said. "She was looking for it before she collapsed."

Nate took it all in, his topaz eyes assessing the room, but he stayed beside Phi. "Let's get her taken care of first."

The first responders arrived shortly after. Thumping up the stairs in their big boots, heavily laden with stuff that didn't make any sense to Pippa.

June tugged her back so they could work. Nate stood beside Pippa, his arm an anchor around her shoulders. Pippa leaned into his quiet strength. He made calls as he held her. First talking to her mother, and then another couple of calls.

Pippa kept her eye on the paramedics. They moved smartly, efficiently, talking to Phi in quiet, confident voices.

Then Phi was loaded onto a stretcher, the clear plastic cup of an oxygen mask obscuring her face. The elastic holding it into place made grooves in Phi's cheeks. A collar held her neck still.

"Come on," Nate said. "I'll drive you to the hospital."

"June." Pippa tightened her grip on the other woman.

"I'll be right there, Pippa." June cupped her face. Dry hands scratchy on her cheeks. "I'll make sure everything is done around here. Tell Wheeler what's happening, that sort of thing. You just go and be with her. She loves you best, you know?"

June's words punched straight through her. Kind words that hurt even more than the bad ones. Words that reminded her Phi was everything in her world.

Chapter Twenty-Five

Nate bundled her into his car and followed the ambulance but Pippa missed most of the journey. Scenery flashed past the windows, and Pippa kept her gaze locked on the flashing lights of the ambulance—red, blank, red, blank, red, blank—all across the top.

They drove fast, Nate's siren a steady wail ricocheting through her brain. He took a corner, fast enough to throw her against the straps of the seat belt. From the dash, the radio blipped and crackled in an intermittent stream that made her want to scream.

The hospital rose up in front of the hills behind it. Nate took her around to the front, while the ambulance thundered down the channel marked EMERGENCY. Bodies in white, green, and blue flew into action. Swarming around the stretcher. The stretcher that was Phi.

Nate took her by the elbow and walked her to the admissions desk.

Hospitals all smelled the same. A sickening waft of antiseptic and illness that clung to your skin. Fluorescent lighting bathed the admissions desk in an unearthly glow. Pippa answered the questions. Luckily, the hospital had a record of Phi because Pippa didn't have the answers to half of the questions.

The admissions clerk looked mildly bored as she typed in all the particulars. Pushed papers at Pippa to sign. An army of troll dolls grinned maniacally from the top of the woman's monitor.

Nate's hand held hers in a warm clasp. It was all that stopped her from knocking those stupid grinning trolls to the floor. Would the bitch behind the keyboard pay attention then?

Her anger wasn't reasonable. A part of her brain kept it under control. Nate's hand was the lifeline of sane she clung to.

Finally, they were done and Nate rose and tugged her to her feet.

"Pippa." Matt's voice came down the stark white passage toward them.

He was in front of her. The blue and green stripes on his plaid shirt filled her vision. He looked like a lumberjack.

He was here.

Nate let go of her hand and she walked into Matt's arms.

They folded around her in a waft of Matt and cotton, and a warm press of strength. His chest felt hard against her cheek, a button from his shirt stamping an imprint from where she leaned.

"How is she?" Matt spoke to Nate over her head.

"We don't know," Nate said. "They admitted her into ER, now we wait."

"What happened?"

"According to June, she got upset over one of her pieces of jewelry being stolen," Nate said.

"Her tiara." Pippa raised her head. "It was a tiara. She wore it when she met Queen Elizabeth. Of England."

"You'll stay here." Nate glanced at Matt then looked at

her. "Matt is going to stay with you. I'll get a description of the tiara from June. You stay here and concentrate on Phi. Okay?"

"Okay?" Pippa burrowed back into Matt. She hadn't realized until his arms wrapped around her how much she needed to be right here.

"Hey." Matt pressed a kiss against her temple. "You doing okay?"

"Nope." Tears threatened again, but she blinked them away.

Matt led her to the waiting area outside ICU and they took a seat.

A young woman with a wan, weary face gave them a sad smile. Pippa smiled back, two strangers united in an intensely vulnerable moment.

Matt put his arm around her and Pippa leaned into his side. He knew what Phi meant to her, there was no need to explain or even speak. He handed her a bottle of water and Pippa thanked him and took a sip. It gave her hands something to do while they waited.

Heels clipped on the hard floor, hurrying in their direction. Her mother headed for the nurses' station before catching sight of her and Matt. She changed direction and bore down on them.

Pippa stood to greet her.

Emily almost looked disheveled in her jeans and T-shirt. She held out both hands to Pippa. "I was in my garden when the sheriff called. Any news?"

Pippa took her mother's soft, elegant hands and pressed lightly. "They took Phi in a few minutes ago. We're waiting."

"What happened?" Emily shook her head at Matt's offer of a seat. Her gaze darted between them, a small frown crinkling the skin between her eyes.

"We're not sure." Matt took over the explanation for her. "June says Phi found her tiara missing."

"The one she wore to meet the queen?"

Matt nodded. "Apparently, it upset Phi so much she collapsed."

"Oh God." Emily plunked into the seat beside Pippa.

"June found her," Pippa said. "She was unresponsive." Her voice shook on the last word and she blinked to clear the tears. *Dear God, let Phi be all right.* Her grandmother was seventy-eight and had lived her life well. Perhaps she should have tried to stop Phi from drinking so much, or running around like a woman half her age. You forgot when you were with her that she wasn't a young woman anymore.

Emily covered her eyes with her hand. "Oh God."

"Nate is looking into the tiara," Matt said.

"Who cares about a bloody tiara?" Emily glared at him, her mouth set in a tight line.

"Phi cares," Pippa said.

Emily's shoulders drooped. "Yes, my mother cares about her tiara. She sent me a picture of her meeting the queen in Buckingham Palace."

Her mother's hand found hers and Pippa held on tight. For all their differences, Emily was her mother and she loved her. She needed her mom right now, and her mom needed her.

"I used to steal the tiara and play dress up with it," Pippa said.

"Did you?" Emily managed a small smile. "That must have been fun."

"It was."

A doctor came in and they all jerked to attention. He offered them a brief glance before moving to speak with the young woman. The woman followed the doctor out of the waiting room.

"I hated that tiara," her mother said. "When she went to meet the queen it was my sweet sixteen, and I wanted her with me."

Phi had thrown a sweet sixteen for Pippa. The Folly had groaned under a ton of pink and silver decorations. Jammed to the hilt with teenagers from Ghost Falls and Phi's friends from her opera days. She suddenly pictured a much younger version of her mother sitting alone while her mother did other things. How Emily must have resented that.

Pippa squeezed her mother's hand. "Phi said something strange to me before she . . ." Pippa couldn't find the words to describe this morning. She waved her hand around the waiting room. "She said she came home to make up for the time she spent away."

Her mother stilled, and then shot out of her seat and paced the length of the waiting area. "I'm going to get some coffee. Would anyone like coffee?"

"I'll get it." Matt stood up. "You stay here in case there's news."

Her mother stood in the doorway, took a step to follow Matt, and then turned on her heel and paced to the window overlooking the parking lot.

The view was dismal. Probably most people sitting here didn't give a crap what was outside, every fiber of their being focused on what was going on inside. The door to the waiting room faced onto the nurses' station. One nurse sat behind the desk, quietly moving charts about and making entries in her computer. Others came and went, some even glanced into the waiting room. Most went about their business as if the waiting relatives didn't exist.

"I couldn't reach Laura," her mother said. "I left a message on her phone and another one with Patrick."

She came back down to sit beside Pippa and took her hand. "How are you doing?"

"Not so good." Pippa dragged in a deep breath. Her mother's caring gaze stripped her bare and she looked away. "I never thought of her as getting old."

"None of us did." Emily patted her hand. "My mother is a force of nature, wild and larger than anything else. I couldn't believe Nate was talking about her when he called."

"Are you okay?"

"No." Her mother breathed the word out on a shaky breath. "There is so much . . . stuff I want to say to her. I drove here and all the way I kept thinking about how that doesn't really matter anymore. All I wanted was to be here. Oh, Pippa . . ." A sob shook her mother's frame. "What if she—"

"We can't think like that." Pippa wrapped her arm around her mother's shoulders. "We just can't."

Her mother took a deep breath and gently pulled away. "You're right. We need to stay positive, focus on the moment." She sat up straighter, and glared at the nurses' station. "Surely they can give us some information."

Her mother got up and stalked over to the nurses' station, elegant and contained, but every inch of her shrieking intent. She had inherited that from Phi. Emily conferred with the nurse behind the computer and came back again. "They say we should have news soon. The nurse says she's stable for now."

Pippa's breath whooshed out of her in relief. Stable was good, right?

Matt returned with a tray of coffee and handed them out. "Any news?"

"She's stable." Her mother took her coffee. She accepted two milks and two packets of sugar and upended them into her cup.

Pippa blinked at her. She'd never seen Emily have her coffee anything but black.

"Mrs. Turner?" A young doctor entered the waiting area.

Pippa started so violently, hot coffee splashed over her hand.

Matt took the cup from her and wiped the hot liquid away with a napkin. He touched a finger to her cheek. "Easy, sweetheart."

"I'm Mrs. Turner." Her mother stepped forward.

"Your mother is stable and resting," he said. He looked so young, too young to have to make the sort of life-and-death decisions that fell on his shoulders. "We think she had a minor stroke, but we'll know more once we've run more tests."

Stroke! The word clattered around Pippa's brain.

Matt eased the coffee cup out of her shaking hand.

"Can I see her?" her mother asked. Thank God one of them was functioning.

The doctor nodded. "We've sedated her for the moment. But you can go and see her."

Her mother turned and held out her hand to Pippa. "Come, darling. Let's go and see your grandmother."

Like she was six years old, Pippa took her mother's hand and trailed her down the passage in the doctor's wake. "She's in very good shape for her age," the doctor said. He frowned and looked down at his chart. "It says here that she's sixty-eight but . . ."

"She's seventy-eight," Pippa said.

Her mother squeezed her hand and turned her charming smile at the doctor. "You will find, Doctor, that my mother is whatever age she says she is."

The doctor led them into a room three down from the nurses' station.

Pippa stared at the frail figure in the bed. That couldn't

be Phi, lying there under those hospital blue sheets with
tubes and wires springing out of her and hooked into vari-
ous machines.

The suck and hiss of a ventilator cut the quiet of the
room, combined with the muted beep from a heart monitor.

"Is this all necessary?" Pippa asked.

The doctor pulled an apologetic face. "Given her age,
we thought it wise to monitor her closely for the next
twenty-four hours."

The first twenty-four hours, the most critical. Pippa ran
the numbers in her head. How far into that twenty-four
was Phi?

She and her mother approached the bed, their hands
growing slick where they gripped.

"Hi, Mom." Her mother dropped Pippa's hand and cradled
Phi's unresponsive one, careful of the drip attached to the
back of it. The veins on Phi's hand stood out blue and
strident against her parchment-pale skin. "I'm here and
Pippa is with me."

The ventilator pump sucked in more air, held it, and
released. A drip hung suspended on an iron pole beside the
bed. Pippa squinted at the label and then gave up. She
wouldn't know what the hell they were giving Phi anyway.

"You gave us a horrible fright," her mother said. "But
the doctor says you're doing much better and Pippa and I
are here."

Pippa slipped to the other side of Phi and touched her arm
lying above the covers. Phi's makeup was smeared down her
face. Someone had attempted to wipe it off and done a piss-
poor job of it. Pippa dug out a pack of facial wipes from her
purse. Her mother motioned for a second one, and together
they carefully removed the streaks of black-and-pink glitter
from Phi's cheeks and under her eyes.

Phi looked vulnerable, fragile, and every one of her years

when they were done, but it was better than the macabre smears from before.

"She needs one of her crazy nightgowns," her mother said. "She will be mad as hell if she wakes up in this hospital gown."

Pippa choked on a half sob, half laugh. "She says blue makes her look sallow."

"She's right." Her mother smoothed back the hair from Phi's forehead. "Stubborn old broad."

They stayed until the sounds of the shift changing made Pippa aware it was night outside. Her mother spoke to the doctor again.

Matt was still waiting for her, his elbows resting on his knees, a full cup of coffee in his hands. He stood when she came in. Some of the dull dread in Pippa's middle unraveled. "How is she?"

Pippa told him what the doctor had said.

Her mother came back into the waiting room. "Matt, I want you to take Pippa home."

Say what? Pippa rounded to argue with her mother. She wanted to be here, near to Phi.

"I'm going to spend the night," her mother said. "Go home, get some rest. In the morning put some things together for her and bring them back when you come."

"I—"

"There's nothing you can do." Her mother cupped her cheek, her face soft and understanding. "I know you want to stay, but I'll be here and I'll call if anything changes. This could be a long wait, darling. I might need you later. You heard the doctor, she's sedated and she's going to need all our strength when she wakes." She turned back to Matt. "Make sure she eats something."

"I'll be back soon." Pippa didn't care what her mother said, she was not staying away long.

Her mother gave her a wan smile. "I know you will. Go and see to the house. June will want to know how she is. Then come back."

She left the waiting room.

"I don't want to go." Pippa resisted the gentle pressure Matt put on her arm.

"Sweetheart." Matt turned her to face him. "She needs this. Your mother needs this and she is Phi's daughter."

"But they're not close."

Matt's eyes warmed. "Exactly. Your mother needs to do this, and you need to let her."

It made a weird sort of sense. Pippa glared at him as the battle waged inside her. She was Phi's "special girl," Phi was sick and she needed to be here. Then again, that was what she needed. What would Phi need?

Her daughter. The answer rang as clear as a bell in her mind. Phi had come back to Ghost Falls on her retirement to rebuild the bridges she'd shattered over the course of her career.

"I am coming back first thing in the morning," she said to Matt.

A slow, sweet smile spread over his beautiful face. "Of course you are, and I'm going to bring you."

"You don't have to do that." Pippa said the words, but her heart wasn't in them. Having him with her was like a rock in a wild sea. Part of her wanted to cling like a barnacle.

"Babe." He pulled her in close. "Where the fuck else would I be?"

Chapter Twenty-Six

Pippa ended the call, and wiped her clammy hands on her thighs. She'd either made the biggest mistake or the best decision of her life. Isn't this where she was supposed to feel all peaceful and resolved? How did she do that when the two parts of her were tearing her in half? The job with Chris had been her dream job, everything she'd worked so hard to achieve, but her family needed her here and for the first time in her life she needed to put them first. All night long the same question had been hammering through her brain. What if next time something like this happened, she wasn't here?

Outside her bedroom window, horses hung out in the pasture cropping grass. God, it must be nice to be like that. Someone to feed you, make decisions for you.

Chris Germaine had listened and said very little as Pippa explained why she needed to stay here in Ghost Falls for the indeterminate future. Accepted her decision not to go forward with quiet understanding.

Pippa needed to get some clothes on her ass. Matt would be here any minute to take her to the hospital. How much of a part had he played in her decision? Stupid to be even thinking that way, when they'd agreed to call it quits. But if she stayed, would things be different?

Fuck, can anyone say "Pippa is Pathetic"? Don't all yell at once, now.

Surprisingly, it was her mother who had pushed her decision into the end zone. Seeing her mother at the hospital, so desperate to make a connection with Phi, had been the clincher. Emily had lived two minutes away from Phi for years and failed to heal the breach between them. It had taken Phi's brush with death to make her realize time wasn't limitless. You couldn't live your life like you had another one tucked away in the pantry.

Maybe the Ray thing did have a silver lining. It had forced her back to Ghost Falls long enough to see what she'd been glancing past for years. She didn't have a relationship with her sister. She and Laura shared a fight cage, and they were getting too old to carry on like this. Pippa didn't have any huge hopes for a Hallmark moment with Laura. She couldn't see them falling into each other's arms and weeping away the scar tissue. She still had to try to find something better than what they had. Build real connections with Daisy and Sam that weren't based on glamour or expensive gifts.

Her job had paid well and she had enough money saved to sit still for a while and plan the next step of her life. And Phi, wonderful, crazy, infuriating diva that she was. Phi was getting old, there might not be that many years left for them.

Pippa dragged on a pair of jeans. Her clothes perfectionist kicked in and steered her away from a T-shirt and into a draped silk jersey top. She slipped her feet into a pair of heeled sandals. Then changed her mind and went with flats. She didn't have enough experience with hospitals to know what worked best. Why did she care about her shoes, again? Because she didn't want to dwell on the decision she'd just made.

"Hey." Matt stood in her doorway. "June let me in. You ready to go?"

The pressure in her chest eased up. Matt had that effect on her. He walked into a room and her shoulders felt lighter. She nodded and grabbed her purse.

"We're taking June to the hospital with us," Matt said as he followed her down the stairs.

Pippa nodded. June must be going out of her mind right about now.

Matt caught her arm and stopped her. He turned her to look at him. His topaz eyes stripping right past her defenses. "What's going on?"

She hadn't sorted it out in her head, yet. "I'm worried about Phi."

"I know that." Matt frowned and studied her. "I get the feeling it's something else though."

"It's nothing." Telling him would make it more real. Also, she wasn't sure how he would react to the news she was staying in Ghost Falls. With the Phi thing, she couldn't take another blow to the gut. The idea that Matt might panic, or be freaked out by her staying, was one she couldn't get her head around right now. Maybe later. Or maybe never.

The ride to the hospital was largely silent. June asked a few questions, which Pippa answered. She stared out the window to avoid the way Matt kept glancing at her.

At June's insistence, they brought a small packed lunch for Emily, and Pippa brought her mother a change of tops.

They found Emily sitting beside Phi in her room. The nurses didn't want too many people in the room, so Pippa said hello to her mother, greeted Phi, and let June have her moment.

Matt was on the phone in the waiting area. "Okay, well, keep trying," he said, and hung up. "Still can't find Laura. Patrick wasn't much help. He thought she was with Phi."

Weird. You could set your watch by Laura. Where the hell could her sister be?

June entered the waiting area, sobbing softly in her hands.

"Why don't you go and see Phi," Emily said to Matt as she hugged June's frail frame.

Matt nodded and left them alone.

"She doesn't look like the Diva." Out of her pocket June produced a crumpled Kleenex and blew her nose. "But she looks peaceful."

"I brought her stuff." Pippa held up the bag in her hand. "As soon as she wakes up, we'll repair her a little."

"I knew she was upset about the tiara." June wiped away tears and more crept down her cheeks. "I shouldn't have left her alone."

"You were only in her bathroom." Pippa would never understand the bond between these two women. Maybe because she'd never taken the time to form those sorts of bonds for herself. When her life had collapsed, Pippa had no June to lean on. No June, just a desperate trip home to Phi. Another point on her list for staying in Ghost Falls.

"But I knew she was upset." June's shoulders heaved up and down in a huge sigh.

"She gets upset a lot," Pippa said. "You know what she's like. It's hard to tell sometimes when she's really pissed or just doing Carmen."

"Ain't that the truth." June tucked her soggy Kleenex back into her pocket. "When Matt comes back, I'll ask him to take me back to the Folly. When she comes home, the

Diva is going to expect everything to be perfect. I can do that for her."

Matt came back shortly after. He pulled Pippa straight into his arms. "She's going to be fine, babe."

Pippa leaned into the spicy, warm heat of him and let it enfold her. For a minute, she let herself be there and be comforted. They might not be an "it," but Matt was a good guy. The sort a girl wanted by her side in a crisis. In happy times, he wouldn't be bad either. But you couldn't rely on the happy times. They didn't amount to anything when a man decided being part of a family wasn't for him.

"I'll take June home," Matt murmured against her temple. "I need to check on a couple of things, and then I'll be back."

"Okay." What the hell was the point in even making a token protest when she wanted him here for as long as he would stay? How long would that be?

Pippa walked into Phi's room. The shock of seeing Phi like this had lessened enough to make breathing a bit easier. She passed her mother a bottle of water and a sandwich. "If I have to eat, so do you."

Emily managed a wan smile. "I'm not sure I can eat."

"Try." Pippa pressed the sandwich back. "Any more news?"

Emily nodded. "They ran a brain scan, now they're not sure it even was a stroke. They're thinking it might have been some sort of seizure."

"That's good news, right?"

"Yes." Her mother's lips quivered and she pressed them tightly together and cleared her throat. "Have you spoken to Laura?"

"Not yet." Laura's cell was turned off too. Another anomaly for Power Mommy. Okay, staying in Ghost Falls was not enough to mend the gap. She would actually have to put some more effort into getting over her shit with her sister if she expected this to work. "Do you have any idea where she could be?"

Emily nibbled at her sandwich. "She does this from time to time."

"She does?"

"The pressure of being a mother, and all her committees and charities, gets a bit much sometimes. I think she goes to a spa in the new casino." Emily wrapped up the sandwich with barely a bite taken out of one corner. "Which reminds me, I need to make some calls and tell people where I am."

"I can do that for you."

"No." Her mother stood and tweaked her jeans straight. "People will only worry if they don't hear from me." She put her purse on her shoulder and strode for the door. "You will stay, won't you? I can rely on you?"

Pippa nodded. Baby steps.

Phi had more color in her face since Pippa had left. She looked peaceful, as if she was only sleeping. A beam of sun streamed through the window and cast an oblong patch of warmth across the bottom of the bed.

"Mom's stepped out to make some phone calls." It felt a little stupid to be talking to an inanimate Phi. This is what you were supposed to do in these circumstances, right? Keep talking, making a connection with your loved one. "Laura will be here soon."

Laura wouldn't stay gone for much longer. Supermom— *Stop it.*

Laura's love for her children would bring her back soon.

A nurse came in and checked the monitors. She smiled kindly at Pippa. "We're going to take her off the ventilator now, if you'd like to step outside."

Pippa got up, her legs creaky underneath her, and left the room.

Her mother was in the waiting area, speaking into the phone and making a list. Funny, she got that from her mom. Phi had never made a list in her life. Not one she'd glanced at after it was made, anyway.

Emily ended her call and looked up.

"They're taking Phi off the ventilator."

"Ah." Emily turned the page in her book and ticked something off. "The doctor said they would do that, as soon as they were sure she was breathing for herself. While I was waiting for you, I made notes of all the things he told me."

Pippa took the seat next to her mom and peered over her shoulder at the list. "I make lists too."

"Do you?" Emily raised her brows.

"Oh, yes." Pippa dug in her bag and pulled out her iPad. "Only I do them electronically." She tapped an icon and pulled it up. "See, and it interfaces with my contacts and calendar."

Emily took the iPad from her and studied it. "Really?"

Look at them, bonding over software for the terminally anal. Pippa bit back a grin. "I use the reminder feature a lot." Pippa showed her mother.

"Well." Mom glanced down at her notebook. "It seems I am horribly behind the times."

"It's the list that matters," Pippa said.

"Yes, it is." Mom smiled at her. A soft light shone in her mother's eyes, tender and hopeful. "Do you think you perhaps get that from me?"

"I'm sure of it," Pippa said.

"All right, then." Emily nodded and put her notebook away. "Do you organize your closet?"

"Like a boss." Pippa grinned. "By item and then by color."

"No." Mom's eyes widened. "Short-sleeved shirts first."

"Then long-sleeved." Pippa nodded. "Followed by pants, skirts, short dresses, and then long dresses."

"Outerwear, coats and jackets at the end." Her mother laughed.

Pippa grinned back at her. "Because you put those on last."

"And one never hangs one's knits."

"Never."

Mom went silent, fiddling with the seam of her jeans. "How did I not know this about you, Pippa?"

"I don't know." Pippa shrugged, but she did know why. Mom and Laura, the dynamic pair with Pippa on the outside. She didn't want to fight and ruin this rare moment like all the other opportunities they'd let go winging past. "Maybe partly because I didn't tell you."

Mom nodded, an unguarded look of sadness pulling at her face. "But mostly because I never took the time to notice." She grabbed Pippa's hand in a clench and brought it to her cheek. "I can do better, Pippa. I can be more than this angry woman."

"We all can."

The nurse entered the waiting area. "We're done."

"Good," Emily said. She took a deep breath and released Pippa's hands. When she stood, Impenetrable Emily was back in place.

Phi woke up late into the evening. Her breathing hitched a couple of times, her eyelids flickered and then opened. She would have been disappointed in the lack of drama.

Her mother and Pippa pressed closer, grabbing Phi's hands.

"Mother," Emily said. "You're in the hospital. You had a bad turn."

Phi frowned at her. She closed her eyes, and opened them again. Her gaze darted from Emily to Pippa and around her.

"What am I doing in a hospital?" Her voice was croaky from the tubes and Pippa brought her a sip of water. She guided the straw to Phi's mouth.

Phi's eyes fixed on her face. "You look fatigued and as if you have been weeping. Was that for me?"

"You know it." Pippa smiled and took the straw away.

Phi glanced at Emily. "Am I dying?"

"Not yet." Emily touched Phi's cheek. "But you scared the life out of me."

Phi grunted and glanced around the room again. "How do I look?"

"Like a woman who's had a brush with death," Emily said.

"Good God." Phi raised her hand to her temple, stopped, and stared at the drip. "Will you do something about that?"

She asked Emily and not Pippa, a strange vulnerability on her features.

Emily blinked rapidly. "Of course I will. Pippa brought you some things."

"Darling." Phi glanced at her and beamed. "You always did know what I would like."

"I'm sure Pippa could help you." Emily folded her hands in front of her and stepped back from the bed.

"Indeed she could," Phi said. "But in times like these, a woman needs her daughter."

Emily blinked. Her mouth dropped open and she shut it quickly.

Phi glanced at Pippa, a world of meaning in one brief

flash of her eyes. Pippa wasn't hurt, and she smiled back at
Phi. Her grandmother wasn't rejecting her. But this was a
time she needed to be with her daughter, because her
daughter desperately needed it to be so. "I'll wait outside
until you're resplendent again."

Pippa might have convinced herself nothing had happened to her grandmother.

In forty minutes, her mother had worked magic on Phi.
How they persuaded the hospital to let them do it, Pippa
was clueless. She shrugged it off. When you lived with Phi
long enough, you got used to strange things happening
around you.

Phi reclined in her hospital bed, resplendent as only a
diva can be. Her hair was coiffed, her makeup flawless—
well, flawless for Phi, which meant far too much glitter and
color—and she was swathed in nasty green velvet. It
seemed unkind to call it cat-vomit green, given the danger
Phi had just faced, but cat vomit came closest to that
ghastly color.

And her mother and Phi had their hands clasped.

Pippa had never seen her mother look so . . . peaceful.
Her striking face lovely in its serenity.

"Everything okay?" Pippa glanced from one to the other
of them. That must have been some makeover session
they'd had.

"Everything's fine." Phi waved her hand. Not with quite
as much energy as normal, but enough to warm the cold
place in the pit of Pippa's belly.

"What happened?" Pippa looked at her mother.

"We—"

"Never you mind." Phi glared at her. "That is between

Emily and me. Suffice it to say, we had a long overdue conversation."

"You need to rest." Emily stood and smoothed the covers. "I'll be back in the morning."

"Thank you, sweet girl." Phi caught her daughter's hand. "I do love you."

Emily flushed a little and shifted her feet. "And I love you."

"Mom." A familiar voice intruded from the doorway.

Pippa snapped her head round. Laura, at long fucking last.

Her sister looked as composed as ever. Perfectly dressed in linen pants, a beautifully tailored blouse with just a pop of color in her shoes and accessories. "Is everything all right?"

"We left messages for you." Emily's mouth tightened.

It felt kind of good not to be on the receiving end of the disapproval for once. "Everything is fine." Pippa took pity on her sister. "Phi seems to be making a miraculous recovery."

"Good peasant stock." Phi beamed from the bed. "None of this interbreeding to weaken the genes."

In fact, Phi looked altogether too well and too pleased with herself. Maybe Pippa would take that young doctor aside and ask him some more questions.

Laura frowned slightly as she glanced at Pippa. "What happened? The messages were hard to decipher. One minute she's collapsed, then she's had a stroke."

"Stroke." Phi snorted. "I had an episode. It is to be expected from one of my artistic temperament."

Ah, hell yeah. A little heart-to-heart with Baby Doctor was definitely in the cards. "They're not sure," Pippa said. "All her tests came back fine, but she was definitely unconscious when the paramedics found her."

"Oh, for God's sake." Laura tossed her purse onto the sole chair beside the door. "I thought she was dying."

"She is right here," Phi sang out. "And she does not like to be referred to in the third person."

Laura wedged her skinny hips in next to her purse. "I got such a fucking fright."

"Laura!" Emily blinked at her oldest daughter.

"Well, I did." Laura raised a shaking hand to push back a strand of hair. "All those messages."

That had to be bad. Pippa wasn't sure what hers had said, but she'd been in shock at the time and not exactly minding her words. "Where were you?"

"At the spa." Laura straightened her spine. "I make it a point to do something for me, once a month. Patrick insists on it." She glared at Pippa as if daring her to contradict her statement.

Pippa was all for women taking the time out to treat themselves. She shrugged and turned back to her mother. "Matt's waiting outside to take us home, do you want to stay a bit longer? Now that Laura's here."

"I can give you a ride home," Laura said.

"I have my car here, but I think I'd like to stay, for a bit." Emily perched beside Phi on the bed.

Pippa leaned over and kissed Phi's forehead. Patchouli oil wafted up and over her. The smell of Phi, and comfort. She almost lost it then. Phi was going to be all right. It was almost too much to take in. Exhaustion slammed into her. "I love you," she whispered past the tears gumming up her throat. "Don't you ever pull this shit on me again. I need you. I forbid you to die on me."

Phi patted her cheek with a naughty grin. "Why do you need me, when you have a handsome stud outside waiting to take you home?"

Oh, yes indeedy, time for Doctor Not-Quite-Old-Enough-to-'fess up.

"I'll see you in the morning," she said. "Don't give them

too much crap. They're busy here. This is a hospital, they have sick people who need attention."

Matt straightened from where he leaned against the wall outside Phi's room. He jerked his chin at her. "You ready?"

"Yup." Pippa slid her hand into the one he held out. "I'm not sure we haven't all been had. She looks great."

Matt raised a brow and narrowed his eyes in the direction of Phi's room. "You think she faked it?"

"We'll never know for sure." Pippa let the warm, rough clasp of his fingers enfold her hand. Their hands fit, like a lock and a key.

They talked a bit on the way home. But it was all small talk, nothing of what was really going through her head.

A knot tightened in Pippa's belly as they got closer and closer to the Folly. This new development in her life was all fresh. Where did that leave her and Matt? Would he find out she was staying, start mumbling excuses, and back out the door? She didn't want him to leave. Tonight. Or maybe any other night.

He pulled up outside the front door, and got out to open her door.

Pippa hopped to the ground.

Matt stayed where he was, wedging her between himself and the truck. His eyes glowed gold as they lingered on her face. "You okay?"

"Tired." She dredged up a smile. She really wanted him to stay. Needy was new to her. She didn't much care for it, but that didn't make it go away.

He brushed the back of his fingers over her jaw. "Get some rest."

"Actually . . ."

"Yes."

"I'm not that tired." She shrugged and tried to keep it

light. "Have you got time for a cup of coffee? A glass of wine?"

"No." He shook his head and curled his fingers through her hair to cup the back of her head. "I don't want coffee. Or wine."

"Beer?"

His breath fanned along her bottom lip. Heat radiated off his powerful body and set up an answering pulse low in her belly.

"Uh-uh." He shook his head. His fingers tightened on her scalp. "Am I an ass for hitting on you right now? Given everything—"

"No." Hitting on her was good. It meant he wanted to stay. She gripped his belt on either side of his hips. There was far too much distance between them. "Stay?"

The word hung in the tiny wisp of air between the mouths.

"God, yes." He crushed the words between their lips, his tongue plunging into her mouth, slick and wet and demanding.

Pippa's knees melted under the rush of heat. Her nipples peaked and she pressed them against him, wrapping her arms around his neck to make sure he stayed where he was.

He edged her away from the open car door. His mouth hot and hungry.

The door slammed.

"You sure?" He leaned back, his color high, his eyes hot and hard.

Was she sure? Sure about the future, no. What this meant? No goddamn idea. But sure that she needed his body on hers, driving into her, surrounding her with his heat? Hell, yeah.

They stumbled through the door, locked at the mouth and shedding clothes as they went. Somehow, they made it up the stairs, Pippa's nerve endings throbbing with need.

Her back hit the bed and he came down on top of her, big, strong, and hot to the touch. His chest pressed into her breasts, the hard jut of his cock through his pants resting between her thighs.

"It seems indecent." He tore his mouth from hers, sat back, and toed off his boots.

Pippa giggled as she followed his sight line to the dancing butterflies on organza. "Phi would have changed it into bordello red years ago if I let her."

His boots hit the floor with a *thunk* and he was back, his weight pushing her deeper into the bed. "Don't let her. It's kind of kinky, like deflowering the virgin."

Pippa arched into him as he slid his fingers between her thighs, locking on the wet heat throbbing at her core.

Grabbing her wrists, he raised her hands to either side of her head. "Keep those there. Let me love you."

Oh God, please, let him love her.

A searing trail of wet kisses marked his passage down her neck, nibbling lightly over her sensitized skin as he homed in on her nipples.

The hot suck of his mouth had her writhing against him.

Pippa wrapped her legs around his hips, and dug her heels into his ass. She needed him closer. His cock throbbed thick and hard against her, and Pippa shifted against him, restless to have him inside her, filling her.

He swirled his tongue through her navel.

Pippa jacked to a sitting position and giggled. She tried to cover up her belly button, but he snagged her wrists again. He raised one dark eyebrow over his glowing gold eyes. "Where did I say these go?"

Pippa dropped her arms up beside her head again.

"Good girl." He continued his slow kiss down her belly and into the tight nest of curls covering her sex.

Pippa's thighs dropped open. Sparks of anticipation shot through her body as he looked at her for a moment, blowing softly on her wetness, before lowering his head to feast.

She rocked and writhed against his mouth as he wedged her legs apart with his shoulders. His tongue dipped and swirled, first over her opening and then up to flick against her clitoris. He took it slow and easy, working her over with tongue, lips, and teeth until she was a hot, panting mess under him.

Her orgasm hit her fast, hard, and dirty, driving her body right off the bed.

Matt sat back on his heels, his glowing gaze on her. "I love making you come."

"Do it again." Pippa's laugh came out low and raspy.

Matt crawled up her body. "Yes, ma'am."

She needed him inside her, and Pippa wrapped her legs around his hips.

He took a moment for the condom and then he was sliding inside her, slow and sure.

Pippa's body welcomed him home, holding him tight inside her.

He took his time, deep, slow thrusts that wrapped her in a slow, steady build. Her climax started way down inside her, sweeping her along as it crashed over her. Matt was right there with her, riding the wave down again.

Tears pricked the back of her eyes as he shifted to her side and got rid of the condom. She couldn't pretend this was just sex anymore. With Matt, it was a soul-deep connection, a celebration of life that she needed like her next breath.

Chapter Twenty-Seven

Pippa lay beside Matt, their breath mingling in the warm night air, moonlight painting streaks of light over the bottom of her bed, tangling through the organza drapery and playing happily across the beautiful lines of Matt's body.

She was starving. "You hungry?"

"I could eat."

She propped herself onto her elbow and looked down at him.

His gaze flickered over her naked body. He stroked the line of her shoulder, over her breast and down her belly to her hip. "You're beautiful."

Damn. How the hell was she supposed to keep it together when he said stuff like that? She rolled away and got to her feet. "I'll see what there is to eat downstairs."

"There's plenty." He climbed out the other side of the bed. "Ghost Falls has been dropping off dishes all day. June put them in the fridge, but there's enough there to keep you fed for a long time."

"Really?" It was the sort of thing that happened in small towns and you forgot about.

He nodded, snagged his jeans, and pulled them on. A tantalizing V peered at her from where he left them only halfway buttoned. "Don't eat the ones in the pink dishes with the flowers and swirly crap down the side."

"Why?" Pippa tugged on a pair of lounging pants and a camisole before she decided to forget about food for the rest of the night.

"Bella made those." He pulled a face. "God love her, but the woman should be kept away from the kitchen."

Now, that was just plain rude. "She went to the trouble of making it. It's the thought that counts."

"Even when that thought is covered in those little pink marshmallows?"

Okay, maybe that would be different. "Surely she doesn't . . . ?"

"Everything." He raised both brows at her.

"It doesn't matter if she can't cook." Pippa felt the need to defend her soon-to-be BFF. "Bella has lots of other great qualities."

He grinned. "All of them covered in fluffy pink and sweet."

Men. They never managed to look beyond the surface. Bella may be all Tinkerbell on the outside, but look what happened to Peter Pan when he messed with Tink. Some lessons were best learned the hard way. "Let's eat."

Matt hauled her back by the waistband of her pants.

Pippa crashed into six-four of solid, hot male.

"And then we come back to bed." He pressed a hot, wet kiss where her shoulder and neck met. "If I only have you for a short while longer, I plan to give you something to remember me by."

He'd done that already. As for the second thing, well . . . "I'm starving."

She threw him a TV smile and hoofed it down the stairs into the kitchen.

Baking dishes covered the table, most of them neatly labeled with instructions.

Matt sorted through them with the eye of a connoisseur. He pounced on a plain glass baking tray with a happy grunt. "Mrs. Mammano's lasagna."

"Good?"

"Oh, yeah." He flipped dials on the oven and the kitchen filled with the hum of the convection fan. "She saves these for hospital visits."

Pippa opened the fridge and handed him a beer. He took it with a smile of thanks and did that manly twist-the-cap-off thing.

It was so him. Was it weird she found that hot? Probably. She shrugged and pulled a bottle of wine out of the rack below the counter.

Matt took it from her and uncorked it. Pippa got herself a glass. That was appealing too. The way he opened doors, carried heavy stuff, opened a girl's wine for her. It made her feel cherished, special somehow. What a dork she was.

The whole scene was domestic, nicely so. She'd never gotten this sort of contentment puttering around the kitchen with Ray. Then again, Ray had never rocked her world with mind-blowing, gut-twisting sex. The kind of sex that made a girl happy to hang around the kitchen with her man. Not her man, she quickly amended. Her pretend, on-loan man.

"So." He handed her the wine. "You gonna hang around a bit longer, make sure Phi is all right?"

Oh boy. Her little bit of domestic happy ended sooner than she'd have guessed. "Um . . . yes."

"You don't sound so sure." He lowered his beer, lion eyes on her like a beam.

Okay, confession was good for the soul and all. "Actually, I'll be hanging around for longer than I thought."

He sipped his beer, eyes still on her. "How long?"

"Indefinitely."

Pippa took a big slug of wine.

Matt lowered his beer bottle and put it on the table with a *thunk*. "Aren't you supposed to start on that series for that Germaine woman?"

Why didn't she just open her mouth and tell him the truth? It's not like she was staying with any expectation of them becoming a permanent thing. Except, his eyes were looking downright cold, and a bit hostile.

"Pippa." It was a low rumble of warning, more growl than anything else.

She took a deep breath. "There's been a change of plan."

He stared at her.

"I turned the job down."

"Say again?" No doubt on the hostile now. Those eyes could cut glass.

"I've been thinking." She had another glug of liquid courage. "I think I need to be here for a while."

He dropped his head, grabbed his beer, and drank. "How long is a while?"

"I don't know." Why was the idea of her sticking around so disturbing it warranted chugging an entire bottle of beer? "I wanted to be nearer to Phi, and my mother and Laura."

He yanked open the fridge and grabbed another beer. "You and your sister can't be in the same room without scratching each other's eyes out."

Pippa tossed back her wine. True, but asshat of him to say so. "We can change."

He snorted and went at that second beer.

"I don't have a relationship with my sister and I want one. My mother and I are finding common ground."

"And this is why you turned down a job you've been

fighting your whole career to get?" Matt shook his head and turned to glare out the window.

"Family has to come first. I've been selfish, ignoring—"

"Stop." He whirled back to her and slammed his beer down. "I can't listen to any more of this crap."

What the hell was his problem? "The door's right there."

She'd been stupid to invite him in last night. All churned up from Phi being ill and mistaking comfort for . . . something else. Pippa whirled around and stalked out of the kitchen.

Only to find a solid wall of muscle in her path. "Listen to me, Pippa." He gripped the top of her arms. "Better yet, look at me. I gave up everything for my family. To stay here in Ghost Falls and take care of them. And what do I have to show for it?"

"You have—"

"Fuck all." He shook her a little bit. "I have *fuck all.* Don't make the same mistake as I did. I'm not going to let you make the same mistake I did. Call that Germaine woman back, tell her you've had a change of heart."

"Get your hands off me." He didn't, so she wriggled out of his hold. "Your situation is not the same as mine. It's way different. You were a kid. Making the best decision you could at the time. I'm a woman—"

"Making a stupid decision."

"Making the right decision." She shoved past him, shoulder-checking him on the way past.

He barely even twitched. "You're not even making a decision. That would be something at least, you're just kind of going with the flow, however crappy that might be. Just like you did when you left LA."

"What?" Pippa gasped as all the air left her body in a rush. He'd sucker punched her. "I had to leave LA. You know what it was like for me."

"Yeah." He grimaced. "Then that Twitter thing sent you running even more scared."

"You have no idea what you're talking about." Blood pounded against her temples.

He raked his fingers through his hair. "Yeah, I do, Pippa. I've been running scared for most of the past seventeen years."

"I see." Pippa gave the words a nasty sneer. "And now Eric has offered you a new job and you've had an epiphany?"

"Something like that." He took a deep breath. "This is coming out all wrong. I don't do the whole talking thing well. Stay because that's what you really, really want. Don't do what I did, and let life roll over you and take you with it."

"I've never done that."

He growled low in his throat. "You're doing it now, and I don't want you here because you feel trapped and like you didn't have any options."

"You don't want me here because you're scared I'm going to think we're a real thing." Pippa glared at him. Insufferable dick. "What's the matter, Matt? Am I cramping your style?"

"Fuck, Pippa." His face grew scary cold. "When you want to shove someone away, you don't hold back, do you?" Matt was mad. Scrap that, furious. His eyes burned bold fire at her, the line of his jaw so tight, his teeth might snap. The tendons in his neck tightened as he dragged in a breath.

"Look." This had gotten out of hand too fast. "You don't have to worry about me. This is my career, and I'm making the right decision."

"To walk away?"

"Yes." Pippa took a step back, out of the arc of those intense eyes. "As for us, you have nothing to worry about. I don't do relationships."

"No, you don't." He shoved his balled fists into his pocket. "Because you don't just walk away from those, either. No, those you run from."

Pippa snapped her open jaw shut.

"I'm sorry to tell you this, but if you look now, you'll see that you're already in a relationship," he said.

"This is not—"

"Yeah, it is. Two people enjoying the hell out of each other's bodies, being together, laughing together, sharing each other's lives . . . loving each other."

Pippa's belly roiled. He couldn't be saying what she thought he was. Her heart set up an uncomfortable tattoo. "That's not us."

"Yeah, Pippa, it is. Or at least it could be if you'd stop running scared from anything in your life that demands you put your heart on the line. This thing with Chris is just a symptom. You're too scared to really let yourself want something, because it hurts like hell when you don't get it." He stalked past her to the door, yanked it open, and stormed out into the night. "Not all men leave, Pippa."

"You just did," she yelled after him.

His wheels churned up gravel as he drove away.

Pippa crumpled like a used napkin. "Fuck." She snatched up the bottle of wine and swigged. "Well done, Pippa. You really are the bitch America thinks you are."

Matt hauled ass out of there. He pounded his hand on the steering wheel.

He was pissed at her on so many different levels. First off, what the hell! Giving up her job to rot in this dead-end town. How dumb could she get? Sure, Phi had scared all of them, but that didn't have to mean the kiss of death on every dream Pippa had ever had.

"Shit!" The needle crept back up into the high sixties and he slowed down and pulled over to the side of the road. She'd hit him where it hurt all right. Kneed him right in the balls. And he'd come out swinging. Maybe because he was doing the same thing about Eric's offer, scared to want something too much.

Eric was being patient, giving him space and time to think about what he wanted to do, but it couldn't last forever. The idea of doing this thing with Eric sparked and rippled under his skin. A new challenge, one big enough to scare him. Scary enough to make him feel alive.

"Damn." Used to be that scared feeling gripped him by the balls and drove him forward. Like the time he'd taken his high school team to regionals. Players got big at regional level. Big enough to make you ache ahead of time for the hits you were about to take. His younger self had loved it, welcomed the challenge with a thump to the chest and a "bring it" ringing through his brain.

The hits had come, and they'd sure hurt. But afterward, standing with his team as they made the play-offs had been pure magic. They'd lost the play-offs to a better team. The Ghost Falls Falcons had him, and Eric, and a couple of useful defenders, but not enough depth to hold off the better team. He'd picked up his college scholarship from the final game. Stood in the locker room with his team and known that their defeat had been his victory.

Some victory. Three weeks later he had backed out of the deal. He'd had a good reason. His mother was a wreck, the business broke, and the family heading straight to hell. He got it all back on track. No clue how, and hours spent staring out at Lovers' Leap and wondering what the hell he thought he was doing, but he'd done it.

Jo had graduated years ago. The business had been running in the black for most of that time. His mother . . .

Matt scrubbed his hands over his face. Cressy was a mess. Way beyond what he could fix. Right now, there were five missed calls from her. Five chances to wrap him in the sticky web of her love and bind him close to her. Their talk in the kitchen the other day had gone right over her head. His mother didn't see the need to change—and why would she? Even though he'd read the denial on her face, he'd said the words. Told her she couldn't lean on him for everything, that he needed his own life. Still, it was going to be all up to him to work some healthy distance between them.

Creating space for him and Pippa. His brain finally rolled around to the biggest thorn in its flesh. He couldn't track back and find the exact point when light and easy had transformed into something else. Hell, maybe he'd never truly seen his relationship with Pippa as casual. They had a relationship all right, as in she was the first face he wanted to see in the morning, and to shut his eyes on the same face at night. He wanted . . . so many things. He wanted Pippa. All of her.

Pippa spent the morning answering calls about Phi's well-being. She finally got to the hospital around lunchtime. Phi had been moved to a private ward, and three nurses stood around her bed as Phi held court.

Phi looked great today. Her color was much more normal and with all her war paint in place, it was hard to believe she had been rushed here by ambulance less than forty-eight hours ago.

"Ma petite!" Phi caught sight of Pippa with a huge smile. "I am delighted to see you. Come and meet the girls." She waved at her gaggle of admirers. "Meet Bethany, Gabby, and Tyler. She assures me this is her first name and not her family name."

The "girls" nodded and smiled at Pippa.

"She should be resting." Tyler gave Phi a half-exasperated smile. Poor woman, welcome to the force of nature that is the Diva.

"My darling Tyler," Phi said with an eye roll. "I once gave three performances to Covent Garden in one day. Hell on the voice, I can tell you." She cocked her head and studied Tyler. "I would have named you . . . Victoria. Such a strong, noble name for a girl with your regal presence. I named my granddaughter, you know."

The girls swung to stare at Pippa.

"Yes," Phi said. "Her mother, my daughter, Emily, had a torturous delivery with her. They had to perform an emergency C-section. Her husband, the poor girl, was a complete waste of oxygen." The girls made the appropriate noises. "Whilst Emily was indisposed, I took up the burden and gave them the name for the birth certificate."

"Yes." Pippa shook her head. And Agrippina had been Phi's idea of a good name for a girl. "Now stop being difficult and let's get you resting."

Phi made a rude noise.

"You're still recovering from a major episode." Tyler gave it a valiant effort.

Phi snorted. "Stamina. All the women in my family have it. Of course, three performances are torturous on the cords." Phi stroked her neck. "But then I have a marvelous trick for keeping the vocal cords at their peak."

Holy crap! Not that story. Pippa didn't think the girls were anywhere near ready for that. "You don't want to know."

"Perhaps it's something we could use on our patients," Bethany, or maybe Gabby, said.

"Uh . . . no." Pippa shuddered. She could only imagine the

lawsuits if the hospital gave Phi's solution a try. "You really don't want to know."

Phi chuckled like a bordello madam and gave Pippa a naughty eye gleam. "Perhaps not, but I did have men lining up to serve on my backstage crew."

"I'll bet." Pippa fixed her grandmother with a stare. "Now, how about resting?"

"I have been resting all day." Phi pushed her bottom lip out. Then her face brightened. "Emily was with me this morning. And Laura. She brought the lovelies with her."

"Sam and Daisy were here?" Pippa dragged a chair to the bedside. The girls filed out of the room, Tyler stopping on her way to check the drip.

"They did not stay long," Phi said. "Hospitals are miserable places for the young. Now"—she smoothed her bedding down over her stomach—"tell me why you're looking like someone ran over your cat."

Pippa sighed. Sick or not, Phi was tuned in to her and her moods. "I had a fight with Matt."

"Why?" Phi's eyes rounded. "Pippa, if I need to tell you that one doesn't spend one's time with a man like Mathieu in fighting, then I have taught you nothing at all."

"He was mean to me." Pippa winced at the whine in her voice. "He said I'm hiding away here and letting life drag me along." The rest of what Matt had said was staying clear of Phi's ears.

"Hmph!" Phi glared at the opposite wall before turning her laser beams on Pippa. "I always did credit that man with remarkable sensitivity, despite the inhibiting factor of the penis."

"You think he's right?" That stung and Pippa blinked away the sudden moisture in her eyes.

Phi leaned forward and grabbed her hand. "You do not?"

"No." The word snapped out of her. "I needed to leave LA because things were impossible for me there. And then, when I tried to do something, nobody would return my calls. Nobody wanted to help me. And don't get me started on the Twitter thing. I tried, I lost."

"Indeed." Phi nodded. "I do not think anyone can deny that. I believe the more pertinent question is what have you done since then, and what you are planning to do from here."

Pippa opened her mouth and shut it when the answer didn't come. "I don't know."

"Precisely." Phi squeezed her hand. "Pippa who flew out of Ghost Falls would have known the answer."

"I was eighteen."

"And you knew exactly what you wanted out of life and had a plan to get it. Good God, Agrippina, you have had your life planned since you were five. Do you remember that nasty Declan Sherman?"

How could she forget? He'd called her Duracell with the copper colored top one too many times. When she got mouthy back, he'd tripped her in the hallway in front of the entire football team. Would that Pippa have simply gone home to lick her wounds? No, that Pippa had made her objection known with a knee to his balls.

"Hello, darling." Emily swept into the room on a floral breeze, her arms full of red roses.

Phi glanced at Pippa. "Think about it, *ma petite*."

"The nurses say you are not resting as you should." Emily placed the vase on a table by Phi's bedside.

"I have been entertaining," Phi said.

Emily smiled at Pippa. "She's impossible." Her smile faded into an almost frown. "You look tired, Pippa. Are you all right?"

"I'm okay," Pippa said. "But I think I will head back to the house now that you're here."

"Make sure you rest," Emily said.

Rest? Wouldn't that be great? If only she could get a pair of blazing topaz eyes the hell out of her head.

Chapter Twenty-Eight

When one person called you a wuss, you could shrug it off. Coming from Matt and Phi . . . the conversations replayed in her mind all the way home. She had made an effort to salvage her reputation, put her life back on track. Hadn't she called around to everyone she knew? They had turned her down, refused to help her.

How would eighteen-year-old Pippa have handled the situation?

She turned into Phi's drive. Sunlight filtered through the trees and painted mosaics on the car hood. Eighteen-year-old Pippa would have kicked ass and taken names later. She had arrived in LA with a huge chip on her shoulder, and used it to shove through every closed door.

Parking the car next to the stables, she dropped her head onto the steering wheel. Somewhere in the fight to build her career she'd lost her hustle. Lost the force that propelled her forward. She'd been running in the same direction for so long, it was hard to pinpoint when she had stopped moving forward and ended up jogging on the spot.

With a sigh, she climbed out of her car. God, if that wasn't her life anymore, and not the life she wanted, then what did she want?

All of it. The thought brought her to an abrupt halt. One of Phi's chickens cocked its head at her, then resumed its pecking closer to her foot.

Wheeler Barrows was packing up for the day and waved his hello.

Nine Barrows kids, eight boys and one girl, most of them still living at home and only half of them working, and they produced a hard-working offshoot like this.

Wheeler approached her as she stepped out of the car. "Is she better?"

He looked like his one sister, blond, tousled good-looking. He must thank God every day for that, because his brothers ranged from homely to skeevy-looking.

"She's nearly back to her old self." Pippa smiled at the look of obvious relief on Wheeler's face. He would grow into quite the looker this one. "They are talking about releasing her tomorrow."

"Good." He nodded. "Will you tell her I said hi?" He shoved his hands in the pockets of his well-worn jeans. "My sister said she'd come with me to the hospital, but . . ." Wheeler shrugged.

Yeah, Pippa got it. Blythe Barrows always had someone better to do. Not much had changed since high school. "Do you want to come with me in the morning?"

A shy grin broke over Wheeler's face. "Could I?"

"Sure." Pippa kept it light and shrugged. "We'll go as soon as the horses are fed."

"Cool." He sniffed and played it cool. "Later."

Wheeler sloped over to his beat-up car. It looked like the same one Blythe had driven in high school.

Pippa let herself into the kitchen and went straight for the wine. She might leave Ghost Falls with a drinking problem at this rate.

She took her phone out and stared at it. Putting it back on the table, she sipped her wine.

Dial him. The phone lit up as she unlocked the screen. Pippa put it down. Not yet, a little more agonizing and the chance to give herself a few more reasons to talk herself out of it.

Pippa keyed her phone on again.

Matt's truck rolled to a stop in the kitchen yard. He climbed out and then leaned back in. Arms laden with flowers, chocolates, and a pink plastic packet, he loped over and let himself in through the kitchen door.

"Hey." He lifted his chin at her.

Suddenly shy and awkward, Pippa nodded back.

Matt put his burdens down on the kitchen table and stood back. "I'm a dick."

Pippa blinked at him, and then the stuff on the table. "Is that all for me?"

"Yeah." He shoved his hands into his back pockets. "I'm not very good at the apologizing thing, so I thought I'd cover all bases." He cleared his throat. "Flowers, always a safe bet, but I wasn't sure what kind you liked. Chocolate." He pushed a gold-wrapped box closer to her. "I hit a snag on the perfume thing, but Bets did have this."

Pippa took the pink plastic packet he handed her. She pulled out a My Little Pony bath and body lotion set, complete with collectible pony. Pippa giggled.

A smile of relief crossed Matt's face as her giggle grew into a belly laugh.

"My favorite," she said when she could manage it. "How did you know?"

"I went with the pony with the orange mane." His face

grew serious and he stepped into her space. "I really am sorry about earlier, Agrippina."

"I hated what you said, Meat."

He grimaced. "Yeah, it was kind of rough." He took a deep breath. "I called Eric when I left here. We're going into business together."

"You are?" Matt didn't waste any time when he got his ass kicked.

"Yup." He nodded. "I gotta tell you, it scares the crap out of me, but I want this opportunity. I don't know what it will mean for the future, where I'll stay—all that stuff—but Eric and I will work it out."

She needed to touch him, help him with the uncertainty lurking in the back of his eyes. "You're going to do great things, you and Eric. Kind of like those Property Brothers."

"Who?" He raised his eyebrow.

"They're brothers, and they have this reality show on TV. One of them is a contractor and the other a realtor." Why was she explaining all this? Pippa waved a hand. "It doesn't matter. The important part is you taking this chance to go after something you want. Plus, you and Eric are much better-looking than they are."

A grin threatened to take over his face. "Good to know."

Pippa let him tug her against his chest and wrap his arms around her. "You know, next time you feel the need to deliver some hard truths, you might bring all the flowers and stuff with you."

"I'll remember that," he murmured against her hair. "If you stay in Ghost Falls, Pippa, I want it to be because there is no other place you would rather be."

"What am I going to do, Meat? All my life I've wanted one thing and gone after that."

"Only you know that, babe. And for the record, I would be very happy if there was no place you'd rather be than

Ghost Falls, but I don't ever want to be something you settled for."

"Really?"

His eyes were full of something she couldn't quite decipher, but it made her heart beat faster and caused a happy glow to flicker into life in her chest. Pippa burrowed back into him, pressing her face into his neck. "We're not keeping this light."

"No, we're not." He kissed the top of her head. "Would it freak you out if I told you there is nothing I would rather do than hold you like this?"

Pippa shook her head. "Nothing else?"

"Nothing." He tightened his hold.

"Not even if I invited you to come upstairs with me?"

"Not even then." Well, that was a bit disappointing, but cuddling was nice. "Pippa," he growled in her ear. "Get your fine ass up those stairs."

She was laughing as she pulled him toward the stairs when he stiffened. His stare locked on something outside the window.

"What is it?"

The sheriff's cruiser pulled to a stop outside and Nate climbed out.

"What the hell?" Matt moved her to his side.

Nate's face was carved into grim lines as he strode toward the kitchen. He rapped on the door lintel.

"Come in." Pippa motioned him inside.

"Hi, Pippa." He tucked his hands into his gun belt.

"Nate." Matt jerked his chin.

"Matt." Nate nodded and turned back to her. "I have some pictures here I'd like you to look at." He pulled a folder from under his arm. "See if these are the things Phi is missing."

"You found them?" Pippa's heart gave a happy leap. Phi's treasures would make the perfect homecoming gift.

Nate spread the pictures over the table. "Have a look and tell me."

Matt crossed his arms and propped one shoulder against the wall.

Pippa glanced through the photos. Man, she nearly kissed Nate. The napkin rings, the silver milk jug, the fob watch, the missing spoons. They were all there. And best of all, the tiara. "Where did you find them?"

"I had one of my deputies do a search of antique stores in Denver and Salt Lake City. He found a dealer in Denver who was a bit nervous about these. Knew they were real but didn't like that they came without any paperwork."

Pippa traced the beautiful lines of the photographed tiara with her finger. "Phi is going to be delighted."

Her smile died as she looked up at Nate. She glanced at Matt.

He straightened and walked over to Nate. "Tell me you were wrong about that."

"I wish I could." Nate grimaced. "You ready for a shock?"

"No." Pippa's belly hit the floor. Why did there always have to be bad news? By the look on Nate's face, the news really, really sucked. "But give it to me anyway."

"The dealer remembered the woman who sold the things to him," Nate said.

"Woman?" *Ah, no, not June. Please don't let it be June.* Phi was going to be heartbroken. "Are you going to arrest her?"

Nate curled his lips down. "I'm not sure. I need to speak with your grandmother first. It could be she doesn't want to press charges."

"Maybe not." June had been with Phi for years. "And if the things are all returned, undamaged, she may just fire June and be done with it."

Nate frowned. "Um, firing June isn't going to fix this." He glanced at Matt.

Matt's jaw tightened and he swore softly. "Are you sure?"

"I double-checked." Nate nodded.

Pippa didn't like that look. "What?"

"Pippa." Matt grabbed her hand from the table and held it. "I don't think June took the stuff."

"Who then?"

"Your sister," Nate said. "I showed the dealer a picture and he recognized it straight away. Laura has been stealing from Phi."

Chapter Twenty-Nine

Pippa shook her head. Not Laura. "No way."

Nate gathered up the photos and put them back in the folder before looking up, face as serious as a winter storm. "I double-checked. Drove to Denver yesterday to make sure. Laura is stealing from Phi."

"Pippa." Matt squeezed her hand.

It didn't make any sense. Her vision got iffy and she hauled her ass onto a chair. "Why?"

"That's what I'd like to know," Nate said. "I'm on my way over there right now. It's not strictly procedure but maybe you could come along and keep an eye on the children while I talk to Laura."

"Sure." And smack the truth out of Laura while she was there.

What the hell! Laura had her hands on Phi's treasures, selling them to some shady dealer in Denver. Quick mental apology to the dealer if he wasn't shady.

"Pippa." Matt got right in her face. "Can you do this?"

Doing this without Matt seemed harder somehow. "Will you come with me?"

"If you want me there, that's where I'll be."

"I want you there."

"Yeah." Nate rubbed the back of his neck. "But you can't go all medieval on her. You have to keep calm."

It all crashed down on her head again. She was tempted to check, one more time, if Nate really had this right.

His handsome, grave face gave her all the confirmation she needed. He wouldn't be here unless he was willing to stake his badge on it. He gathered up the pictures on the table. "Let's get going. This isn't going to get any easier."

What the hell was Laura thinking? Nate damn well better ask her that because Pippa really wanted to know. Then she wanted to know how Laura got off thinking it was okay to steal from her own grandmother. Their grand-mother.

Pippa called her mother from the car. Emily was at the hospital and didn't want to leave Phi. Pippa told her she'd be by to see them later. She needed the full story before she broke Phi's and her mother's hearts.

Laura and Patrick's home was a ranch-style showpiece set in a neighborhood that whispered its affluence in mani-cured lawns and imposing front facades.

Nate parked the cruiser at the curb and they approached the door together.

Patrick opened the door on a waft of savory cooking smells that reminded Pippa she hadn't eaten yet. Trust Laura to be an excellent cook. Her sister did everything well. Including theft, apparently.

"Pippa." Patrick gave her his shy, sweet smile and swept her into a hug. Of medium height, with an attractive combi-nation of dark brown hair and blue eyes, Patrick looked like what he was—the original good guy. "Laura said you were home and I was waiting for you to show your face here."

Oh God, Patrick wouldn't be wearing that happy face for long.

Matt took her hand and threaded his fingers through hers. A silent gesture of support she appreciated more than she could say.

"Patrick, is Laura home?" Nate took over the conversation.

Patrick's smile faltered as he looked at Nate's set features. He stepped back to let them in. "Yes, she's in the kitchen. Is everything all right? Is it her grandmother?"

"Phi's fine." Pippa tried to put a note of reassurance in her voice. "But we need to speak to Laura, alone. Do you think you could take the kids for a walk or something? Maybe an ice cream?"

"Laura doesn't allow them to have ice cream before dinner." Patrick slid his hands in his pockets. "What's this all about?"

"It really would be better if we spoke to Laura alone first," Nate said.

Patrick rocked on his heels, frowning slightly. "Daisy," he called over his shoulder.

Daisy's voice rose inside the house in answer.

"Take Sam upstairs to watch a movie." Patrick turned back to them. "Your mother and I have something important to discuss."

Pippa tensed. "Patrick, we—"

"I don't know what the hell this is about, Pippa. But when the police show up at my door asking to speak to my wife, there is no way in hell I'm not going to be there beside her."

Laura had found herself a good man, one who might just stick around through this.

Matt increased the pressure on her hand. "Let's get this over with," he said to Nate.

Nate nodded and motioned Patrick to show them the way.

"Hey, Pippa." Daisy clattered past with Sam at her heels.

"Matt. Sheriff Evans." She went red to her hairline, grabbed Sam, and rushed up the stairs.

"Patrick?" Laura appeared at the kitchen doorway, a dishcloth in her hands. "Why are the children going to watch television before dinner?" She stopped halfway down the gleaming wooden hallway floor. The wood looked like she polished it every day. Knowing Laura, she probably did.

Laura had stolen from Phi. It seemed incredible to Pippa, looking at Laura, so perfect and composed in her tasteful, beautiful home with her wonderful husband. The same wonderful husband who bristled like a pit bull in front of them.

Laura glanced at Nate, then Matt, and finally, Pippa. She went pale and scrunched the dish towel in her hand. "Phi didn't—"

"Your grandmother's fine." Patrick rushed to her side and put an arm around her waist.

Pippa stared at her sister, trying to jam the pieces into a coherent order. How could Laura look so concerned about Phi when she'd been stealing her treasures? When, in fact, Laura and her sticky fingers had caused Phi's collapse? Pippa wanted to punch her sister so badly. Her free hand balled into a fist. Words came out of her mouth in a low growl. "Don't you dare pretend to care about Phi."

Matt gripped her hand tighter. "Easy," he murmured. "If you can't keep it under wraps, I'm going to have to take you outside."

Take her outside? No fucking way.

Laura's gaze locked on Nate. Her throat worked as she swallowed.

"Let's take this into the kitchen." Nate took the lead.

Laura nodded and turned to go back the way she'd come.

"What the hell is going on?" Patrick rounded on them

as they entered the airy, spotless kitchen. Stainless steel appliances nestled between dark wood and gleaming granite.

Laura moved around to the far side of a large central island. Her fingers turned white against the dark granite as she gripped the edge. "Am I under arrest?"

"Under arrest?" Patrick swung his head from Laura to Nate. "What the hell could you be under arrest for?" He thrust his chin out, his arm protectively wrapped around Laura. "This is bullshit, coming into my house and threatening my wife."

"Tell him," Pippa said. Patrick was a good man, standing there ready to defend Laura without even knowing why. He didn't deserve this shit. Phi for damn sure didn't deserve this shit. Perfect Laura, not a hair out of place and a thief. Lying to them, all of them. Their mother, Phi, her, Patrick, and those two great kids upstairs. *"Tell him."*

Pippa snatched her hand away from Matt.

Nate stepped into her path, throwing a quick glance over her head at Matt.

Matt moved behind her. Ready to grab the madwoman in case she lost it. Pippa was perilously close with Laura looking like she might try and lie her way out of this.

"I paid a visit to some antique dealers in Denver yesterday." Nate put his folder on the island.

Laura thrust her hands behind her back. Her mouth worked but no sound came out.

"As a courtesy to your grandmother, I'm here to give you a chance to explain." He sent the folder skittering across the gleaming granite surface to Laura. "But you should know that the dealer positively identified you."

"So, you're not here to arrest me?" Laura stepped back. "What—"

"Give her a chance." Nate cut Patrick off gently. "Then if you still have questions we can answer them later."

"Why?" Pippa tried to yank her shoulders free of Matt's restraining hold. His grip tightened. "Why would you do that to Phi?"

"You wouldn't understand." Laura's eyes glittered at her, her face so angry it took Pippa's breath away.

Laura was mad at her. *Laura* was mad at *her*. It took a moment for her lame brain to make sense of the information. Who the hell did Laura think she was? Pippa's voice burst from her, getting louder with each syllable. "You stole from Phi."

"Keep it down," Matt muttered. "We don't want the kids to hear."

Pippa checked her volume but the anger soared through her, hotter now that she knew she couldn't yell. "She trusted you, loved you. She's your grandmother, for fuck's sake, and you took her treasures. You put your grubby hands on her special collection and—"

"Pippa." Nate cut a glance at her. "Get it under control or take it outside."

No way she was letting them kick her out now. She wanted to hear what her sister had to say. Pippa clenched her teeth together so hard, her jaw ached.

"Laura would never steal anything." Patrick gave a choked little laugh. "This entire thing is ridiculous. She loves her grandmother."

"Love?" It got away from Pippa before she could stop it. She snorted and stepped back into Matt. His chest pressed against her back, solid and dependable and the only thing keeping her from losing it.

"I do love Phi." Laura's voice trembled. Her shoulders collapsed and she dropped her head forward. "I do love her. I mean, she's weird and eccentric and drives me nuts, but I love her."

"Then why?" Her sister's words carved a path through her chest. "Why?"

"I needed the money, and I couldn't think how else to get it."

"Laura?" Patrick glanced at Nate, emotions chasing so fast across his guileless face it was difficult to keep up. Disbelief, confusion, anger, hurt—Patrick was an open book. "Why would you need money? We have money." He made a truncated movement with his hand. "We have money."

"Not the sort of money she needs." Nate said it so quietly Pippa almost missed it.

Nate had been holding out on them.

Wet splotches appeared on the countertop in front of Laura. Her sister was crying. She wanted to shake Laura and yell at her, and she wanted to rush over there and comfort her.

"She owes money to some nasty people," Nate said. "Once I found the stolen items, I made some inquiries. Most of the time, if you want to know why, you follow the money."

"Laura?" Pippa winced at the raw pain in Patrick's voice. He was pleading with her sister for answers. Begging her to put him out of his misery.

Laura shook her head, silent sobs ripping through her torso, shaking her shoulders and coming out her mouth in sawing gasps.

"She's been gambling," Nate said. "And she got in over her head. I'm guessing she didn't want you to know, and she took the stuff from her grandmother to cover her debt."

"No." Patrick stepped away from Laura. He shook his head and took another step back.

Laura stood alone, so small and defeated and in so much pain. She wanted to be furious at Laura and she was, but a sister was a sister. Pippa ripped free of Matt and ran around the island. Her hip jarred against the corner as she reached for Laura. God, she wanted to kill her, but she wanted to love her more. She grabbed Laura and pulled her tight, as if she could suck some of that anguish into herself.

"I don't understand," she whispered into her sister's hair. Roses and lilies drifted in a subtle fragrance from Laura. Her body felt tiny, insubstantial and not strong enough to bear the weight of the emotion ripping through Laura. Pippa clenched her arms around her sister, holding on to her for dear life.

Laura collapsed against her and Pippa braced and took her weight.

"I don't know why." The words were pressed into Pippa's shoulder. "I couldn't stop. I knew I had to but I couldn't stop."

"How much?" Patrick jammed his hands in his pockets, his jaw worked convulsively.

"A little over three hundred kay," Nate said.

Oh, *dear God*. Pippa held Laura tighter. The desire to shake Laura again grabbed hold of her and she had to dig her nails into her palms to stop herself. That was a mountain of debt. Would Phi's treasures even cover a fraction of that?

"Laura." Patrick nudged Pippa's shoulder, pressing her away from his wife. "You need to start from the beginning and tell me all of it."

Pippa let him take his wife. Patrick helped Laura onto one of the wrought iron counter stools.

Laura scrubbed the tears away with the dish towel. Dark smears of mascara made macabre stripes down her cheeks. She glanced at Nate. "What will you do?"

"That depends on your grandmother. If she's prepared to be lenient, I can get this pleaded down. You're a first-time offender, a mother, a respectable community member. I can probably persuade the DA to let you off with a fine, maybe some community service. The items were extremely valuable, so that makes your case a lot weaker, but they are all here and you will have to pay back whatever you got from the antique dealer."

"I don't have it anymore." Laura grabbed a pack of Kleenex from the counter.

Of course Laura would have Kleenex close at hand. She was the perfect mother. Perfect mother who stole from her grandmother to pay her gambling debts. The kitchen dipped and swayed around Pippa and she pulled up the stool three down from Laura. She didn't trust herself to sit any closer right now.

"Will she have a criminal record?" Patrick glanced at Nate.

"It will go on her file for sure," Nate said. "The items were reported stolen and I investigated the crime. There's no way to make that go away, and even if there was, I'm not sure I'm inclined to. Laura stole and however close I am to your family, there are repercussions to that sort of thing."

"I understand." A muscle ticked in Patrick's jaw. He shook his head as if trying to make sense of this.

It didn't make any sense, none of it did. Why would Laura be gambling in the first place? Pippa voiced the question aloud and Laura's head dropped again.

"I don't know," she said. "I can't explain it, but when I was there, I didn't have to be me."

"What the fuck does that mean?" Patrick gripped the sides of his head. "What the fuck is so wrong with being you? You have a perfect life here. A beautiful home, great kids, I give you everything you need."

"It's not that." Laura held her hands out in front of her, pleading with him.

"We should go." Nate turned to her and Matt. "They need to talk and then we'll see what needs to be done next. I need to talk to your grandmother."

Oh God, Phi. This was going to kill her.

Phi was asleep when they reached the hospital.

Pippa felt like a bitch for having to break this to her now. She even tried to plead with Nate to see if they could wait, but Nate—followed by Matt—got stubborn. Phi needed to be told and by them before she heard it elsewhere. Also, Nate wanted to act before the DA got all excited by the idea of putting Laura in jail.

Emily sat by her mother's bed, her chair pulled into a large pool of sunshine.

Pippa told her mother first. Emily paled but took the news quietly. Almost as if she didn't quite grasp what she'd heard. She kept glancing at Nate as Pippa spoke.

"Are you certain?" she asked when Pippa stopped talking.

Nate nodded. "I drove to Denver with a second picture of Laura, just to make sure."

"Poor Patrick." Emily shook her head. "He will be devastated. And the children." She glanced at Pippa. "Do they know?"

"We didn't tell them. We left so Patrick could talk to Laura alone. Have you any idea why Laura would be gambling?" Pippa tried to see past the smooth facade her mother wore. It was her mother's troubled face. When Emily got that smooth, impenetrable mask, it had been a signal as a girl that she was in deep, deep trouble. Had her mother developed that in reaction to Phi's theatrics? Phi's emotions were large, on a cosmic level that vibrated through everyone who came near her. Emily went dead still, the exact opposite.

They waited for Phi to wake before they told her.

Nate and Matt left them to it.

Pippa watched Matt walk away down the long, antiseptic corridor. The words to call him back, beg him to stay caught in her throat.

She left the telling to her mother. Emily in her calm, efficient voice gave Phi the truth. Pippa locked her gaze on Phi's face. Ready to leap in with the inevitable explosion. Except it never came.

Emily fell silent and Phi nodded once, and then turned her head to stare out the window. "It's the pressure, you know," she said. "Of being Laura. The perfect one. The good girl. She's always been that way, and I am surprised she didn't break before this."

"What do you mean?" Emily frowned.

"I mean Laura is trapped inside a person she created." Phi turned back to them. Her green eyes glimmered with tears. "My poor darling girl. How she must have suffered to end up so desperate."

Pippa perched on the end of Phi's bed. The day kept bringing one surprise after another and she was all out of mental stretch. "She always seemed happy to me."

"Because that is what she wanted you to believe." Phi swung her gaze to Pippa. "All her life Laura has done what was expected of her."

"Are you saying this is my fault?" Emily stood at the foot of Phi's bed, her body vibrating with tension.

Phi tilted her head and gave Emily a sad smile. "No, dear, I am saying this is my fault."

Okay, someone should start explaining because Pippa was lost as all hell here. How could any of this be Phi's fault? Laura had stolen from Phi, and sold those things to pay off her gambling debts.

"I created an imbalance," Phi said. "I did not intend to,

but I did it all the same. It was so easy to relate to Pippa. She was so like me and I got to pretend I was not a terrible mother when she was around."

Emily sank into the seat by the window. "I don't understand."

Thank God, Pippa wasn't the only one lost as hell here.

"I left you to your father to raise." Phi looked at her daughter. "You were a shy child and you didn't fit into the world I so desperately wanted to be a part of. It was easier to do that than come home and make the sacrifices I needed to make as a mother."

A tear slid down Phi's cheek. "You married and had your children and I convinced myself you were happy. Laura was such a good baby and your joy in her was clear to see. I was a bit jealous of that. Then Pippa was born and she and I became a unit and I left you out in the cold again. Laura, bless her heart, tried to fill that gap. She wanted to be the one who would make everything all right for you," Phi said to Emily. "Then that idiot left and you were even more alone than ever. Laura knew you were hurting and took it upon herself to ease that pain. Laura never discovered who Laura was, she tried to be what everyone wanted her to be."

Pippa's head ached for all four of them. What a tangled mess they'd managed to make of their relationships.

Emily felt rejected by her career-driven mother, rejected by her husband, and then again when Pippa chose Phi over her. And Laura. Not really belonging anywhere and trying so hard to make a place for herself. Hadn't Pippa done much the same thing? Except her box was labeled "career woman," and she'd never even allowed herself to consider there might be more. Been too frightened of ending up alone like her mother. Funny, she'd ended up alone anyway. Until she opened the door a crack and Matt charged through.

"I should have seen it," Emily said. "How could I not have seen that my child was in so much trouble?"

"At least you tried," Phi said. "I refused to see what was right in front of me when it came to my child."

"Laura's stealing is a symptom," Emily said. "And the gambling was an expression of how unhappy Laura is." She pleated her skirt with her fingers. "Mom is right. Laura never went through a wild phase. She was always good little Laura. Everybody has a breaking point and Laura reached hers."

"But how is any of that Phi's fault?"

"Because I created the whole screwed-up dynamic in the first place," Phi said. "I made Emily feel rejected, which is why she clung to Laura. Then when you and I became close, Emily felt more rejected and Laura needed to make that up to her somehow. She did that by being the perfect daughter."

"And the sperm donor didn't help," Pippa said.

"Pippa!" Mom looked at her with wide eyes.

"Well"—Pippa shrugged—"he didn't do much more, even when he was around."

Mom's lips twitched, humor lighting in her eyes. "True, but what a terrible way to describe your father."

"A father raises his children," Phi said. "He does not merely beget them. The sperm donor." Phi crinkled her nose. "I rather like it."

"You would." Mom chuckled. "Laura has been trying to fix the world around her since she was little."

It made sense, in a strange way. When they were kids, she got muddy and Laura always kept her dress clean. Pippa got into the cookies and ate the entire batch. Laura had one with her milk. Pippa chased her dream. Laura stayed home and married the right sort of guy. "What about Patrick? She loves him, right?"

And where the hell would that leave Daisy and Sam if the answer was no?

"She loves her family," Emily said, smoothing her skirt. "I'm sure of that. As unhappy as she is, Laura still chose well for herself. She loves being a wife and mother. It's about the constant pressure she puts on herself to be perfect, all the time. I know a little something about that."

Phi snorted. "I'll bet you do."

Emily looked at her mother and laughed.

This was not Pippa's family. Her mother and grandmother did not sit quietly and joke about each other, tease each other and not react. "What did you two talk about the other day?"

"Never you mind." Phi sent her an arch look. "That is between Emily and me. Now we need to turn our attention to Laura. You know the district attorney don't you, Emily?"

Emily nodded. "Yes, she chairs the committee that oversees the community center. I will talk to her, assure her we can get Laura sorted out."

"Can we?" She had to ask because it didn't seem such an easy fix to Pippa. Basically, these two were saying Laura's entire life was in the toilet.

"We have no choice," Phi said. "The alternative is too horrible to be contemplated. But we will do it together."

It felt good to hear Phi say that. Even better when her mother nodded and smiled. "I'll be here to help, in whatever way I can," Pippa said.

"No, you won't." Emily looked across Phi's covered legs at her. "I already have one daughter making bad decisions to fix what is not hers to fix. You need to go and do what is right for you."

"This is right for me." Pippa looked to Phi for support.

Phi rolled her eyes and snorted. "Living in Ghost Falls for the rest of your life is right for you?"

"But you said family was more important than career."

"Yes, dear." Emily stood and fussed with Phi's sheet. "But there is a balance. Family is vital, but it's not all there is to life. Can't you see that with what happened to your sister? There's something missing in Laura's life and the gambling is a sign of that. You were never meant to stay here. What would you do?"

It was a fair question, one Pippa had been avoiding. "I could take care of Phi."

"You would drive me mad within the month," said Phi. "All the energy you have. Fussing and fuming around me all the time. Making those lists like a little dictator. No."

"I want to be here for you." Pippa was beginning to feel the sting of rejection.

"Then be here for us by being the best you that you can," Emily said. "Do the things that make you happy, and the rest will follow. Come home more often. Call more often, but don't go flying off to the other extreme."

"And what about Matt?" Phi raised her eyebrow. "You're going to sit there and tell me you're happy about walking away from him?"

Emily frowned over the bed at Pippa. "What happened with Matt?"

"It's complicated." Pippa had to stand and pace. "We were supposed to be a casual thing."

Phi snorted. "You spend a lot of time together for two people who are casual."

Emily rounded the bed. "Find the middle ground, Pippa. Don't do what my mother and I have done our entire lives. Don't blindly charge off in one direction to the detriment of everything else."

"Have you ever asked Matt if he wants to make space for you in his life?" Phi folded her arms over her stomach. "Or have you been too frightened to admit your feelings. Even to yourself?"

"I haven't told you everything." Pippa swore she felt her back against the wall.

Phi snorted. "Do you want that man?"

"I do." Saying it out loud brought it ringing home to Pippa. She did want Matt. With his lion eyes and his bad boy grin. The way he could make her laugh when everything was going to shit around her. The way he got her on a cellular level that made everything all right. "But his life is complicated and so is mine."

"Then uncomplicate them," her mother said. "Do what you do best, Pippa. Find the thing you want and go after it."

Chapter Thirty

Pippa sat in a pool of warm sunlight. Chest rising and falling in a steady rhythm, Phi slept peacefully. Mom had finally agreed to go home for a few hours, and left Pippa in charge.

Tyler came in, smiled at Pippa, and went through the routine of checking on Phi. Her pen scratched across the chart as she made her notations.

"Did you always want to be a nurse?" Pippa kept her voice low enough not to wake Phi.

Tyler stopped writing and cocked her head. "Not always." She glanced at Pippa, then finished her notations and slid the chart into the slot at the end of the bed. "I wanted to be a doctor, but halfway through my first year something changed." Tyler clicked her pen and snapped it onto the top pocket of her duckling-yellow scrubs decorated with a swarm of bumblebees. "I discovered that I liked taking care of people more than I liked curing them. I like helping people."

"I wanted to be famous," Pippa said. "Like my grandmother. I couldn't carry a tune in a bucket, didn't like acting, so TV seemed the next best thing." Wanted to shake the dust of this nowhere town off her, and show them it didn't matter that she was different, didn't matter that her father had left. She was somebody.

Shifting her weight, Tyler leaned her hip against the end of Phi's bed. "I used to watch your show."

"Did you?"

"I miss it," Tyler said, and straightened. "I loved watching what happened to those women. It was like you gave them their own magic potion." Tyler blushed, as if embarrassed by her statement, and jerked her scrub top straight. Bumblebees rippled across her chest. "I'll see you later. I've got other patients to check."

"Okay." Outside Phi's window a man stepped into the courtyard and lit a cigarette. His cheeks hollowed as he sucked on his smoke. He looked like he really needed that nicotine hit.

Pippa had started in television to be famous, but it wasn't the fame she missed. She missed the transformations, the change she made in women's lives. The magic—and the magic was worth fighting for. Her magic potion was worth any risk, and that potion was made up of many different ingredients. Family, career, home, and a man to share that home with her.

Without the thought having fully formed, she pulled out her phone.

"Pippa." Chris Germaine answered almost immediately.

"Um, hi." The man outside tossed his smoke and ground it beneath his heel. "About our last conversation . . ."

"Yes."

"I've been thinking."

"Dammit." Chris barked down the phone. "Can't you sort that out without me?"

Relieved laughter bubbled up Pippa's throat. "I thought you were talking to me."

"You haven't said much yet."

This was true. "I was wondering how set in stone your ideas for the show are."

"In terms of what?" Chris's tone sharpened.

"Me," Pippa said. "I was thinking we could come up with something that suited both of us. A way in which I could be the best me along with the women we transform."

"Do you know what the best you is?"

"I'm getting there," Pippa said. "I know what it isn't."

Chris chuckled, her throaty laugh. "Just a minute." The phone crackled as Chris moved it. "Shut the door," Chris yelled. "Pippa and I are negotiating."

Deep inside, a spark of excitement flickered into life. A tiny twinkle of pure magic.

Matt stopped so fast, Nate trod on the back of his heels. "You have got to be shitting me."

"What the hell is she doing here?" Nate breathed deep.

They were on their way to Phi's ward, to wait for Pippa to finish breaking the news about Laura. If there was a chance Pippa needed him, then by her side is where he wanted to be.

Matt's mom sat in the large hospital reception area with a nurse handing her Kleenex.

"You must think I'm crazy." Mom took the Kleenex and dabbed at her eyes.

The nurse heaved a big sigh. "Cressy, I'm a mother myself. I know exactly how you feel."

Cressy, was it? Mom had been making time with the nurse, which didn't answer the question as to what the hell she was doing here.

"My boys have always been so popular with the young ladies." Mom's top lip wobbled. She pressed the Kleenex to her eyes and dabbed at her tears.

"Fuck," Nate breathed. Matt couldn't have said it better.

"I just never thought my Matt would fall for a woman like this." Matt's blood pressure geysered up and a red haze covered his vision. His breathing sawed through his lips, hitting the air in a harsh grate.

Nate grabbed his elbow. "Take it easy. You know what she's like."

"It breaks your heart." The nurse squeezed her arm and handed her another Kleenex.

"Mom." Matt shook Nate off and entered the room. He was proud his voice still sounded vaguely normal. "What the fu . . . what are you doing here?"

Nurse Carver, by her nameplate, stood and buckled into her armor. You had to hand it to his mother, if she were a Christian in a Roman amphitheater, she'd find a lion to champion her cause. "Your mother came to check on the condition of Mrs. Philomene St. Amor."

"I had to see for myself." Mom shredded the Kleenex. "Ever since your father died, there's nothing but drama with that woman. She's always dragging you into it."

"Nobody drags me into anything, Mom. I owe Phi everything, and I go because I want to."

Mom gave a desperate wail and tears streamed down her cheeks. "You see how it is, Belinda?"

"Boys." Nurse Carver, Belinda to his mother, apparently, threw him a look filthy enough to stain his shorts.

"Would you mind?" He didn't exactly blame the woman but what he had to say to his mother wasn't going to be pretty. "I need to talk to my mother alone."

"Why don't we wait out in the hall?" Nate threw down his pretty boy smile and Nurse Carver followed him out like she'd just sighted Nirvana.

"You're angry with me." Mom blinked up at him with damp eyes.

The old fix-it urge rose up in a chokehold. Matt breathed deep and channeled his inner Eric. "Yeah, Mom, I am mad at you. We might have lost Phi, and she and Pippa . . . they mean a lot to me."

Mom's breath hitched. "You see, that's why I'm here. You've always put her above me. That ridiculous old woman."

Inner Eric wasn't helping right now, and Matt paced to the far end of the room. He had seen it with his dad, yelling didn't work with her. Cressy would collapse into a mass of inconsolable jelly. "That ridiculous old woman is the kindest, most sincere and bighearted woman I know. She saved our asses giving me the job to build her house after Dad died." See, he could do this. "There wasn't any money, Mom. Dad died leaving us with a huge mortgage and the business about two steps away from the bank foreclosing on their loans. Nobody around Ghost Falls wanted to trust their construction project to a nineteen-year-old kid with no experience. Until Phi let me build that huge house. We all owe her, not only me."

"Do you love her more than you love me?"

God, not even Jo with rampaging teen hormones had been this needy. "You're my mom, and I love you. Nothing and nobody can change that."

Cressy perked up a bit and a tremulous smile appeared on her face.

"But." Matt needed her to hear him. "I can't be your everything, all the time."

Her face dropped so fast, it was nearly comical.

Matt crouched down in front of her and took her hands. "I'm always gonna take care of you, Mom, but that doesn't mean there's no place for other things in my life." He squeezed her hands to get her to look at him. "You need to find a life outside of me, and the others as well. You make friends easily. Hell, you were only in here for five minutes and already you have Belinda ready to string me up."

"She's a very nice woman." Mom sniffed.

"I'm gonna be building my own life, and some of that is not going to involve you."

"Like the job with Eric?"

"Like the job with Eric." He nodded. "I want this, Mom. I want my chance to do something outside of the legacy Dad left me. I'm excited about this, like I haven't been excited about anything in a long time. And then there's Pippa."

Mom's eyes flashed wrathful fire as she stuck her chin out. "I knew it had something to do with that girl. I suppose she's been whispering in your ear, telling you to leave your mother and go off to LA with her. That spiteful woman—"

"Be very careful." Matt rose and put some distance between them. "This is a nonnegotiable. Pippa is the woman I love, and I don't care if you like her or not."

"But, Matt—"

"She makes me happy. When I'm with Pippa I feel alive. I'm crazy about her and I'm gonna do whatever I can to make sure she stays in my life from here on out. If it means I have to travel to New York to be with her, or live in LA, that's what I'm gonna do." He met his mother's startled stare. "I love her, and I need her around for as long as she'll have me."

"Are you going to marry her?" Mom's eyes were like circular blades in her pale face.

"I haven't gotten that far yet, but I will and I'll do whatever I must to make sure she says yes."

Mom got to her feet, her body vibrating with pent-up emotion. "No, Matt. I cannot accept that. You saw what she did on that television program. The whole world saw what I've always seen. She's cunning and manipulative and controlling. That girl has hunted you for years. You didn't see her when she was younger, always casting her lures your way. I won't let you fall into her trap."

"You don't have a choice." Matt hauled back hard on his fraying temper. "I won't discuss that television program with you. If Pippa chooses to tell you, then you'll hear the truth. But listen and listen well. Don't make me choose, Mom, because you won't like the choice I make."

Nate appeared as Pippa said good-bye to Chris and hung up.

"Is the Diva okay?" He jerked his chin at Phi's room.

"She's amazing." Pippa gathered her things and stood. "She's a tough old broad."

"It runs in the family." Nate gave her a smile sweet enough to melt her bones.

"Did you just call me old?"

Nate blushed. "Never. Matt's waiting for you downstairs."

She and Nate left the ward, and took the long corridor to the reception. People bustled past them on a calm, steady hum.

As they turned the corner into the reception waiting area, the tension between Matt and Cressy was thick enough to cut.

"Hey?" Matt strode toward her and took her hand. "How did Phi take it?"

Cressy glared at her, arms crossed over her chest and chin stuck out.

No change there then. Pippa let Matt pull her into a warm hug. "Well. Actually, both Phi and my mother feel badly for Laura and are deciding which one of them is most to blame."

Matt gave a soft huff of laughter, his eyes gentle. "That's the Diva for you. The biggest heart in the world."

"Then they told me to get off my ass and go for what I want," Pippa said.

His topaz eyes gleamed at her, full of something that gave her hope her next negotiation would go as successfully as the last one. "And what is it that you want?"

"I think we should talk about that." Behind Matt's shoulder, Cressy sneered. No way she was doing this with that kind of attitude beaming at her. "Walk me to your car."

As she walked out of the ward, Matt dropped into place beside her. "You doing okay?" He cocked his head, studying her. "You look . . . different."

Butterflies grew into bats in her gut, flinging themselves around. "I feel different. I've made some decisions."

Matt followed her into the elevator and pressed the button for the parking garage. "Good ones?"

"Yup."

The elevator stopped and an elderly couple climbed aboard. The man nodded at Matt and her before the couple turned to watch the numbers above the elevator door.

Pippa used the ride down to get her stomach bats to stop. The doors swished open and they all stepped out.

"I'm doing the show with Chris," she said.

Their footsteps rang through the dim garage.

Matt grunted. "It's a great opportunity and everything you ever wanted."

"Everything I ever wanted for my career," Pippa said.

They reached Matt's truck, and he beeped the locks.

"So, you're leaving?" Matt caught hold of her arm and turned her to face him.

Everything was right there for her to reach out and grab. Her happiness, her future, her everything. A future she wanted to build for herself, certainly, but with this man by her side.

"I don't want to go back to LA," she said. "I called Chris and talked to her about how we could do this. I need to stay closer to Phi, and to my mom. Laura might not admit it, but she's going to need me in the coming months and I want to be here for her."

Matt gave his head a small shake. "And Chris went for that?"

"We haggled some," Pippa said. "But we both walked away happy."

"And this is what you really want?" He cupped her face in his palms.

"It's part of what I want." Pippa leaned her cheek into the warmth of his hand. "And I know you're going to make this thing with Eric a huge success." Pippa couldn't bear standing here much longer and not being closer to him. She put her hands on his chest and stepped into him. "I'm done being scared, Meat. I want more than my career. I want everything life is offering me right now."

Matt's chest rose and fell on a huge breath. "Have we got to the 'us' part?"

"I've got a plan for us too."

Another smile ghosted over his features. "Am I part of that plan?"

"The biggest part." Pippa slid her arms around his waist. "My plan is that we keep this casual thing between us going."

He groaned. "Pippa—"

"For the next twenty years or so. Then we can reassess and see if we have another twenty years in us."

"I see." He smirked and tugged her flush with him. "Would this include making an honest man of me?"

"In a completely casual way." Pippa grinned back at him.

"Of course." He lowered his head to whisper in her ear. "Only, I get to do the asking, Agrippina."

"I wouldn't have it any other way." Pippa shifted her face into his neck and drew in a deep breath of Matt. "I'll probably say yes."

"Okay." His grim expression transformed into a breath-taking softness. "Marry me, Agrippina."

"Yes, Meat."

Epilogue

Epilogue

Matt rescued a plate of canapés before Pippa dumped them on the floor. She was nervous as hell. Jumping this way and that, making sure everyone had everything they needed before the program aired.

Laura smiled at him, the expression not quite reaching her eyes, and rearranged the items on Phi's sixteen-seater mahogany dining room table. "You have enough food for twice the people here," she said.

"I always expect a crowd." Phi bustled in wearing some kind of silver thing that rustled like a paper bag. She caught sight of him and trilled, like they hadn't seen each other in the kitchen two minutes ago. "Mathieu, is this not thrilling?"

She grabbed his face and kissed him. Matt dodged the silver feather sticking out of her hair. "It's great, Phi. Pippa is going to knock this right out of the park."

"I'm going to puke," Pippa said, and slumped against the table.

"No, you're not." Emily grabbed her and pressed a martini into her hand. "You're going to drink that and greet your guests like the star you are."

"People are coming." Sam roared through the room, almost

slamming into Matt's legs. "There are, like, a thousand cars out there."

"That's because we invited them." Matt straightened the kid and sent him shooting off on his way again. It was a pity Patrick wasn't going to be here. Pippa told him things between Laura and her husband were still very strained. Patrick had settled her debts, Pippa didn't know how, but he'd done it. Laura had finished her community service about nine months back, and then elected to stay on working with at-risk teens. Right now, she was fighting with all she had to keep her family together.

"I hate these pants." Daisy sloughed past him with a glare. "They make my thighs look fat."

"No, they don't," Pippa said, drawing her niece into a hug. "Do we really have to have that talk about the way we speak about ourselves?"

"God, no." Daisy rolled her eyes but returned the hug. "I told everyone at school about your new show."

"You did?" Pippa's eyes got a bit watery, and Matt slid into place beside her. This new show of hers meant the world to Pippa. It had taken two years to get to this point. Allie was selected as the first participant. Even with the Chris Germaine clout behind it, the network had come on board slowly.

"Don't start bawling." Laura handed Pippa a Kleenex. "Or I'll have to disown you as my little sister."

Pippa snatched the Kleenex and dabbed her eyes. Things with Laura went even slower than the network. Basically, she and Pippa were too different to ever be best friends, but they managed to be there for each other through the big shit.

"Hey there." Eric waved to him from the doorway.

Damn, did his brother not own a pair of jeans that weren't designer? Stupid question, because Matt knew for a fact

Eric didn't. Working closely with his brother over the last two years had brought all sorts of revelations. Not the least of which was that Eric wasn't the only Evans brother with the Midas touch. Matt kept his smug grin off his face, but just barely. This was Pippa's day. He'd had his moment eighteen months back when they broke ground on the first Evans Property development. Sales were driving him and Eric to work sixteen-hour days and weekends. It meant he didn't spend as much time with Pippa as he would like, but she'd been as busy and they both made sacrifices for their future.

A future that was looking brighter and brighter. Along with a beautiful five thousand square foot home perched right on the edge of Lovers' Leap. He, Eric, and Nate had worked side by side to build it.

More people flooded in and pretty soon he and Pippa were caught up in a sea of excited faces and chatter. Most of Ghost Falls had shown up to watch the first episode of *Your Best You*.

Matt nodded to Nate as his brother slunk past a group of single women and disappeared into the salon, which Phi had kept them busy rearranging for the past week.

Jo led his mother into the room, and Matt sent her a heavy stare.

Jo rolled her eyes.

Yup, Cressy was doing her thing, but at least she was here. Isaac had started basic training two months ago and wouldn't be able to make it. Still not sure what he wanted to do with his life, Isaac had joined the Army. The Cressy meltdown following that one had been epic. But her posse, led by Nurse Belinda—who still hated his guts—had clustered about her, and clucked, cooed, and soothed his mother back into a better mood.

Bella popped up right in front of them, her big blue eyes lit up and dancing. "I'm so excited for you, Pippa."

Pippa and Bella seemed to spend a lot of time together. Fortunately, it kept Bella out of the kitchen a bit more. He tuned out of their conversation and took stock.

It had been a helluva two years. Pippa would be great. He had no doubt about it.

"It's starting," Sam bellowed from the other room.

With an excited ripple the crowd moved toward the salon.

Pippa tugged him back. "I love you," she whispered. "In a totally casual way."

"And I love you." His own shit-eating grin took over his face.

How lucky could one guy get?

Love Ghost Falls?

Keep reading for a sneak peek at

BECOMING BELLA,

available soon from
Sarah Hegger
and
Zebra Books!

Bella cranked the volume on Bing Crosby crooning Christmas carols until it carried into her yard. Let Ghost Falls hear that Bella Erikson was busting her mold and coming out. Not out-out, but letting her freak flag fly. Besides which, Christmas wasn't Christmas without the Binger.

She wanted—no, *invited*—her neighbors to peep out their windows and see Bella, the new and improved version, taking charge of her life. Timer and lighting cord—ready. She rechecked the length and made sure she'd bought the right one. Normally, Dad did this, but Bella had launched into taking control, starting with Christmas, and these suckers were going up because she put them there.

Ladder propped up against the side of the house, extension cord curled up like a forest green snake beside it, she got down to item one of her Spending Christmas Alone checklist: *Decorate.*

"You've got this." The ladder loomed above her. "There is nothing to fear but fear itself." And heights. Heights made her knees shaky. No, heights used to make her knees shaky. This Christmas Bella laughed at heights; she climbed ladders in stiletto heels if she wanted to. Bing hit the chorus and Bella joined in.

"Pick a focal point." She consulted the pamphlet she'd picked up from Lowe's when she bought her string of warm white Christmas lights. Reading it out loud to the tune of "Silver Bells" made it less daunting.

With a telltale squeak her neighbor's door opened, and Liz Gunn stepped onto her matching porch. Bella waved, and this being the holidays, gave her voice a dollop of goodwill to mankind. "Hi, Liz."

Liz, known as Headlights Gunn throughout Ghost Falls because of her propensity for pointing her surgically enhanced chest at anything with a penis, tugged her cardigan over her painted-on sweater and nodded. "Whatcha doing?"

"Hanging Christmas lights." While Bella didn't like the nickname, Liz did always have her perfect double-Ds rounded up and pointing.

Liz stepped off the porch onto the dried winter grass of her lawn. "On the house?"

"Yup." Waving her pamphlet Bella tried to sound more competent than she felt. "It's easier than you would think."

Apparently, you still had to test the lights even if they were new.

"You're going to hang lights on the outside of your house?" Liz crossed the small strip of driveway separating their lawns.

"Yup!" She tossed Liz a chipper little smile. "It's Christmas."

"So I can hear." Toeing the dark green box of new lights, Liz came to a stop next to her and stared at her house. "You didn't hang lights last year."

"No, I didn't." Because last year she had spent most of Christmas, like so many Christmases before, wallowing in the bitter knowledge she would spend another Christmas single and stuck in her rut. This year, no more wallowing. No more pining, and definitely no more bemoaning her single state. As for the rut, that ended today and it all started with Christmas lights. "I'm getting into the holiday spirit."

"Aren't you spending Christmas with your family?" Liz peered over Bella's shoulder at the pamphlet. Those breasts stuck straight out and Bella moved her arm out of the way.

"No." She stomped on the residual all-alone pang and forced another smile. Being alone for Christmas didn't mean being miserable. "My family went to Florida, and I stayed behind to look after the store."

Liz looked vaguely skeptical. "They left you here."

"I'm fine with it." Actually, more than fine. Not that she'd admit this to Liz, or anyone, but escaping Nana's gruesome turkey dinner didn't hurt in the least. Her plan for Christmas started with these lights and ended in a glorious new epoch in the life of Bella Erikson.

Liz eased the pamphlet out of her hand. "It says here you have to check the lights, even if they are new."

"I'm about to do that." Bella took her pamphlet back.

"You need to plug them in."

"I know that." Plug in hand, Bella marched over to the outside power outlet. Three years she and Liz had lived side by side, barely spoken a word to each other after the incident with the tree—which Bella still didn't quite believe hadn't been deliberate—and now Liz wanted to chat. Still, Christmas, goodwill, peace on earth and all that. She shoved the plug in the outlet. Her lawn lit up in a magical sprinkling of warm white. Bing provided the soundtrack and she loved it. "Did you need something, Liz?"

Liz bent down and connected another string to the lit string. More warm white sprang to life. "Looks like those are fine too." She flicked her Christmas-themed nails at the ladder. "Why don't you get up there and I'll connect the lights."

"Really?" Liz wanted to help? Maybe the magic of Christmas got to Liz, too.

"Why not?" Liz shrugged. "I've got nothing better to do."

Bella's guilt monitor crackled. "You staying here for the holidays?"

"Like I have anywhere to go." Liz waggled her head and jammed her fist on her teeny-weeny hips. "Are we going to hang these lights, or what?"

"We're going to hang these lights." Bella put her foot on the first rung. She needed a little mantra reinforcement first. *Thinking will not overcome fear, but action will.* Gripping the higher rungs with both hands, she climbed. First one rung, then two, and away she went. This really wasn't that bad. Before she knew it, the gutter came within easy reach. "Hand me those lights."

"Aye aye, Cap'n." Liz grinned up at her.

When she smiled like that, and not the coy lip smirk she did whenever a man wandered into view, Liz looked really pretty. An opportunity to bridge the gap with Liz opened and Bella took it. "Maybe when we get done here, we can hang lights over at your place," she said.

Liz pulled a face. "I don't do Christmas."

"Why not?" Everybody did the holidays in some way or other.

"Doesn't seem much point." Liz fed her the string of lights. "With just me on my own."

Bella clipped until she ran out of reach, then came down the ladder again. She'd never thought of Liz as lonely. With her flashy clothes and brassy attitude, Liz didn't strike her as the sort to have vulnerabilities. But then, everybody had a soft underbelly somewhere. Even if they kept it buried beneath a titanium exterior. "I'm on my own."

"It says here you need to make sure they're all either pointing up or down." Liz squinted at the gutters.

"Are they?"

"Yup. Pointing down."

"Okay then." Bella moved the ladder across. "Let's keep at it."

Talk about weird. Her and Liz hanging Christmas lights like they didn't spend most days giving each other a tight-lipped how-are-you from safe sides of their yards.

They fell into a rhythm that took them all along one side of the house and into the front. When they reached the porch, the focal point, Bella stepped back and eyed the sloping gutter line. "We need to do something different here."

"Like what?" Liz stood shoulder to shoulder with her.

"A focal point."

"Huh."

"We could wrap the lights around the poles holding the roof up."

Liz scrunched up her face. "Nah! They're too skinny. A wreath would be nice."

"A wreath?"

"Yeah, hanging in the center there. Do you have one?"

A wreath would be great. "No."

"I do." Liz nodded. "I'll run next door and fetch it."

"I thought you didn't do Christmas." Bella raised her voice as Liz dashed across the lawn.

"I don't." Liz turned and trotted backward. "But I used to be married and we did Christmas. I got the Christmas decorations. He got a twenty-three-year-old blonde who looks like she should be decorating the top."

Ouch. She'd known Liz was divorced, but the younger-woman thing must bite.

"And these." Liz pointed to her chest. "Can you say 'alimony'?"

Bella laughed. Turns out spending time with Liz didn't suck. Who knew? See, this is what came of opening yourself up to new experiences.

Liz reappeared with her wreath. "If you wrap lights around it, you can hang it in the center there," she said.

"Are you sure?" Bella took the wreath. "We could always hang it over at your house."

"I'm sure." Liz pursed her lips. "Are we gonna stand here all night or get this shit finished? It's so cold out here my nipples are gonna break through any second."

Bella blushed. She couldn't help it. Nobody in her world spoke about nipples or boobs, or—God spare them—down there. Even in her head the phrase came with Nana's wide-eyed, furtive glance southward.

Daring to go where she never had before, Bella said, "Mine too."

Perched on top of the porch overhang, leaning forward to hang the wreath, Bella made the mistake of looking down. The ground rushed up at her, dipped, and heaved to the side, taking Bella's stomach with it.

"What are you doing?" Liz peered up at her.

"Ummm . . ."

"Hang the wreath, and then we can get a glass of wine." Wine would be lovely. "Er . . ."

"Bella?"

"I'm stuck."

"No, you're not." Liz moved to right beneath her.

"Am too."

Liz's eyes widened. "Are you scared of heights?"

"Yup."

She crossed her arms. "Then why didn't you let me go up the ladder?"

Because she hadn't exactly planned on freezing and sticking to her roof like a demented icicle.

"Edge back." As if directing traffic Liz waved her hands. "Move away from the edge and you'll be fine."

"I can't." Was the ground getting closer? Or was she leaning even farther over? A whimper escaped her and she shut her eyes. Dear God, that was worse. She popped them open to find Liz frowning up at her.

A smile suddenly spread over Liz's face. "You're really stuck?"

"Yup."

"As in can't move?"

"Yup."

"You know what this means?" With glee Liz whipped her phone out. "I'm going to have to call the sheriff."

"Don't." It came out in a breathy hiss. The idea of Nate Evans having to rescue her off her roof burned through her. Ghost Falls would have a field day if that happened. She could hear them all now.

"Did you hear Nate Evans rescued Bella Erikson from her roof?"

"What was she doing up there?"

"Waiting for Nate to rescue her." Snicker, snicker. *"Is that girl ever going to wise up and realize she will never catch Nate Evans?"*

She'd wised up—mostly—and she could do this. All she had to do was edge back the tiniest bit to where she couldn't see the ground anymore.

"Hi, Sheriff Evans," Liz purred into her phone. "This is Liz. Liz Gunn." She growled. "Liz Gunn from Grizzly Drive. I have a problem."

One, two, three . . . edge back. Nope. Bella's hands refused to let go of the roof lip. Years of limiting contact with Nate, and now this.

"No, it's not like that time." As she spoke, Liz paced beneath her. "Actually, it's not me. It's my neighbor."

From up here Bella could see the darker roots of Liz's platinum do. Nowhere in her grand visions of conquering Christmas had she needed a rescue.

Liz nodded. "That's right, Bella."

Oone . . . twooo . . . and three. Oh God, she was going to fall. She knew it.

"She's stuck on her roof."

All she had to do was release the edge of the roof and scooch back. This time, her butt scooched but her fingers stayed stuck.

"Hanging Christmas lights." Liz hummed and glanced up at Bella. "Actually, right now she looks a bit like she's twerking on her roof."

Bella lifted her left index finger. Then her middle finger. The index finger snapped back around the ledge. Darn! Bella did not get beaten by a roof. Bella, for certain, did not get caught twerking on her roof by Nate Evans.

"Right you are." Liz keyed off her phone. "They're on their way. Do you need anything?"

"A frontal lobotomy."

Liz grinned at her. "Nate said to keep talking to you." She stopped right under Bella. "So? How you doing?"

"Not so good."

"I can see that. Let's take your mind off the fact that you're about twenty feet from the ground."

"Erp." Twenty feet? Her head went woolly.

"I know." Liz cocked her head. "Let's talk about our yummy sheriff."

"Um . . . no."

"Um . . . yes." Liz tucked her hands into the pockets of her bright pink cardigan. "Just how long have you been in love with him?"

"I'm not . . ." Everyone in town knew anyway. "I did have a crush on him. For most of high school." And a little bit after, but she wasn't confessing that. "It started in first grade, but it ended when he joined the police academy in Salt Lake."

"Wow." Liz winced. "That's not what they say."

Oh, Bella knew that, only too well. And Liz had no room to talk, calling Nate out at least twice a week and answering the door in her negligee. "And you?"

"Oh, I'm in lust, not love." She waved a breezy hand. "I was married, remember. I don't want anything more to do with love, but lust . . ." She chuckled like a bordello madam. "Now that I've got time for."

Nipples and down there and sex, definitely sex, were not things Bella had been raised to talk about. Ever.

"You all right, Bella?" Mr. Powell from across the road stepped onto his porch.

Her situation plummeted from bad to hideous as Ghost Falls's biggest gossip followed her husband onto the porch. Bella was supposed to be launching her new epoch, darn it.

Bella put as much chipper into her voice as she could manage. She did not need the Powells coming over and getting a front-row seat of the action. "I'm fine, Mr. Powell."

"She's stuck on the roof," Liz called out. "We were hanging Christmas lights, but Bella didn't tell me she was scared of heights."

"Oh dear." Mrs. Powell came across the road toward them. "I had a cousin who was afraid of spiders."

"Vertigo," announced Mr. Powell as he led the charge. "Irrational fear of heights."

"Isn't that a movie?" Mrs. Powell tucked her hands into her pockets.

"Hitchcock." Liz scrunched her shoulders up around her ears. "Man, it's cold. How you doing, Bella? Hang in there."

"Yes, dear." Mrs. Powell's face crinkled with concern as she gazed up at Bella. "I'm sure help is on the way."

"Did you call Sheriff Evans?" Mr. Powell stared up at her.

"Sheriff Evans?" Giggling, Mrs. Powell smirked at her. "Are you sure you're scared of heights, Bella?"

"Oh, she's scared all right." Bless Liz for coming to her rescue.

Mr. Powell took hold of the ladder and gave it a shake. "Just hop on the ladder, Bella. Seems sturdy enough."

"Mike." Mrs. Powell stood on her tiptoes and whispered in his ear.

Bella dug her fingers into the roof. She didn't need to be clairvoyant to guess what was being said. Would Ghost Falls, for the love all of everything, just let this go? She was not wasting away for Nate.

"Oh." Mr. Powell scrutinized her. "Are you sure that's a good idea, young lady?"

Maybe she should end it now and throw herself off the roof. Then again, they'd only whisper over her coffin how she'd killed herself for unrequited love.

"Sometimes a girl has to take matters into her own hands." Mrs. Powell tossed her a conspiratorial wink. "It's not like you have all the time in the world, dear. You can't keep waiting for that man forever."

"I'm not—"

"It's a dreadful waste of taxpayers' money." Puffing his chest, Mr. Powell stalked to the ladder and gave it another good rattle. "Now, buck up, Bella. You can't call the sheriff out unless it's a genuine emergency."

"Really?" Liz examined her fingernails. "It's one of the perks of living in this town."

"Disgraceful." Mr. Powell flushed. "The man is the

representative of law and order in this town, not . . ." He sputtered and huffed for a bit.

"Man candy?" Liz looked smug.

Turning his back on Liz, Mr. Powell harrumphed and put his foot on the ladder. "I'm coming up."

Dear God, save her that.

"Oh no, Mike, your back." Mrs. Powell fluttered over to her husband. Small and compact, she could easily fit under his armpit.

"Perhaps you're right." Mr. Powell made a manful show of regret. "I would hate to risk her by dropping her."

She didn't want to be ungrateful or anything, but how was this supposed to help her climb off the roof?

Mrs. Powell patted her husband on the chest. "That's so like you, Mike, always thinking of someone else first."

Liz looked up at her and rolled her eyes.

Bella stifled a giggle, and then choked on it as blue and red flashing lights turned into her street.

Oh boy. Nate couldn't be subtle about this, now could he? He'd delighted in tormenting her since he'd first dipped her waist-length braid in purple paint.

Connect with

U S

Visit us online at
KensingtonBooks.com
to read more from your favorite authors, see books
by series, view reading group guides, and more.

Join us on social media

for sneak peeks, chances to win books and prize packs,
and to share your thoughts with other readers.

facebook.com/kensingtonpublishing
twitter.com/kensingtonbooks

Tell us what you think!

To share your thoughts, submit a review,
or sign up for our eNewsletters, please visit:
KensingtonBooks.com/TellUs.